Racing Hearts

Racing Hearts

ANN ADAMS

DELL | NEW YORK

Dell
An imprint of Random House
A division of Penguin Random House LLC
1745 Broadway, New York, NY 10019
randomhousebooks.com
penguinrandomhouse.com

A Dell Trade Paperback Original

ISBN 978-0-593-97651-7
Ebook ISBN 978-0-593-97652-4

Printed in the United States of America on acid-free paper

1st Printing

BOOK TEAM: Production editor: Annette Szlachta-McGinn • Managing editor: Saige Francis • Production manager: Meghan O'Leary • Copy editor: Whitney Bak • Proofreaders: Allison Lindon, Hope Clarke, Vicki Fischer

Book design by Betty Lew
Oar art by Evgeniya Vasileva / stock.adobe.com

The authorized representative in the EU for product safety and compliance is Penguin Random House Ireland, Morrison Chambers, 32 Nassau Street, Dublin D02 YH68, Ireland. https://eu-contact.penguin.ie

For my mom,

who gave me the confidence
to dream the biggest dreams.

AUTHOR'S NOTE

Dear Reader:

When I read a book on a topic I know well, I'm quick to notice if it has inaccuracies. That's why I want to be upfront with you about something: This story blends realism with imagination. While I worked hard to authentically capture the culture and emotional intensity of elite competition, I've also taken creative liberties to better serve the narrative and characters' journeys. To those deeply familiar with rowing, I hope you find this story reflects the heart and spirit of the sport you love.

ANN

Racing Hearts

One

1 DAY UNTIL WORLD CUP FINAL

There's nothing but a lemon bar standing between me and financial ruin. That's why, the evening before my last World Cup final, I'm powering over quaint garden parks and through sweeping alleyways, light mist glossing my face. If I don't get that bar, it won't matter if I sleep like a rock, or crush my pre-race routines, or wear thirty pairs of lucky Powerpuff underwear—I'm losing the final, the rest of my sponsors, and all my remaining income.

My foot snags on an irregular cobblestone and I glare at it as I speed past. I can't afford to face-plant in a piazza full of Italians sipping wine.

Sofi, a few paces behind, leaps over the threatening stone. "I always knew one of your superstitions would be the death of me. What I *didn't* predict was that it would happen while sprinting to a bakery in Varese."

"Okay, first off," I say, falling into step beside her. She's usually faster than me—both on and off the water—but this evening her wildly impractical strappy sandals are holding her back.

"Our pace clearly puts us in the 'power walking' category. And second, as I was told on my fourth call to one of these places, the preferred term is *pasticceria*."

"I notice you're not taking issue with my untimely demise."

"Oh, this situation is absolutely going to ruin us both," I say. "You because of those shoes. And me because of my ridiculous Olympic dreams."

Sofi sighs. "Your Olympic dreams will be fine."

"If I choke again tomorrow," I say, ticking off fingers as I list my points, "I won't make the World Championships team and then my last two sponsors will dump me. I'll have to work a part-time job between practices. I won't properly recover. My performance will keep spiraling. And I'll never make it to the Olympics."

When I stop, I notice that my heart rate has accelerated despite my world-class cardiovascular fitness. Maybe it's because our route has started to curve uphill. Or it's that laying it out makes it feel even more real.

Sofi lowers her chin. "Okay, then. Let's do this thing."

"Thanks, Sof, but I think we're already doing it."

"Nah. Before, I was here for aesthetics and comic relief. Now, I'm committed."

"Aesthetics?"

She swivels and jogs a few steps to the side so she can motion at her outfit. "*Aesthetics*."

I laugh. Even though she's one of the fastest rowers on the planet, and has the stacked quads and chiseled back to prove it, Sofi's muscles have a softness that allow her to look conventionally feminine, especially when she's not wearing spandex. It's a feat I never even try to pull off, thanks to my high forehead, angular jaw, and hips so straight you could use them like a giant ruler. That's not to mention my hair, which has basically been ironed onto my head in the shape of a French braid. But, as I glance at her again, I notice that tonight Sofi's also wearing earrings, a flowy skirt, and golden eyeshadow that looks like stardust against her brown skin.

"You look good, but right now my only priority is speed." I swivel my wrist to glance at my watch. "Although we are making decent time."

"How long 'til they close?" Sofi peeks around my elbow at the electronic display. "Wait, you have the watch set to *training mode*?"

"I needed to actively monitor our progress!" I slap the screen with my palm, darkening it, and move my hands back into walking position. "I'll delete the data later."

We skitter around a set of café chairs and Sofi vaults over a sidewalk planter to evade a woman walking a dachshund at approximately the speed of a sedated turtle.

"They'll still be open for a couple of hours," I say when we've cleared our obstacles. "The problem is that lemon bars are some kind of rarity here, so it took me approximately a billion calls to find a place that sells them. Also, the lady mentioned they had only one left and she 'definitely won't hold it,' no matter how many times I asked."

"Did you try begging?"

"Repeatedly. Also cajoling and a little insisting. I think that made it worse."

"I mean, fair," Sofi says. "Americans are already obnoxious and you are . . ."

"A carefully curated brand of neurotic and inflexible?"

"I was going to say 'determined.'"

I snort. "That's kind of you."

The good news is the hill has leveled out and we're really cruising now—leaping over sidewalk edges and zipping around motorbikes. The bad news is our mist has turned into a light drizzle.

"So," Sofi asks, "why didn't you already have a lemon bar with you?"

It's a solid question. The last time I was caught without food pre-prepared was probably in high school before I started insisting Mom let me handle our groceries.

Still, I hesitate before answering. The truth is sure to open up an argument.

"I did bring a stash on the flight," I say finally. "But, Maxwell threw the last one away."

"He *WHAT*?"

I grimace. The fact that my best friend and boyfriend don't get along is probably the greatest source of discomfort in my life right now. Except, of course, for my monthlong string of spectacular defeats that are putting my entire future in jeopardy.

The whole Maxwell situation is yet another reason tomorrow's final needs to go well. Whether I win or lose, Maxwell always goes through videos of my races with me—pausing after key moments to lecture me about stroke rates and connection. I used to look forward to our debriefs, but now that my performance has started spiraling, these conversations have become more stressful than helpful. Inevitably, I end up snapping at him, and he'll throw up his hands and storm out of the room. Once I get back to normal, *we* can get back to normal.

Sofi bumps a rain-slicked elbow against mine. "Seriously, Kath, what was Maxamillion thinking?"

"Maxwell."

She snorts. "Right, right. What was Maxwellington thinking?"

I repress a laugh. When they first met, Maxwell made a big

show of correcting Sofi for calling him "Max," and she refuses to let it go.

"He said"—I pause as we zoom around a towering statue—"that he forgot about that particular superstition of mine."

Sofi releases a signature groan. You know how some people have a way with words? Sofi has a way without them.

I would cross my arms if we were standing still but instead resign myself to pumping them even harder. "Even you've been saying you can't keep up with my 'rapidly expanding list of neuroses.'"

"I have expressly prohibited you from adding yet more superstitions to your list," she says pointedly. "A decree you have flagrantly disregarded."

She's not wrong—since I first qualified for Worlds last year, I have tacked on one or ten more. Still. "Because they've all been solid additions! And you agreed daily affirmations are a good idea."

"None of this excuses Maxattack's behavior. The lemon bar thing is one of your oldest and most sacred superstitions."

"To be fair," I say, "he had a good reason. Namely that it's not a good idea to eat so much sugar before a race."

Sofi rolls her eyes and, honestly, I can't blame her. Maxwell is usually quite helpful—he goes over my pre-race checklists with me, shares his own sponsor-provided supplements, and even bought me a top-of-the-line sports watch for my birthday—but it still frustrates me that he's always been skeptical of my superstitions, especially those he's deemed illogical.

"He only did it because he cares about my success," I argue, as much to myself as her.

"Maybe too much," she mutters.

My eyes whip toward her. Sofi's suddenly absorbed by her

footwork, as though this pace requires concentration. Cobblestones aside, this girl can run for miles without getting winded.

"What does that mean?" I ask.

My phone instructs us to turn right. As we bank hard past a street vendor huddled under a wide canopy, Sofi's lips snap open and closed, like she's fighting with herself about how to answer my question.

Finally, she says, "Don't you ever think he cares a bit too much about whether you're winning or losing?"

I consider this for long enough to do it justice, waiting for Sofi's usual wisdom to seep in. It doesn't. Like me, Maxwell is disciplined and hardworking. We both care about rowing—and making it to the Olympics—more than anything else. Maxwell pushes me to be a better athlete instead of questioning my dreams. The fact that he wants me to succeed is literally the reason I started dating him in the first place.

"I don't see why that's bad," I say.

"It's bad if he doesn't want that for you, but because he sees your success as a reflection on him." She watches me as she says the next part, clearly choosing her words carefully. "Things have been rocky between you two for a month now—ever since that first regatta. I don't think that's a coincidence."

I purse my lips, unswayed. So what if Maxwell cares about my success for selfish reasons? He still cares about my success. It's far better than the alternative: a man who forces you to choose between the person you love and the thing you love to do. I should know. I've had a front-row seat to that kind of relationship disaster.

"Things will get better," I assure her. "Once we're back in the training center and in our normal routine."

Sofi nods, resigned. Besides, the thick smell of sugar and dough has heralded our arrival. Beyond an expanse of slightly fogged glass, clustered café tables dot a terrazzo floor. I use a finger to squeegee rainwater off my forehead as Sofi yanks open the door.

It's time to get that lemon bar.

. . .

Unfortunately, two minutes later, Sofi and I are gaping at an irritated woman and a nearly empty display case.

"What does she mean she just sold the last one?" Sofi's voice has gone up about forty-five octaves. "Tell her you need that lemon bar and you're not leaving until you get it."

"*Scusi,*" I whisper to the cashier, thankful for my single year of Italian in college. I'm suddenly self-conscious about my damp braid, stuck to the back of my neck, and gray racerback darkened with rainwater. "*Siamo Americani.*"

We're American—as though that explains it.

The woman presses her lips together in an expression that falls somewhere between a respectful smile and an irritated frown. "*Si vede,*" she says. *That's obvious.*

I'm about to ask if she knows of any other establishments in this city that sell lemon bars when Sofi hooks an index finger into the hem of my shirt, pulling my attention to the high-back chairs behind us.

"He's got it," she hisses and points.

The man at the other end of her blue fingernail is hunched over a thick book, notebook to one side and the lemon bar on the other. He scribbles something furiously, seemingly too preoccupied to have yet touched his baked good.

"Oh, and he's a hottie," Sofi adds enthusiastically.

"Why is that relevant?" I ask, even though she's unequivocally right. He looks to be a few years older than us, maybe just touching thirty, with a tight jawline and high cheekbones. His brown hair sweeps low, nearly into his eyes, and his concentration is so intense I think he could snap a pencil with his gaze. I'm probably the only one who finds that last bit attractive.

"Go ask him for it," Sofi whisper-commands. "Use your charms."

"What charms?"

Sofi sighs and theatrically jabs an elbow into my rib cage. "Then use your determination. I know you can white-knuckle your way through pretty much anything."

Still, I hesitate. I'm willing to do some weird stuff to achieve my goals, but begging a stranger for his pastry is a step beyond normal behavior, even for me.

"Didn't you say it was important? That you'll race poorly without it?"

"Yeah," I say as I picture myself approaching tomorrow's starting line. Lately, my races have felt wildly unpredictable. It's like, at any moment, my body could betray me and my performance could spiral without an ounce of my consent.

But this? This I can control.

"All right." I suck in a deep breath and set my chin like I would just before the start of a race. "I'm going to get that lemon bar."

Two

As I approach him, the stranger with my lemon bar is crossing out long lines of his own notes like they've done him a personal injustice. I brace my hands against the high-back chair across from his table, taking in the littering of espresso cups, insides coated with a brown film, and snapped pencils—casualties, no doubt, of his assault on these notebooks.

I clear my throat. "*Mi scusi.*"

His eyes rise to meet mine. They're an unexpected shade of effervescent green, like slices of polished jade. The words I had planned to stammer out in Italian flee my mind. I fumble to regain them, like I'm grasping for droplets of water skittering across sand.

"Do you want that chair?" he asks after another beat passes and I still haven't spoken.

"No, sorry, I—Oh. You're not Italian," I say as I place his accent. He's almost certainly American, maybe from the West Coast or some Northeastern city.

"Fortunately not," he says. "If I had daily access to this espresso, I'd spend my life in a half-delirious caffeine high."

I re-scan his empty cups, mentally tallying the milligrams of caffeine he's consumed in this sitting. "Do you need to stay awake for something?"

"Nah," he says. "I just think this stuff tastes like they've found a way to liquefy a rainbow and pour it into an espresso cup."

I smile, even as I speculate about the nutritional value of liquid rainbows. "You sure that would taste good?"

He tilts his head. "Why not?"

"Sounds a bit saccharine."

"You're not a sweets person, then?"

"Sweets are usually useless to me, but—Well, actually." My eyes fall on his untouched lemon bar lingering at the edge of the table. "That's what I want to talk to you about."

He lets his pencil drop between the pages of his book. "You have my attention."

"Right, well, the thing is . . . is that . . ." I fumble through my cross-body bag for my wallet. "I'd like to buy your lemon bar. Please."

"Even more interesting."

"I'll pay you whatever you want." I shove a handful of coins toward him. "That is, as long as you'll take euros. Otherwise, I'll have to use an app or something."

He leans back in his chair. "Honestly, now I just need to know why someone who is not a sweets person so desperately wants a lemon bar."

I drop the coins and they tinkle to the ceramic table with a soft clatter. "Okay. I assume you've seen the signs around town? The last regatta of the World Rowing Cup is here in Varese."

For a fleeting moment, the stranger looks genuinely surprised, and not just in an amused kind of way. He quickly hides the expression, though, wringing it out with an exaggerated frown.

"Rowing . . ." he says. "Is that the one where you huck yourself off a waterfall?"

I snort. "That's kayaking."

"Oh," he says, but there's mirth tugging at the corners of his lips. "Then you mean the one where you face the wrong direction and a short person yells at you from the back of the boat."

This draws a smile out of me. "I race singles so the only person yelling at me is my coach, and she's nearly six feet tall." I flatten my lips. "I guess you don't know much about rowing, then?"

He exhales a laugh and flips his book closed. It's not a textbook at all, but *Dunbar's Training for Elite Rowers*.

"Clearly, not as much as I should," he says, motioning to his mangled notes.

Now it's my turn to be surprised. I survey his torso with new appreciation. He's wearing a loose windbreaker, so I can't gather much about his build, but he has a rower's stereotypically broad shoulders. He also has telltale signs of someone who spends their summers on the water—in his case, a mess of brown hair that's lightened at the ends and white skin tanned to a light taupe.

"You're a rower?" I guess.

This time his smile is more forced than genuine. "Let's just say I'm a passionate fan."

That seems purposefully evasive, and I pause, waiting to see if he'll say more. The door chimes in a cascade of bells, and a laugh rings out over the clatter of plates and cutlery. The stranger watches me, his expectant gaze unbroken by these distractions.

I guess it's time to explain.

"Here's the thing. I'm in the B final tomorrow, and it's important that I do well. I mean, it's the World Cup, so of course it's important. But it's bigger than that for personal reasons."

"How does a lemon bar help?" he asks.

"It's one of my rituals."

"One of them?"

"You want an inventory?"

His lips tick. "No, but I'm curious about this particular one."

Even though the bar is on the line, I hesitate. It's not like I believe eating this pastry will *guarantee* victory. It works because it gives me a feeling of calm and confidence—a knowing that I've done everything I can to prepare, which puts me in the right mindset for victory. Still, I know how this sounds. I get judgmental reactions to my detailed sleep plans and food logs from pretty much everyone except Maxwell.

"I've been eating a lemon bar before every race since my first Youth Nationals," I explain, bracing myself as I walk through my logic. "I ate one the night before a final and, very unexpectedly, I won gold. The next race, I didn't eat one, and I got fifth. I've been doing it ever since. Every race. No matter what."

He raises an eyebrow.

"Lots of athletes have superstitions," I bite out. "It might sound strange but—"

"I don't think it's strange."

"Oh. What's with the"—I circle a finger in the direction of his eyebrow—"skepticism?"

His lips tick. "That's not skepticism you see."

"What is it then?"

"Let's call it *intrigue*."

A tingle traces between my shoulder blades. "Oh."

He taps a finger against his notes, fixing me in place with those jade eyes. I avert my own gaze toward the counter. In the last few minutes Sofi has procured some kind of chocolate-stuffed pastry. She's now fervently tearing it into tiny pieces and casting glances at us from behind a curtain of curls. At least *someone* is enjoying this.

"Here's the thing," the stranger says, drawing me back to our pocket of the room. "I want the lemon bar, too. Not for the same reason, but still. A good one."

I frown at his dessert. "You haven't had a bite yet."

"I'm saving it."

"For what? An art installation?"

He smiles softly. "You eat lemon bars to win competitions. I eat lemon bars to cheer myself up."

I squint at his lingering smile. "You don't look like you need cheering up."

"Not yet, but I will after tomorrow morning."

"What's happening tomorrow morning?"

He shakes his head. "I don't usually share deeply personal shortcomings and coping strategies with strangers in Italian bakeries—"

"Neither do I."

"To be fair," he says, "you still haven't."

"Haven't what?"

"Told me why this race is so important."

"Oh," I say.

He seriously wants more? I guess he's right that I haven't shared anything truly personal. Nor was I planning to. But it seems this man is just stubborn enough that he isn't going to give up his dessert without the messy details.

"Can I sit?" I ask.

"Please."

The chair lets out a high-pitched whine as I pull it across the tile. I lower myself onto the creaky leather and brace my elbows against the cool table. "Here's the deal. I've been competing in the World Cup regattas and my last few races—the ones in Germany and France—were bad. Really bad. I barely made it to the C final in Germany and I didn't make it out of the repechage in France."

My memory of that day is as vivid now as it was when it happened. The finish line in sight. The buzzing in my ears, drowning out the roar from the sidelines. The burning filling every muscle. The exhaustion that felt both all-consuming and also wholly inadequate.

I take another breath, keep my gaze fixed on my fiddling fingers. "Two of my four sponsors dropped me after that. This Italy event is the last one—and the last-chance qualifier for Worlds. If I do worse than third, I doubt I'll make the team, and that will mean losing my last two sponsors."

I sneak a glance upward, ready to find pity or dismissal in the stranger's gaze. His lips are flat in a way that's almost purposefully neutral. But the lock of his eyes on mine sends a prickle across my bare arms.

"What happens if you lose the last two sponsors?" he asks.

"My friend and I"—I tip my chin toward Sofi—"we live in the training center in Southern California. That covers our living expenses and coaching. But we have to pay for everything else ourselves, like travel and equipment."

"Hence, sponsors."

"Right."

The stranger traces a finger across the edge of his notebook, considering. "So you're saying that winning this race isn't just about the thrill of victory?"

I swallow, considering how openly to answer. Unlike Sofi, who competes with a team, I race alone. While Sofi always internalizes far more of the boat's mistakes than she should, she's still training and racing with eight other women. In my case, it's just me and the boat and the pain. I have no one to blame but me. I have no one to answer to but me.

I suck in a long breath through my nose, trying to let the ambient scent of espresso and sugar calm my nerves.

"I don't race to win," I say. "I mean, winning is good. It feels good. But, for me, a race is always more than a race. Because a loss is always more than a failure."

The stranger sits back, some other emotion unspooling onto his face.

"That's more compelling than I expected," he says.

"Are you going to tell me your reason, then?" I ask. "Since I shared."

He drums his fingers against his book, perhaps weighing his response. Like me, deciding how much to reveal to a stranger in an unfamiliar place.

"My dad always expected a lot from me," he says finally. "And he was never much of a coddler. So, I didn't always get much . . ."

He pushes a hand through his hair.

"Anyway. You get the idea. But once in a while, when I was going through something tough, he bought me a lemon bar. The last one was about two years ago. When he went into the hospital for the last time."

Holy shit. My problems suddenly feel so small.

"I'm sorry," I whisper.

"I didn't tell you that for—I only told you because I didn't want you to think I was being a jerk."

He closes his eyes briefly and rolls his shoulders. When he opens his eyes again, the expression that meets mine is clear and light, all traces of consternation erased.

"How about we split it?" he asks.

It's a fair and decent offer. The problem is that I've tried it. Ahead of the demoralizing heat in France, I was so nervous I could barely choke down a few bites before my stomach revolted. Clearly, I paid for that mistake.

"It only works if it's the whole bar," I say, sincerely apologetic. "And your reason is really good. As much as I hate to say it, better than mine."

He frowns. "Why do you think it's better?"

"You have that whole dad thing . . ."

He shakes his head. "I shouldn't have played the dead dad card."

"It's a good card."

He chuckles. "That's why it was unfair. But I have an idea." With an index finger, he slides one of my euros to the middle of the table. "We'll flip for it."

I frown. "I know that sounds good, but I'm not a fan of leaving stuff like this to chance. Random chance is just *random*. Not divine."

He nods like he might have been expecting that. "A competition, then. Rock, paper, scissors?"

"Still pretty much just luck."

"Fair." His eyes roam the table, the chairs nearby, and then touch on my arms, just for a moment. "How about we arm wrestle?"

He must be joking, but it's an interesting proposition and not as unbalanced as it might seem. I am *excellent* at arm wrestling. It's not just about upper body strength, which obviously I have, but also leverage and technique. Back at the training center, one of Sofi's favorite pastimes is to challenge male athletes to arm wrestling matches with me in the dining hall. I can't beat the swimmers or the gymnasts, but Sofi revels in the expressions of utter defeat that dawn on cyclists and soccer players alike when they get bested by a woman.

Plus, I'd strongly prefer a competition where my own effort will control the outcome. This might be the best offer I'll get.

"All right," I say. "You're on."

A few moments later, we've cleared the table of his books and cups and perched our lemon bar on a chair, like a trophy awaiting its victor. Sofi has procured another baked good. At this point, she's lost all pretense of minding her own business. Instead, she has a bit of chocolate muffin dangling from her fingers and one of the café chairs scooched so far forward she's practically breathing on my opponent's shoulder.

He pushes up the sleeve of his windbreaker, revealing a sinewy forearm, and extends his hand. I slide mine into his. I can feel the rough edges of his calluses, and his palm is bigger than I expected, with fingers so long they nearly envelop my wrist. Strength radiates not just from his forearm, but his whole shoulder.

Well, shit.

"Ready?" he asks.

Over our clasped hands, his gaze settles on mine. The room collapses, like our table is bathed in a spotlight and everything else—chattering customers, grinding espresso machine—has fallen away.

"I was born ready," I whisper.

We push. His forearm flares to life, long lines of muscles raising across tan skin. Pressure rockets me back. Balancing to one side, I fight to regain my ground. My chest heats as I recruit stronger muscles. Our palms tremble, but remain aloft.

He's even stronger than he looks. I'll have to use leverage to hold my own until I can catch him off guard with a burst of power. So, I angle down my wrist and tuck my elbow into my body, pressing hard enough to keep the balance from tipping against me, but without giving away my true strength.

My pecs and biceps burn, forcing a tremble into my hand. I distract myself by watching my opponent's expression. He's bent forward, hair fallen nearly into his eyes. I can tell he's trying to keep his face neutral, but there's a strain in the slight flex of his well-crafted jaw.

He purses his lips to let out a breath. It shakes just slightly. My opening.

With sudden ferocity, I push. My shoulder screams. I nearly levitate out of my seat, but keep myself rooted to the cushion.

This is the part of the race—the competition—that I love most. The finish.

His arm descends, hard and fast, toward the table. With a thud, his knuckles land against ceramic.

"YES!" I leap out of my seat.

Sofi lets loose the same battle cry she makes when her boat is picking up speed.

I sneak a glance downward, expecting to find the hurt, bewildered expression of the male athletes I best in the training center. Really it should be doubled, given that this guy had something at stake other than his ego.

He's rubbing the back of his knuckles and staring up at me. Yet the look on his face is anything but resentful. In fact, he seems . . . impressed?

All propriety gone, Sofi leaps to my side and drags an arm around my shoulders. "That's my girl!" she says, squeezing me close.

The man scoops up the plate and, when he extends it, maintains eye contact. Heat flares through my fingertips. It's residual, surely, from the competition.

"I think this is well earned," he says.

I blink at his plate. "Are you sure?"

Ignoring both of us still staring at each other, Sofi scoops up the pastry and slips it into a white paper bag, probably leftover from one of the several desserts she's consumed in the last twenty minutes.

He raises a shoulder. "This was worth it."

The smile he gives me is as warm as his hand felt covering mine.

"Thanks," I say, breathlessly, as Sofi tugs me toward the exit, clearly ready to move on with her evening.

"Victory again tomorrow, then?" the man asks with a grin.

I raise the pastry bag like I'm making a toast. "Already planning on it."

Three

DAY OF WORLD CUP FINAL

My pre-race routine goes almost flawlessly. According to my watch, I hit my sleep metrics like a champion bowler bagging strikes. Then, this morning, I somehow convinced the hotel's kitchen staff to let me cook eggs on their industrial stove. I boiled the eggs for seven minutes and twenty-two seconds before shoveling them down with two pieces of wheat toast and four ounces of banana. That breakfast is exactly as delicious as it sounds—that is, not at all—but it's tradition.

Like I said, it goes *almost* flawlessly. The problem is Maxwell.

He was supposed to meet me by the trailers before I head down to the lake. A month ago, Maxwell would have been there ten minutes early, notebook at the ready, prepared to impart last-minute advice. Sure, these pep talks have recently been devolving into laundry lists of the problems with my technique and race strategies, but his support is still vital, nearly as important as a lemon bar.

When I arrived, though, I found only Sofi—coffee cup clutched in one hand and a cardboard sign reading *KILL IT, KATH* in the other. Twenty minutes later, I've finished my dry-land warm-up and had a final conversation with my coach about my race plan. As I make my way to the docks, boat lofted on one shoulder, I still haven't seen a single hair of Maxwell's perfectly coiffed head.

Heart skittering, I set my boat in the water and tap the oarlocks six times for good luck. Despite the encouragement from Sofi, my stomach churns like a washing machine set to high. I'm just lowering myself onto my seat, taking another breath to ease my jangle of nerves, when I hear my name.

I look up to find a familiar spike of gelled hair and neon green sunglasses descending toward the dock.

"Maxwell," I say, exhaling his name like a sigh of relief.

The dock bounces slightly as he steps across it, then he crouches low next to my hull, resting an arm against a knee so his bicep muscles bulge. Maxwell isn't racing today, but he's still wearing a unisuit like he might need to spring into action for an emergency training session.

"Hey there," he says.

I search his expression for remorse or anxiety but find neither. He looks neutral, almost like he's steeling himself in indifference. "Why weren't you at the trailers?"

"I—" He flexes his shoulders. "I came, okay? I'm here now."

"Okay?"

I roll a hand against my oar grips as I wait for him to impart some words of wisdom or tips for the race to come. Instead, he keeps staring at me, mouth working like he's chewing on his words.

"Any thoughts you want to share?" I ask. "Advice on my race plan?"

He pauses. I can't see his eyes behind his sunglasses, but I swear I can *feel* him roll them. "I can't keep wasting my time giving out advice that you're only going to ignore."

"I don't ignore you."

He frowns. "You haven't fixed your chin—"

"That's unfair," I say, interrupting him. This is not the time to bring up my worst technical issue. "You know I've been working on that for *years*."

"All the more reason you should have fixed it by now."

I slap the surface of the water, sending a splash across the dock. "I can't just change my technique halfway through the World Cups!"

He frowns at my outburst. "And that's why I can't do this anymore."

I look from his face to a group of four rowers marching toward the dock, a shell lofted on their shoulders. Behind them, a race official is frowning at me, probably wondering why I haven't pushed off yet. "You can't give me notes?"

Instead of answering, Maxwell lets out a long exhale that's tinged with a sigh. That's the noise he makes when he's going to lay out one of his "difficult truths." *I know you're working hard*, he said after we watched the tape of my heat in France. *But some rowers peak in their twenties. Maybe it's time to face what's on the horizon.*

When he still doesn't say more, I tug off my sunglasses and shove them on top of my visor. "I don't understand what's going on. Tell me what's happening."

He splays out a hand, gesturing toward me, my boat, the dock. "I can't do *this* anymore."

The men's single sculls are already flying down the shimmering lanes, judges streaming behind them in a roar of engines and wake. That's only five events before mine. I should have already started my warm-up.

"Do *what* anymore?"

Maxwell tips his chin. "Us."

The lake tilts. My oar slips wrong into the water, nearly dragging me over. I slap the dock to catch myself.

"You . . . what?"

"You know we're not right for each other, Katherine." He's using that slow, patient voice, like he's explaining how to share to a small child. "That's been clear for some time now. It will be better for both of us, in the long run, if we go our separate ways."

There's a low buzzing in my ears, like someone stuffed cotton into them. The announcer, the wind, the clang of cowbells—it's all muffled.

"Now?" I say. "You want to do this *now*?"

Maxwell tightens his lips into a conciliatory smile and nods slowly. I imagine that behind his mirrored sunglasses, his eyes are drenched in pity. "This is somewhat overdue."

My knuckles whiten on my grips. "Maxwell. I'm sitting in a boat about to go race. It's maybe the most important race of the year. You could have talked to me about this at any other time. Later this evening, or tomorrow, or when we get back to the training center. Why in the actual hell did you pick the worst possible moment to have a *breakup*?"

He folds his arms around a knee, and in that level, reasonable voice, he says, "I doubt it would have made any difference."

"What's that supposed to mean?"

"I think it's clear enough."

My blood has gone hot and sticky. "Because you think I'm going to race poorly?"

He pauses. Then nods. "It has nothing to do with belief. Past performance is highly correlated with future success."

Tears prick my eyes. I have a completely irrational urge to whip my oar out of the water and slap it against his smug face. Instead, I bottle up every emotion inside. I have never cried in front of Maxwell. Not when he threw away my lemon bar. Not after France or when he called me "a ball of anxiety" or when he told me my Olympic dreams were already dead.

"I need to go," I say. I don't trust my voice enough to say more.

Without another glance in his direction, I slam my sunglasses over my eyes and heave off the dock. My shoulders burn as I start the long, slow strokes toward the warm-up area. My heart pounds like a boxer laying into a punching bag. My lungs blaze with fire. And I haven't even approached the starting line yet.

Thirty minutes later, the start judge calls for attention.

I race, but I don't just fail to make the top three.

My bow crosses two boat lengths behind fifth.

Dead last.

. . .

I don't bother with a cooldown. What's the point?

When I make my way back to the docks, my lungs are still burning like I lit one of my mom's incense sticks and shoved it down my throat. My vision blurs at the edges so all I can see are Sofi's curls framed by fake wood. The lactic acid in my arms and legs makes my limbs so thick and heavy that I have to let my boat coast the rest of the way.

Sofi grabs my blade and pulls until she can catch my rigger. I slump forward, elbows crushing my knees.

"I'm so sorry," she says as I heave myself off the seat and she folds me into her arms.

I take a deep breath, fighting back the tears that threaten to spill onto her curls. There are people everywhere—athletes clamoring into boats, officials hopscotching over oars. The Canadian woman who won my final is shouting breathlessly into a phone that her coach is holding up.

I can't lose it now. Not in front of all these people.

So, I wordlessly extricate myself from Sofi's hug. She silently squats to lift my bow. Together, we trudge up the long grassy hill toward the trailers. When we finally loosen my boat into its slings, I drape myself over it and let my temple rest against the cool surface.

"I heard him telling one of his teammates about what happened." Sofi's voice is so sharp it could slice through rock. "He's a *dick*, by the way."

"This isn't how it was supposed to go."

"I know," Sofi says. "But that doesn't mean you won't get through it."

"I would have never done something like this to him. He was never supposed to do something like this to me. That was the whole *point*, Sof. He supported my goals instead of questioning them. He understood who I am and never tried to change me—only tried to make me better. Those were the reasons I took a chance on this ridiculous relationship in the first place. And it *still* backfired."

Sofi sighs, but doesn't respond.

I ball up a fist and push myself away from my boat, then root through my duffel bag until I find my phone. Any moment now, it will fire to life, carrying more bad news. "I'm not going to Worlds. I definitely lost my last two sponsors."

She lays a hand across the screen. "Don't worry about that right now."

"But it's going to happen. And then what? I have no marketable skills. What employer wants me to work a few hours a day for eight months a year?"

"I think you need to stop trying to leap fifteen paces forward and instead focus on what's next. Tomorrow, we'll fly back to California and we'll be back in the training center. You'll get to sleep in your perfectly made bed, and eat your perfectly ratioed meals, and row on our perfectly flat lake with Carla shouting at you from her launch."

My lips crack into the slightest smile. I do love it when our coach shouts at us.

Sofi squeezes her hand against my clammy skin. "And maybe you'll have to get a part-time job. That's okay. I know you can handle it. You can handle pretty much anything, Kath. *Including* getting over Maxwell." She grabs me into another firm hug. "But you'll cross all of those bridges when you get there."

I let myself melt into the strength of her embrace. She's right, as always. I just need to get home, get back to normal. This isn't a death sentence for my Olympic dreams. I can't let it be.

My phone buzzes.

I pull away and wipe my cheek with the back of my hand as I peer down at the name on an incoming message. COACH.

Come to my tent. We need to talk.

Hovering by my shoulder, Sofi grimaces. The phone buzzes again.

Now.

Four

Inside her white vinyl tent, Carla is perched in a director's chair, her windbreaker's declaration of TEAM USA facing me. She lets out a snort of laughter directed toward the laptop balanced on her knees. Which is playing . . . a TikTok video?

It's the last thing I'd ever have expected to find my coach watching. Actually, no, the *last* thing is one of those sappy rom-coms with an ensemble cast of famous people. *But* TikTok would have been a very close second. And yet, here she is, watching a screen with a profile video of young kids in unisuits doing some coordinated dance.

I clear my throat awkwardly. "Coach? You wanted to see me?"

Carla slides her laptop onto the stack of papers and clipboards adorning her makeshift desk—a card table—and tosses her reading glasses on top. She bolts upright to face me, fists on her hips like a superhero. Even from this angle, I have to crane my neck to look her in the eye. I don't dare look down. Carla's athletes hold their chins high on and off the water.

Her eyes roam my face, and my breath stills.

"Kath."

"Coach?"

She rubs the back of her head where her hair is buzzed close to her scalp. "Tough break on that race. What happened?"

I shake my head, trying to sort through the tangle of memories from the last hour. "I was fast off the line and settled into pace, but when I hit the thousand—"

She folds her hands, steeples her index fingers, then tilts her head. My shoulders stiffen. This is Carla's X-ray vision pose—the one she assumes when she's examining my soul. Or whatever is even more core to my being than that. My to-do lists, maybe.

"No," she says. "What *happened*?"

I'm not sure how much I should share. I hate that she's looking at me like she's wondering how much disappointment I deserve. Then again, Carla has very little patience for excuses and interpersonal drama, so oversharing might backfire.

I keep it vague. "I—I had some bad personal news. Right before the race."

She fixes me with a purse-lipped stare. "I'm sorry to hear that. But we both know this has been going on much longer than just today."

Despite my best intentions, my eyes drop to my cracked red, white, and blue toenail paint. I suppose that's true. I don't have the breakup to blame for the race in France. Or the ones in Germany.

"Kath." When I look up, Carla nudges her chin toward the director's chair. "I need you to sit down."

My heart freezes. Carla has been my coach for nearly four years and, for all the tough talks she's given me, she's never once asked me to sit down. She delivers bad news with the swift precision of a surgeon cutting out a diseased kidney. This woman has never even heard of the word *coddle*.

"This is about the Worlds team, isn't it?" I ask.

She shakes her head minutely. "This is about your residency."

"My . . . what?"

"Your performance in this regatta has brought down your standing rather significantly." Her voice is uncharacteristically soft. "You no longer meet the minimum qualification for Olympic Training Center residency."

These words punch a hole through my center. My scalp tingles and fingers go numb. It's like my body is responding before my mind even has a chance to process what's happening.

"You mean . . ."

"You're going to have to find somewhere else to train."

There is no air in this tent. I'm floating, like the sensation that sometimes happens during a race, in those moments when I'm in such intense pain that my mind disconnects from my body as some kind of demonic self-defense mechanism.

The training center is everything to me. Everything. It's my home, my coaching, the literal roof over my head. The weight room, physical therapy, medical care, all of my meals. I can't be a rower without the training center. I don't know where I'll *live* without the training center.

"I've . . . You're telling me . . ."

How did this even happen? How did I miss that this was a possibility? A few years ago, when I first qualified for training center residency, I was tracking my standing obsessively. But I guess I've been so focused on everything else—my sponsorships, qualifying for Worlds, Olympic trials next year—that I started taking what I already had for granted.

"You can re-establish residency at the next qualifying event," Carla says, not unkindly. "That would be Pan Ams."

"Pan Ams," I whisper.

I would have to *win* the Pan American Games to make a straight qualification there. And winning seems unlikely at best, impossible at worst. I can beat the Argentine and Chilean women when I'm at the top of my game. But the Canadian is like a tank on a Jet Ski. I couldn't beat her if Carla sprinkled me with fairy-coach magic dust.

My coach squints at me like she's reading all of this mental calculus. "This isn't a death sentence. Pan Ams won't be until the end of September. You have two months to train."

Train where? My sponsorships barely pay for my travel needs, so I have almost no savings. No money for rent or dues at a top-tier club. Crashing with a friend is impossible—they all live in the training center. "I don't even know where I'll go."

"You're from Berkeley, right?"

"Yes, but . . ." I haven't lived in Berkeley since high school. I'd have no other rowers for pacing, no dining hall for meals, no trainers to tape my shoulders and wrists. I'd have to move back into my mom's house, which can best be described as the landfall of a tropical storm. "There's nothing for me there. I'd be all alone."

"Actually, you wouldn't." Carla moves to her desk and flips through a stack of papers until she finds a business card near the top. She hands it to me. "There's a solid youth club in the East Bay. It's currently headed up by Adrian Crawford, a very promising coach. I can talk to him for you, see if he'd be willing to let you work with his team. Plus, I think going back home and training in a less demanding environment could be good for you. Get away from the pressure of all this—just for a while."

I stare down at the plain-looking card—inscribed with the

address where I first got on the water. Carla is looking at me expectantly, like I'm supposed to be grateful. I try not to look incredulous. I've been living in the training center for four years. Before that, I rowed on my college varsity team. Before *that*, I made the Junior Worlds team. And, still before that, at the very beginning of it all, I learned to row at this very youth club.

"I'm sorry"—I splutter out—"you want me to train with teenagers?"

Carla purses her lips. "Is there something wrong with teenagers? Are they offensive in some way?" I'm about to stammer out an explanation but she folds her arms and plows forward. "You need a coach and other boats to pace you. The guys will be about your speed when they're in doubles. And, from everything I've been able to tell, this coach is excellent, which is why he's currently under consideration for a position with the junior national team."

"*Junior* national team," I repeat.

I'm not trying to be arrogant here. Really. It's just that there is an order to things, a *progression*. In rowing—in all sports, really—you take certain steps forward, pass certain milestones. I've earned my progression. I had to train, race, and win for my spots. Going back to training with a youth club isn't like taking a step or two backward: It's like nearing the end of Chutes and Ladders and getting sent back to the start.

To make it all worse, somehow, I'll have to go from that starting place to *winning* Pan Ams. In two months. I know Carla believes her athletes can do anything we set our minds to, but right now it's like she's saying this Adrian guy in Berkeley will teach me to sprout wings and fly over the course. It's impossible. It's—

I remember something. A few years ago, one of the men's pairs lost their training center residency, but their ornery coach urged USRowing to keep them on anyway. They got to stay.

"Overrule." I whisper the word like a prayer.

Carla blinks. "I don't have that power."

"Right, but you can make a recommendation. You can ask the board to override the rules."

Carla's scowl burrows deeper. "They won't go for it."

"You won't even ask?" I say, voice rising because this is the only way forward that doesn't involve growing a pair of wings.

"Not without concrete evidence of improvement that I can give the board to back up the recommendation," she says. "Because it's not just your performance that's the problem. It's your lack of adaptability."

My insides flare as a frustrated growl nearly escapes my throat. I can't believe *this* is the reason she's giving up on me. For the last month, Carla has been obsessed with this idea that my routines have gotten too involved and are now working against me. But every time we discuss specifics—changing how I spend my rest day, modifying my sleep schedule—I can point to clear reasons why I have the system I do.

"My routines make me a good athlete," I say for approximately the thousandth time. I wouldn't need to keep repeating myself if Carla listened.

"Clearly they don't or you wouldn't have strung together so many questionable performances."

I step back, surprised by the sting in her voice. "There have been extenuating circumstances."

"Such as?"

"Such as getting *dumped* on a *dock*." I'm losing my professional cool here, but I can't help myself. The unfairness is as palpable as fire ants coursing down my limbs.

Carla gives me a fleeting, sympathetic smile before launching back in. "And France? Germany?"

"My relationship has been on the rocks for weeks." As soon as

I say the words, I can feel the truth behind them. Sofi was right about Maxwell. He *has* been the problem. The last few weeks have been tough on me and Maxwell has only made that worse with all his pressure and opinions and disappointment. He's made my emotions more volatile. Thrown me off focus. "If anything, what I need is more stability and predictability. *More* routine."

Carla massages the bridge of her nose, looking like she's counting to ten in her mind. Distantly, an announcer crackles over the loudspeakers, calling out finishes.

"All of that only hurts you," she says. "Particularly when it starts spiraling out of control. Your refusal to see that *is* the problem."

Spiraling out of control? How does that make any sense? My routines give me control.

"I need an example," I say. When my coach narrows her eyes, I add, "Let's discuss an example. Please."

She taps a long finger against her folded arm, eliciting a soft whisper from her windbreaker. "Why were you arm wrestling with a stranger for a lemon bar last night?"

"How do you know about that?"

"Answer the question."

I smooth a hand across my braid and tug at the frayed end. "I needed to eat one before my race. It's a pre-race superstition. All athletes have them."

"Right, but not all athletes have so many. Not all athletes have beliefs so deep-seated that they can never be changed. Not all athletes are certain they'll fail if they don't follow their plans precisely. Obviously, this isn't about a lemon bar. It's about how you eat, recover, and train. It's about how you prepare for races and whether or not you make real changes when you lose or if you just keep doubling and tripling down on the same failing strategies."

She presses her hand to my shoulder. "Having routines is good. Being so dependent on those routines that you're unwilling to change them, even if they aren't serving you anymore? That's not. I want you to find a way to be okay without lemon bars in your life. Maybe some time away from the training center will help. Maybe Adrian can help, too."

My ears ring with a high-pitched whine. She's abandoning me. I'm going to lose my spot. I've already lost my spot. And—barring magic or a miracle—there's nothing I can do to get it back.

There's sandpaper scraping against my eyeballs. Outside, music fires alive with a pumping bass, punctuated by shouts and whoops of glee. The races are ending and the after-parties are getting warmed up—a loud, jarring overtone to the misery inside this tent.

I blink hard against the coming storm. After all of this, I'm sure as hell not going to let Carla see me cry.

Chin up. Chest forward.

"I appreciate your consideration," I say quietly.

"I know this is tough, Kath," Carla says. "Try to relax tonight. Get your mind off it. You can pick back up in a few days."

I nod, fighting back tears. Carla releases me, stepping back. I'm sure she knows I want to be alone and she's not about to stand in my way.

As I hurry toward the exit, she calls after me. "This isn't impossible."

Without turning, I nod and draw back the flap, using an elbow to shield my eyes from the blinding sunlight. I want to believe that, too.

But I don't.

Five

64 DAYS UNTIL PAN AMS

"You know what relationships are, Sofia? Chaos. Fucking chaos."

Sofi looks at me like I'm drunk. I take another drag of Long Island Iced Tea through my straw, strobe lights turning the glass neon blue. Around us, sweaty athletes pound their feet and sway their hips as electronic dance music pulses so loudly I can practically hear it in my kidneys.

"You can't hear the music in your kidneys," Sofi says, which is when I realize I've said that last bit out loud. "How are you already this drunk? You've barely had half of that."

I glare at her. "One of these is like three drinks."

She rolls her eyes and shoos me backward, angling toward one of the black booths framing the room. I fall onto the sticky leather, holding my drink aloft so it doesn't slosh onto this ridiculous outfit Sofi somehow convinced me to wear. I wanted to stay in spandex. She argued for sequins. We compromised on cutoff jean shorts and a strapless top.

"Besides," I shout over the pounding music, "I'm not drunk. I'm pissed."

Every national team rower on planet Earth has descended on this *discoteca* for our World Cup after-party, including Maxwell. Thankfully, I've easily avoided him so far. He's been holding court in a corner booth, surrounded by the other guys in his eight and a few Australians. I bet he's spent the night shouting lectures about rhythm. Maybe I should feel jealous that they're getting his full attention now, but all I feel is smoldering rage.

"You have every right to be angry," Sofi says.

I nod. Angry, at least, is better than the devastation that's threatened to hollow me out since my conversation with Carla. Until Sofi dragged me to this club, I'd been comatose all day. The same thoughts skipping through my mind for hours. It was already going to be hard enough to come back from this slump. Now I'm going to have to do it with some untested, brand-new coach? Without my teammates or any supportive resources?

On top of it all, I'll have to *win* Pan Ams. It's enough to make me want to collapse in a puddle of despair.

Fucking Maxwell. This is entirely his fault. Dating him was the single worst decision I've ever made. And I *knew* better.

My hand clenches around the icy cold glass. "I'm going to lose rowing because of him."

Sofi lays her fingers on the rigid lines of my forearm. "You're not."

"And then I'll have nothing. I'm a rower. That's it, Sof. That's all I've got. I can use an oar to move a boat through water. And apparently I can't even do *that* very well."

When I look up, Sofi is frowning, but silent.

I grip the straw with my teeth and pull liquid until I hit the bottom of the glass. It vibrates with a mixture of melted ice and air. "I'm getting another."

Sofi eyes me. "Really?"

I don't usually drink, even after races. I've never seen the value in it. Maybe it feels good or whatever, but that's just temporary. It won't help my performance and, if anything, dehydration and a hangover will only hurt me, even if marginally. Tonight, though, I don't know. Taking the edge off the sharp pit of all these emotions feels worth it.

From the dance floor, one of Sofi's teammates waves frantically at us.

"You should go be with your team," I say. Despite some drama lately, Sofi's boat won gold two days ago. It's the only good thing that's happened in weeks. "Celebrate. Please."

Sofi's eyes cut to her teammates and she lets out a heavy sigh. I follow her gaze toward the smallest person in the tight pack of bodies—Missy, who is now twirling, one hand up, while she cluelessly sloshes her open drink on everyone within spitting distance. She's a tiny thing, even for a coxswain, and super talented, but she's also younger than everyone else. And, as we discovered over the course of this regatta, she's wholly inexperienced with alcohol. Usually, Sofi and I keep an eye on Missy together, but tonight I'm useless.

"You don't need me?" Sofi asks.

I stand and snatch up my empty glass. "Please don't worry about me."

"Okay," Sofi says. "But promise not to get all weird and tense without me around?"

"Don't be ridiculous, Sofi. I'm always weird and tense."

She laughs, hip checks me, and darts off.

When she's gone, I scythe across the dance floor, dodging gyrating bodies and athletes yelling over the music in a dozen different languages. As I move, I keep my eyes fixed on my target—the bar, glowing purple with up-lights—so I can avoid any glances toward Maxwell's booth. If he gives me another one of those pitying looks, I'll probably scream.

My elbows land against the sticky surface at the far end. It's somewhat quieter here—probably because we're not facing any of the giant speakers—and I'm out of the way. Just me and a guy hunkered in a high-top chair, nursing a drink in silence. He looks about as dejected as I feel. I guess this is the loser section of the club.

A bartender with cropped blue hair and chipped black nail polish lands in front of me.

"What do you want?" she shouts in only slightly accented English.

I should probably chill with the Long Island Iced Teas, but I don't know many other drink names. I glance down at the guy's glass next to me, which has a promising slice of lemon among the ice cubes. "I'll have that."

The bartender rolls her eyes. "I don't remember every drink I've made in the last hour."

"Whiskey sour," the guy with the tight shoulders supplies.

As the bartender wheels away, the man lifts his drink. His eyes catch mine over the rim and his eyebrows shoot up. My insides flare as I register a familiar green hue.

"It's you," I say.

"It's *you*," he responds.

"What are you doing here?"

He takes a long sip, considering me with those intense eyes. Maybe it's because I'm tipsy, but I feel like I'm being sucked into his pupils, light and sound collapsing in their depths.

"The pastry didn't hit hard enough." He sets down his glass. He's wearing a light blue button-down, but he has the sleeves rolled up to the elbows and the top button is undone, like his chest is trying to escape the restrictive fabric. "I'm here for something stronger."

He's still facing the bar, wide shoulders shadowing his drink. I'm not sure why I'm so struck by them. He's not built like a swimmer, with a frame so broad it's practically offensive. But maybe that's just it—this guy is attractive in a well-rounded way. He's tall, but unlike a volleyball player, it's not his *only* striking feature. He's got a broad chest, but I can also see the thick rise of quads underneath his dress pants. And then there are those eyes.

"So, your thing didn't go well?" I ask.

He lifts a shoulder, but not his gaze. "Not exactly."

"And you came to a *nightclub* for a drink?"

"It was in walking distance."

Does he mean from the course? He must. I guess that's the reason we picked this place. He said he's not an athlete, though. A spectator? But he's dressed so sexy finance man.

I'm about to ask when he says, "What happened with your race?"

"I bombed," I say. "And then I lost my training center residency."

"Damn," he says. "I'm sorry."

The lasso that's been wrapped around my chest since my conversation with Carla tightens.

"You know what the most bullshit part is?" I ask.

"Tell me."

"A year ago, I won this race."

I close my eyes, swaying slightly despite my elbow anchoring me to a steady surface. That day ruled. It was the first time Carla told me she thought I had what it took to go all the way. The day Maxwell asked me out. Even though I'd never said yes to a real date before, I knew him well enough to know that he was the right match for me. Everything was clicking into place. My life was on *schedule.*

I blink open my eyes. "And now here I am." I flap my hand around to our sad little corner and repeat what Maxwell told me two weeks ago. "I've peaked. The end is in sight. On the hor-i-zon."

Music thuds, pulsating the bar under my elbows. Despite it, the silence between us stretches, tightens. I keep my eyes down to avoid whatever look of pity the man must be casting my way.

To my relief, the bartender materializes and sets a pale yellow drink by my fingertips. I snatch it up, take a chug of tangy liquid, and immediately get another rush of lightheadedness. An advantage of exercising for six hours a day and hardly ever consuming alcohol? Extremely low tolerance.

"Losing." At the sound of his voice, I swivel to find the man fully turned toward me, leaning against an elbow so his shirt is tight against his biceps. Those green eyes settle on me, practically glowing in the neon light. "Losing fucking sucks."

The lasso around my chest eases, just a touch, and my lips crack into a half smile. "That it does."

"But." He shifts, leaning in so he can say the next part close to my ear, like he doesn't want me to miss it over the music. "It's one thing for a loss to be a loss, and it's another to let it be more than that."

"What do you mean?"

"Losing is painful and terrible. But that's all it is. It doesn't mean there's something wrong with *you.*"

My stomach twists with an almost painful emotion that I can't name. Not with the jumble of thoughts and alcohol clogging up my brain.

"How did you know to say that?"

He shrugs and sits back.

"Well," I say, "that was good. And totally untrue."

He exhales a laugh. "Yeah, this stuff is always easier to tell other people than it is to hear yourself."

"Regardless." I hunt for the tiny straw with my tongue and suck down more cool liquid. "I want my life back. So, now I have two months to get good enough to win the freaking *Pan American Games.*"

The guy stares at me for a long moment, strobe lights bouncing off his cheekbones. Warmth from the alcohol purrs through my limbs.

"Can I ask you something?" he says.

"Shoot."

He blinks his eyes closed. "There's a chance this is a wildly inappropriate question from a stranger and I'm *just* drunk enough to ask it."

"I'm an open book," I chirp. Not generally true, but whatever, right now it is. "Fire away."

"All right." He traces a finger across the rim of his glass. "Do you think you'll quit? Like, not make yourself go through all of that."

"Nope." I haven't thought about it and I don't need to. "It might all feel impossible right now, but I will only quit rowing when someone pries my oars out of my cold, dead hands. Or . . ."

"Or?"

"Or when I get trounced at Pan Ams and I have no other choice. But I'm not going down without a fight. I will work every minute of every day to claw my way back, no matter how long the odds."

A laugh eases out of him. "Fuck, that's impressive."

"I think you mean stubborn."

"No." He looks at me, holds my gaze. Despite the sticky heat practically radiating off the walls, goose bumps race across my bare arms. "I meant what I said."

There's acid coursing through my veins now. I'm loopy, slightly out of control. At least I don't feel hollowed out anymore.

"Do you want to dance?" I ask.

His mouth explodes in a grin. "Hell yes, I do."

I polish off the rest of my drink in one clean gulp, slam down the empty glass, and spin. I don't usually do this. But right now, with the residual heat of anger and the sparkle of alcohol in my veins, I want to dance until my toes go numb.

The two of us forge a path through the cramped dance floor until I find a sliver of empty space. Circled by sweat-slicked bodies, I raise my hands and let the music take over. It vibrates through me, guiding my hips back and forth, my shoulders up and down. Lasers crisscross the crowd, speckling my arms in neon green. I chase them like a cat, finding the beat in my fingers and my toes.

I'm lost in this moment, in everything. All the shit has fallen away—Maxwell, the race. Even the talk with Carla. There's nothing left but this moment. And a man.

I spin, searching for my dancing partner. When I've made nearly a full revolution, I find him moving with the music, a surprisingly respectful distance back.

And, damn, he's gorgeous.

His green eyes, his tight jawline. The way his hair falls forward as he moves, and the way he shakes his head to pull it back. Those shoulders—so wide I don't know if I'd be able to get my arms comfortably around them, but I'm suddenly extremely interested in trying. Obviously, I noticed all of this before. It's electric now, though. Air fizzes around him, pulses with his energy.

I step toward him. Our eyes lock. He hesitates, so I reach out, green lines zigzagging the expanse of my skin. He catches my wrist, thumb pressing to the skin just below my palm, and draws me into his body.

I release myself into the hard planes of his torso. Our bodies zipper together and we move as one. We're so close that I can smell him—sandalwood and citrus. Our knees lock together: mine, his, mine, his.

His palm goes flat on my low back. Through the thin fabric of my shirt, my skin prickles under the feathery touch of his fingers. I'm reminded of the way they engulfed my wrist when he took my hand yesterday.

The music changes. Hard bass melts into a smooth rhythm, guiding us in a synchronized harmony. His hand hitches up my shirt and his fingers trail across the smooth skin at my low back. The touch sends shivers chasing one another along my spine.

In return, I twine an arm around his neck. He instantly escalates, running his knuckles down my bare arm. My skin melts in the wake of his touch. I arch into him, threading my fingers into his hair at the nape of his neck. A low, guttural sound escapes his throat. Heat pools between my legs.

My forehead is in line with his throat. His breath warms my cheek. I twist, my nose bumping his jawline. Music fires around us, intoxicating and smooth. His eyes drop to my mouth and I tip my face upward, edging closer to his lips.

Then he inhales sharply, so loud I can hear it even over the thumping music.

"Are you sure?" he whispers.

He draws himself back.

Heat vacuums out of my limbs, and collects in my cheeks instead. I recoil, stumbling away from the all-consuming moment. Embarrassment rushes to fill the space left by the warmth of his body. What the hell am I doing?

I don't do this. I *never* do this.

"I—" My head is spinning. I don't even know this man's name and I just tried to make out with him in the middle of a dance floor? "I should go."

"What?" His eyes are unfocused as he pushes his hand into his hair. "I'm just not—"

"It's okay!" I blurt out. "Don't worry about it. I'll see you some other time."

It's a lie and we both know it. Tomorrow, I'll fly back to California. He'll go wherever he goes. Either way, we'll definitely never see each other again.

Before he can say another word, though, I turn and flee.

Six

63 DAYS UNTIL PAN AMS

The next morning, I repress the urge to gag as our airplane bumps and swoops over the Atlantic. Shoved in the narrow seat with earbuds jammed in my ears, I suck liquid from a gallon jug of water squeezed between my knees. It does nothing to drown out the pounding in my head, the ache in my chest, or the lurch of embarrassment I get every time I think about *last night*.

Those green eyes forging a tunnel right into my soul. The citrus smell. And . . . the sharp inhale when I angled my face upward.

What the hell was I thinking?

I wasn't. That was the whole problem.

This is the *exact* reason I have rules. Limits. Without them, a single misstep can turn into a catastrophe.

That said, I hardly have the emotional bandwidth to focus on embarrassment, because I have deep, penetrating sadness to deal with, too.

With tears threatening my eyes, I spend my last evening in the training center packing up everything I own. My array of unisuits and a handful of favorite photos and medals fit into two large suitcases. The rest of my belongings get stashed into a comically small storage container.

Early the next morning, I try to hold it together as I say my goodbyes. When I tell the athletic trainers I'm leaving, they blink in shock before filling my backpack with free samples of Tiger Balm and medical tape. The hulking weight room coach, who rarely shows emotion except to pump his fist when I add a plate to my weight belt, engulfs me in a bearlike hug before gruffly informing me that he's always admired my discipline. In the cafeteria, one of the chefs insists on making my favorite, most nutrient-packed omelet and writes NOT GOODBYE, YOU'LL BE BACK in ketchup around the edge of the plate.

Saying goodbye to Sofi is the worst, of course. She insists on accompanying me to the airport and white-knuckles my hand until I reach the end of the security line. Even then, she doesn't let go until the TSA agent has shouted "*Next!*" for the third time.

"Train your ass off," she whispers as she pulls me in for a last hug. "And come back faster than ever."

Mom doesn't own a car, so when I land, I order an Uber with savings from my now entirely former sponsors. I got the last two calls while in the air, so at least I received the bad news with the sterile transactionality of a voicemail message. Officially, it means that I'll be living for the rest of the summer on the limited funds I've saved over the last few years. If I'm extremely frugal, it might be *just* enough to pay for food this summer, plus my travel to Canada for Pan Ams in September.

My forehead is still lolled against the cool glass when the Uber comes to a stop in front of my childhood home—a single-story bungalow in North Berkeley. I practically have to squint to make out a house-shaped building behind the thick vines scaling the porch railing, succulents spilling from chipped pottery, and dozens of mismatched wind chimes. Despite the disarray, it's a fairly nice house in a very nice neighborhood, attributable to the only good financial decision my mom has ever made: She never sold her grandparents' house.

Just as I'm hefting my second suitcase out of the trunk, Mom bursts out of the turquoise door and throws open her arms. Her array of scarves and shawls spread open like a pair of mottled fairy wings. "Home at last!" she shouts.

I thank the driver and abandon my suitcases so I can leap up the porch steps and bury myself in her embrace. My chin presses to the top of her head, avoiding the two sets of reading glasses perched in her gray curls.

"Hi, Mom," I whisper and breathe in deeply, savoring her smell of spiced tea and jasmine.

Around us, wind chimes sing a symphony in the summer breeze. Her giant philodendron, still overgrowing its chipped ceramic pot, tickles my shoulder. Standing on this porch is like stepping back in time. It's nostalgic in a way that makes me ache with regret. I can't help but feel like I'm living in reverse. Going backward instead of forward.

"Let me get my eyes on you." Mom lowers a pair of glasses to her nose and pushes back my shoulders with surprising force. Her gaze snags on the bags under my eyes, then the exhausted hunch of my upper back. She purses her lips. "This breakup has taken too much from you."

I repress a sigh. Mom sees the whole world through the lens of heartbreak. She cycles through men like a track star turning laps. For her, each beginning is full of optimism and hope. Every time, it's followed by a crash—usually involving hours of tearful phone calls. I have no idea how she's had the stamina to keep that up for decades. After what Maxwell did, I don't want to give someone else control over my emotions ever again.

"It's not the breakup," I say. Well, not *only* the breakup. "But, yeah, things are rough right now."

She smooths back a wisp of hair that's come loose from my braid. "Nothing a little cacao ceremony can't fix."

Smiling patiently, I trudge to the sidewalk to collect my suitcases. As much as I want to collapse on the creaky twin bed in my old bedroom, I need to get unpacked and send an email to Adrian, my new coach. His last message indicated he'd prefer me to take a few days off before getting back on the water, but I can't afford the break. So, I need to make sure he'll have a loaner boat ready for me tomorrow morning when I head down to the boathouse.

The distinctive smell of burning sage greets me when Mom throws open the door. I toe off my sneakers next to her pile of moccasins, heeled boots, and a few pairs of clogs. We forge through the familiar features of her living room: the well-loved red velvet couch, the cloudy bronze-framed mirror, and, in the corner, a colony of dust bunnies so large it has probably established a governance structure. I'm making a mental note to deal with those later when my eyes catch on the kitchen countertops.

I freeze.

"Why is there a jungle where your sink should be?" I ask.

Mom spins slowly toward me. "Sweetheart, I need you to take a deep breath for me, okay? I didn't have time to get the house in *Kath-ready* order after you called yesterday."

I abandon my suitcase and tiptoe into the kitchen, shoulders already tensing. The walls are still that faded amethyst—a color my mom grabbed out of a discount paint bin after a particularly bad breakup, insisting a purple kitchen would brighten her mood—and the ancient Frigidaire is still rattling in the corner.

But an indoor garden filled with overgrown herbs and wilted flowers has sprung up across the butcher block. When I yank open a drawer, I find paintbrushes mixed in with the spoons. Inside the nearest cabinet, fake spiderwebs and an array of plastic pumpkins pile high on top of serving platters.

My head falls back and I try not to hyperventilate. Memories of my high school years tumble through my mind like a rockfall. Waking up in the dark to cook eggs before practice, only to find Mom had hurled them into the sink in a fit of rage. Trying to get to sleep while Mom and her latest guy played music in the living room, laughing over the booming stereo. Getting rides to races from friends because Mom never paid her parking tickets and couldn't keep a job long enough to afford a car, anyway.

"Please stay centered here," Mom warns from over my shoulder.

The worst part is that the problems at home also had very real consequences. This fridge has always oscillated between too full and too empty, usually alongside Mom's relationship status. As a freshman, I went to my first regionals in Oakland when Mom had just broken up with some guy from the bank where she worked at the time. She'd forgotten to buy groceries even though she promised a dozen times over that she would, so I had nothing to eat that morning but pudding and a handful of olives. My blood sugar crashed halfway through my heat and I barely crossed the finish line.

Rowing was my escape from this house, but I forgot all the ways this house challenged my ability to row in the first place.

With a harsh breath, I cut off the train of thoughts. I'm not a teenager anymore. It's not like I was expecting to find protein powders and electrolytes in her cabinets. All I need is a budget and a plan. And maybe some elbow grease.

"Can I organize things?" I ask, even as I dig out my phone

and pull up my email chain with Adrian. I'd wanted to carefully craft my next response, but I don't have time for all that. "Make an inventory of your food so I can figure out what I need to buy?"

I need to get right back on the water, I type out quickly. Will need a loaner boat, too. See you for morning practice tomorrow. I stare at the message and then add, Looking forward to it!

I don't usually do exclamation points, but I should at least attempt to get things off on the right foot here.

"I can help," Mom says as I stuff my phone back into my crossbody bag.

"Really?"

She shucks off one of her longer scarves, the one with tassels that nearly brush her knees. "We'll conquer it together."

"Okay, then," I say, moving to the countertop. The surfaces that aren't covered in wilted plants are overfilled with appliances, including a bread maker that looks like it hasn't been used since I was in diapers. "We'll need to get this cleared so we have—Mom, why do you have a hair curler stored with the Cuisinart?"

"I don't own a panini press."

"You . . ." I stare at her, then sigh and pull forward the stand mixer, which seems to be made of pure steel as it weighs approximately a metric ton. "Never mind. Can I put this out of the way? Maybe on top of the cabinet?"

Mom materializes next to me with an antique chair and clasps the neck of the mixer. When I try to wave her off, she flexes a twiggy arm. "Yoga has made me strong."

"Yeah? How many push-ups do you think you can do?"

"Pfft, push-ups. Yoga is about functional strength."

I step back. "Let's see it, then."

To my surprise, my graying mother hops atop the rickety

chair, lifts the mega stand mixer, and presses it on top of the cabinets. She spins, crossing her arms with the triumph of a gold medalist.

"Impressive," I say. "I guess owning a yoga studio has more practical benefits than I'd realized."

"The studio isn't quite profitable yet. Something about paying bills with loans—I don't know the details. But it certainly has nourished my soul." She puts a hand on my shoulder, at first to steady herself as she descends from the chair, but then to pull me in close for another inspection. "One of my classes might be just what you need to restore your spirit."

I break away so I can yank up shriveled brown plants from their chipped pots behind the sink. "My life isn't just about this breakup, you know. I have training to think about, too."

"I don't just mean the breakup. There are serious athletes in my classes. Yoga could be the key to unlocking your inner strength."

"Yeah? What kind of classes do you have?" Even though I doubt vinyasa is going to be the secret ingredient that helps me beat the Canadian powerhouse, I'm happy to visit her studio. She opened it six months ago or so—right after my last visit home. I doubt it'll be around much longer, so this will probably be my only opportunity to see it firsthand. "We have power yoga at the center, and something like that might work for . . ."

When I turn to toss a wilted basil plant into the countertop compost bin, I see that Mom's lips are curled, like she smells something bad.

"What's wrong?" I ask.

"*Power* yoga." She says it like it's a synonym for *corporate* or *factory farmed*.

"And power yoga is bad because . . . ?"

Mom yanks a cabinet open and shoves her slow cooker in front of a stuffed elf that I think I won at an arcade in middle school. I guess I'll reorganize that one later, then.

"Our classes are a sacred journey of the soul," she says. "A dance with cosmic energies that transcends this mundane realm. We stretch, we chant, we sing, and through that harmonization, we unlock the hidden chambers of our souls."

I blink. "So . . . not really yoga at all."

She wheels on me. "It is more *yoga* than some boot camp regimen of squats and lunges. You would like it if you gave it a chance. Plus, there are nice-looking men there."

I bottle up a sigh and turn to the refrigerator. I'm somewhat surprised it's taken her this long to bring up her latest man. I've been home for at least four minutes, so she'd usually have found a way to tell me about the new Leonard, Javier, or Magnus in her life. That is, if he wasn't hanging on her arm when I arrived.

"Tell me about him, then," I say.

"Who?"

"The guy," I say as I riffle through the fridge. To my surprise, instead of candles and sweaters, I find actual food. Not the array of high-quality proteins or fresh vegetables that I'll need, but two kinds of nondairy milk, hempseed hummus, and a glass container filled with a sprouted grain that doesn't seem to have molded yet. Odd. "The new man in your life. The one who you are meeting up with at the yoga studio."

"Why do you think that?"

I bump my hip against the fridge door to shut it. "The thing you just said. About the men."

Plus, she's not currently cocooned on the couch clutching a paper napkin soaked in tears, so that means she's in a new relationship, not getting out of an old one.

"I was talking about *you*," she says.

I eye her, noticing, for the first time since I arrived, the healthy glow in her cheeks and the confidence in her posture. Come to think of it, I can't even remember the last time Mom mentioned a boyfriend or even a casual date. Months, at least. Maybe even a year. Could Mimi Rose Parker possibly have been *single* for all this time? "You're not dating anyone?"

"You don't need to sound so impressed." She purses her lips and, only because I'm her daughter, I can read the hurt in her eyes.

"Right. Sorry," I say reflexively. "I'm just a bit negative on this whole 'relationship' thing right now."

"That's not new for you."

"Yeah." With a sigh, I add, "I took a chance on Maxwell. We see how well *that* worked out."

"You must have seen something in him."

She says it like she agrees with Sofi—like she's not quite sure why I dated him in the first place. She met Maxwell only once, at a race in Oakland. We got dinner afterward—at a dim sum restaurant Mom suggested—and Maxwell spent about a half hour deliberating over which orders would meet his precise dietary specifications. At the time, even though I knew Mom was a bit annoyed, I took it as evidence of how well we were going to work for each other.

The truth is that kind of behavior, as cringeworthy as it was to other people, was the reason I dated him in the first place. It wasn't that I had particularly deep feelings for him. He was never the one I wanted to talk to after a tough race—that's always been Sofi—or the one who pushed me to find my secret reserves of strength—that's Carla.

He did, however, want to talk about rowing all the time. He never flinched when I customized my orders at restaurants. He was always up to compare notes on journal articles and go over training logs to find patterns and better methods for recovery.

"I thought he was the right match for me," I say finally.

"How so?"

"Well, you know how Dad was about your dancing career?"

She half laughs, half snorts. "Of course."

"Right. Well, Maxwell was the opposite. We shared the same ambitions. He was just as invested in my success as he was in his own."

"You need someone who supports you."

"But he did," I say. "And it still didn't work."

"No, not like that. Not someone invested in your success. You need someone who can fill in your gaps. Someone to pick you up when you fall."

I shake my head. Like I told Carla, the breakup wasn't the only problem. It was the relationship, too. If I hadn't ceded so much control over my emotional state to Maxwell, my performance wouldn't have derailed. I'd be in the training center right now, probably drinking a specialty smoothie in the dining hall and laughing at something Sofi said. Not here, trying to clear my mom's kitchen of holiday decorations, further from my dreams than I've been in years.

My phone buzzes. I fish it out and swipe open an email from Adrian.

> You need a few days off, at least. We can talk in my office once you've had a chance to rest, get some extra sleep. Maybe do something fun? Get your mind off rowing for a bit.

I release a groan. Maybe Adrian thinks I have unlimited time for resting and diversions, but I'm at a huge disadvantage and time is running out. If I'm going to beat the unbeatable Canadian, I can't afford to lose a single session.

"We'll see about that," I mutter to myself as I shove the phone away.

It doesn't actually matter what he says. I'm going to morning practice whether Adrian likes it or not.

Seven

61 DAYS UNTIL PAN AMS

I arrive at the rickety old boathouse just as the first splashes of orange sunrise soak the horizon. Although someone has given the place a new coat of paint recently, it's otherwise just as I remember: all cupolas and gables and ancient wood siding, dotted by white-trimmed and thinning windows. It's a far cry from the sleek lines and shiny aluminum infrastructure of the training center. Maybe I should feel at home here, like cozy or nostalgic. Instead, I have that Chutes and Ladders feeling again, like I've been sent back to the starting line.

The bay doors are still firmly padlocked, but I'm glad to be the first one here. It means I have at least a few minutes to do a dryland warm-up with visualizations before the team arrives. As a freshman in high school, I started stretching daily on a grassy knoll, under the sprawling branches of a copper beech-tree, that overlooks the expanse of water spilling into the San Francisco Bay. My quiet moments alone by that tree, listening to the gentle lapping of waves against the shore and the call of a seagull overhead, became a meditation for me. A peaceful place away from the whirlwind of my mom's life. A place that belonged just to me.

The tree is still here, and I find a flat section of sandy earth where I can finish my pre-workout drink while I run through my warm-up routine. As I sink into a hamstring stretch, I picture my oar dipping into the surface of the water, a spray of water kicking off the blade. Then, a micro-pause at the base of my stroke, and—

Discordant music assaults my ears.

I whirl to find a gaggle of high school rowers descending the rickety wooden stairs from the upper levels of the boathouse. They're yelling and dancing to a cacophony of music—a pelting mixture of pop and rap—blasting from portable speakers clipped to their backpacks. At the bottom of the stairs, one kid holds his phone up to snatch a video as two others perform some kind of fake boxing match.

"*This* is what's wrong with teenagers," I mutter under my breath, like I could go back in time and land the perfect comeback to Carla. "Maybe they're not offensive, but they definitely aren't serious."

I scan youthful faces and lanky bodies, searching for an adult. Adrian doesn't seem to have arrived yet, so I root through my bag until I find my earbuds. Then I jam them into my ears, crank the volume, and focus on my lunges. If I turn my back to the group, all I can see is the trunk of the beech-tree and a stretch of placid water. It's not quite peaceful, but it's almost like being alone.

That is, until I'm bent in a calf stretch and someone slams into my back.

I topple. My hip lands on the grass with a whack of pain.

Still too surprised to be angry, I untangle my limbs and search for the source of my sudden engagement with the ground.

Above me, a kid with a constellation of acne is still midway through a backward dance move, phone held high in selfie mode.

"You ran into me?" I splutter.

Only then does the breakdancer look down.

"Sorry," he mutters. As though to prove the point, he tosses up a hand in an utterly unconvincing apologetic wave. Without another word, he resumes his dancing.

Involuntarily, my teeth gnash. I bet that vein in my temple is pulsing. The one Sofi calls my "anxiety-indicator light."

I press myself to my feet and dust off my unisuit, searching again for my new—very *temporary*—coach, who, as far as I can tell, hasn't lifted a finger to impose order on this dance party at dawn. Over a mass of heads and shoulders and oars, I finally spot a tall person with messy brown hair and a clipboard clasped behind his back. I beeline toward him, ducking out of the way of a quad precariously lofted on scrawny shoulders and a set of oars wielded like accidental spears.

I land behind the coach's wide shoulders, which are shaking with a chuckle. For reasons I can't quite place, his posture is vaguely familiar.

"Hello, Adrian?" Do I sound shrill? I probably sound shrill. I'm annoyed enough that I don't care.

The man turns.

And my gaze hiccups on a pair of familiar green eyes, crinkled in a laugh. The sound cuts off as my stomach plummets through my toes.

What the hell. This isn't happening. This is a dream.

My coach—my actual *coach*—is a man I once arm wrestled for a lemon bar? Danced with while I was drunk? Tried and, very importantly, *failed* to kiss?

Did I say dream? I meant nightmare. This is a nightmare.

"Kath, hey," Adrian says with too much ease. "I told you to wait a few days before coming down here."

"You—" I blink as I scrutinize his expression. He doesn't look sufficiently surprised. "You already know who I am?"

Adrian's eyes flick to his athletes, still parading around to their cacophonic beats. "Carla mentioned the World Cup and the finishes, the disqualification from residency."

I can't tell whether or not I should feel relieved or even more embarrassed. My mind retreads the emails we sent each other, even as my stomach clenches, decision made without me. More embarrassed. Definitely even more embarrassed.

"When, exactly, did you find out?" I ask. "Did you know when we . . ."

Adrian shakes his head. "No. Not until Carla messaged me a couple of days ago. And I was really hoping we could—"

"Who're you?" A gangly kid with gapped teeth pops up behind Adrian, regarding me with unconcealed curiosity.

I stare back mutely, still dizzy from the dawning reality that I got *drunk* and *rejected* by the man who is supposed to be coaching me for the next two months. How can I look at Adrian without remembering the way I lost control that night? How can I listen to his coaching cues without thinking about the way his hands felt on my waist?

"Do you need me to repeat the question?" the kid prompts. "You kind of look confused or, I don't know, maybe like English isn't your first language?"

When my mouth continues to work soundlessly, Adrian shoots me a sympathetic look.

"This"—he waves a hand like he's introducing a famous singer—"is Kath Parker, a national team athlete who just raced in the World Cups. And lucky for us, she'll be training with the performance team for the next two months."

More heads spring up. A few of them must have lowered the volume on their music, because the ambient ruckus dampens, and the group seems to be growing exponentially.

"Oh, shit."

"Really, World Cups?"

"How'd you do?"

Saving me from answering that last, rather loaded, question, Adrian interjects again. "She raced in the B final in Varese. In singles. That means you're looking at one of the twelve fastest women on the planet."

This elicits another chorus of reactions. I'm trying to figure out how to dispute Adrian's claim, to tell them that really World Championships is a more definitive measure of international rankings, when another kid tilts his head and says with a wide grin, "Really? What are you doing training here with us, then?"

Someone laughs and my stomach trips.

Another shout: "Hey, have you been to the *Olympics*?"

I blink into a sea of silent faces and watchful eyes. These kids look so innocent and yet they're finding my weak spots like archers aiming for bull's-eyes.

"No," I force myself to say. "One day I hope to go."

Two kids whistle. Someone flashes a thumbs-up. My eyes snag on a kid near the back of the group with knobby knees and pale white skin that looks as if it's been repeatedly burned into a permanent pink. Through a pair of wire glasses that take up most of his slight face, he's staring at me so intently it's almost unsettling.

"Any of you hoping to make it to the Olympics one day?" Adrian asks the group, and I'm thankful that he's pulled their attention away from me.

The question mostly elicits a chorus of *nahs* and shakes of the head.

"Too much work!" someone yells.

"I like video games too much," another supplies.

Some of the kids laugh, but the serious one holds himself completely still, except that, behind his glasses, his eyes widen.

"Isn't that kind of an unrealistic goal?" His voice is so low that, if I hadn't noticed him already, I would have missed it.

A kid wielding a phone like a searchlight leaps in front of his coach. He has umber skin and a mess of black hair that's been shaped into a surprisingly stylish quiff for a teenage boy. "Coach is going to say that no goal is unrealistic. All of us can do anything we set our minds to."

Adrian playfully punches his shoulder. "Thanks, Rohan. Actually, I was going to say that *nearly* all of you can do anything you set your minds to. Some of you are beyond hope."

"Ah!" the phone wielder—Rohan—yells. "Why did you have to say that when I wasn't recording? Everyone loves a snarky coach."

"He has to say that, though, right?" The serious kid is still looking at me, like nothing else has been said for the last few moments. "But it *is* unrealistic."

The question reminds me of the time I tacked up my first poster of an Olympian. I'd kept it rolled up under my bed for weeks, like my dreams were some sordid secret and if I declared them publicly, they'd never come true. One day, Mom saw the poster peeking out from under my duvet. When I admitted the truth, she took my hands in hers, looked me in the eyes, and told me about *the fire.* That was back when she danced professionally, and she said among dancers, there were some people who had it and some who didn't.

"When I look at you," she told me, "I don't see a few flames. I see a whole bonfire."

Mom might not have been great at signing permission slips

or remembering to make cookies for bake sales, but she gave me something better: the confidence to tack up that poster and dream bigger dreams.

I'm not saying anything about "the fire" to a bunch of teens, though. Instead, I lift a shoulder and tell them, "Yeah, probably."

Rohan's mouth drops open. "*That's* what you have to say? 'Yeah probably' our dreams are unrealistic?"

"Sure," I tell him, even though I shouldn't. I'm too honest with myself and everyone else to be good at these kinds of motivational speeches. "All big dreams are unrealistic. If you care enough, you'll try anyway."

A bunch of the kids, including Rohan, bury their gazes in frowns, but Adrian's eyes catch mine and his lips tweak into a crooked smile. It's the same look he gave me when I told him I had no thoughts of quitting rowing.

"Nahhhhh." A voice pierces our pocket of silence, and Rohan lifts his phone toward my face again. "We're gonna need something way more inspirational than 'this shit's hard, but try it anyway.'"

Adrian's eyes shift and he clears his throat. "Okay, that's enough. You'll have plenty of time to pester Kath later. Right now, you all need to start getting on the water."

Rohan groans, but clicks off his phone. The group scatters toward their awaiting shells.

Adrian remains by my side, though, which means we're alone again. I sink to a seat in one of the empty nylon slings behind me, partly because my legs have been so fatigued lately that they feel as substantial as Jell-O. Also, partly to get out of Adrian's proximity and the memories it induces. We have exactly one relationship now: coach and athlete. Nothing more.

"It's going to be great for these guys to train with you this summer," Adrian says. "Peter, in particular, I think."

I frown after the mess of heads bobbing down toward the dock. By my account, so far, we've only managed to all make one another uncomfortable. "Peter is the serious kid with the glasses?"

"Yeah. He sits stroke seat in my fastest quad. He's serious about everything, but he's most serious about rowing."

I nod. That tracks.

"So," Adrian says, sinking into a crouch in front of me, possibly so I don't have to get up from my makeshift seat, but putting himself firmly at my eye level again. "Can we talk quickly? There were a couple of things I was hoping to go over alone."

"Sure," I say.

He glances around at the guys who seem to be a safe distance away or at least too preoccupied with their equipment to be listening in. Then he says, "I know Carla has mentioned that I applied for the junior national team, but I'd rather you don't share that with anyone else. The kids, specifically."

"Won't they find out eventually, anyway? If you get it?"

"Unlikely," he says with a terse finality. "Can I have your word?"

I nod slowly. "Okay, sure. I won't say anything."

His expression softens. "Excellent, thank you. And the second thing. Are you feeling okay about everything? Now that you know who I am, too. Comfortable? We can also talk about this later if you need time to collect your thoughts."

I blink with surprise and search his expression for a hint of insincerity. In my experience, coaches barely acknowledge the existence of emotions, let alone ones directed at them. I don't remember the last time a coach asked me if I was comfortable with them, even though there are unique circumstances here.

"I'm fine," I say when Adrian still hasn't given any indication he's anything but serious. "But I do want to talk to you about that loaner boat. I'm not sure if your delay was about all this"—I wave my hand around vaguely—"but I don't have time to waste here."

Adrian tilts his head and studies me with an expression that suggests he's doing long division in his head. "You're ready to get back to it. Just like that?"

"Why wouldn't I?"

He lifts an eyebrow. "I hate to be crude about it, but you did experience an unfortunate series of losses."

"I bombed, you mean."

"Right."

I shrug. "Doesn't matter. I can't change that. All I can control is what I do today, tomorrow. That's why I'm here."

Emotion passes over his face like the roll of wake across the edge of a dock. He holds my gaze for long enough that a breeze kicks up around us, swirling the light morning mist over my skin. Goose bumps race down my arms.

"Well, that's something else, Parker," Adrian says, voice low. Then he stands, putting distance between us. "But still. You'll need to wait. I didn't tell you that because of anything to do with us. I said it because you've just spent the last month racing and you need a physical and mental break."

"I'm rested. It's been, like, three days of resting."

"You mean while you took a transatlantic flight and then packed up all your belongings and then took another flight across the state?" he asks.

"Exactly."

He shakes his head, another smile caressing his lips. "It's not enough. You're overtrained."

I cross my arms. Overtraining is real, but it's a feeling more than a diagnosable condition. Carla flags it for me when she sees my split times worsen, but without a metric like that, it's hard for someone else to identify it.

"How can you tell?" I challenge.

Adrian's eyes trace my face, my shoulders, and dip down my torso to my toes. I feel warmth prickle each body part his gaze touches, like he's extracting something from my exposed skin. "Your complexion is pale. When you talk, the ends of your sentences are clipped. Your feet drag when you walk and you're sitting at every opportunity."

I lurch to a stand. "Maybe that's just how I am."

"We've met three times," he says. From this vantage, we're suddenly close again. Too close. "I know how your face looked from the first and how you move from the second."

More heat climbs up the back of my neck. I fight to inhale properly. I try to take a step back, but my thighs brush against the sling, trapping me. "Those are all just—just subjective measures."

Adrian's eyes flick to my watch. "I bet your resting heart rate is through the roof."

As though on instinct, my wrist swivels to point my watch face upward. The numbers blink in yellow instead of green—more consistent with a light walk than standstill. The textbook would say that's a signal of cardiovascular stress and a good indicator of overtraining.

I slap the screen and drop my hand. "That could be from the travel and the time change."

"Yeah? What's the number, then?"

Before I realize what he's doing, Adrian reaches toward me and envelops my wrist with his long fingers. I'm so caught off guard I do nothing but stand limply as he gently swivels my watch upward again, drawing my hand toward him. My heart takes off at a gallop. The watch face careens through colors—dark yellow, then bright orange.

I yank back my hand.

"That's not—" I splutter. "It doesn't matter what my heart rate is."

Adrian finds my eyes and my chest lurches like the traitor it is.

"Of course it matters," he says.

I shake my head, some combination of defiance and embarrassment moving my chin before conscious thought. My heart wouldn't be dancing around in my chest like a rhythmic gymnast if we hadn't arm wrestled or danced. If I hadn't tried to kiss him. If he didn't have those eyes or those damn shoulders.

"I'm ready to get back on the water," I say firmly. "This is my call."

Adrian's eyebrows squeeze together as he studies me again. This time, though, he's not examining anything on my face or my body, but something deeper. Something that sends another shiver right through my spine.

He clicks his tongue and his body language shifts—arms crossed, back straight, smile gone.

"Rest, Parker. You need rest. And then you need to do something else. Something fun. Don't think about rowing. And that's not your call. It's mine." With that, he turns and strides down the hill toward the docks. "You can get back on the water when you can stand upright and the watch stays green."

I gnash my teeth even as I let myself slide back into the sling. Kids filter down to the docks, shells lofted high on shoulders. One by one, they pile onto their seats, push off, and stroke away.

As the boats recede into pinpricks, I run through mental math. I have sixty-one days until Pan Ams. It might sound like a lot, but in training terms, it's nothing. A blink. Plus, to get my heart rate down to baseline, I'll need *days* off. So, Adrian is saying I should skip—what—twelve percent of my on-water sessions?

I can't give up that much precious training time if I want to beat the unbeatable Canadian.

Resolved, I march into the boathouse and hunt for a shell that no one will miss. I find my prize crammed into the back. Its faded gray cover is thick with dust, and it has a cracked footplate and a missing bow ball.

Better than nothing, I think as I settle my boat into the water, strap in my feet, and push my fingertips off the dock.

Eight

60 DAYS UNTIL PAN AMS

After I'm berated for "using club property without permission," Adrian starts locking the bay doors when his team gets on the water. In answer, I start pacing the shoreline until I can pepper my so-called coach with questions, like: "When will you release me from this purgatory?" and "Is this some kind of conspiracy to tank my performance?" and "Are you secretly a Canadian plant?"

My questions barely faze him. In fact, they seem to fuel his resolve. I don't know what happened to the enthusiastic smiles and kind words. Now, he's all crossed arms and wordless shoulder shrugs. He even snorted when I asked him about being a Canadian plant. *Snorted.* He then retorted that the Canadians are winning plenty of medals without an ounce of his help. Frankly, I find this offensive given that I have to beat one of them to get my damn life back.

I've spent hours hatching a plan to break into the boathouse, heist-style. Most of the windows are firmly locked or, I don't know, sealed shut with grime and dust, but there's a possibility I can scale the wood siding and get in through one of the small ones up high. Yet, after picturing myself getting stuck like Winnie the Pooh, resulting in a broken ankle or, even worse, a rescue from Adrian, I shoot down the idea.

Instead, I manage to convince Peter—the serious kid with the glasses—to leave a set of dumbbells outside the weight room so I can do weighted lunges. This earns me my second reprimand from Adrian, who's all scowls and finger pointing as he wrests "East Bay Rowing property" out of my hands.

"You said I can get back to strength training!" I protest as I relinquish the dumbbells. "Today!"

"I *said*," Adrian growls as he hoists them onto a shoulder, "that I would consider letting you join us for the weight room session this afternoon. The one *I* have programmed. Where *I* will be present. But now you'll have to wait until tomorrow at least."

"WHAT?" I scream at his tight shoulders as he strides away. Adrian keeps saying stuff about "mental health" and "emotional bandwidth" but never acknowledges this actual *torture* he's putting me through. "What about a racing shell? When do I get one of those?"

He points a finger toward the road. "Get some rest, Parker. Have some fun."

Terrified he'll add yet more time to my sentence, I stop stalking the bays.

Instead, I stalk his office.

At the very least, I argue, he should let me read his training program. Ostensibly, I'll be doing this program for the next two months and I need to mentally prepare. After much cajoling, Adrian begrudgingly agrees to give me an hour with it and forks over a stack of papers. This is the first red flag. Back home, my programs are on electronic spreadsheets where they belong.

With raised eyebrows, I heft the jumbled pile to the team lounge and prop myself on one of the faded couches.

My eyebrows climb into my hairline as I keep reading. Adrian's program isn't a "program" so much as it is a *Choose Your Own Adventure* novel. The sheets are littered with a wild array of matrices, printed text, and handwriting in different colored pens. Big sections have been scratched out with ugly slashes and replaced with nearly nonsensical scribbles. Plan A's and B's and C's abound. There are decision trees scrawled in margins and contingencies mentioned on every other page. It's all so indecipherable that I give up, trudge back upstairs, and ask Adrian to translate. With that enigmatic smile, he tells me he's happy to answer any specific questions, but ultimately, I shouldn't get too "wedded" to any single approach because he might decide later to "adapt" the program as needs arise.

"Adapt," I say, dripping with skepticism. "A training plan is a *plan.* It's based on analysis and evidence. You can't change it because you feel like it. That's called winging it."

He lifts a shoulder like my entire future isn't riding on the next sixty days. "I prefer to call it 'intuition.'"

"Intuition. Whose? Yours?"

"Yes." He leans forward, arms crossed on his desk. "And half my team went to Youth Nationals last year, so the proof is in the pudding. Time's up, by the way."

I bottle up a scream and power walk home, stomping with every step, but avoid an actual jog lest I fail another one of Adrian's resting heart rate tests. When I careen through the door, Mom makes a whispered suggestion that I should try one of her yoga classes for relaxation. I tell her I'm in no mood for chanting, then cloister myself in my room and stare at the Olympic rings on my ceiling, feeling farther from my dreams than I have in years.

. . .

"It can't have been *that* bad," Sofi says through my phone, which is leaning against a shampoo bottle.

I'm sitting on a shaggy mat attempting to turn Mom's claw-foot bathtub into a cold plunge. If I were in the training center, Sofi and I would be sitting in adjacent tubs, as we do every day after strength training. Here in Berkeley, I have nothing but a bucket of ice, a meat thermometer, and simmering rage over my first official workout with Adrian.

"Yeah, it was worse," I say as I tip another handful of cubes into the already icy surface. "Remind me what temperature it's supposed to be?"

Sofi sucks in a breath through her teeth, then wades across her sleek, stainless steel contraption held at a constant temperature with a continuous filtration system. She peers at the LED display.

"We're at fifty-one degrees."

I glare at my meat thermometer. "Crap. I'm at fifty-four."

"That should be fine."

"There are studies on this." I shovel another few handfuls of ice into the tub. "The temperature needs to be precise."

Sofi balloons her cheeks as she settles back. "I'm only here because Carla thinks it builds character."

"Not what I said." Carla's voice floats in from the background.

Sofi waves her off. I'm pretty sure she's the only one with the confidence to tease our coach. To her face, anyway.

"Carla's there?" I whisper.

Sofi angles her phone so I can see. Carla seems to be dispatching advice to one of Sofi's teammates. Oh, the irony of missing that woman. I always knew I loved the training center, but I never appreciated how good I had it until now. Real, consistent training programs printed out and pinned to a bulletin board? Specific metrics and predetermined goals? A rowing coach who actually lets me *row*?

Heaven.

The pair disappear as Sofi sweeps back into view, tugging at her red bathing suit strap to keep it from falling off her shoulder. "So, why exactly was the first practice such a disaster?"

"First of all, it wasn't even practice," I grind out. My tub has now reached fifty-one degrees. I dip a foot into the icy surface. Cold slingshots up my leg. I let out an involuntary hiss. When I get myself under control, I stick the next foot in. "It was strength training because Adrian hasn't deemed me worthy of anything else. And, second, he wouldn't let me do the right number of sets."

For some reason I couldn't fathom, Adrian told me to stop after four sets of squats, instead of the typical six I do during the on-season. But I still felt good enough not just to keep going, but even to add another couple of plates to my barbell.

"Cut it out, Parker," Adrian growled from across the room, even though his eyes were glued downward as he spotted Peter on the bench press.

I glared at him from over the bar, thoughts seething. He never does this dictator routine with any of his kids. As he cued Rohan on his triceps extensions, he joked about his advice even as he dispatched it. With Peter, he squatted to meet him at eye level and coaxed him through his final reps. When another guy slipped off the pull-up bar and nearly ate it on the rubber mats, Adrian helped him up, drew him aside, and gave him a pep talk about falling that sounded like it was copied straight off a motivational poster.

So, it's just me that gets domineering Adrian.

Of course.

Adrian turned to cue a kid on the bench row. With his back turned, I racked my weight, curled my fingers around the coarse grips, and dropped below the bar to start my sixth set.

"Parker!" Adrian's voice bit out over the clangs of iron and thuds of barbells against wood. "Don't you do it."

I cursed under my breath before glowering at him. He scowled right back with equal obstinance—all the gentleness that he'd just been administering to his young athletes evaporated. Still, I didn't let go. I've researched this. I've done the repetition maximum tests and calculated the right load coefficients factors. I do six sets because of science and evidence, not winging it.

"I always do six," I bit back.

"Today you're doing five."

I tensed my shoulders and lifted the bar off its hooks. Adrian flew across the room, landing in front of me. Eyes burning, he pressed his hands on either side of my barbell, hemming me between his arms. Then he pushed backward until I heard a click of metal on metal.

I stared up at him defiantly, neck still pressed to the cool bar. The proximity of him, the way his body seemed to engulf mine . . . With him this close, I could even smell him—all sandalwood, and citrus, and *opinions*. On either side of my shoulders, Adrian rolled his hands against the grips, as though fixing the bar—and me—in place.

"Enough," he growled. "That's enough."

My heart thudded, low in my chest, and heat spread up my neck.

Around us, the clangs and thuds of an active weight room quieted. Dozens of pairs of eyes descended on my squat rack. With another frown, I released the bar and stepped back, extricating myself from Adrian's overwhelming nearness.

He exhaled, and it sounded almost like relief, then spun around. "Back to work, boys!"

"You sure this is about the squats?" Sofi asks from her perch at the edge of the tub.

"What's that mean?" My teeth involuntarily chatter again. I glance at my timer. Still nine minutes to go, which sounds shorter than it'll feel.

Sofi's eyes get closer to the screen, like she's trying to inspect me through the tiny window. "You're more agitated than usual. And that's saying something."

"I'm agitated," I say, pivoting to avoid her scrutinizing gaze and so I can scoop up one of my hard-boiled eggs from the Tupperware on the bathroom tiles, "because I have to beat the Canadian to get my life back and the person who is supposed to be helping me do that is holding me back instead."

"Hmm," she says, leaning yet closer. I can barely see anything but one of her brown eyes. "*Or* you're feeling embarrassed about the dance floor incident, but that emotion makes you uncomfortable so you're channeling it into rage instead."

I narrow my eyes. Sofi might be my best friend, but I still hate that she witnessed that moment. No one should have seen that because it never should have happened in the first place. "I'm not."

She nods like I just agreed with her. "Right, so it's both, then. And maybe some repressed attraction?"

I fight a sigh, which quickly turns into a shudder. "I am not repressing attraction. Adrian is my coach. Besides, I don't have any attraction to repress."

"Yeah. Right, totally," Sofi says. "It's probably also why you kept yourself a respectful distance away from Citrus Adonis on the dance floor."

"*Citrus Adonis*?"

She fights a grin. "You don't like that? I've got more. Hunk o' Lemon? Tarty Squeeze?"

I bite off half an egg and roll my eyes aggressively enough that she can see me do it. "Can we talk about you now? Surely you have some emotional wounds we can pick at instead."

Her gaze pings around her med center room before she pinches the bridge of her nose.

"What's wrong?" I ask, realizing I've elicited more consternation than expected.

"It's just . . . Missy melted down after practice this morning because she feels like the boat isn't 'respecting her calls,' but that led to a huge fight with everyone about how emotionally she responds when things aren't going her way and I, of course, ended up in the middle when I tried to talk everyone down. Now I'm lightheaded and fed up."

"That's frustrating," I say, genuinely sympathetic. Every time something like this happens with Sofi's team, I feel grateful I have only my own drama to deal with. "How are things now?"

She puffs her cheeks as she resettles into her seat. "Fine, I guess. Missy apologized for her outburst, but it's been an hour since I left her room and I'm *still* dizzy."

"Yeah? When's the last time you ate?"

She regards me skeptically. "You've only been home for a few days. How have you already turned into your mom?"

I laugh darkly. "Well, first off, you're thinking of *anyone else's* mom, not mine. But second off, I always bring eggs and bananas to our afternoon cold plunges"—I lift the banana peel that I dropped on the floor earlier—"and you're both lightheaded and empty-handed."

She balks. "Will you be mad if I admit that I haven't eaten since second breakfast?"

I sigh. "I'll text you tomorrow to remind you of our snacking times."

"And to think people call you overbearing."

"Those people should meet my new coach."

She guffaws before shaking her head. "You know, you could try his method. To see if it works."

"I can't afford to experiment right now. I've lost *days* and I have no idea how much longer this is going to go on. I'm considering quitting the whole thing."

"Quitting what whole thing?"

I wrap my hands around my triceps as though it will do something to dispel the deep chill. "Training with Adrian. Or *not* training with Adrian, as the case may be. The kids are more of a distraction than a pacing help, anyway, so I might as well get on the water alone. I can talk to the boathouse's equipment manager to get a permanent loaner shell and then make my own program."

Sofi's eyes drag between me and something off-screen. "You sure that's a good idea? Wouldn't you want to talk it over with Carla first?"

I open my mouth to retort something very acerbic and convincing about how I shouldn't have to loop Carla into my plans when she's cut me out of all of hers, but Sofi grimaces. My stomach sinks.

"She's listening, isn't she?" I ask.

Sofi nods.

I lean back and instantly regret the way the cold water sends another shiver up my spine.

From the background a voice bites out, "Let me talk to Kath."

Nine

"I can't do this anymore," I say, grinding the words out with more confidence than I feel given the intensity of Carla's frown now filling my screen. "No amount of hypothetical coaching is worth this."

Carla doesn't respond. Instead, I think she must drop the phone and start walking because she disappears, and the screen bounces erratically as the background, with Sofi in it, recedes from view.

"Coach!" I hear my friend shout. "You have my phone."

"I'll be back in a minute," Carla says without slowing. "I need to talk to Kath alone."

I shiver as I wait, willing the final minutes to tick away on my apple-shaped timer. Through the screen, I catch a glimpse of dark gray carpet and the metal legs of Carla's desk. A door clicks closed. A leather chair creaks.

My coach's face reemerges on the screen, but she's now framed by a black leather chair and the massive set of Olympic rings on her wall.

"I was going to call you later today about this, but if you're going to broadcast your intention to quit in front of Sofia and half the team, we might as well talk now." Carla leans her elbows on her desk and eyes me heavily. "The board voted to move Adrian forward in the hiring process this morning, but it's a bit of a complicated situation."

"Complicated how?"

"He'd be an unconventional hire for this particular job." Carla sounds like she's choosing her words carefully. "He's never coached above high school, although I have it on good authority that he's turned down three varsity jobs, so it's not for lack of opportunity. Also, I like him for the job. Still . . . some are concerned that he's too risky of a pick."

"Okay," I say, "what does this have to do with me?"

"You can't quit on him. You have to train with Adrian."

"Because . . . he might be a junior national team coach someday?"

Carla blows out a breath. "No, so you can provide an independent review of his performance. You've had elite coaching in multiple age categories. You could tell us more about his style and whether or not he has what it'll take. And, despite all the hiccups lately, you still have a reputation as a straight shooter, so the board will listen."

Blessedly, at that moment, my apple timer screams. I shoot out of the bathtub and spring onto the mat, wrapping my pink, raw skin in one of my mom's fluffy robes. The moment gives me a reprieve to collect myself and consider exactly how I'm going to turn down Carla's request without aggravating her.

"Coach," I say into the phone, trying to be as professional as possible given that I'm dripping on a bath mat. "His coaching style doesn't work at all for me. I appreciate that USRowing has hiring needs, but I have to think about myself, here."

"Kath." She says my name like it's made of a sigh. "I *am*

thinking about you. You might not be able to see it, but forcing yourself to change up your routine is exactly what you need to improve for Pan Ams."

Ugh, not this. The silver lining of being sent home was that I wouldn't need to have this argument with Carla yet again. My *routines* worked just fine for the years before I started dating Maxwell. Carla wasn't complaining about my *routines* a year ago when I was making A finals.

"Routines and schedules make me successful," I say. "Sticking to the plan is how I perform my best."

Carla pinches the bridge of her nose. "I'm trying to offer you an opportunity here, and if you could yank your head out of your backside for a moment, you'd see that."

I inhale sharply, stunned by her tone, but even more angered by her words.

"I'm sorry, an *opportunity*?" I say, channeling the last seventy-two hours of frustration into my tone. "To train with *this* guy? You want an honest review of his coaching style?" I start pacing circles in the bathroom, holding the phone up with one hand and my robe closed with the other. "We don't need to wait eight weeks, I can tell you right now. He's stubborn and opinionated. He doesn't value the importance of hard work or time on the water. Instead of a structured training program, he relies on, I don't know, stream of conscious, nonsensical notes, and probably some astrology for good measure. Oh, and he smiles way too much to be taking his job seriously. So, yes, I can already tell you what it will be like to train with him and, no, I don't think it's much of an opportunity at all."

When I finish, I'm breathing hard from emotion, pacing, and keeping my voice just below a shout. Thankfully, my mom is at her yoga studio, so I don't have to worry about her bursting into the bathroom out of concern.

Carla doesn't speak, her serious brown eyes boring twin holes into my face. My neck pricks under the thick silence, punctuated only by the screech of brakes as a garbage truck comes to a stop outside and then hums and clangs. The engine revs again and the sound fades. A shiver races down my spine and I hug the robe closer.

"Are you done?" Carla asks.

"Yes," I say.

"Good. Because those subjective opinions aren't going to cut it when you submit Adrian's evaluation in two months." I raise an incredulous eyebrow and she puts up a hand. "Enough. Let me finish. The reason I said this is an opportunity is because I have a deal for you. You haven't talked me out of it, but only because you still have an ounce of my goodwill left.

"If you do this—if you spend the next two months training with an entirely different coach, and one with such a clearly different style than what you're accustomed to—it will go a long way to proving you are more adaptable than we all thought. It would help change the board's position on your residency."

Wait, what? Everything freezes. My breath. My feet. The shaking of the phone in my hand.

"What are you saying?" I ask. "If I do this, USRowing will give me my spot back?"

"I can't guarantee it. You'll still have to perform well enough at Pan Ams that the board is willing to accept my recommendation. I think that would be top two. But if you do that, and participate fully in Adrian's programming, and give us an *unbiased* account of his strengths and weaknesses at the end of the summer, I will be able to submit a recommendation that they are likely to accept."

My breath is coming in short gasps now. Holy crap. Top two. Difficult, but doable. I wouldn't have to beat the unbeatable

Canadian. I'd still have to place above everyone else in Central and South America, but I've done that before.

"Would I be able to tell Adrian what's going on?"

"Yes, I already told him about this possibility. But you cannot share with anyone else."

"I can't tell Sofi?"

"*Especially* not Sofia."

"Why not?"

Carla runs her tongue over her teeth. "These kinds of things are fodder for rampant speculation. Athletes will get a say through the formal channel—their representative on the board. Otherwise, this is USRowing's decision."

"But you're evaluating him for the junior national team," I say. "No one I know would care about that job."

Carla doesn't answer for a moment. Then she says, "Just promise me, Kath. I don't want this getting out too early."

"Okay," I say, already moving on. I'll just have to be careful of what I say to Sofi. "I promise."

It doesn't matter anyway, not compared to everything else. Obviously, training under Adrian is not ideal. I'll have to keep modifying his program so I don't lose a huge amount of fitness this summer. I still have Olympic qualifiers next year to think about. But. This bargain is way too good to refuse. At this point, it's my only real shot to get the spot back.

"I'll do it," I say aloud.

Ten

57 DAYS UNTIL PAN AMS

When I mention the evaluation—in conjunction with yet another request to get back on the water—Adrian lifts a shoulder and asks about my resting heart rate.

"You don't care?" I splutter. I'd thought the whole tenor of our conversations might change, ideally make him more accommodating to my requests. Our power dynamic should have completely changed now that I'm the one with control over his destiny. At the very least, I thought he'd have a few questions about how the evaluation is going to work. "How can I evaluate you without, you know, *training* with you?"

Adrian shrugs again. "There's time."

So, I spend another thirty-six hours aggressively resting. I've always been good about my nutrition and sleep, but I become maniacal. I track every ounce of water, every gram of macronutrients and milligram of electrolytes that pass over my lips. I monitor my sleep, not only with my watch but also a heart rate strap for more accuracy, and I scrutinize the graphs before plunging into yet another nap. Any minute that I'm not sleeping, I'm stretching, or visualizing, or eating as much protein as I can conceivably stuff into my mouth.

Finally—*finally*—Adrian deigns to let me back into a racing shell.

My new loaner is a big upgrade from the dusty boat I pirated, but it's still slightly wider and therefore slower than the one I have at the training center. I don't care. I'm so relieved just to be touching carbon fiber again that I practically sob when I set it into the slings.

Heart climbing up my throat, I start running through my warm-up stretches: lunges, toe touches, some dynamic rotations. Probably because I'm so relieved, I feel incredible. It's like there are secret reserves of strength and energy flowing under my tingling skin, powering every swing of my nearly weightless arms and legs. Then I jam in a pair of earbuds and blast David Guetta, and, as Sofi would say, I'm ready to run through a fucking wall.

I missed this so much.

Yet this floaty, happy feeling lasts about three minutes. Because Adrian always has a catch.

He materializes behind me, holding out a lockbox like a collection tin awaiting its tithe. One by one, the guys form a line and toss their phones in the outstretched box with a series of thunks. I've seen them do this ritual over the last few days, but this rule shouldn't apply to me. It's so that young athletes aren't, like, on TikTok in their boats.

For some reason, Adrian smiles at me from beneath a section of hair that's fallen in his eyes and nudges the box toward my wing riggers where I've already mounted my phone.

"You can't be serious," I say.

"I'm always serious," he says with a grin that is anything but.

Peter darts up to lay his cell phone in the box, then watches me from around his coach's shoulder.

"The rule is *everyone, every time,*" he says, like he's repeating something that's been engraved on a stone tablet, not at some point mentioned by a high school rowing coach.

Adrian nods solemnly.

I purse my lips as I relinquish my phone. It's not ideal—I prefer to have it so I can monitor advanced metrics, like distance using GPS—but what I really need is my StrokeCoach: the small device that monitors my most important stats, like splits and stroke rate.

I'm already moving back toward my boat when Adrian says, "The StrokeCoach, too."

Slowly, I turn back. "Excuse me?"

"Just for this practice."

Another cell phone thuds into Adrian's box. I'm still staring in disbelief.

"I have to have it," I stammer.

"Oh yeah? Why's that?"

It's like asking me why I need a *seat*. I've used a StrokeCoach since I was a teenager. It's one of my most important pieces of equipment. Especially today. We're doing three by three thousand meters—one of my keystone practices. It'll establish a baseline for the rest of the summer. "I need to know my interval times."

Adrian plucks up the stopwatch hanging around his neck. "I actually have a device capable of keeping track of time."

My mind flicks through the rubric Carla sent me and I mentally pen in the places where I can write *intransigent* and *demanding* and *possibly cracked in the head*. You know, in an unbiased way. "But . . . in real time. If I know my speed and stroke rate, at any given moment, I can calculate how I stack up to the splits I need to get second at Pan Ams."

"You think that's a good thing?" Adrian asks. "Living with that in your head every second of every practice?"

"It keeps me focused."

"That's one word for it."

Rohan, who has just reached the top of the line, drums his fingers against crossed arms. Instead of scattering toward their shells, he and the rest of the guys are watching me. Maybe waiting to see who will win this standoff or possibly plotting to take me down in defense of their coach.

"You're one of us now, ma'am," Rohan says. "You have to do what Coach says."

I narrow my eyes at him as one of the other kids guffaws.

Rohan throws up his hands in mock surrender. "Ma'am! I said *ma'am*! That was a hundred percent respectful."

Adrian nudges his athlete away with an elbow. "I think you're making it worse, dude." He holds the box toward me once more, voice hardening. "StrokeCoach, Parker. I'm not asking again."

Heat rises up my neck as watchful eyes track my every movement, but I still unlock the device from its mount and drop it into the box. Then I turn and march down to the water, boat firmly on my hip and left hand facing away from the team.

Because Adrian didn't ask for my watch.

The first interval goes poorly. Even though my body feels light, I'm opening my trunk too early and missing water at the catch. I also have to keep angling my wrist so I can surreptitiously glance at my watch. Every time I see a number that displeases me, my next stroke falters, and I fight to regain momentum.

All in all, this practice is going exactly as well as I'd have expected considering I lost multiple days of training and I don't have my most important tech.

"Damn it, Parker!" Adrian yells from his launch as I finish the second-to-last interval. I'm hunched over, elbows crushing my knees as I suck in air, trying to calm my burning lungs.

His boat accelerates toward me in a storm of wake and roar of engine.

"What?" I yell, even though I know exactly what. I hit a button on my watch moments before Adrian's outburst.

He kills the engine and strides to the edge of his platform, towering form casting a long shadow that nearly reaches my deck.

"Watch," he demands. "No more games. Give it to me now."

"I told you—"

"No." He points a finger at it. "No more. Take off the watch."

There's actual pain in my jaw from how hard I'm clenching my teeth. My mind flits back to that rubric and I can't wait—I *cannot wait*—to tell USRowing exactly what kind of coach Adrian is.

"Now, Parker," Adrian says again.

I refuse to look at him as I unclasp the band and throw the watch at his chest. He catches it with one hand before tucking it into his pocket.

"Thank you," he says, tone lower. "We'll start again in a few minutes."

I channel my rage into my last interval.

Every time Adrian's green eyes flit into my mind, I jam my legs harder, driving the boat forward with strokes as vengeful as they are powerful. My blades splash under each precise catch, my core flexing as I drive, my lats and biceps burning with the finish. A salty breeze swirls around me as the oars glide back and forth. Catch, drive, feather, recover. Over and over until it isn't just a rhythm. It's a poem.

We hit the halfway point, and my breaths start coming in

harder. There's acid building in my limbs, but I'm so focused, so intent, I barely feel it.

I glide, skating on the water like a kid on a swing: light, weightless. I'm floating, each stroke propelling me forward, taking me feet instead of inches, like my boat has a life of its own. Like my equipment weighs half as much as it should. The pain is there—always there—but it's overshadowed by joy.

This right here. It's one of the reasons I love rowing. Yes, there's the control and the routine and the life I get to live because of my devotion to the sport. But there's also this feeling. Like I'm flying. I never get to choose when it happens, but when it does, it's magic.

We finish the last interval in a whirlwind of sweat and pain and breathtaking exhilaration. I brace my elbows against my knees, droplets of sweat and briny water dripping from the tip of my nose. Instantly, I turn my wrist, searching for my phantom watch. My gaze flicks up to Adrian's launch a few boat lengths away. He's grinning.

"Time?" I ask with my next lungful of air.

His smile widens.

. . .

Adrian makes me wait until all the guys have left, filtering away to idling cars in the parking lot, before he'll share the last interval time with me.

"Want to guess?" he asks, a devilish grin playing across his lips.

I swallow a heavy sigh. I take my splits way too seriously to play these games. Even worse, I'm annoyed by the way his eyes dance when he's smiling.

"Can't you just tell me?"

"Did it feel faster or slower than the others?" Adrian prods.

I don't have to think about it, because it doesn't matter how it felt. For the last few months, whenever I've done this workout, the pattern has always been the same. The second interval is slower than the first and the third is slower than the second.

"Slower," I bite out. "So, what was it?"

Very slowly, and with that damn grin spreading even wider, Adrian shakes his head, maintaining eye contact like he needs to witness my reaction. "Faster."

"Faster than the second?"

"No," he says. "Faster than both."

I stare at him for another beat, trying to figure out if he's lying or exaggerating. "Sounds like a mistake."

He hands his clipboard to me. "See? Resting. Getting out of your head. It works. Are you ready to start taking my method seriously?"

I tilt the page. It's filled with notes and times layered together with errant observations about conditions and technical cues. Adrian reaches over to tap a finger against my initials near the bottom. I squint at the numbers scrawled there.

"The second interval is off by about a second," I say, slapping the clipboard against his chest.

He frowns at the paper, then up at me. "That's about how much time it would take you to look at your watch. Besides, you beat your time by almost ten seconds on the third one, so we're well outside a margin of error."

"Yeah," I say, "but now I don't know if I can trust your notes."

Adrian leans his head back and stares at the boathouse rafters for so long I wonder if I've taken this too far. It wouldn't be the first time a coach quit on me. During my senior year of high school, I started refusing to do my coach's elementary, often recycled on-water programs. After some months, that coach, Darlene was her name, stopped fighting me. Eventually, she stopped coaching me entirely. I think I might lose my deal with Carla if Adrian actively quits on me, though.

Just as I'm about to try to, gently, take a step back, Adrian's eyes sink to my face. He blows out a long breath, gaze softer than it has been in days. "Maybe I'm taking the wrong approach here."

"What does that mean?"

"Maybe I'm coaching you wrong."

"I don't understand."

Adrian folds his arms around his clipboard and tilts his head. For the last few days, his expression and demeanor have been filled with visceral authority, demanding and stern. But . . . his body language has shifted again. More open somehow.

"I thought you might be an athlete who does well with rules and boundaries and firm lines," he says. "I also thought you'd change your mind if I gave you clear reason to do so. Like today, without technology getting in the way, you were able to connect with your body instead of being so fixated on all the tangential stuff. It worked, too, or at least I can see that it did. But you still haven't changed your mind about me or my coaching. So, maybe it's time to switch gears."

Connect with my body? Technology "getting in the way"? It all sounds suspiciously like something my mom would say, but with less talk of chakras and healing spirits.

"What do you mean 'switch gears'?" I ask.

"Coach you differently. Quit doing the iron fist thing."

My brain stumbles. "Wait, sorry. 'Iron fist' thing? You're saying you've been *acting*?"

He frowns, but his tone remains more open than stern. "No, I've been *coaching*. Different athletes need different styles. Some need firm rules and limits. Some need smiles and pep talks. Some need high standards and specific praise. I'm trying to figure out what you need."

I blink at him. I've trained with a lot of coaches and, yes, they all had different approaches, but that was about them as individuals. Carla has sky-high expectations that most people fight to try to meet. Darlene doled out praise like candies while my varsity coach withheld it except in the rarest of occasions. Those styles work better or worse for different athletes. But I've never seen a coach change *themself*.

I shake my head.

"You don't believe me?" he asks.

"It doesn't sound possible."

Adrian regards me for another beat, finger tapping against his clipboard. "Well, I guess it doesn't matter."

"It doesn't? How about for the evaluation?" I ask.

"I can't keep having every practice be a fight like this and, apparently, the iron fist isn't working," he says, clearly ignoring my question. "You're not one of my actual athletes. I can't actually tell you what to do. So why don't you tell me. What do you need to start taking all of this seriously?"

"What do you mean you can't really tell me what to do," I say.

"I have no actual power in our relationship," Adrian clarifies. "I can talk loud. I can shout demands. But I can't withhold anything from you, like a seat or race placement. I'm not going to make a recommendation about your future team selections. I can't impose any consequences on you like a real coach would. I need you to decide to work with me, to take me seriously. So, why don't you tell me what you need to start doing that?"

I swallow a gasp as I realize what he's offering. "Give me control over the program."

Adrian chuckles. "I'm the coach, Kath."

"Okay, well you asked what I need to take you seriously, and that's it. I want routine and structure and matrices. I want plan A's, which never morph into plans B or C based on someone's whim or— "

"Intuition?"

"Yeah, intuition." I fold my arms, but I'm relieved to finally be given an opening to state my preferences. "I'll design something structured and predictable. Your team can do it, too."

Adrian's eyes dance across my face even as he shakes his head. "I'm not doing that."

I shrug. "Well, then, I'm not taking it seriously."

Adrian watches me for so long I wonder if I've broken him. Hopefully, I have. This man could use some breaking.

Abruptly, he says, "Let's compete for it."

"What?"

"We compete. Like with the lemon bar. You win, I'll let you design the program. I win, you have to start following my instructions without arguing about every decision or trying to find loopholes in every rule."

The edge of excitement lifts my chest. For the first time in days, I have a real opportunity to determine my own fate. And a competition is exactly the way I want to resolve this.

"We can arm wrestle again," I say, nearly breathless with excitement.

Adrian barks out a laugh. "No, Parker. The offer is only good for the erg."

I can tell he thinks he's got some kind of upper hand here, but adrenaline still rushes through my fingertips. Little does Adrian know, the *erg* is my forte. Using an erg is like rowing—pulling an oar through water—but there is no water and there is no oar. It's just a machine with a handle, a sliding seat, and a display screen. No crosswinds, no waves, no confounding conditions. Just pulling.

"Yes," I say, trying to hide the eagerness in my voice. "It's a deal."

Adrian's mouth explodes with another grin. "Let's race right now."

Eleven

Adrian practically skips to the lockers. From one of the wooden cubbies, he extracts a gym bag like a handyman retrieving a well-loved toolbox.

"Meet you there?" he asks. "I'll change."

That enthusiastic grin has reinvigorated his face. This time, a certain deviousness simmers just under the surface. It reminds me of Sofi's wolfish grin when she's about to crush me at pinball. Wariness rises up in me, like my body has internalized a mistake before my mind has caught up.

I sling my own bag onto my shoulder and scale the rickety old wooden stairs toward the upper levels of the boathouse, forging toward the erg room.

I'm not a religious person, but if I were, this place would be my house of worship. Dust motes dance in the rectangles of light spilling from the massive bay windows. They illuminate the row of ergs like pews awaiting their parishioners. The room smells like sun-warmed wood and old varnish and I'm bathed in a prayer shawl of silence, entranced.

The first time I ever felt the sensation of rowing was on one of these machines. It was the summer before I started high school, Mom was between jobs, and no two days were the same. One night she'd wake me up at midnight because she was craving waffles, and the next she'd be canceling our plans to go back-to-school shopping so we could do a candle-making workshop at the YMCA.

On a whim, Mom signed me up for Discover Rowing Day. The coach, Darlene, led our awkward group of shuffling teens through the trophy room to tell us about the club's long, decorated history, and let us each hold an oar. I was already awestruck by what she described: the discipline, the routine of early mornings, the consistency of long-distance sessions.

It was the erg that sold me, though. When we got upstairs, Darlene said we could all give them a try, so I sat on a seat and pulled at the handle, awkwardly lifting it over my bent knees. The flywheel came alive in a whir and the display screen lit up to monitor distance, stroke rate, and splits. My technique was all wrong, even inexperienced I could tell that, but as I watched the little screen, I started experimenting, moving my arms differently or pushing my legs harder. I loved the way the numbers jumped or stabilized in response to my movements, the smooth feeling of the handle in my fingers, and the droning, constant purr of air.

Standing over me, Darlene asked what I planned to do with the rest of my summer.

"This," I told her through panted breaths. "I want to keep doing this."

That night when I got home, it didn't even matter that Mom was still asleep, snoring softly on the couch. I tucked a blanket over her toes, made myself dinner, and searched for rowing videos on a laptop in my room. In the soft glow of that screen, I watched, mesmerized, as oars skimmed the surface of placid water in the same regular, rhythmic movements I'd just made on that whirring machine.

In the erg room now, I sip on blue liquid from my blender cup and consider the room. So much has changed and yet so little. Despite all the difficulties and hurdles and unending heartache, rowing has always felt like an escape and a privilege. It's just as true now as it was when I was fourteen.

Now, I just have to win this erg race to get it all back.

The stairs creak. The door cracks open and Adrian bursts into the room.

And, oh shit.

He's donned a spandex unisuit, but he has the top folded down so he's basically wearing nothing but fitted shorts. Clearly, he's kept himself in shape. Not the gym rat way with bulging (read: useless) biceps. He's got the long muscles of an athlete: defined abs, broad, muscular shoulders. He even has that deep V shape cut into his lower abs that trails into the top of his shorts. My god, in Italy, I ran my hands over those abs and I had no idea what was lingering right under his dress shirt.

More bad news.

It's not just Sofi's prodding or my alcohol-soaked memories. Adrian isn't just objectively attractive.

I'm attracted *to* him.

"Do you want to go first?" he asks, startling me from my train of thoughts.

Okay, even worse. I've been staring. Also, my mouth is open.

I snap my lips closed and lift my gaze to his face. His eyes dance with another devious smile. So, he caught me staring. This has actually become the worst-possible-case scenario.

"I—" Shit. Shit. Shit. "I'm so sorry."

Adrian sucks in his bottom lip and furrows his eyebrows in exaggerated confusion. "For what?"

My cheeks might be made of fire now. This man is supposed to be my *coach*. "You know."

"I really don't."

"I'm sorry for . . ." I hate this. But when I've been on the receiving end of this kind of thing, I've wished the dudes and occasionally ladies would fess up and apologize. So, I take a deep breath and say, "I'm sorry for ogling you."

Adrian's smile draws wider. "Ogling? I thought you were merely perusing."

My gaze sinks to my neon yellow running shoes. "I regret everything."

"I, for one, am nothing but thrilled."

"Do you accept my apology or not?"

"Oh, yes. Apology accepted."

"Do you want to, uh . . ." I point a tentative finger at his upper body. "Put the top part up? Just so it doesn't happen again."

I'm not sure I'll be able to pull straight if I know Adrian's exposed abs are in the same room as my eyeballs.

When I peek up from my shame-stare, Adrian has obliged. The problem is that the top of his suit is so tight I can still make out the ridges of his muscles. I force my eyes back down.

"Better?" he asks.

Sort of. I nod at the ground. "I can go first."

I take a breath and try to get my head in the game. So, Adrian has been keeping himself in shape, but that doesn't mean he's guaranteed to win. I have some control here. I can still choose my own destiny.

With as much confidence as I can muster, I peel off my sweatshirt, set the erg's heel cups, and strap my shoes into place. I take a deep breath and—to the best of my ability—push thoughts of Adrian's *abs* out of my mind.

Then I put my hands on the smooth, plastic handle. And it all gets easier because I'm lost.

In fluid motions, I move. My quads flex as I press down, powering into my first stroke. As I round the top, my abs tense, shoulder blades pinch, and hands snap into my torso, sharp and quick. I hit a microscopic pause. Then I release it all in a rush of air and breath, now barely audible under the purr of the flywheel. In an instant, I'm pulling again, inhaling back up the slide in motion after glorious motion.

Press, flex, pause, repeat.

It's a song. A prayer. The pain builds, but I'm in the zone now. Committed. It's not just this moment on the line, but the next eight weeks. Control over my own program and an end to the otherwise endless cycle of frustration and consternation. If I give in to the burning in my lungs and the fire in my legs, I'll lose it all forever.

So, I pull with everything I have. Sweat slicks my face. My breath heaves in fiery inhales. Up and down, I glide. I fly.

Seconds tick. I push my legs harder. On the display screen, meters blur like sand flowing through an hourglass. Press, flex, pause, repeat. I'm nearly there. Two hundred meters to go. A hundred. The last burning ounces of pain extracted like a sacrifice to a sadistic god.

My neck lifts out of neutral and I hear Carla's voice screaming at me to get my chin down. I force myself to drop it. Chest up. Heart forward. Pull. Again. And again.

I let out a gasping yell. And cross the finish.

My hands release the handle. I gulp down air, forcing my lungs to relax, before swiveling to examine the display. It's far from my personal best, but it's the best I could have hoped for today.

I glance up, suddenly remembering Adrian is here, too.

He's staring. Lips slightly parted. Hands limp by his sides. Chest rising and falling, like he's also out of breath.

The heat that had just eased from my body rushes back like a swollen river overtaking a bank.

Memories of our night in Italy spring from their carefully contained box: A bead of sweat descending Adrian's collarbone. Our synchronized movements in the deep thrums of bass, bodies glued together from chest to knees. My arm curling around his neck as his knuckles trail along one of my triceps.

"That looked good," he says.

He steps toward me and crouches next to my erg. Every inch of my skin is magnetized, like I can feel the molecules of air humming over me.

"Except for one small issue." He hooks his index finger under my chin and tilts my head up. My vision fills with nothing but his face. "Your chin rises when you're pushing hard."

He's so close. I'm breathless, quivering from head to toe like a tuning fork. Adrian is imparting technical advice here, but all I can think about is the pressure of his finger, gently lifting my chin. And his lips, soft and just a shade lighter than red. I wonder how they taste.

"I—" I clear my throat. Try to get a grip. "I'm working on it."

"Don't," he says softly.

"Don't what?"

Adrian releases me. Air rushes back into my lungs and reality floods my system.

Coach. He's my *coach.*

Despite our brief but memorable history, I can't let my mind wander into musings on what he tastes like.

Probably citrus, though.

"Stop trying to fix it," Adrian explains. "It works for you. It's like you're looking to the sky for your power. Like you can't be contained to just the water and the boat. Why not let it tilt?"

I squint at his forehead. With some distance between us, I can finally put my tumbling thoughts into a coherent order. The fact that I have to explain this doesn't bode well for Adrian's level of knowledge or my future recommendation to USRowing—and that's not to mention the strange nonsense about sky and power.

"Because that's not proper technique," I explain. "The chin is supposed to remain neutral throughout the stroke to keep the athlete's airway open, maximizing the efficiency of breath."

Adrian snorts as he pushes himself onto the seat of the erg across from me. "Did you just quote verbatim from *The Rower's Guide*?"

Okay, never mind. If he knows where the quote came from, then he knows the technique advice. "Yeah. Which is exactly the reason I'm trying to do it."

"Well, notwithstanding *The Rower's Guide*"—he lets himself glide down the slide, crashing into the base like a kid riding a swing—"sometimes you need to do what feels right instead of what the textbook says."

"*Notwithstanding*?" I spin so I can face him down and administer exactly the right level of indignation. "You can't *notwithstand* the seminal text on rowing technique."

"Sure I can. It's not like you're losing your eyeline. But you *are* wasting mental focus fighting what comes naturally to your body."

I cross my arms and my chin lifts slightly, just the way it does when I'm at the top of a stroke. I force it back down. "With enough time and work and discipline, I can get my body to do what's *right* instead of what's natural."

Adrian stills his pseudo-swinging and folds his arms over his knee. I avoid noticing the way his forearm muscles crease.

"How many years have you been rowing?"

Ten years, three months, and twenty-two days. "Ten."

"And for how many of those ten years have you been trying to correct your chin?"

The answer, unfortunately, is all of them. It's *basic* technical stuff. I've heard this correction from at least five different coaches, even Darlene. *Drop your chin. Relax your forehead. Eyes down.* One of my coaches even made me hold a rolled-up towel under my chin during endurance sessions.

Admitting all this to Adrian, though, would be like saying that I'll never have the textbook technique. "I don't want to give up."

"That's fine. I have the rest of the summer to change your mind."

I gape. "Wait. So, you're conceding, just like that?"

Adrian nods thoughtfully. "Here's the way I see it. I'm trying to coach you for the next couple months. So, if it has to do with how you're training or what you're doing in that time—it should be my call. At least if you let it. Afterward? That's squarely your domain. Or, hopefully, Carla's. And correcting your technique isn't just about the next two months. It's about how you row for the rest of your life."

This is surprisingly reasonable from my wannabe personal dictator. "So, I'm free to keep working on my chin?"

"Yep. And I'm free to keep telling you to let it tilt." Then he stands swiftly and that wolfish grin returns to his eyes. "And, also, to win this erg test."

. . .

Adrian wins by four and a half seconds.

I saw it coming. I knew it was happening as soon as he started pulling the handle, legs and arms gliding with strength and precision. The inevitable barreled toward me as I remained frozen on my own seat and the meters ticked down on his display. He's kept himself in shape, which means that, even though it was close, I was doomed from the start.

When Adrian releases the handle, a mess of emotions strangle my throat. I've lost the bet. I have to return to the mercy of his scrawling handwriting and plans B and C. This summer could set me back months if not years. I have goals—big goals. Olympic ring–sized goals.

"Kath?" Adrian's cheeks are still red from exertion, and a glaze of sweat has dampened the edges of his dark blue Lycra. His concern is palpable.

My eyes sting and I clench my jaw like it'll force the tears from seeping out. I don't cry in front of other people, especially coaches. I can't count how many times I've seen my mom break down in front of a confused bank teller or grocery store clerk. I once watched her sob to her boss, clinging to his shoulders in the drizzling rain outside a concrete-lined office building. He stared out over her shoulder, stone-faced, and idly patted her back until she pulled away. I have always promised myself I will never be like that.

Still, I can feel that sharp prick at the back of my nose. Tears are threatening to leak out despite the set of my jaw and the tight balls of my fists. So, I bolt upright, snatch up my gym bag, and start backing away. My calf whacks against the long slide of an erg.

"I need to go," I say, not looking at Adrian.

"Kath. What's going on? Talk to me."

I spin, nearly toppling over another slide, and beeline toward the stairs. Adrian's footsteps pound after me. I pick up my pace. I know how ridiculous I am, bag thumping as I practically sprint out of the erg room, but the tears are coming.

Just as I drop down the first step, Adrian's fingers glance against my shoulder.

"I can only help if we talk," he says softly.

This does stop me. "What do you mean 'help'?"

Adrian's hand finds my elbow and he tugs me around, gently, until I'm facing him. Then he drops his hand again.

"I'll listen. I want to know why this scares you so much. And I want to try to reassure you—in whatever way I can."

I squeeze my eyes shut, feeling seasick. I didn't even realize it until Adrian said it, but he's right. I'm terrified. I've felt that way ever since I stood in Carla's makeshift office and my future crumbled before my eyes. The last few days—being literally locked out from everything I know and love—have only made that fear more palpable.

"I just lost everything," I say, and I hate the way my voice nearly cracks. "And I *know* what I need to do to get it back. But you're—you're not letting me do those things. And now—I had a glimmer of hope, but you won and I lost and now I have nothing again."

I blink my eyes open, raw with repressed tears.

Adrian gazes back at me with more sympathy than I expected. "Okay. I see. Maybe I can help."

"You'll let me do my program?"

He shakes his head, but there's a soft, inviting smile tugging at his lips. "You give *determination* new meaning, Parker. But no. You have to do my program. Still, I think there are two things I can do."

"Okay?" I sniff.

"As a coach, I can see now that firm rules and boundaries are all wrong for you. I'm not going to cave to your demands, but I also think you need more explanations than what I've given. You need to understand my decisions so that, even if you don't agree, you also know they're not based on whim. So, no more declarative coaching. I mean, I still want you to hold up our end of the deal, but I'll also try to explain things. And I promise to listen when you have a different view."

My first instinct is that this is hardly a concession at all. But if I really think about it . . . I do like to understand decisions and, if there is a method to Adrian's madness, I certainly want to know it. I've also never had a coach offer to completely change their style for me before, and while I realize this is part of Adrian's shtick, it is moderately heartening. Besides, I suppose this new approach will at least give me some opportunities to make my case.

"I'd like that," I say. "What's the second thing?"

Adrian's eyes crinkle. "You need a chance for a win."

"A win?"

"Against me, specifically. It's only fair, given what you've been going through."

Not for the first time, I search his face for insincerity, but find none. "What kind of win?"

"What was in the basement when you were in high school?"

I lift an eyebrow. "That's possibly one of the top five creepiest things you could have said to me right now."

He laughs. "Seriously."

"Um, dirt floors and cobwebs."

Adrian nods as though that answer is satisfying in some way. Then he bolts down the stairs and motions for me to follow through a door at the back of the team lounge. When he flicks a few switches at the top of the stairwell, my jaw drops.

The basement springs to life in an array of bright lights and discordant sounds. We descend the stairs, unveiling the full scope of the transformation. It's not a dusty, empty basement anymore, but an *arcade*. The air sizzles with clatters, clangs, and whirrs. Against the backdrop of unfinished brick walls, I find everything from pool to air hockey, Ping-Pong to pinball. There's even a basketball hoop next to a Skee-Ball track. Everything's worn at the edges, well loved. But it's incredible, like a grittier version of our sleek game room in the training center.

"What is this?" I ask. "Where did you get the money for it?"

Adrian drops off the bottom step beside me. "Fundraisers, but it wasn't that expensive. I organized a few work days last spring and a bunch of the parents came to help lay flooring and install lights. I bought the machines secondhand from an arcade-bar that was going out of business uptown."

I stopped visiting the boathouse regularly when I moved to the training center, and the last time I practiced here was a few years ago. But contrary to what I thought when I first arrived, there have been tons of improvements beyond that fresh coat of exterior paint. The weight room is cleaner and better stocked, the wood flooring in the trophy room got a polish, and the countertops in the kitchenette have been replaced. I guess those were all Adrian's doing.

But this? This takes the cake.

"Holy shit," I say.

Adrian purses his lips. Shrugs again. "I want everyone to enjoy themselves when they're here. We work hard, but I don't want this place to be only about hard work."

"It's impressive. Seriously."

Adrian's chin drops and I think I catch a tinge of pink on his ears. "So, what do you say? You want a win?"

I look back at him. "You're not going to let me, are you?"

"Parker." His expression goes serious. "I wouldn't dare."

My mouth cracks with a smile. As much as everything is dark and crumbling around me, the idea of crushing Adrian at one of these otherwise meaningless games sends a surge of excitement through me that's so intense, I can barely suck in a deep breath.

"Challenge accepted," I say.

Twelve

Adrian extends a hand toward the array of games. "You pick."

I spin a slow circle, appraising the neon flashing lights, chiming interfaces, and glowing screens. As I scrutinize the options, I catalog the number of hours Sofi and I have spent on each, and weigh my probability of victory. The truth is, though, I have a clear favorite.

"How about Skee-Ball?" I ask.

Adrian's eyes dance. "That works."

Through the clamor of dings and flashes, we march toward the machine. Adrian punches a button and worn balls tumble forward. Thankfully, the coin slot has been disabled—otherwise I would have had to skip a snack or two this week to afford an hour on it.

Balls rattle to a stop with a familiar, satisfying clamor. That familiarity, more than anything, is what I love about this game. Success in Skee-Ball is about finding a reliable strategy, minimizing confounding variables, and then repeating that strategy with perfect fidelity. And I am nothing if not consistent.

"You want to go first?" Adrian asks.

"Please, go ahead," I say, eager for a benchmark to work toward.

I settle just over Adrian's shoulder—a spot with the best view—as he sets his foot so that his shin touches the alley. He plucks up his first ball and pinches it with long fingers and practiced certainty. With a straight wrist and flawless, upright posture, he drives it forward. The ball rumbles up the alley, sails high in the scoring section, and plunges into the forty-point hole.

Well, then. Amateurs—and cocky men—will always go for the fifty or the hundred. The hundred is the flashy one that looks the most impressive when you sink it. And the fifty is the best of the smaller fish. Yet mastering this game—like rowing—is about being consistently good, not getting distracted by always trying to be extraordinary.

Adrian sets his feet and lets loose another ball. It tracks the same arc as the last, and burrows into the same hole.

I raise an eyebrow. "You're not giving this one away for free."

Another plunk. Another forty. Another consistent performance.

"I told you I wouldn't dare." He glances at me. "Impressed, then?"

"Very," I grudgingly admit as his next ball rolls forward, a hair off its arc. It skims the edge of the forty cup and lands in the twenty instead. Finally, something less than perfection. "I didn't expect this level of devotion to control from a guy who approaches his training programs like Jackson Pollock attacking a canvas."

Adrian snorts. "I'll take that as a compliment, then."

"The Jackson Pollock thing or the control thing?"

Adrian tucks his chin to glance at me. "I can't imagine you have much reverence for an art form that principally relies on spontaneity and improvisation."

"I do rather prefer order and consistency."

"Rare exceptions notwithstanding," Adrian says.

"Rare exceptions?"

"You know." He raises his chin in my direction, suggestively implying something he doesn't want to put into words.

My stomach tightens as I register what he means. The rare exception: the only time I've lost control around him. Suddenly, unwanted memories have again hijacked my mind. Me: chugging a whiskey sour like it was water and slamming down the empty glass. Me: turning loops on the dance floor with the fervor of a fidget spinner. Me: tilting my face up toward my future coach, right before he sucked in a breath and stepped away.

I steady myself with a lungful of air. I need to put a stop to this conversation and all the messy emotions it's dredging up.

"Clearly," I say, reaching for crisp and businesslike, "that was a one-time-only mistake."

Plunk. Thirty. "I thought you've been doing it for years?"

"What?"

"Your chin. I thought you've been tilting it for years."

Oh.

Ohhhh.

That's why he lifted his chin at me.

"Right," I manage, trying to reorient. "That. Yes. I have."

Adrian steps back without picking up another ball, studying me like he's just found an oar with two blades. Upright, he's standing close—too close. But I'm the one who staked this ground so I could watch his gameplay from the best angle. I can't surrender it now.

"What were *you* talking about?" he asks.

My eyes drop to an oil spot on the rubber-matted floor, and I scuff my toe against it. I'm irrationally terrified that he can read my thoughts.

"I—Uh. It doesn't matter."

"Parker?"

I don't want to talk about this.

But also, shoot. Maybe I need to acknowledge the awkwardness of our history? Of my behavior? Maybe this is how I can keep my blood from roaring in my ears and my heart from skipping every other beat when he gets too close.

I take a long, controlled breath. "The club. I was talking about the club in Italy. And. Look. I . . . I know I was a mess that night. I'm usually in better control of myself. But I hope you can forget about it."

Adrian's brows pull together. "What do you mean 'a mess'?"

"Emotional. I'd just lost that race. Gotten dumped. I spilled my soul out to you by a bar top."

The alley is still lit, score impatiently flashing, but Adrian's looking at nothing but me. "I remember we had a conversation about racing and quitting. I don't see why that is *messy*. In fact, I also shared some personal things with you the day we met."

He's still not getting it. "Right, well, also the other stuff."

"What other stuff?"

"You're going to make me say it?"

He tilts his head in question, zero glint of recognition in his expression.

"I have no idea what I'm making you say," he tells me.

"We danced." My whisper is barely more than a hiss. "And then—and then I tried to *kiss* you."

I burrow my face in my hands. This is not a conversation I want to be having with my coach, even a temporary one. Games still buzz and whirl around us, a melody of cheer that stands in almost ridiculous contrast to my haze of embarrassment. Still, Adrian hasn't said anything.

When I peek out from between my fingers, he has one eye closed like he's seeing double. "You mean before you ran away from me?"

"Because you turned me down!"

"Turned you . . . what?"

"You backed up."

Adrian stares at me for so long it's like he's struggling to translate my words from another language into English. "We had both been drinking, Kath. I was trying to check in. To see where we were on, you know, *consent*."

Oh. "Oh." Really? "I thought . . ."

"You thought I was rejecting you?"

I nod.

Very slowly, with almost painful deliberation, he shakes his head, eyes locked on mine like he needs to see my recognition.

"No," he says. "That night. Right now. I find you nothing short of extraordinary."

A breath gusts out of me. Adrian's gaze drops to my lips. Something thumps over inside my chest, a heavy, rhythmic movement like a boat keeling to one side. I'm suddenly aware of the already too-narrow space between us. He's so close I could touch him with less than a step. So close I can see his chest rising and falling with each breath.

The Skee-Ball alley lets out a high-pitched ring.

I startle backward, glance up at the screen.

"It's going to time out," I say, voice disintegrating.

Adrian pauses, gaze tracing my face. Then he lets out a

breath that sounds like half a sigh. He steps back. Turns to pick up his ball.

It rumbles up the alley, skips wide. For the first time, Adrian doesn't sink any of the higher-scoring cups.

With his back turned, I release a shaky exhale.

Three balls later, a respectable score of 220 flashes in red above the alley. Adrian sank a few forties, and otherwise had an assortment of tens, twenties, and one thirty. He never went for fifty, not even once.

Now that I've had a moment to collect myself, I know how I'm going to beat him. Yes, playing this game straight and consistent is the right strategy. But *winning* is about taking the occasional risk. You have to wait for the magic moment when everything aligns and success feels imminent. This isn't controllable—the opportunity either arrives or doesn't. But when it happens, you slam the gas.

Adrian steps to the side. He doesn't insult me by offering any technique advice, as Maxwell would have done. He just wordlessly waits for me to fulfill my promise. Despite my jitters and all the ways my new coach throws me off like a compass confronted with a roomful of magnets, I know my true north.

Victory.

I close my hand around the soft, almost leathery surface of my first ball and soak in that earthy smell. Then I set my foot and let the ball fly.

The ball skips off the edge of the forty pocket and buries into the twenty. I allow myself a single moment of disappointment before I sink back into my racing zone—a state of mind that hovers above emotions, positive and negative, only achievable under the right circumstances. With a clear mind, I grab another ball, loosen my wrist, and fling it forward. It rumbles aloft, pitches off the edge and arcs, landing in the forty.

My chest purrs. And then I've grabbed the next ball, satisfaction forgotten, focused anew.

Thirty. Ten. Forty.

The next ball feels light in my fingertips. The neon lights fade, whirring sounds quiet, and the lingering smell of basement musk recedes. Anticipation pricks over my forearms. Magic.

I adjust my aim higher and loose the next ball.

It lands with a satisfying plunk.

Fifty.

I've stopped caring about the score. It's just me and the alley. It's the same feeling I get in a great race—when everything drops away. The world narrows to a pinprick and there are no competitors, no spectators, no finish line. It's just me and the boat. And we're dancing.

I sink another. And another.

When the last ball disappears, I step back. Above me, my score blinks in red. 250.

"YES!" My arms fly above my head.

Behind me, Adrian claps. "Impressive as hell, Parker."

I spin and he puts his hand up for a high five. I slap it with relish, so hard my palm stings. When our hands drop, Adrian's middle finger hooks into mine.

"You leave me no choice but to ask for a rematch," he says. Ever so softly, he runs his thumb over the back of my knuckles. My skin tingles under the feathery touch. "A chance to redeem myself."

"I can do this all night," I whisper.

He nods, another smile unfurling, and releases me. My chest feels two sizes too large for my rib cage.

Several rounds later, I'm still ahead. Adrian is nothing if not consistent—his score is nearly always around 200. The variance on my scores is much bigger. I don't ever quite hit the 250 mark again, but I do get a couple near 220 and one under 200. This, it would seem, mostly has to do with our very different strategies. We both are remarkably consistent in form, it's just Adrian *never* goes for the fifty. I do, but sometimes I miss.

"Bet you thought you were going to cruise to victory on the basis of having these machines at your disposal twenty-four seven," I say as Adrian's third ball of this set rumbles up the alley.

"You are unexpectedly good," he says. "Although I should know better than to underestimate you. Is this your natural aptitude for anything competition-related?"

"We have a game room in the training center," I admit.

He sends another straight up the middle. "Ah. So, you do occasionally let yourself have fun."

"When it doesn't interfere with training."

"See, I think you have that backward." His eyes cut to me like he's about to say something else when my watch buzzes.

My stomach rumbles in response, and I realize I haven't eaten since before the erg test. I drop to a knee and dig around my bag for my dinner: cold chicken, vegetables, and brown rice, all weighed and measured. I'll have to get in one more snack tonight to hit all my minimum nutritional benchmarks for the day, but I'm nearly there.

"Mind if I eat?" I ask.

Adrian shakes his head with a smile. "I haven't forgotten what it's like to be training and hungry all the time."

"Good," I say as I click open the plastic travel case holding my utensils. "Then you also know why I won't share."

Adrian eyes my meal with no hint of disappointment. "We have some leftover pizza upstairs if I get really desperate. So, tell me, does the training center's game room have as much character as this basement?"

I snort. "What it lacks in character, it makes up for in massages and state-of-the-art training equipment."

"Sounds nice."

Homesickness washes over me as I saw at my chicken with a fork and knife. I can practically hear the gentle hum of the halogen lights in the dining hall, smell the faint musk of the lake when it's heavy with morning mist.

"It is," I say quietly.

Adrian cocks his head. "What makes it special?"

He once again looks like the man I met in the *pasticceria* and not the tyrant who has subjected me to his modern-dance interpretation of a training program.

I swallow my bite. "I can't imagine you care."

"I do, actually."

Maybe because of the job. If Adrian gets the coaching position with the junior national team, he'll move to Florida to head up a series of development and selection camps. It's not exactly the same as my training center in Southern California, but I guess the setup is similar enough that he'd be curious.

"The facilities are incredible. The conditions are always basically perfect. But I think what I love most is . . . being surrounded by excellence, you know? Like, living there, I'm constantly inspired. The athletes, the coaches, the trainers, the chefs. It's like, we're all in it together, living and breathing the motto."

"The motto?"

"The Olympic motto. *Citius. Altius. Fortius.* It means 'Faster. Higher. Stronger.' It's like . . . always strive to be better. The goal *is* improvement. You're never done, but also, you're always getting somewhere."

I take a deep breath, trying to push out the negative thoughts that this inspires, too. Until recently, I always felt like I was living that motto. Until I started going backward.

"Anyway," I say as I lift a forkful of vegetables, trying to focus on what I can control, "it also has a game room, as I mentioned, and the best-stocked weight room I've ever used. I'm sure the facilities in Florida will be similar."

Adrian smiles. "That does sound pretty epic."

"Yeah? I didn't peg you for a state-of-the-art-facilities type of guy."

"You're right," he says, turning back to the game, "but I like what you said about having a team."

"Is that why you applied for the junior team job?" I ask as I shovel up some rice. "So that you'd have other coaches working with you?"

Adrian's ball sinks in the ten cup and he winces. "That would be nice, but no. I'm happy with the job I have."

"Then why did you apply?"

"My dad." He sends another ball rumbling up the alley. For the second time tonight, it misses widely. Adrian lets out an impatient sigh and pushes back his hair, like he's chastising himself. Then he spins toward me without picking up another. "He always wanted me to try my hand at higher level coaching. After he died, I applied. My mom thought it would be a good way to honor his memory."

"Oh," I say eloquently. I wish I had my own mom's ability to say the right thing—something deep and impactful and loving, but still specific and totally not generic. Or Sofi's ability to tell a joke that somehow dissipates tension while making me feel supported. "I'm sure she appreciates it."

He smooths the front of his shirt, expression blank. "She's happy when he's happy, even now that it's hypothetical."

I watch him, unsure of how to respond to that. "She must be

proud, though. It's a big deal you've gotten this far in the process."

Adrian turns to his final ball of the set. "It's not that serious, only been a couple of interviews. I won't get it."

I squint at the side of his face. "USRowing flew you out to Italy. They're asking me to evaluate you over the next two months. Carla wouldn't make you jump through all those hoops if the board wasn't serious about you."

Mechanically, Adrian lets his ball roll. Sometime in the last couple of minutes, his shoulders have gone stiff and his arm has lost its smooth, fluid swing. The ball plinks against the thirty cup, flies wide, and buries into the lowest-scoring section.

He frowns after it before blowing out a long breath and turning back to me. "You're saying I should take this more seriously."

I wrinkle my nose. "Not at all. It's your application. Take that as seriously as you want. I'm saying, regardless of how you feel, Carla and USRowing are clearly taking *you* seriously."

Adrian's eyebrow rises as he stares at me.

"What?" I ask, and wipe at my mouth with the back of my hand, wondering if I have food on my face.

"Nothing. I just thought . . . I don't know. I assumed you'd be exacting in your standards. Expect other people to meet the same high bars you do."

"Why, because I push myself?"

"Yeah."

I lift a shoulder and stab at another chunk of chicken. "I push myself because I want to push myself. I always hate it when people tell me to lay off the gas or not take myself too seriously or lower my standards or whatever else. My standards are mine to set where I want and so are yours."

Adrian doesn't speak for a long moment, but he's still looking back me with so much heat and heaviness in his gaze so that I can feel a tingle tracing up my neck. The game chimes, threatening another time out, but this time he ignores it.

"Well," he says finally, breaking through the noise.

"Well, what?"

He tilts his head and a lock of hair falls over his eyes. My heart flutters. No idea when I started finding partial vision impairment so attractive.

"Well," he says again as he leans in closer. "I'm glad USRowing is deluded enough to think I'm a good candidate for this job."

I swivel to look at him in the eye. "Because you've always had a deep-seated, yet inexplicable desire to get crushed at Skee-Ball?"

"No. Because it means I get to spend the next two months with you."

We hold each other's eyes and heat unfurls over me, so intense it's almost uncomfortable. I can hear the blood pounding in my ears, and I'm too aware of my pulse, which is now skipping every third to fourth beat. I feel completely out of control, like I'm falling. Like I'm standing too close to a fire.

My watch blares. I startle away, swivel the screen to see what scheduled activity I just missed. Then do a double take.

It's nine forty-five. I should have already done my pre-bed routine.

"Crap!" I nearly scream. How have *two hours* passed? I've already missed my evening stretching and hydration session. Already moving, I slam my Tupperware closed and stuff it on top of the heap of dirty clothes filling my bag before wrestling the zipper closed. "I need to get home."

I back up toward the stairs.

Adrian abandons our game, moving with me.

"Let me walk you," he says.

Bad idea. That's a bad idea. I should have ended this evening nearly two hours ago and *not* neglected my evening recovery routine. I open my mouth to say so, but instead what comes out is: "Okay." And then: "I'd like that."

Thirteen

The last traces of sunset have already drained from the sky, casting low buildings into indigo silhouettes. The fading warmth of daytime soaks my limbs even as a cool breeze ruffles my braid. Maybe it's the summer air, humming with possibility, or the high I'm still riding from my string of Skee-Ball victories, but I'm relaxed in a way that I shouldn't be, especially considering the fact that I missed my evening foam-rolling session.

"Can I ask you something?" Adrian says as we pick our way past a pair of street musicians throwing a melancholy song into the twilight sky.

He presses a bill into the velvet lining of an open guitar case. It's the tiniest gesture, but it reminds me of my mom and her sincere appreciation for anything artistic. I think she would like Adrian, if they ever met.

"Sure," I say.

"I don't want this to sound wrong, though."

"Go ahead," I say. "I've already pried about you and the job."

"Okay." He hesitates for a moment longer, then says: "In Italy . . . when I asked if you were considering quitting, you said no."

I snort. "I believe what I said was someone would have to tear my cold, dead hands from my oars."

It's one of the only things about that night that doesn't coat me with embarrassment.

Adrian smiles. "That's right. Well, what I'm wondering is . . . why not?"

I pause, considering.

"I have a lot of goals for rowing. Making the finals at Worlds. Racing in the Olympics. In my biggest dreams, standing on the podium there, too. And, yeah, all of those goals involve winning, but to be honest, that's not why I row. Or why I *keep* rowing. Like, despite all the pain and heartache, I row because I love the predictability of my daily routine, the calm I feel when I get on the water. Rowing makes everything else go quiet." I glance at him. "Winning is good, too. My collection of medals is probably the first thing I'd save in a fire. But even if I somehow knew that I would never stand on another podium, I would still want to row."

A bus exhales a group of chattering college students as Adrian considers.

"I still remember the way you said it in Italy. That winning is about more than the thrill of victory. I'll be honest, I didn't believe you at the time."

"Because rowing isn't just my life," I say. "It's *me*. Quitting it would be like quitting a part of myself."

Adrian's eyebrows flash upward. "Damn."

"Too much?"

"Not at all. As usual, you're just the right amount of extremely fucking impressive."

My cheeks heat to the point that I'm relieved for the cool evening air. "Well, anyway. That's why I'm here. Living with my mom. Taking three hundred steps backward so maybe one day, I can go forward again."

"I'm sure it's nice for her," he says, and I'm relieved he's letting me change the subject. "To have you home, I mean."

"That's true," I say. "And it's nice for me, too. To be home with her. Between training and racing, it's been years since we've spent more than a few days in a row together."

I can feel Adrian's next question radiating in the thud of his footsteps, the faraway rumble of traffic up Shattuck Avenue. The next question is obvious: What about your dad? Most people don't have any reservations about asking that question—it's as natural as asking if you're married, if you have kids. But for someone who is recently divorced or who lost a child, those simple questions are anything but harmless. It's the same with a parent, no matter how many years have passed since you spoke to them.

Adrian doesn't ask. But his silence, and the dispassionate way he's asked his questions, make me want to keep talking.

"My dad left when I was young," I explain. "Mom was a professional dancer. She was on the verge of making it big—she had been a guest with San Francisco Ballet and was offered a permanent spot. It was all too much for him, though. The long hours, the travel. She quit dancing to save their marriage. But by then, it was too late."

Of all my mom's breakups—the dozens of small chips that have torn away at the foundation of her life—that is the heartbreak I'll never forget.

Mom and Dad were supposed to go to a New Year's Eve party, but they'd been arguing all day. Dad kept slamming cabinets and shouting about priorities. Mom was sobbing, then yelling back about how much she'd already given up. When the babysitter rang the doorbell, Mom was still in her robe, cheeks blotchy and stained with mascara-black tears. I heard Dad say they weren't feeling well, then the babysitter's car rolled away. I spent the night shivering under my bedsheets, listening to them argue over the occasional percussive thud of a distant firework.

The next morning, I awoke to the echo of the front door slamming. Downstairs, Mom stood in the living room, fingers shaking, sobbing so hard she could barely breathe. When she saw me, she lost her balance and crumpled onto the carpet. I knelt next to her, patting her back, and puffing up my slight shoulders, hoping I'd be strong enough to hold her weight.

"I've lost them both," she sobbed into my hair. She repeated those words, over and over, until they branded onto my skin. "They're both gone."

Without looking at Adrian, I shrug my bag higher on my shoulder, trying to get it to stop feeling like it's dragging me backward. "My dad and I haven't talked in years, not since he got remarried. I mean, he sends me birthday cards or whatever. And a few years back our address somehow ended up on his Christmas card list and we got a glossy postcard with photos of him and his wife and three sons in matching sweaters. Luckily, I was home for a break and could toss it in the trash before Mom saw it."

It's not painless for me to see pictures like that, but I can handle it. If Mom had been the one to open the card, she would have been on the couch for weeks.

"It's been, what, almost twenty years since he left," I finish. "But she's never really been the same."

I don't know what possessed me to just unleash that all at once, and I glance up to see if Adrian is bored yet. But his eyes are soft with interest, like he actually cares.

"She's been heartbroken all this time?" he asks.

I tilt my head and watch my moving feet as I consider. "Yes and no. She was devastated, obviously, but him leaving wasn't only about him. It was that she'd given up her life, too. Her passion. And she never really found her footing again—after she quit dancing and Dad left, she powered through jobs like she powered through relationships. If you can think of the profession, she's probably done it."

"Nothing wrong with figuring out what you enjoy," Adrian says. "Was she the one who got you into rowing?"

"In a way," I say, thinking of Discover Rowing Day. It was one of about a hundred activities she signed me up for over the years, at least when she had steady employment and we could afford it. "She was always trying to get me into some low-cost class at the YMCA or the library. Dance. Pottery. Reading. Some Junior Ranger thing. Find my passion, she said. Rowing was the one that clicked. What about you?"

"What about me?"

I nudge my elbow against his to signal our next turn, and we drop onto a narrow alley with decorative brick paving. "Well, you used to row, that much was clear from the erg." And the fact that most coaches are former athletes, so it was a solid assumption, anyway. "Did your parents get you into it?"

He nods. "My dad."

"A rower?"

Adrian releases an unsteady laugh. "My dad was a rower well after he stopped rowing."

I smile because I can relate. "Boat?"

"Eight. Varsity crew at Stanford. He got a scholarship and it changed his life. Not just because of the degree. The *life lessons.* The teamwork and focus and, most of all, the mental toughness born from the 'inferno of pain,' as he called it. I can't count how many times he reminded me that rowing is the most physically challenging sport to exist, and that's what makes it the best."

I laugh hollowly because this is where Adrian's dad and I unequivocally differ. I know his type well. They form big groups of sweaty men who run through pull-ups on a makeshift bar hanging from boathouse rafters, one-upping one another until they drop to the dusty floor because their shoulder muscles stop contracting. The guys in the national team eight once disassembled their fifty-seven-pound ergs into two pieces, latched those to their backs, and hiked up a literal mountain so they could do a workout on the summit. The idea was "teamwork," but there's more to it than that. For a lot of rowers, the pain of our sport isn't incidental. For them, it *is* the point.

This attitude is backward, of course. The pain is nothing more than the price we pay for the privilege of sitting in a rowing shell.

Now, I'm curious if Adrian was ever like that, and I'm about to ask what varsity crew he was on, but he says, "How's your mom doing now?"

I blink, surprised he's turned back to what I assume is a boring topic for him. "Better, maybe. She opened a yoga studio this year."

"Yeah? What's it like?"

I wince. "I haven't seen it yet, honestly. I know. I know. She keeps asking. I should have gone already. If it sounded like regular yoga I would have. But this sounds like it's all . . . I don't know. Chanting and singing and heavy breathing."

Adrian hums like he knows something I don't.

"What?" I ask.

"There's empirical evidence about the benefits of that kind of yoga. Studies showing it can lower stress and reduce anxiety."

"So, just mental stuff," I say.

"Just?" He bumps his shoulder against mine. "I don't have to explain the very well-established connection between improved mental health and performance, do I? Especially when it comes to stress and anxiety."

I bite the inside of my cheek. "No, you don't. Are you telling me I have to go?"

"No, in this case, I'm going to explain the research and hope you make the right choice."

"I'll think about it, then," I say, fully planning to spend some time googling this supposed research. But I also know I need to be supportive of my mom, chanting aside. This is the first job she's truly seemed to care about in years. "If nothing else, I'm sure her classes are an *experience*. The woman is like a ball of fire disguised as a white lady with graying hair and twiggy legs."

Adrian snorts. "She sounds fun."

"Oh, she is. My mom has more passion in her pinky finger than I do in my whole body." I pause in front of the steps of her redwood porch. A dozen wind chimes sing into the evening air. "This is—"

When I spin, Adrian's expression confuses me. The traces of his mischievous smile, usually omnipresent in the corners of his mouth, have evaporated. His head is cocked, eyebrows squished together.

"What?" I ask.

"I'm trying to figure out if you're saying you don't have passion."

I ascend one of the stairs and lean my low back against the handrail. "I'm not passionate, I'm obsessive. If you took an X-ray of my bones, they would be made of lists and neuroses. I thought that was obvious by now."

"Not to me."

I let out an impatient sigh. I'm not embarrassed about who I am—I'm realistic about it. "The first time we met, I literally *arm wrestled* a lemon bar off you because I'm so obsessed with ritual and routine. Routine works for me. It makes me a better athlete. But I'm well aware of how all that stuff comes off to other people."

Adrian frowns at me for so long I wonder what's happening in his mind. Maybe he's finally seeing the full picture of my personality? Maybe he's trying to figure out a way to extricate himself from this conversation—and possibly the rest of the summer—now that the pieces are clicking together?

I half expect him to hunch his shoulders and bolt back into the night. It would be fair. It's the way most people react to me. *Grating*, I've been told many times—sometimes even to my face. *She's just too much.*

Maxwell was one of the first—and only—people in my life who wasn't always trying to fix me for being rigid. Given that Adrian is basically Maxwell's opposite, it's hard to imagine he'll appreciate my flaws for what they are: important, albeit socially awkward, tools for success.

Adrian moves up the stairs and presses his hands to the railing beside me, gazing down at the vines like he's lost in their pattern. "I want to tell you a story."

"A . . . story?"

"About a woman I met in Italy."

Goose bumps raise on my arms. "Okay."

"So," Adrian shifts so he's leaning against the railing, facing me now. "I was sitting in a bakery—"

"*Pasticceria*," I whisper.

He nods, unthwarted by my attempt to deflect. "Of course. I was sitting in a *pasticceria*, trying to prepare for an interview that

I was . . . well, let's just say I was not ready for it. And suddenly this woman with a blond braid and striking brown eyes marched up to me and demanded to buy my lemon bar."

His eyes flicker between mine and I can practically feel the anticipation crackling in the places where his gaze touches me.

"That was you."

"I got that," I manage.

He continues, low: "Glad for a distraction, I asked her why on earth she wanted a lemon bar so badly that she was willing to bribe one off a stranger. To my surprise, she brought up rowing. Yeah, I knew something about that sport. Then she just laid it all out for me. I thought my anticipation was bad? She was confronting a string of failures, one worse than the last. She was staring them down and powering through. She was ready to take on more."

He drops down a step, angling toward me. There are only inches separating us now, and all I'd need to do is lean forward to erase them.

"Sure," he continues, "she seemed a bit stubborn and maybe a little inflexible. But I also saw her passion. Her power, her confidence. I felt it, too, when I got her to agree to touch my hand."

My chest tightens like Adrian's words are wrapping around my middle.

"And then you saw me bomb," I whisper. "And lose it in a club."

He shakes his head. "That was the most impressive part of all. You were knocked down. Hard. A few days after that, you fought me to get back on the water with the same grit and determination as before. Without a single thought of quitting. Of letting yourself get defeated." Slowly, he reaches his hand toward my forehead and sweeps a strand of hair off my face, like he's worried it will distract from the intensity of his eye contact. "You might be the most stubborn woman I've ever met, but if that's not *passion,* then I don't know what is."

I'm not sure whether it's the thick summer breeze or the warmth of Adrian's approval or the way I feel so *seen,* but my body seems to have floated up from the porch, untethered. I'm drifting in the specks of gold flickering in his green irises, sinking and rising.

Adrian is so close I can feel the warmth radiating off his skin. So close that when I take another breath, I inhale his scent of citrus and sandalwood. I'm huddled in this pocket of his body, enveloped like I've found a peaceful eddy even as a river rushes around our shoulders.

I lean forward.

Our lips touch. Heat ignites between us, so sudden that I startle backward.

"I'm sorry," I stammer out. "That was so unprofessional of—"

Adrian's expression cuts me off, hunger in his eyes. I go silent as my legs loosen, like my knees have been replaced with mousse.

In slow motion, he lowers toward me until his breath warms my temple. He squeezes a hand to my cheek, fingertips pressing into the back of my head. His other hand follows, framing my face. I tip my chin higher. Adrian leans in until his lips touch mine, a kiss that's gentle but firm. My lips part for his tongue. Our bodies flatten together, drawing heat across my chest.

My hands coil around his shoulders, tugging him yet closer. He responds to my touch with equal energy, fingers crushing my braid to the back of my head. Desire rolls through me. One of my hands circles his arm, my fingers notching into the indent of his triceps. He flexes under my touch.

I sigh and this seems to unlock something else inside him. With one motion, he lifts me up and sits me on the railing. My legs curl around his torso. I press myself into the warmth of his body, slotting into him like a puzzle piece clicking into place. His heart hammers at my collar bone.

The railing groans. I tug him toward me, like I can't get him close enough, and he meets my urgency with his own, pressing harder into our embrace. Holding me tighter. I bite on his lip and he moans. I try to silence him with another kiss, tight against his lips.

But then he's trailing a hand up my shirt, leaving fire everywhere he touches, and I can't care about how much noise we are making or which of Mom's neighbors might hear. I arch my back into his hand, relishing the feel of his skin against mine, my head falling back—

The railing shifts. I nearly topple backward. I clutch at Adrian instead. He shoots his arms out to catch me, but loses purchase. We both tumble onto the steps in a heavy, crumpling echo.

A porch light clicks on, bathing us both in a harsh illumination.

"Kath?" Mom's voice filters outside.

The kiss is still jamming up my throat. "Yes! Mom, it's me. Everything is fine!"

"Are you reorganizing the patio furniture again?"

I try to push myself backward from my awkward position, now straddling Adrian—one of his legs underneath me the other splayed out onto the stair above us.

"Sorry," I call out. "I dropped something. I'll be right in."

Untangling myself from Adrian's limbs, I find my way to my uneasy legs. I fumble for my discarded bag, and hug it to my chest, like it could slow the erratic beats of my heart. Adrian slings himself upright, looking decidedly less rumpled than I feel.

Regret fills the empty space that now hangs between us. *Coach.* I just made out with a coach. How am I supposed to look him in the eye the next time he reads out my splits? The wind chimes peal around us, discordant and harsh, like they are judging us, too.

"I should go," I say, motioning to the door, looking anywhere but his eyes. His chin. I can handle his chin.

The chin nods.

"Okay, then." Adrian's voice is low and rough.

"Goodnight," I say.

Without waiting for a response, I flee to the door and let it thunk closed behind me.

Fourteen

56 DAYS UNTIL PAN AMS

"You don't *look* tired," Sofi says. Via FaceTime, she's been circling me like a vulture stalking a wounded hamster. She can definitely tell something happened between me and Adrian last night. And she's trying to bleed it out of me, drop by painful drop. "You look all . . . ruddy."

"What do you mean, ruddy?"

"I don't know. Dewy. Like you've been wearing eye masks or something. Have you finally started moisturizing?"

"No," I say. "But I did drink about a gallon of water this morning."

I've been trying to drown out the regret. That, and make up for last night's lost recovery time. I'm sure it hasn't been enough, though. Not only did I stay up past my bedtime by a full half hour, but I also missed at least twelve ounces of water from my hydration log. Maybe what I should do is recreate the epic smoothie I have in the training center on my make-or-break recovery days.

Sofi snaps her fingers as I pad down the stairs toward the kitchen. "It's your eyes," she says. "Usually they're puffy in the morning."

"Thank you."

"Well, today they're not."

"Do you want to just come out and ask instead of this prying thing you're doing?"

Sofi snorts with mock indignation. "Prying. You are my best friend, you are contractually obligated to answer my questions. And *I'm* contractually obligated to ask you the questions everyone else is too intimidated to broach."

The screen bounces as Sofi turns a corner. She's walking the perimeter—the trail that laps the circumference of the training center. It's one of my favorite morning jogs. I miss that place. I miss her. I'd give nearly anything to be jostling elbows with her right now instead of trying to carve out a corner of this kitchen to make a smoothie—one, by the way, that will be lacking at least six different ingredients I couldn't afford to buy for the summer.

Still, there's no point in giving up before I've even gotten started. So, I extract my mom's ancient blender from the perch I assigned it and root around for the almond butter.

"You are going to have to tell me what happened, though," Sofi says. "And don't you dare insult us both with another vagary about your string of Skee-Ball victories."

Despite myself, a smile flickers onto my lips.

"I SAW THAT!" Sofi pounces. "You tell me all about it right now, Katherine Parker, or you will sorely regret the consequences of my wrath."

"You're, like, five three."

"I'm five four and a half and I could drop you like a pool noodle."

That's probably true. Even though I have four inches on her, Sofi has an Olympic bronze medal. And she's scrappy.

"All right," I say as I break a banana in half and drop the pieces into the blender. "So, we made this bet about the training program and raced for it on the ergs. I lost and, well, you know how I'd feel about that." I'm still pissed, obviously, though the sting seems to have softened. "But there's this really great game room in the basement. So, we played Skee-Ball, which I destroyed, obviously. He walked me home and—I'm talking about Adrian, by the way. Maybe I should have started there."

"I CLEARLY KNOW WHO YOU ARE TALKING ABOUT." Sofi pinches the bridge of her nose. "Rowing gods, give me strength. What happened?"

"We kissed."

"And?"

"And nothing. We kissed. Now it's over."

"I knew that already on the basis of the fact that your lips are not currently attached to his. What was it *like*?"

"It was . . . nice." That damn smile is back.

"I knew it." The phone jerks and suddenly all I can see is blue sky and Sofi's pumping fists. "I FREAKING KNEW IT."

She hovers back into the screen and triumph blazes in her eyes. It's the exact expression she had right after her boat crossed the finish line in Tokyo. Head back, eyes pointed skyward. I know because she has a picture of it framed above her bed.

Sofi raises the phone so her eyes nearly fill the screen. "I knew you and Citrus Dreamboat were perfect for each other. I literally made a bet with myself that you two would fall in love."

"First of all, you can't make a bet with yourself. And second, we are *not* falling in love. In fact, there will be no more kissing. This was strictly a one-time-only situation."

"What? Why?"

I have about a trillion reasons, some of which I'm not even allowed to mention to Sofi. He's my temporary coach. I'm supposed to be evaluating him for a job. And that's not to mention how a relationship would negatively impact my performance. It was literally a relationship—and a breakup—that landed me in this mess in the first place.

With as much casual indifference as I can muster, I tip a scoop of protein powder into the blender. "I have to get second at Pan Ams."

"So?"

Without my permission, my mind leaps back to the docks at World Cups. Maxwell's patient face. My emotions spiraling out of control. My crushing defeat. "I lost control last night. I knew it was a bad idea and I kept going anyway. And now look what's happened."

"What's happened?"

"I lost valuable recovery time."

Sofi makes a noise that sounds a bit like a skeptical goat.

"I'm serious," I say.

"So am I," she retorts.

"You didn't even say anything."

"You knew what I meant."

I did, actually. "Well, your skepticism aside, I know what I need. And it definitely does not involve evening walks, Skee-Ball, or any sort of kissing."

"Mm-hmm."

"No more kissing," I say, more confidently now. "I might be attracted to Adrian or whatever, but that's all it is. And I can ignore attraction no problem. I have *excellent* self-control."

"Are you trying to convince me or yourself?"

Both. "Neither."

I slap the lid on the blender and press start. The machine's high-pitched whir puts a violent end to the conversation. Sofi glares at me over the din, mouth working like she's warming up to launch back in as soon as I turn it off.

Fortunately, just as I do, footsteps sound behind me. I spin to find Mom hovering in the doorway. She's wearing an all-white ensemble, complete with billowing pants and an airy, just barely sheer top. She even has her hair gathered in a white headband. Her eyes ping to my phone and she motions like she's going to leave, but I wave her into the kitchen.

"Can we finish this later?" I ask Sofi.

After last night, I've realized I need to rectify the fact that I haven't been to my mom's yoga studio yet. And possibly apologize for being a neglectful daughter.

"Fine," she says. "But don't think for a moment you're off the hook."

She ends the call.

"Hey, Mom," I say as I pour my smoothie into a glass. "Can we talk about something?"

"Of course," she says as she lowers herself to the kitchen table, as elegant as a white butterfly perching on a stick. "I wanted to talk to you about something also."

"What's up?" I ask.

"Please, you first."

I lean against the counter and sip my smoothie. "I want to apologize for not visiting your studio yet. I know it's important to you."

A smile lights up her face like she's on a dimmer that's just been turned to full blast. "That's sweet of you, my darling."

"Does that mean you accept?"

She tilts her head and her salt-and-pepper curls cascade from her headband onto her shoulders. "I will if you come to my Elevate and Radiate class in thirty minutes. I know today is one of your recovery days and it'll be perfect to help rebalance your mental state before a week of tough workouts."

I'm about to protest that my mental state doesn't need any rebalancing when I remember what Adrian said about the science-backed benefits of my mom's yoga. Then I promptly shove that memory out of my mind. I'm officially on Adrian abstinence.

"Let's do it," I say.

"Wonderful!" She springs up from the chair in a billowing cloud of white.

"Did you want to talk to me about something, too?"

Her eyes crinkle as her smile widens. "We can after class."

. . .

I knew, from the way Mom has talked about the studio, that it's been positive for her. Still, I wasn't expecting it to be quite like *this.* Wood-paneled walls frame floor-to-ceiling windows, which look out on a courtyard garden brimming with green plants. Himalayan salt lamps droop from the vaulted ceiling. The faintest scent of lavender hangs in the room.

As I sit cross-legged on my cool rubber mat, waiting for the class to start, I watch my mom. She flits from student to student, inquiring about health issues and asking for requests. She seems to remember everyone's name and their lingering aches and pains. When she passes, the students tip toward her like flowers searching for the sun.

I can't help but smile with them. Mom is radiant. In her element. Completely in control, but brimming with energy and love. She struggled for so many years that I always hoped—but never believed—she'd find passion in life again. And now, look what she has.

The soft chords of a flute float around us. Mom takes up a

spot in the center of the room, ready to start the class. I'm grinning at her like a maniac, probably just as I did as a very young child, watching her begin a dance performance.

It's wonderful—the distraction I needed to stave off the memories of last night.

Just then, the door creaks open.

"Room for one more?" a familiar voice asks.

I spin.

Adrian's broad shoulders hover into the entrance.

"Of course!" Mom exclaims. "You can put your mat right here. In front of my daughter."

Fifteen

The worst part of this class isn't the breathwork (strangely uncomfortable), my singing voice (laughable), or the various stretches (unexpectedly difficult, but oddly relaxing). It's Adrian's shirt. At least he's wearing one, I guess. The problem is it's made of some kind of stretchy material that clings to the muscles lining his back. Pulls tight across his shoulder blades. Tucks into the underside of his arm because it can't seem to fully contain the bulk of his biceps.

I swear he did this to me on purpose. Every time he swivels around on the mat, I try to glare at him questioningly. Like *Why must you make my life physically and irredeemably painful?* but said with my eyeballs and general aura of anger. Adrian just smiles innocently like this is all a big coincidence.

Fifty minutes and four peace mantras later, Mom instructs us to lie on our backs. I close my eyes and try to focus on the faint lavender smell and the soft chimes in the music. All I can smell is Adrian's cologne. All I can hear is that groan he made when I bit his—

Breathe, Kath. Focus on your breath.

As soon as Mom ends the class with a bow and a *namaste,* I shoot up from the mat. This isn't going to be a graceful or polite exit. Still, I cannot be in the same room as Adrian and that blasted *shirt* for a single gong beat longer.

"Kath!" I'm halfway to the door when Mom's voice halts my steps.

I mutter a curse as I turn. Mom is standing with a small group of people in a semicircle near the front of the room. Adrian is, of course, with them. Because apparently, I haven't suffered enough.

Mom gives me another enthusiastic wave, gesticulating like she's marshaling an airplane to a runway. Still, I hesitate, trying to find a way to leave without crushing her. Completely of their own volition, my eyes flit to Adrian's face.

He's smiling, but it's tentative. Like he's bracing himself for what I'll do next.

My heart sinks. I've been so focused on Adrian's muscles that I didn't stop to think about his feelings. I bolted away last night without a word of explanation, and probably left him confused at best or pissed at worst. I can be an adult and have a conversation with him. I can be an even bigger adult and explain why I ran out. First things first, I guess.

Clinging to my yoga mat like it's something between a comfort blanket and a shield, I slink toward the group.

"Did you have somewhere you need to be?" Mom asks as I approach.

I position myself so that Adrian is standing as far from me as possible and mumble something about a calorie deficit.

Mom rewards me with a patient smile.

"Kath," she explains to the others, "needs to eat a lot."

The assembled students nod like this is a perfectly reasonable explanation for Mimi's daughter sprinting out of her own mother's yoga class.

"But now that you're here," Mom continues, "I'd like to introduce you to some friends."

She motions first to a muscular woman with a crop of gray hair that rings her headband like a mane. "This is Susan. She's a retired firefighter."

Susan flashes a chipped-tooth smile. "It's great to meet you, Kath. Your mom brags about you constantly." Her voice drops into a conspiratorial whisper. "But I think she has a right."

"Thanks, Susan."

Next, Mom motions to an older man with a smartly trimmed beard and brow-line glasses. "And Rob, my business partner."

He reaches out a hand to shake mine in a firm grasp. "I've heard so much about you that this is a genuinely exciting moment for me."

Mom beams at him. "Rob is responsible for this dream becoming reality," she explains. "He's got the head for the business side of things. And he's very comfortable with a spreadsheet. You two would get along."

I nod and smile, even as some kind of demonic leprechaun kicks off a dance party in my stomach. Because Adrian is the next, and last, person in the semicircle. Mom is going to introduce him. Then he'll make eye contact with me. I might vaporize.

"Mimi is being far too modest," Rob says tenderly. "She's the heart of this operation. I'm just the support crew."

Mom elbows him, and then catches my gaze pointed at Adrian's bare feet.

"Right," she says warmly. "This is Adrian. He's a rowing coach!"

"Hey, Kath," he says. His smile looks easy again, no traces of tension haunting it anymore.

"Hey," I say, striving for the same level of nonchalance, but I'm positive that *hey* was approximately two octaves higher than the last couple.

Mom clearly doesn't miss any of this because her eyes cut between us. "You two already met? At the boathouse?"

"Actually, we fought a duel for a lemon bar," Adrian says.

"And I won," I add.

Adrian squeezes his lips to repress a smile. "That seemed self-evident."

I forcibly beat back the surge in my stomach. "How is it that you two know each other?"

"I offered some free yoga classes to teachers and coaches as one of the opening events for the studio."

"They were a huge success," Rob adds. "Just one class with Mimi and they're hooked."

"Nonsense." She swats at his shoulder, but I can't miss the glow in her eyes.

She *should* be proud. If I can cast Adrian's expanse of pectoral muscles out of my mind for five seconds, I remember to be awed, too. Her studio seems to be an unequivocal success and, in the few moments during class when I wasn't incapacitated, I enjoyed myself.

"This class was great, Mom, and the studio is beautiful. I can also see why yoga is a solid recovery tool."

From the corner of my eye, I catch Adrian beaming. My neck warms.

Mom is now glancing between us, a small, twisted smile on her face.

"Rob!" she says suddenly. "I need to talk to you about year-end accounting."

Rob's bushy eyebrows draw together. "It's July?"

"Or, you know, the other number things. The numbers we

have to think about in July. We'll just be off!" With sudden intensity, she rams Rob and Susan with her tiny hands and whisks them away.

"Wait, didn't you need me for something?" I call after her. "You said you wanted to talk after class."

"Oh, no," she says over her shoulder without pausing her escape. "Rob and I have very important numbers to attend to. You and I can talk later."

I detect the barest wink in one of her gray eyes.

God, not her, too.

Adrian shifts his weight and runs a hand through his hair. "Were you serious about being calorie deficient?"

As if on cue, my stomach growls. I wince.

"I could use another breakfast." I pause. *Adult, Kath. You're an adult.* "Also, we should talk about last night."

Adrian nods, face inscrutable again. "I'd like that."

. . .

Adrian takes me to a brunch place with mismatched vintage furniture and an open kitchen that's soaking the air with the smell of freshly brewed coffee and sizzling bacon. I would have asked him to meet at my mom's house to avoid the expense of eating out, but I wasn't eager to return to the scene of our fiery make-out session. Plus, we need to have this conversation approximately a million miles away from Mom's eardrums.

"The pancakes are top-notch," he says, nudging me with an elbow as I scrutinize the handwritten menu on a chalkboard above the register. "The ones with apple butter have the power to make my knees weak."

"Well," I say, "since strong joints are quite important for rowing, I'll stick with the eggs."

Adrian laughs like I'm joking, but I blink back at him, not

letting my expression crack. It's not like I have a problem with apple pancakes. It's just that they have no value to me. They'll give me, what, a rush of pleasure? That doesn't help me train harder or row faster, not compared to something more nutritionally dense. Besides, if I fill up on apple pancakes now, I'll miss an opportunity to hit some of my nutritional benchmarks, and I really don't want to be sitting up in bed eating deli meat tonight.

Adrian's laugh fades to a wry smile as he evaluates my expression, like, somehow, he finds my obstinance more charming than irritating. And that smile—not to mention the tender look in his eyes—somehow *does* make my knees feel weak.

"Suit yourself," he says and steps up to the counter.

We perch ourselves at a high-top table under the shade of a trellis dripping with jasmine. It's quiet, with only a few other patrons back here—some students, earbuds jammed in their ears, furiously clicking away at laptops, and an older woman with sunglasses sipping a latte and reading on a tablet.

Across this very small patio table, Adrian eyes me steadily. For the first time since last night, we're staring at each other head-on, and I have no distractions, no menus, no other people to buffer me against his presence. It's already too much. His soft smile while I'm talking. The tilt of his head and hair whispering against his forehead. The way his forearm muscles tighten when he crosses his arms.

I grip my fingers around my steaming tea mug, trying to distract my hands from the memories of the way those arms felt under my fingertips.

"You ran away quickly last night," Adrian says at nearly the same time that I say, "We can't kiss again."

Blast him for being a thousand times better at this adulting thing than I am.

He raises an eyebrow. "I don't know what you think of me, Parker, but I wasn't planning to toss this table aside and—"

"Don't finish that sentence." My heart beats like a furious bird trying to escape a too-small cage. "Let me try again. I'm supposed to be evaluating you for a job. My coach was very specific that I need to be unbiased. So, it would be inappropriate for us to get involved."

Adrian presses his lips together, more serious. "That job and I . . . we aren't going to work out."

Why does he keep saying this? Does he not want it for some reason? If that's the case, it's slightly annoying I'll have to spend so much time on Carla's very extensive evaluation rubric. Then again, the evaluation is my ticket back to the training center, so I can't complain too much. "Why not?"

He shrugs. "I don't know. Who knows what will happen. But you and me?" He leans forward and his eyes don't leave mine as he says, "I'm much more interested in what could happen with us."

A tingle traces up my spine and into the back of my head. Like fingers softly drumming into my hair. Like the sparks I felt when he—

Pan Ams. The spot.

It's all more important than the fluttering subsuming my body.

"You're coaching me," I say levelly.

"That's true." He leans back. "I wouldn't want to make you uncomfortable."

"Hold on, that's not what I meant." The words crack out of me. I want to put up boundaries, but I don't want to make him feel that he's taken advantage of me. "It's like you said before—you're not really my coach. This is a temporary arrangement and you don't have any real power over me. I wasn't trying to say I think there's a consent issue."

"Then what were you saying?"

I lift my mug and blow steam off the surface in a little riot of waves. "That coaches and athletes should be professional with one another."

"Even when one of them isn't really the other person's coach?"

At that moment, our server arrives in a whirlwind of plates, giving me a chance to organize my thoughts. She sets the assortment of dishes on the mosaic tabletop, each one clicking definitively, before she whisks away.

Across the table, Adrian's pancakes ooze with apple butter and he slathers them with syrup and whipped cream before taking a heaping bite. I watch as he pulls the fork away from his mouth and runs his tongue along the edge of his bottom lip to catch a drip of syrup. I force my gaze away.

"You were saying something about professionalism," Adrian says as he adds another stream of syrup to his pancakes.

"Yes." I straighten my back. "Kissing is unprofessional."

"And the two of us must remain strictly professional because . . . it's the principle of the thing?"

I realize I don't *owe* Adrian an explanation. If the answer is no, that should stand regardless of the reason. Yet I can't help but think about his tentative smile in the yoga studio. He might be assuming he did something wrong or that my reaction was somehow about *him.*

I should tell him the full truth.

I clear my throat. "Look. I am *attracted* to you. But I need to be one hundred percent focused on training this summer. I can't afford any complications or distractions."

"Because of Pan Ams?"

"Yes. I need to get top two to win back my spot."

"And kissing is a problem for that because . . ."

His skepticism reminds me of Sofi. But neither of them seems to understand that this is my shot. Carla's deal, the evaluation, and the race—it's my *only* shot. I'm walking a tightrope, with one single, very narrow path to getting my life back.

"Let's say I don't make it," I tell him. "I know how my brain works. I'll go back over every minute from this summer, cataloging each missed stretching routine and off practice. If you and I are—if I'm *involved* in that time, I'll wonder if that's the reason. Even if I might have lost anyway, I'll always second-guess myself and wish things had gone differently. I need to do everything in my power to get that spot back. That way, even if I lose, I won't have any room for doubt."

Adrian nods slowly, considering.

"That makes sense," he says.

"It does?"

"I wouldn't want to hurt you. I wouldn't want you to regret us."

I still for a moment, then regain my words. "Great. It's settled: There will be no us."

Declaration done, I shove a bite of eggs into my mouth to prevent myself from immediately taking it back.

Sixteen

51 DAYS UNTIL PAN AMS

I have come up with a rule to stick to my professional commitment with Adrian. It's a simple question that I ask myself before I say something, or anything, to my stand-in coach.

Would I say this to Carla?

If the answer is no, then I don't say it to Adrian.

It's working quite well. We've had no more heart-to-heart conversations. I've given him no additional openings to tell me how he finds me inspiring or passionate or "extremely fucking impressive." This has, in turn, reduced all my lip touching and abdominal staring to the acceptable level of zero.

The new maxim has a pleasing side benefit, too. It's allowed me to also keep the promise I made with the erg race: to stop fighting Adrian's coaching style. One morning, when he spontaneously decides to reduce the number of intervals in our workout, I grit my teeth and bite my tongue but refrain from complaining and tacking them back on out of spite. I do grumble—but only *internally*—when Adrian shouts at me to let my chin tilt up. And when the guys all pile into the game room one evening and Adrian asks if I'd like to join them, I say no as quickly and politely as I would if Carla asked. Well, to be fair, Carla would probably rather shave her eyebrows than spend an evening playing air hockey with a gaggle of teenagers. But, you get the idea.

It's all manageable. Expected. There are no further temptations or distractions. I'm able to focus on training to the exclusion of everything else, which on the whole, means things are good enough. Well, my boat still feels like a barge dragging a partially submerged parachute, but my splits are still good enough for top two. I just have to stay the narrow course.

Inevitably, Adrian finds a way to throw me off.

The performance team and I have just finished our cooldown, sweat- and water-slicked unisuits clinging to our backs. My quads and shoulders are still throbbing, but giving way to the sweet relaxation of post-exertion. As we start piling toward the docks, though, Adrian unexpectedly cuts off his engine, stopping in a sheltered inlet.

"Who's up for the standing challenge?" he shouts over the faraway whine of boat traffic.

To my utter confusion, the guys all cheer.

Without further instruction, one of the rowers in the bow seat of a quad gathers his oars in one hand, tucks his feet in close to his chest, and begins to stand. The boat rocks slightly, sending a ripple of waves vibrating off the hull, but it's still relatively stable with the other three bracing. Once he's upright, the lanky guy in two starts going vertical, as well.

Rowing shells are built for speed, not balance. Standing in them is difficult—more like trying to stand on a floating log than a surfboard. I haven't tried since college—not after I saw some guys in a double doing it and one of them had a very close call involving his nose and a misplaced oar.

Adrian maneuvers his launch until he's close to my blade. The hum of the engine dampens as he shifts to neutral.

"This isn't in the program," I say. "This isn't even in your contingency notes."

I crane my neck to look at him. Above me, his mess of brown hair, flecked in glistening droplets, is framed by an endless blue sky.

"This exercise transcends the program," Adrian says as Peter—who sits stroke seat in this quad—tucks his feet under his torso.

"What does that mean?"

Adrian grins back. "It means I like to make it a surprise."

With his three other teammates nearly vertical now, Peter's shell rocks and teeters, at this point closely resembling a mechanical bull with four crouching riders.

"LET'S GO!" Rohan shouts. In the last few minutes he has raced back to the docks, and is now jumping from foot to foot, phone aimed at the rebelling quad. "You've got this, Pete!"

Some of the others yell encouragement and friendly taunts. Peter's teammates, each hunched and wobbly, stare at the horizon in concentration. Peter pauses for a moment more before drawing himself higher. Cheers ring out. Rohan whoops and pumps the fist not holding the camera.

"There it is!" Adrian yells.

Peter flexes, but the motion is too much. The boat lurches. The guys spill out in a cascade of arms and legs, the shell flipping upside down as they hit the water with splashes and half-panicked laughter.

"Can you do it?" Adrian asks me as the guys swim their boat toward the dock, hollering for another crew to try.

"Of course," I say. "But I don't see the point. Explain your reasoning?"

It's a new thing between us. Ever since the erg race, whenever Adrian catches me off guard with a new training strategy, I ask for an explanation. As promised, he always delivers. Although I don't always agree with his logic, at least I can see where it's coming from. On rare occasions, his explanations are even compelling.

Though I doubt today will be one of those days.

Adrian starts ticking off points on his long fingers. "It tests balance. It will help you get out of your head and connect with the boat on a more subconscious and intuitive level. And . . ."

"And?"

"And it's fun."

I side-eye a double now wobble-standing, grins plastered to their faces as they brace for the inevitable crash. "What about the potential for injury?"

"You've seen someone get hurt doing this?"

"No," I say, "but I saw someone almost get hurt."

Adrian chuckles. "Let's not live our lives overly worried about 'almosts.'"

I frown. "Does that mean I have to do it?"

The way Adrian's lips lift has me forcing my eyes away from him. I hate that, even when we're arguing, I find his smile infectious.

"Yes, Parker. You have to." Another cry rings out as more guys flail and stutter. Water crashes yet again.

"Fine," I say and snatch up my oars. I haven't tried in years, but one advantage of the loaner boat I'm using is that it's wider than my normal racing shell and therefore a bit more stable. "My turn."

The guys cheer as I paddle toward a clear section of water, away from Adrian's launch and the other boats.

Rohan trains his phone on me as I angle my stern toward the

docks. "Get it, Kath!" he screams, fist pumping again. "The people want to see you fuck this up!"

He flashes me an enthusiastic—or maybe sarcastic?—thumbs-up.

"He means it in a good way," Peter clarifies as he flutter-kicks the stern of his quad past my shoulder.

My lips crack as Rohan starts dancing from foot to foot, muttering, "Get it, get it, get it."

"All right," I yell back. "Let me show the people how it's done."

He whoops in return.

A breeze flutters across my damp shoulders. I suck in a deep breath and let the omnipresent smell of brine and motor oil calm my racing heart. Then I organize the handles below my legs—regardless of what Adrian says, I don't need one of my oars impaling me—and press a foot to them to keep them level. With as much deliberate control as I can muster, I push myself upward.

The boat shudders. I keep my gaze locked on one of the irregular wood planks jutting up from the dock. My legs extend a bit more. And . . . yes!

I'm standing.

Hands splayed, I steer my triumphant smile toward Adrian. "Easy."

The boat rocks, but I manage to stay upright, riding the movement. Around his shoulders, I hear the distant smattering of applause.

Adrian folds his arms, his boat swaying slightly in the gentle waves. "Great. Now close your eyes."

"What?" I yell back, not quite sure I heard him right.

"Close your eyes."

The boat lurches, but I'm determined to say upright. "I'll fall."

Adrian's smile twitches. "Probably."

I bottle up a frustrated growl and survey each piece of equipment around me, trying to memorize their positions.

"No more stalling," he says.

Right, then. I give the dock one last fleeting look before I jam my eyelids shut.

For the briefest of moments, I'm triumphant. The world is dark, but I'm aloft, riding the boat like a teeter-totter. Thank god. Now I can get back to the dock and my post-workout routine. I want to start stretching before I—

My hip thrusts to the side. My legs tumble. Water envelops me as I crash through the surface in a cannonball of limbs and tidal wave of bubbles.

I kick toward the surface. Next to my overturned shell, my face thrusts into air. Water pours off me and I cough out salty liquid.

From the docks, Rohan flashes another thumbs-up. "GREAT CONTENT!" he yells from behind his phone. "Keep up the good work!"

Adrian navigates the launch to my side, joy dancing in his eyes.

"Almost," he says.

I wipe a hand down my wet face. "This is ridiculous."

"And here I thought it was 'easy,'" Adrian says with a wink.

I know what he's doing. He's manipulating me. (I guess he would say "coaching" me.) He's appealing to my competitive instincts to get me to work harder. I know that and yet . . . all I want is to flutter-kick this boat to the dock, slam myself back onto the seat, and prove this man wrong. No matter how many tries it takes.

An hour later, the guys have slowly streamed toward their impatient parents idling in the parking lot. Rohan seemed particularly difficult to tear away, but Adrian managed to convince him he had enough content for the day. Frankly, this has to be true. At this point, Rohan has probably caught me plunging into the inky water a dozen times.

Despite these many tries, I have so far been unable to hold a standing position, eyes closed, for more than a moment. Yet I'm sure as shit not done trying.

Adrian, for some reason, hasn't tired of watching me fail.

By the time I'm paddling out for my next attempt, the sun hovers low in the sky and the air has quieted with a gentle dusk. Moments later, the boat yet again tips out from under me, possibly even sooner than last time. Without the kids around anymore, I let out the scream that's been simmering in my chest for the last hour.

"This isn't possible," I say as I heave myself back onto the dock, water streaming off my braid and shoulders heating from the repetition.

"You're not committing to it," Adrian tells me. "You're not connecting with the boat. You have to lead with your heart instead."

I press my lips together and narrow my eyes over the expanse of water, darkening to charcoal blue with the setting sun. "None of those words make any sense in the order you've put them in."

Adrian laughs. "Out of your head and into your body. It's the same thing I tell you in practice—this is just a different format for learning it."

I let out an exasperated groan. Of all the coaching cues Adrian has given me over the last week, this one is the most confusing. Every time I try to ask him to break down what he means—to explain it to me in terms of leverage or handle height or torso hinge—he interrupts to say I need to stop thinking with my head so much and just *feel* it all more.

"I have no idea what that means," I protest impatiently. "I'm *in* my stupid body. There's literally nowhere else I can be. I bet this is actually impossible and you're just trying to break my spirit or something."

"*Impossible*?" Even from a few dozen feet away, I can hear the challenge.

With one foot on the hull of my boat, I thrust it toward his launch. "Show me, then."

Adrian grins like he was hoping I'd say that.

A few moments later, he's leaped onto my seat and is moving away from the dock. A puddle accumulates beneath me as, knees pulled into my chest, I trace his movements.

He's wearing a light-colored Henley, better suited to coaching than crewing, and even though the rigging is wrong for him, he looks perfectly at home in my boat. He handles the oars with easy confidence, forearms flexing as he arcs the stern toward me. He's just as strong and balanced as he was on a yoga mat, but now there's a self-assuredness in the flex of his arms and a smoothness to the press of his legs. He rolls a hand against the oar grip and, for a sudden confusing moment, I wish it were the back of my head under his fingers.

Adrian flashes me a smile, clenches his eyes shut, brings his feet beneath his body, and stands. The motion is wobbly, yes. He's a rower, not a gymnast. Still, his movements are sure and precise. A moment later, he's fully upright, eyes closed, with arms splayed out to his sides.

It should make me feel jealous or maybe even defeated. Instead, I'm just impressed.

"How are you doing that?" I yell across the water.

Eyes still closed, Adrian lists to one side, but quickly recovers. "Practice. And connection. You have to get out of your head and connect with the boat."

"Okay there, Sensei," I say with a laugh even though I'm still grappling with the growing knot in my stomach.

There's an aliveness to him that I've either never seen before or never fully appreciated. His energy is striking. Infectious. I want it near me. I want to breathe it in with deep, gasping inhales.

"Ready to try again?" he asks.

"I'm fine sitting here and watching you."

The words pop out of my mouth before I can check them against my mental rubric.

That's not something I'd say to Carla.

Adrian's eyes fly open. They grab me over the glimmering water: him still riding those faint waves, me soaking wet and unbearably warm despite it. A shimmer of electricity passes between us, a cord connecting us that I thought I'd severed days ago. It sends a rush of heat down my spine, a tingle all the way to my still-damp toes.

Adrian's mouth unfurls in a smile.

And then his boat tips.

Seventeen

47 DAYS UNTIL PAN AMS

I vow to use my next recovery day to get my head back in the game. With a full day at Mom's house, I can alternate napping, foam rolling, and stretching in forty-two-minute increments. I can mix up all my recovery beverages using my favorite recipes, and sip on them as I scroll through updates from Rower's World. I won't have to think about the way I awkwardly bolted from the boathouse the day of the standing challenge or the uncomfortable fluttery feeling in my stomach that I've had every day in practice since. Today, there won't be disconcerting eye contact, random interruptions, or sudden changes in plans.

This is a good thing.

Obviously.

Yet as my massage gun digs into my quads, Adrian's infuriating smile invades my mind. His forearms as he smoothly glided his oars across the water. The way he so effortlessly and confidently pressed himself upright and the way his eyes danced before he tipped.

Fuck.

To distract myself from both the intensity of the vibrations and this parade of memories, I pull up Carla's rubric on my phone and grope around on my desk for a set of Post-its. I haven't made much progress on the evaluation, so I scan the options, resolving to draft at least a couple of responses.

How would you describe Adrian's coaching style?

My pen hovers above my red Post-it. Two weeks ago, I would have written "domineering" and moved on. Since the erg test, though, it's become clear that Adrian's commanding attitude was an act—or, as he would say, a *coaching strategy*. But that introduces a whole set of other problems. If he's adapting his style to his athletes' needs, then what is his style in the first place?

I decide to skip that one for now and move on to the next.

Have you seen any improvements in your performance?

Maybe marginal? That one workout where I beat my own splits comes to mind. But otherwise, I'm basically in the same place I was when I got here. Fortunately, assuming I can actually complete this evaluation, this should be good enough to get top two and win back my spot. Still, in the interest of the objectivity I promised Carla, I should give Adrian most of the summer before I answer this one.

Another skip for now, I guess.

Describe Adrian's level of interest in the job.

Honestly, we've hardly talked about it, which is strange. Adrian is so enthusiastic about so much, especially anything to do with rowing. This job should be a huge deal—a massive step forward in his career. It makes his nonchalance, or even disinterest, confusing. At the same time, I haven't asked him explicitly if he wants it and I should probably wait to answer this one until I do.

I stare down at my empty stack of Post-its and groan. Clearly, I need a break from Adrian. A real one.

I roll over so I can massage my other quad—vibrations slackening skin and muscles—and flip my phone to Rower's World to get my daily dose of updates. There's some news from a few collegiate programs, including next year's race scheduling and various signing announcements. Then, a lengthy tribute written up about the decorated career of the retiring men's national team coach. I start reading it, but abruptly flip back to the main screen when I reach an adoring quote from Maxwell. My fingers keep scrolling, desperate to find something interesting enough to distract me from memories of Adrian's smile.

And that's when I get my wish.

Not in a good way.

Campeonato Brasileiro de Remo. Updates from the national championships in Brazil, which just wrapped yesterday. When I click on the link for the women's single sculls final, and have Google translate the page, what I see freezes me.

The winning time. It's not just good.

It's Canadian-level good.

I bolt upright, massager spitting out discordant circles on my carpet.

What the hell?

My fingers shake as I click around to see the other times clocked by the winner—Camila Gomes. Surely, the conditions must have been extremely favorable, like some massive tailwind or maybe a slightly short course. Or maybe something got lost in the automatic translation.

I mean, I barely even recognize this name. I think Camila

went to World Cups this year, but I remember beating her handily in the heats.

What is even happening?

Maybe it's something about her lane. When she clocked this ridiculous time in the final, she raced in lane five, but she was in lane three for the heat. On certain courses, some lanes can be considerably faster or slower, depending on current or wind. I could look at the times from the eights to see if there's a similar pattern. I don't know offhand how fast the Brazilian eights *should* be, but I know someone who would.

I switch off the oscillating massager, finally stilling it, and pick up my phone, then pace across my narrow carpet as FaceTime chimes.

"Have you seen the race times from the Brazilian Nationals?" I ask while the video is still loading.

"Good morning to you, too," Sofi replies. Her camera comes alive and the room around her is dark enough that all I can see is her silhouette, illuminated by the blue light of her phone.

"I woke you up?"

"I should get up anyway." The sleep is still heavy in her voice and she rubs at her forehead. "I've been having trouble waking up from my naps lately, so I probably need the extra time."

I hum. "Fill that sixteen-ounce water bottle you keep by your bed and put an electrolyte tab in it. One of the pink ones, though. The blue ones will only make you feel worse."

A flicker of something like annoyance passes over her expression before she presses her lips together and pushes off her bed. "I didn't even know I *had* pink ones," she mutters.

I watch the underside of her arms as she hunts through the stack of sponsor-provided supplements and protein bars on her desk. If I were there, I would have already handed her the water bottle with the correct tab dissolved.

Finally, though, she props up her phone so I can see her again, drops the tab into her bottle, and takes a sip of fizzing liquid.

"Now," she says, already sounding more alert. "Let's get back to your midafternoon panic."

"Brazil. Have you seen the times?"

Sofi sighs, but she takes another swig as she nudges a box of protein powders off her laptop. I hear the telltale sound of the ancient machine roaring to life. "I mean, I *saw* them. I didn't memorize them in anticipation of an interrogation, which I'm guessing this will be."

"How did their winning eight look?" I ask, breathlessly. "They were in lane five in the final. Was it faster than you'd expect?"

"Actually, that I can answer without looking," Sofi says. "It was a bit slow. Their stroke seat decided to race singles, so they had to make a switch midway through the season and it's costing them."

That knotted feeling in my stomach tightens. "Is her name Camila? Their stroke seat?"

"Yeah, that's it. What I heard is that she'd been trying to race both events, but decided she was spreading herself too thin. Why?"

"Take a look at her final," I say pitifully.

I watch as Sofi clicks at the screen, then sits back in her chair.

Her expression goes flat. "Oh," she says quietly. "I see."

I let the phone flop out of my hand as I collapse back onto my mattress and stare up at the Olympic rings on my ceiling. "Yeah."

"Have you watched any video from her race?" She clicks some more and I hear a rattle of Portuguese—I don't know what they're saying but I assume Sofi has pulled up the video of the final on YouTube. "Damn. Camila is pulling like her stern is on fire."

"Does it look like it could be a fluke?"

"Probably not," Sofi replies. "Her natural technique works better for sculling. In the eight, she was dropping into the water too aggressively, using more brute force than finesse. In the single, she's letting it flow naturally. It's working for her."

"Shit," I say.

So, the massive jump in her performance has a reasonable explanation. In fact, it's so reasonable that I should fully expect Camila to race just as well, if not better, at Pan Ams.

Which means . . . my spot is in jeopardy again. Now, I have to beat either the unbeatable Canadian or the, apparently, almost-as-fast Brazilian.

It's not enough. My mediocre progress, my handful of halfway decent workouts. It's not enough.

"How's it been going?" Sofi asks, her voice soft. "With Adrian's coaching?"

She doesn't know that I'm evaluating Adrian for the job, but she does know about my deal with Carla—that if I prove my flexibility by training with Adrian over the summer, and finish in the top two at Pan Ams, she'll ask USRowing to give me my spot back.

"About the same," I say. "Not that I can expect much better. I waste too much time doing irrelevant stuff like *connecting with the boat* and *getting out of my head*."

"That's not helping?"

I roll over to keep the ceiling rings from taunting me. Sofi, I think, is lying back down again because all I have is a view of her chin.

"It's kind of hard to 'get out of my head' when I'm counting down the seconds until I can get back to a real training program," I say.

I expect Sofi to laugh or sigh or make a joke about my absence or the distance between us. Instead, she hums.

"What?" I ask.

"It kind of sounds like you're not really doing his program."

"What do you mean?" I protest. "I've done everything that beautiful maniac has asked of me. I haven't done any of my own workouts. I keep my mouth shut when he suddenly changes our metric goals halfway through practice. I even did his cursed standing challenge last weekend. Even though there is approximately zero chance that tipping a boat three dozen times is going to make me row faster."

Sofi lifts the phone so her expression is bathed in the harsh light of her screen. Her eyes are flat and serious, no trace of her usual mischievous smile. "Yeah, but you haven't been *committing* to it."

I frown back at her. "You sound like Adrian."

"Maybe because he's right? You're going through the motions. It's not going to work if you're doing it half-assed."

I don't know about that. I mean, I'm not even really sure what his approach *is*, other than something vague about getting out of my head. "So, you think I should, what?"

"Apply that big, beautiful brain of yours to understanding his method. And then apply your extraordinary discipline to executing it."

We sit in silence as I tap my fingers against the comforter and consider that.

I suppose I have three options, here.

One: I quit on Adrian, write my own program, and lose my deal with Carla. That would mean I'd need to beat both the

Canadian and the Brazilian to get my spot back. At this point, a near impossibility.

Two: I keep doing what I have been for the last couple of weeks. Admittedly, that has gotten me nowhere.

Or . . . three: I take Sofi's suggestion. I really apply myself to Adrian's approach and take it just as seriously as I would if it were a program I'd written myself.

I glance back at my phone screen, click away from the call, and flip back to Camila's race times. I'm not going to beat this woman if I don't make a change. A big one. Maybe Adrian's method will work, maybe not. Either way, what I said to him at brunch is true. I don't want to look back on this summer and wonder: *What if?* At least this way, I'll have given it my all. I'll have tried every conceivable option. I won't have any regrets.

"At this point, Kath, what do you have to lose?" Sofi asks like she's reading my mind.

I clear my throat. "You're not wrong."

"I know," Sofi says. "Although that hasn't stopped you from ignoring my unusual but effective advice in the past."

"I don't care how many times you tell me to, I'm not going to start whispering affirmations to my boat."

"Suit yourself," Sofi says. "You're only hurting you."

"And you, just a little bit, every time I don't listen."

She laughs. "You're not supposed to know that. I should go. I have a physical therapy appointment in ten. I'm glad we had this talk, though."

She hangs up.

I stare at my phone for another long moment, sigh, and pull open my text message chain with Adrian. Our entire exchange is comically brief considering how much mental space this man has occupied. I have one group message from him from last week, when he let the team know that he'd be late to practice the next morning, and one direct message with a link to an article he found on blood oxygen testing. It's a topic we'd debated furiously earlier. I thought maybe the article would support his position, but to my surprise, it supported mine.

Question, I type. Let's say I wanted to really commit to your program. How should I rest today?

My phone lights up with his response almost immediately. Parker? Blink twice if you've been kidnapped.

I chuckle as I type. I'm desperate here.

Clearly.

I'm about to follow up when Adrian's dots dance again.

Moments later, his message appears. Recovery is enhanced with endorphins. And endorphins are best produced by fun.

Fun?

I can practically feel Adrian smiling as I read his response. "Fun" happens when you engage in an activity purely for pleasure, instead of following the advice of Rowing Quarterly.

As opposed to the advice of my temporary coach?

There's a long pause, long enough that I listen to Mom downstairs, where she's singing along to something upbeat on her speakers as she careens around the kitchen. Finally, Adrian's response comes through. Good point. It only works if it's something you'll enjoy.

Any suggestions, then?

You need suggestions on how to have fun?

I stare at those words because, yeah, I kind of do. If I picked for myself, I'd probably end up choosing something that isn't *fully committing*. Like . . . going for a trail run. Or getting a massage. Or reorganizing Mom's kitchen.

Yes, I enjoy these things, but it's stuff that I do all the time. Maybe committing means trying something totally different.

Yes. I write, finally. Please.

Adrian's response is almost immediate. How about I show you instead?

Eighteen

Adrian kills his engine in front of a neon red sign promising FUN, FUN, FUN!

I lean out of the open window. "I didn't know we were being so literal."

"I am a man of my word." He runs his hands in an arc against the steering wheel. "So, you promised you'd commit to this?"

"Commit to having fun?"

He nods gravely, like we're talking about rehabbing a serious injury, not an amusement park.

I put up my right hand as the video of Camila's final resurfaces in my mind. "I commit to having fun."

Adrian grins and yanks open his door.

We drift toward the bright primary colors splashed across the entrance like boats tugged downstream. Beyond the gates, the air is filled with a discordant song made up of whacking baseball bats, heavy clanks from roller coasters powering uphill, and the errant dings from a shooting gallery. Couples in damp T-shirts sprint toward the entrance for the bumper boats and throngs of kids tear at clouds of cotton candy with sticky fingers and pink-stained teeth.

"Wait," I say, grabbing Adrian's elbow as my eyes roam over signs for the *Fun-O-Lympics* and *Aim, Shoot, and Fun!* "Is this really about helping me? Or are you secretly looking to redeem your string of Skee-Ball defeats?"

Adrian lays a hand on his heart, feigning innocence. "I have no idea what you mean, Parker. I promised fun, which is the primary offering of this establishment. Besides, if there's one thing I know about you, it's that you enjoy competition."

"And winning," I say.

"That's too bad," Adrian says.

"Why?"

"Because"—he fights a grin—"I intend to crush you at everything we play."

My lips twitch. "It's cute that you think you stand a chance."

Over the next few hours, we trade breathless victories.

Milk bottles explode off their stand, clattering in the wake of my projectile like they were hit with a hand grenade. An amply pierced college student throws a petrified glance in my direction. Adrian looks impressed. My heart swoops like I've just hit the drop on a roller coaster.

Then Adrian convinces me to get on an actual roller coaster and the experience is far less pleasant. Much more high-pitched clanging and terror than I'd expected. When the safety restraints lift off my chest, I guzzle my first breath of free air and stagger toward the neon exit sign, clutching a handrail for balance.

"Again?" I ask, still panting as we spill back onto the park's brick walkway.

Adrian studies me with a tilt of his head. "Do you *want* to go again?"

"I promised to commit to your method."

He offers me an elbow. "The method is fun, Kath. Whatever that means to *you*."

My chest lightens as we forge back toward the games.

In the shooting gallery, Adrian's aim is much steadier—probably from his superior patience. Predictably, I slaughter him at Whac-A-Mole, which is mostly about reflexes and brute force. Adrian bests me in the batting cages. I realize this is not technically a competition, but I can tell who's winning based on how loudly our bats crack against our balls. Adrian's next high five is electric, sending a crackle down to my toes.

When my watch buzzes, alerting me to my snacking hour, he disappears and reemerges with two golden brown corn dogs.

I study the red-and-white checkered paper boat tray he's holding out.

He must have caught my hesitation because he pulls it back. "No pressure. If you don't want one, I'll gladly eat both."

"Is this part of the 'fun' protocol?" I ask, thinking of the preportioned snacks in my bag. "Because if I eat that, I probably won't be hungry for one of the other meals I planned."

"Sure, but I'm not going to tell you what to eat." Adrian tucks one of the boat trays into an elbow so he can lift a corn dog off the other. "Have the corn dog. Have your special ratioed meal. Have both. It's all valid and they all have benefits."

"Yeah? What's the benefit of a corn dog?" I ask, skeptically.

"It gives you joy," Adrian says. "And joy has to be a part of rowing. And life. Otherwise what's the point?"

I consider that for a long moment, listening to the ambient chiming of bells, mechanical clanking of gears, and the shouts from a carnival barker. Then I grab for the other stick. As I sink my teeth into the fried dough, my tongue springs alive.

"Holy shit, this is good," I say around a second bite. Weirdly sweet? Why is it sweet?

Adrian offers me a paper bowl smeared with mustard. It doesn't seem like it should, but somehow, that makes the next bite even better. "Mini golf next?" he asks.

I stuff the half-eaten corn dog in my mouth and sling my bag over a shoulder, already taking off toward the clubs. "Race you there!"

By the time we've started our second round, a deep, resonating stillness fills my bones. Mini golf is another one of those sort-of sports that I enjoy, probably because it involves precision, repetition, and deep focus. I love the smooth feel of the club in my hands, the tiny crack of the club, and the absolute exhilaration I get when everything lines up perfectly and that little ball sinks into its cup.

"So," Adrian says, almost like he's reading my mind, "best day off or *very* best day off?"

I settle my purple ball into its tiny divot. "I have to admit, it's the best I can remember."

"Ah." Adrian sounds borderline triumphant. "I thought I was at least playing second fiddle to Mimi's yoga class."

I square my shoulders, eyes zeroed in on my target. "That was not a good day off."

"Why not?"

"That damn shirt."

"Which damn shirt?"

With a thwack of my club, the ball skitters forward, plunking definitively into my hole. Heck yes. I pump my fist as I raise my eyes to Adrian. "The one you wore to class."

"What was wrong with it?"

I don't know whether it's the hole in one or the way I'm still zinging from the corn dog, but I'm suddenly feeling bold. I drop my miniature club and step toward Adrian, close enough that I'm practically pressed against his body. He inhales sharply. I circle an arm around his back, and pull his shirt tight until it's stretched across the hard planes of his abdomen.

"*This* is what was wrong."

His chin drops so that his mouth is nearly brushing my ear. Lightning skitters down my spine as his breath warms my cheek. "I have absolutely no idea what you're talking about, but I absolutely like it."

"You did it on purpose, though, didn't you?" I whisper, still holding the back of his shirt, still so close to him I can practically feel his heartbeat through it.

"Wear a shirt?"

"Show up to my mom's yoga studio."

He chuckles and the sound skitters over my skin. "It crossed my mind that you might be there."

I shake my head and step back, letting cool air between our bodies again. "I still can't believe you already knew my mom before we met. Your turn."

Adrian sets his ball. "And *I* still can't believe Mimi Parker of Enchanted Asana fame is your mom. If I'd known, I would have asked for your autograph."

"More impressive than 'national team rower'?"

"Nearly."

I clear my throat. "I should thank you, by the way, for pushing me to go to her studio. I probably wouldn't have otherwise. But it was great to see how well she's doing. I mean, I knew it's been good for her. But I wasn't expecting her students to be so doting or—if we're being honest—the studio to be so well organized."

Adrian shifts his weight and pulls back his club. The ball flies forward, slightly overshooting the target. "So, your love of spreadsheets doesn't come from your mom?"

I laugh, thinking about the frozen-deer look Mom gets when

confronted with a checkbook. "No. She's always been more interested in having dance parties in our living room than signing permission slips. I'm blown away that she's running a successful small business."

I tip my chin toward the cobalt sky, thinking about that morning in the yoga studio and her surprisingly well-stocked fridge. I haven't seen her cry once since I got home, either. It can't be a coincidence that this stability and happiness has coincided with a noticeable absence of the "latest guy."

"She's finally found purpose and success again," I say. "Probably because she's finally abstaining from love."

Adrian squints at me with more skepticism than I'd prefer. "Well, she might be abstaining from love, but she's certainly giving it some glances, if you know what I mean."

"Ew. No, I don't."

Adrian puts up a hand in mock surrender before striding after his ball. "I've seen the way she looks at Rob, that's all I'm saying."

Rob? An image flashes to my mind of the tall man with salt-and-pepper hair and glasses that nearly melt into his thick eyebrows.

"Wait." I hurry after him. "You mean her *business partner*?"

Adrian taps his ball into the hole and lifts a shoulder. "You can ignore it all you want. Doesn't make it less real."

I'm about to retort something very convincing about how Mom has finally gotten serious about her career and isn't going to mess it up by getting involved with Rob, *her business partner*, when my watch buzzes again. Time for my late afternoon self-massage session.

I click it to silent, pluck my ball from its cup, and forge toward the next hole.

A few hours later, the sun begins to set, basking the hot pavement in an orangish glow. My stomach grumbles and I ask Adrian if we should get more corn dogs.

"I have something better," he says.

"Funnel cake?" I ask.

"Better than that, too."

"Really? My best friend says funnel cake is the root of all happiness. I sort of want to find out what the fuss is about."

He laughs. "I'll make you dinner."

I meet his eyes with a seductive jolt of possibility. Although he's offered this meal so casually, I know what it means. Saying yes here isn't just about his approach to training and recovery. It's about abandoning my plan to keep things professional. It's about *us*.

"I'd like that," I say.

. . .

Sipping on a fizzy water, I lean against Adrian's wooden kitchen island while he cooks. He moves expertly between his stainless steel fridge and graphite countertops, a hand towel slung casually over one shoulder. To my surprise, he wields a paring knife with the precision of a professional.

"I wasn't expecting you to be such a good cook," I say as Adrian presses his thumb into the side of a fleshy scallop and pulls out some kind of muscle, like he's peeling a petal from a rose.

He flicks it into a bowl. "There was a time I wanted to be a chef."

"Really?" I slide to a seat on one of Adrian's barstools. Chef seems like an odd detour along the path from rower to coach. "When?"

"After I quit rowing, I took a year off before college. Everything in my life was up in the air, so I ran through a lot of options. I've always loved to cook. Chef was on the short list."

"Oh. You quit rowing after high school? I've been assuming you were on some varsity crew." Adrian's splits on the erg were way too good for him to have topped out as a high school athlete.

He nods, but doesn't look up from the rhythmic thuds of his knife against the chopping block. "I had an athletic scholarship to Georgetown, but I ended up turning it down. Much to my dad's dismay. But, as it turned out, he hated the culinary school idea even more. So much that he eventually offered to pay for part of my tuition if I still went and got a degree in exercise science."

I tilt my head, watching him. I know a lot of people whose parents got them into rowing. Most ended up resenting the sport. "Did you, er, like crew?" I ask. "As an athlete."

Adrian's knife sails across a stack of herbs and he considers the question for so long that I wonder if the answer is no. Then he says, "Yes. I loved being part of a team."

"But?"

"*But* there was a lot of pressure."

"From your dad?"

He looks up sharply. "Did I already say that?"

I lift up a foot onto my stool and rest my temple against my bent knee. "No, but you described his personality. Plus, I know a lot of athletes from 'legacy' families."

"Right. I guess you'd know the type." He blows out a long, controlled breath. "Yeah, you're right. My dad . . . Well, you already have a picture. He always wanted me to be the best. Race up age categories. Medal at Youth Nationals. Get on the best varsity crew."

He tosses a clove of garlic onto his chopping block and crushes it hard with the flat side of his knife. "The better I got, the closer the races got. The harder I had to work. The more he expected perfection instead of merely excellence. My last couple of years of high school, he started coaching me himself. Not on the water, but cross-training sessions in the weight room and on the running track."

"That's never a good idea," I say.

Adrian laughs hollowly. "It certainly was not. One time, I forgot my heart rate monitor after school, and Dad decided that he would also 'forget' how many intervals I was supposed to do. Every time I finished a lap, I'd ask him how many more and he'd say 'I forget' and make me do another."

"Horrible," I whisper. "What did you do?"

"I kept going. Dad never brokered any disagreement. But, eventually, I guess he decided I'd learned my lesson when I was barely dragging my toes across the ground. He took me home. And yet— "

He cuts himself off and turns to the stove, clicking it on.

"And yet?" I prod.

Blue flames spring to life, reflecting in his pupils and casting across the hollows of his cheekbones. The light illuminates an emotion lingering there. Sadness? Regret?

"And yet it still wasn't enough. He never said good job or that he was proud of me for sticking it out. We got in the car and went home. Mom asked me how it went, and I told her it was great, just like I always did."

"I'm so sorry."

He lifts a shoulder as he gazes down at the pan, waiting for it to heat. Then he pours in a stream of oil and lays his scallops in the shimmering liquid. The pause lasts long enough that I assume his next words will be consequential, but all he says is: "It is what it is."

"It's not," I insist, trying to catch his eye, but he's too focused on the olive oil, the popping scallops. "What he did to you was unfair and cruel. You didn't deserve that."

"Maybe not. It was easier then, though."

"How so?"

But Adrian's shoulders have gone tight. It's like he requires all his focus to spoon little puddles of liquid over the crisp, brown surface of the hunks of meat. His jaw is clenched so hard I wonder if he can breathe properly. Maybe I shouldn't prod. Selfishly, though, I want him to keep talking.

"You don't have to tell me," I say. "I know there isn't anything I can actually do to help. But I promise I'll listen. Whatever it is, I won't judge."

It's something Sofi sometimes says. Like, *Do you want opinionated Sofi or nonjudgmental Sofi?* With the toughest stuff, nonjudgmental Sofi is the easiest to talk to.

Adrian flicks off the stove and frees his browned scallops from their hot liquid. I wait in silence as he sprinkles the meat with salt and uses a mitt to pull a tray of crispy-looking asparagus from the oven.

"We should eat now," he says, motioning to the pair of plates with scoops of brown rice already laid out. "The scallops are best fresh off the heat."

As a person who fights to show nothing but composure to the world, I know what it feels like—and what it looks like—to face down an avalanche of emotion and turn away. So, I push myself off from my seat and circle around to his side of the countertop. I stand between him and the scallops.

"It's just you and me here," I say.

"You," he says quietly, "are never *just* you."

"I am right now, though."

He draws in a sharper breath and his eyes find mine. I nod encouragingly and he exhales as though steeling himself.

Finally, he says, "It was tough when he was alive. But it's all harder now."

I blink. He's just revealed something, something important and possibly deeply hurtful. And yet I have no idea what it was.

"Why is it harder now?" I ask as gently as I can manage.

He rocks his lip between his teeth. "Because he's gone. And now I'll never have his approval."

His words knife into my sternum. Without a moment of thought, without worrying about job evaluations or Pan Ams or all the other reasons I shouldn't cross yet another line with him, I run a hand down his arm. The muscles of his forearm are clenched tight as I grab his fist.

His breath gusts out, but before I can pull away, his fingers twine with mine.

"Listen," I say. "Obviously, I can't tell you that your dad was proud of you. I can't know that. But here's what I do know."

I press the tip of my thumb into his palm, like I'm anchoring myself to him. Like I want to impress on him the gravity of what I'm going to try to say.

"You have some unconventional strategies, but you are a hardworking and diligent coach. You're willing to change to fit the needs of athletes, instead of demanding they adapt to you, which is so unique I've never even heard of it before. But, much more importantly than all that, you are a good man. You have great taste in pastries and a mean swing in a batting cage. You're strong and steady, but also energetic and honest and, unlike every athlete and coach I've ever met, you have no trace of ego."

I squeeze his hand tighter. "I have no idea how much of that your dad knew, and I'd be lying if I said it doesn't matter, because it does. Of course, it matters. But, also, those things are true. Whether or not your dad saw them."

His hand tightens around mine until I can feel the calluses on his palms and the heartbeat in his fingertips. "Kath."

The way he says my name, like it's full of hurt and want and need and hope. It unspools the last little bit of thread wrapped around my heart.

"Adrian," I say, and my voice trembles.

"I would like to kiss you," he whispers.

In answer, I lean forward and press my lips to his.

Nineteen

Adrian cups my face in his hands and kisses me. My lips part in invitation and his tongue brushes against mine. A tingling warmth descends over every inch of my skin. He tastes as good as I remembered, like mint and citrus. Our next kiss is fuller, rounder, each of us giving ourselves over to the motion of it. I sink my teeth into his bottom lip and he groans.

The sound stirs deep inside me. Heat pools between my legs and *want* uncoils in my chest. I want him—desperately. It's not just today or right now. This feeling has been with me for days. I've just repressed it, beaten it back. Forced it into hibernation.

Now that I see the scope of it, it's almost startling. In the past, moments like these were always part of a plan or a schedule. I've kissed other men, slept with other men, because it made sense or because I felt I needed the experience or because it was the logical next step in the natural progression of a relationship. It's not to say I've never felt attraction or lust. But this—this is different.

That was like lighting a candle and watching the flame dance. This is like becoming the fire.

I'm desperate for him now and that flickering flame infuses every movement of my body: the tug of my hands against his neck, the press of my tongue against his, the murmur of a sigh on his lips. Adrian, clearly, notices the shift because his movements change, too. His hands are suddenly everywhere: pinning my braid to the back of my head, running up the smooth skin under my shirt, cupping the back of my thigh and hitching my leg between his. I can feel his desire. Not just in the way that he captures my mouth or murmurs against my neck. But in the way he breathes me in, like he's been waiting for this moment for just as long as I have. The thought is a puff of air on an already billowing fire.

Adrian presses me backward until my low back hits the edge of the kitchen counter and I can feel the cool surface just beyond my thin nylon shirt. I want more of that—more sensation, more friction. My hands find the hem of Adrian's T-shirt and he moves his arms so I can pull it free. His expanse of muscles gleams in the low light. I run my hands against his velvety skin, touching him in the way I've wanted to since that day on the ergs. Since the first time I saw him do an arm balance on a yoga mat or sit in a rowing shell. I revel in the contours of his chest, smoothing my fingers across the dent in the middle of his sternum, the pocket beneath each of his pecs.

We meet each other's eyes and before this goes any further, I wrap a hand around his wrist and angle our bodies toward the door that I think leads to his bedroom. But Adrian remains solidly in place. Instead, he scoops two hands under my backside and lifts me until I'm sitting on his kitchen island.

"You cook food on this surface," I remind him, even though the scallops are a safe distance away.

He laughs against my throat. "I also own a variety of countertop sanitizers. Besides." He pushes back from me slightly, two hands pressed on either side of my legs. From this vantage, he has to tilt his head to look up at me. "I've spent a long time thinking about all of the things I can do to you in this position."

"How long?"

He takes my mouth in his and then moves his lips to my ear. "You thought you were tortured by my shirt? I've been tortured by that damn porch."

Adrian runs a hand along my inner thigh, pushing my legs open wider.

"You were like this," he murmurs as he moves closer, slotting into the space between my knees. Flattened together, I can feel he's hard through his jeans. "And I was like this," he adds and runs a hand up my spine, cupping the back of my head.

Heat gathers in all the places he's touching, sending waves jackknifing through my fingertips.

"And then I almost fell," I say.

Adrian's arm tightens around my waist. "Nowhere to fall this time."

Then his lips are on my skin again, traveling across my neck, running up the crease of my jawline, finding the sliver behind my ear. And, oh, it's heaven. Every one of his touches sends a cascade of tingles over my skin, a rush down my spine.

Still. We can't just *do it* out here. Beds exist for a reason.

"Adrian," I say again. I tug at his elbow. "This isn't the place."

His lips loosen from my throat and he pulls back enough that I can see the smile in his eyes. "You have a pre-approved list of acceptable places for sex?"

"No. Well. I mean. I guess, like, a *rough* list."

Adrian's chuckle is low.

"What?" I ask.

He smooths his hands down the backs of my bare arms and there's this *thing* in his eyes—like I'm something precious that can't be broken. "That is just so perfectly you."

And for the first time in a long time, it is as I said. Right now: It's just me. I've never felt so exposed or so seen. I'm neither whole nor unbroken, but Adrian makes me feel like my cracks and splinters are something to admire. Like they are battle wounds that prove my worth. I'm dizzy with this feeling, head untethered and floating.

My need for him deepens. It's a cliff. An abyss. Something I can sink inside. A place I can lose myself. I'm desperate to feel his skin against mine and the gloss of our bodies moving together. I curl my fingers under the hem of my racerback and tug it off.

Adrian's eyes skim over the surface of my torso and I try to keep my head high. I don't want to be surprised when I see the inevitable disappointment in his eyes. I know what I am—a body built for racing and lifting and sprinting. I'm hard where other women are soft; my body resists where it should give.

But Adrian's fingers notch into the phantom edges of my waist, draw across the contours of my back muscles. And when he tugs the edge of my sports bra down, freeing one of my nipples from the tight fabric, he lets out a moan so guttural that I can practically feel it reverberate between my legs.

His mouth finds my nipple and his tongue flicks over the surface until it hardens. The sensation draws an involuntary sigh from my lips.

"Adrian," I say desperately.

With his mouth still pressed to my aching skin, he pries the other side of my sports bra down, too. It's tight, so tight that I nearly think he won't manage it. But with a pop, both of my breasts come free—two swells rising above the line of neon blue that was once my sports bra.

Adrian pulls himself back and his eyes trace over every inch of me, working from my backside on his counter, up my exposed chest, and then settling on my eyes. His pupils are so blown out that his eyes are practically black. His teeth sink into his bottom lip.

"Tell me the places on the list," he says.

"What?"

"Tell me." He presses each of his hands to my waist and my heart kicks up a scattered rhythm. He hasn't issued a command like this since the days I was first training with him. Back when he wrenched those dumbbells out of my hands and caged me out of the squat rack. "Give me a list of places where I'm allowed to make you come."

Everything is tingling, shivers racing and melding and multiplying so fast I'm not sure I even know what a list is anymore. I've probably never made a single list in my whole life.

Only one word loosens from my lips. "Bed," I say. "The bed."

Adrian traces a finger across the skin of my collarbone, dipping until he hits the crease between my breasts, and then traveling up my throat. He anchors the finger to the edge of my lips and kisses the place it's touching.

"And?"

His hand travels lower, this time sliding into the waistband of my pants. Everything is on fire in the wake of his touch. My hips roll against him, but he refuses to dip lower.

"A couch," I insist. "Adrian. Maybe the couch?"

His fingers find the edge of my underwear. Gently, slowly—far too slowly—he pulls the fabric aside and slides his finger underneath. I let out a moan. That single touch—that mere breath of contact—it's enough to loosen my spine. I sink into his arms like I'm boneless, my head pressing into his bare shoulder.

"Kath," he says gently. "Let me show you the things I can't do to you on a bed or a couch."

"Okay," I manage.

"Yes?" he asks gently, finger running up and down just below my underwear so lightly it's like I'm being tortured from the inside. "I need an enthusiastic yes."

"Yes," I say. "Enthusiastically."

Adrian smiles and it's so eager and hungry that my heart stammers again. He presses one hand to my back to lift me from the counter and draws my pants free. Goose bumps rise instantly on every inch of my now exposed skin. He slides down my body and drapes each of my knees over his shoulders.

"Okay?" he asks.

"Yes," I say again.

Then he grabs me from behind and hitches my hips forward until I'm nearly slipping off the edge of the counter, but I can't because my legs are anchored to his wide shoulders. He smooths a hand just below my navel, tugging upward and pulling the skin taut. Then he finds me with his mouth.

His nose nudges while his tongue swirls. My hips buck against his face and he presses a palm to my stomach, anchoring me down, so all I can do is writhe against it.

"Adrian," I whine. I'm whining? I don't whine. Not like this.

He laughs, and the tip of his nose dances against my nerve endings, and all I can think is that I've never had an orgasm with a man's mouth on me like this. It's never even felt *good* like this. It's always felt like something else on a checklist—one of the bases I'm supposed to cover at certain points, like making sure I get enough fiber in my breakfast. Never like I'm vibrating from the inside.

Just when I think it can't feel any better—like this is good, but not orgasm good—Adrian hooks a finger inside me. My head falls back and a moan rips out of my chest. I dig my hands into his hair as he keeps moving, alternating short and shallow with long, devastating strokes that draw tingles across my skin. I'm teetering on the edge of a cliff, about to rip apart at the seams. Adrian keeps pumping his finger and tongue—shit, that tongue—holding me right on the edge, like he's found every single one of my lines and he knows exactly how to keep me on his side of ecstasy. My knees curl against him. Gasps escape between my pants. I haven't breathed this hard since the last time I was on the erg.

Adrian's other hand travels higher, hitching my hips into his mouth. My head falls back, spine arching. My gasps turn to moans even as my body blooms with heat and vibration.

I'm close—so close—and Adrian knows it because his finger glides faster now, tongue rolling and swirling in escalating rhythm. I'm cresting like a wave, force and pressure building up in the arch of my back. He adds a second digit. I contract around him—a sudden and completely involuntary seizing that leaves me shaking. Adrian doesn't back down. It's like he can sense this crack, this splinter, and he's wresting me fully open.

His rhythm intensifies, fingers picking up their pace, and tongue moving still faster. I clench again and almost twist away, but his arm around my back tightens, keeping me pressed close. And there's so much pleasure and vibration and movement and rhythm and—

The wave crashes.

Everything explodes. Lightning bursts in my mind, splitting apart in raining shards of glass. My vision spots and blurs even as pleasure racks through me in glittering confetti. My fingers pull at Adrian's hair but he keeps moving until I shudder, then murmur out a sigh. Only then does he let me go.

I'm panting and Jell-O and so utterly wrung out that I think my insides might be made of nothing but fizzing bubbles.

Adrian runs his nose across the skin of my thigh and I can feel his smile. "Worth all the sanitizing I'll need to do tomorrow?"

My brain is still making its way back from somewhere around the ceiling, so for a long moment I'm not even sure I know my name, let alone what needs to be sanitized.

I struggle up to a real seat and Adrian releases my legs. I'm so lightheaded that I nearly lose my balance. He catches me with an arm around my torso.

"I said I wouldn't let you fall," he tells me as I slump against his wide frame. "So maybe it's time for that bed, after all."

And even though I'm still boneless and wrung out, his words send another lick of heat up my middle. I pull back so I can look him in the eye. "The bed?"

Adrian smiles and kisses me softly. "For sleeping," he says. "For resting."

"But . . . you."

"Kath." His fingers flutter against the edge of my face, drawing down to my chin. He kisses the divot of skin between the swell of my cheek and the ridge of my nose. "I'm fine."

"But," I say again. This isn't how it's supposed to go. These aren't the steps.

Adrian's tongue skims against his bottom lip and, even though it's his arms and his torso that are holding me upright, he gives me a look that can only be described as vulnerable. Like, suddenly, he's the one who might break.

"I want to wait for next time."

Somehow, I understand what he's leaving unsaid. He only wants to do that with me if there *is* a next time. He's not ready to give up this piece of himself unless he has some assurance that this first time won't be our last. I think I know all that because, even as he says those words—*next time*—I know there might not be one.

Tomorrow, I'll have to go back to the reality of my life. Training. Pan Ams. Winning back my spot. These are my goals.

Relationships—and all the complex, uncontrollable emotions that come with them—are not compatible with these goals. Worse, my feelings about Adrian are already more intense than they ever were for Maxwell. Today, and what just happened this evening, has made that terrifyingly clear.

I can't afford to get too invested and end up like my mom—curled on a couch, clutching a paper napkin as I sob. I can't afford to lose focus. I can't let myself get distracted and emotional in the weeks before the most important race of my life.

On the other hand, I'm not sure I have the willpower to stay away. I've tried that. Multiple times. I only ended up half naked on Adrian's countertop.

So, I have no idea what I think about "next time."

"I'm—I'm evaluating you for a job," I say, because it's the closest approximation of an excuse that I can give him right now. Besides, it's true. Unbiased, Carla told me. I'm not sure doing what we just did counts.

Adrian tips his forehead forward until it touches mine. "I'm not going to get that job."

"You've said."

"So, what's the problem?"

"You've never said that you don't want it."

I feel his forehead shake. "It's the same."

"It's not."

"Okay. How about this: I trust you to keep it all separate."

"Separate?"

"Separate, like, when I do this"—he drags his thumb down my collarbone—"it has nothing to do with my weight room routines. And when I do this"—he presses his lips to the exposed skin just above my neckline—"you don't have to think about splits. Are you thinking about splits?"

"No." The word quivers out of me.

"Good." I can feel his smile tight against my skin. "Because right now, all I'm thinking about is you."

Inexplicably, my body aches for him all over again.

"Does that mean we can do bed things?" I ask.

Adrian lifts me into his arms and my hands coil around his neck. He carries me toward the closed bedroom door, as he again says, "Next time."

Twenty

Despite all the things we won't be doing in the bedroom, Adrian convinces me to spend the night. He also convinces me to change into one of his oversize T-shirts and eat dinner on his comforter. The scallops are objectively delicious—browned and crispy on the outside, soft on the inside—although Adrian keeps complaining that they would have tasted better fresh out of the pan.

Even though it's nearly an hour past my usual lights-out time, I'm energized. Instead of sleeping, I find myself lying awake on my side, mesmerized by the photographs on Adrian's bedside table. There's one of him in his launch, a quad in the foreground. A group shot where he's standing behind a long line of young athletes. A candid shot from Youth Nationals last year where he looks particularly gorgeous glowering at a clipboard.

"You don't have any pictures of yourself in a boat," I observe, thinking about all the ways Adrian was tortured by our sport, but also his limitless capacity to still love it.

He cups his face in his long fingers. "Not everyone finds rowing shells so appealing, Kath."

I roll toward him and smile, but I'm still watching his eyes. "Why'd you quit?"

I've been wondering since we talked about his dad. He alluded to a sudden and possibly dramatic breakup with the sport. I don't want to push him on it, but I'm too curious not to ask.

His gaze drops to our feet before finding the ceiling again. "I did poorly in a race."

"I see." I bump his toes with mine. "I know the feeling."

His smile tightens, but there's still no levity to it. "You didn't quit, though."

"Only because I have no other choice."

"How so?"

I twiddle with the frayed end of my braid, considering how to respond. Adrian always seems impressed that, in the wake of what happened in Italy, I never considered quitting rowing. While that's factually true, it's not because there's something special about my spirit or backbone. The truth is less glamorous.

"Here's the thing." I push myself to a seat and swivel so I'm facing him, cross-legged, my bare knees jutting out from under his shirt. "I know how unusual this is, but I didn't graduate from college because I dropped out when I got a spot on the national team. I never took any more classes or tried to transfer to a university near the center because I knew it would interfere with training, even though pretty much everyone else does just that. Maybe they take extra years to graduate, but they do it. I didn't.

"I've barely had a real job. Part-time work as a front desk attendant at a gym hardly counts. I have no other passion or skills. No other abilities or pursuits. I have no choice but to hold on to this sport."

Adrian shakes his head. "You're not being fair to yourself. You have tons of skills that would work in other areas of life. Organization, communication. Discipline and dedication, especially to the degree you have it, are extremely rare. Any employer would be lucky to have you."

My mind flashes to a handful of Olympic medalists who now work for bosses a decade their junior. "Maybe. But I don't know if I'd be able to be as disciplined or dedicated to something else. I'm disciplined because I love rowing. Rowing is the perfect manifestation of who I am—it's *everything* I am. It's order and control. It's calm in the chaos."

"That's not true."

"What?"

Adrian's eyes flick to mine. "There is so much more to you than 'order and control.'"

My chest fizzes with his words, like I'm a bottle of soda water that's been shaken and slightly cracked.

"Well," I say, "the point is I've had plenty of races that went bad enough that I probably should have quit after them. That race in Italy tops the list. But I *can't*. I haven't seriously considered it since I got injured as a junior. At this point, I don't have any other choices. And the fact that you did, well, that's nothing to be ashamed of."

Adrian is quiet for so long that I worry I've said something to hurt him. His mouth is turned down, in contemplation, as he runs his fingers against the edges of his sheets.

"I caught a crab," he says finally.

His tone is so serious that I repress the urge to question his non sequitur. Catching a crab means a stroke has gone seriously wrong. It can happen easily enough, especially to less seasoned rowers. The oar buries a hair too deep or clips against the surface on the recovery, and suddenly the whole thing sticks. With really young rowers, it can cause embarrassing disasters, like forcing the entire crew to stop and wait while the rower pries out their blade. In the worst-case scenario, it'll tip an entire boat.

When Adrian doesn't elaborate, I ask as gently as I can, "In a race?"

"In *the* race," he says, still not looking at me.

Now I get it. He's explaining why he quit rowing. I don't know what changed, but I'm grateful it did. I curl my legs into my chest, press my temple to one of my knees, and wait.

"It was my last year of high school," he says. "I was supposed to go to Youth Nationals, but my dad pulled a favor to get me to fill in for a higher-level boat, one in a U-23 race. They'd just lost one of their guys to an injury and were scrambling at the last minute. The others were all *a lot* older—or at least, as much as early twenties feels when you're a teen."

He massages the back of his neck like he's trying to physically expel the memory. "I should have said no. I should have gone to Youth Nationals with my crew. But I didn't. So, I ended up in this big, high-pressure race. Near the end, we were holding third place. I was weaker than the others and struggling to keep pace. I caught the crab. The boat veered out of the lane and we were disqualified. The other guys didn't say anything after, but they didn't have to. We all knew whose fault it was. My dad was—well, you can imagine. I didn't just blow it for myself. I embarrassed him, after he put his neck out to get me in that boat."

He rubs at a callus on his palm like he's trying to push it off. "After that, I don't know. I couldn't force myself back onto a seat again. The only thing that was worse than never rowing again was . . . rowing. I gave up the scholarship. I deferred college for a year. I quit training. The truth is, I wasn't strong enough to do anything else."

I cover his agitating hands with mine and then braid my fingers through his, wishing I could erase his pain with touch alone. I know it's not enough, though. So, I search my brain for something helpful to say. He's certainly not the only one who's ever choked in a high-pressure situation. I know so many athletes who have been in his position. I can name about a million times that Sofi has blamed herself for her crew's failures.

Yet, I also know that none of those words would help. You don't dislodge guilt like that by pointing to someone else's flaws.

So, all I have to offer him is this: "I say this with absolute love and affection, but sometimes rowing is actually the worst."

Adrian closes his eyes and laughs through his nose. "It really is."

"Also, you *were* able to get back into a boat eventually," I remind him, thinking about his steady confidence as he crushed the standing challenge. "Maybe you quit racing, but you didn't quit rowing."

He nods, but it's laced with a frown. "Eventually. But only a single. And only once I figured out how to turn off the part of my brain that approached rowing as a competition and sculling as nothing but practice for a race. I've never gotten back in a team boat. But, yeah, I missed the sport way too much to be away from it forever."

I shake my head, still impressed. Given that horrific history, he should have ended up resenting shells and oars for the rest of his life. Instead, he's been enthusiastic and joyful about a sport that has caused him so much pain. "And you're a coach now. A job that you love."

He nods, even though I didn't pose it as a question. "I do."

"That's impressive, too," I say. "To get back to it like that."

His eyes glide away from mine and unspoken words glimmer under the surface of his neutral expression.

I nudge his knee with my toe. "What?"

His mouth ticks. "How do you know I have something to say?"

"You always have something to say."

Adrian laughs at that, then runs his tongue across his bottom lip. "Yes, I love my job. I love my teams. It's rewarding to get to be the coach I never had myself. But sometimes . . . I don't know. Sometimes it feels like I can't always be everything to everyone."

I consider that for a long moment, thinking about all I know about Adrian's coaching. The ways he changes himself to fit the kids. The ways he takes on a wide variety of roles—head coach, trainer, assistant coach—that at higher levels are separate jobs. He's got all of those kids, but hardly any adults. He's surrounded by people without having a team of his own.

"You mean it's lonely."

He glances up sharply. "Why did you say that?"

I lift a shoulder. "Probably because I know how you feel. At the training center, I'm surrounded by all these teams—pairs and quads and eights. They all have their crews. They're all in the thing together. But singles? You have your coach and your training partners, but no one is *with* you. It's all on you. Success. Failure. In some ways, it makes it worse, being surrounded by people but still feeling alone."

"Sure," Adrian says. "But coaching is different from racing."

"Yeah," I say. "Coaching could be worse. When things go right, the athletes get the credit. When things go wrong, you bear the blame. You're in *charge*, but you're not in *control*. I bet that's as isolating as it gets."

A long pause stretches between us. Finally, Adrian swallows, raises his eyes to mine. "I don't think anyone has ever said it like that before."

His expression feels like a key setting into its tumblers.

I swallow. "Do you ever talk to people about this stuff? Your mom maybe?"

He shakes his head softly. "My mom is a good person. Kind and gentle and loving and wonderfully supportive in so many ways. But, when it came to rowing . . . I don't know. Whenever I've brought it up with her, especially when I was having a hard time, she'd always brush it off and say she didn't want to get involved, or she'd tell me 'That's your dad's domain.' I think, ultimately, she always had a slightly warped picture of him, sugarcoated maybe. And she loved the idea of rowing as something he and I did together—a way for us to bond. She couldn't really see it as anything else."

"What about other rowers?" I ask. "You didn't stay in touch with any of your teammates after you quit?"

"Over the years, yeah. But I haven't seen any of them in a while. Not since I moved to California for this job."

"I see. And . . ." I hesitate because I want to ask him about his previous relationships. With some benefit of hindsight, I know Maxwell's support wasn't really support, but at the same time, I did appreciate having someone to talk to about everything. Big and small. "You've never dated a rower?"

Adrian raises an eyebrow. "Are you asking for my dating history?"

I playfully backhand his shoulder, but he catches my hand and twines his fingers through mine. He watches our joined hands for a moment, then answers.

"It always felt like it would be too much to get involved with someone in the sport. Dating is already hard enough. I just didn't need to add that kind of pressure to it, you know?"

"You made an exception for me," I observe.

"Because . . ." He runs his thumb across my knuckles. "Because you push yourself and *only* yourself. Your dedication is already unique enough, Kath. But it's even more unique, and even more beautiful, that you have it but don't force it on anyone else."

He's looking at me. And, oh god, I think I could lose myself in his irises. The feeling is so much more than magnetism, or his sharp jade of beauty. It's about what I see reflected back. The weight of his approval and respect. The connection between us.

And me.

A new version of myself that I have only ever seen reflected in Adrian's eyes.

Twenty-One

46 DAYS UNTIL PAN AMS

When I wake, predawn light filters through Adrian's shutters, casting the room in an indigo sheen. It's the same cool light that has illuminated breakfasts spent standing in the kitchen, smoothies drunk on the way to the boathouse, an expanse of unbroken water, misty in the warming air. It's the light of discipline and hard work. The light of my real life.

Carefully, I extricate myself from the sheets and hunt down my clothes. My sports bra lays discarded by the bedside. My yoga pants and tank top are still in a crumpled heap below the granite countertops. When I return to the bedroom fully dressed, Adrian's chest rises and falls with the soft ease of sleep, his hair whispering against the pillowcase. I won't see him at practice this morning—he's going to a recruiting event in San Francisco today—so if I leave before he wakes, I'll have a few hours to think about "next time" before we talk again.

I hunt through the living room until I find a pad of paper and a pen in the drawer under the coffee table. I scratch out a quick note, trying to keep my scrawl as legible as possible:

> *Thanks for an amazing day. Needed to change for practice. See you soon.*
> *Kath*

It's true, but also purposefully neutral. Hopefully, it'll also keep Adrian from worrying before I have a chance to sort through my feelings.

When I get to the boathouse an hour later, I expect to be the only one there. With Adrian away, the performance team has the morning off. Yet when I drop off the last creaky stair beside the bays, I find Peter running through a set of warm-up lunges underneath my beech-tree. He's facing the pale expanse of water, watching the mist rise from it with intense concentration etched between his eyebrows. I observe him for a moment, thinking about a young teen girl who used to stretch in that same spot, feeling like she'd finally found a place where she could be *herself*.

"What are you doing here?" I ask, stopping next to his shoulder.

Peter startles and his glasses slip down the bridge of his nose. He shoves them back up and tugs his earbuds out.

"Sorry to sneak up on you," I say. "You didn't want to take the morning off?"

"The other guys are but . . ." He chews at his bottom lip, gaze sailing toward the long expanse of water before pinging back to me. "We only have a month until Nationals."

I nod, because that's explanation enough. Youth Nationals are the weekend after Pan Ams, so I have a rough idea of how much urgency Peter feels right now. I shrug my bag higher and motion toward the bays. "Right. Good. Well, I'll just . . ."

"Hey, do you—" Peter starts, then ducks his head. He rubs at the back of his neck, looking somewhere over my shoulder. "Do you want to, maybe, paddle together? Today? I'll do whatever workout you want and I know I won't be able to quite keep up, but . . . If you're up for it."

I smile. "Yeah, okay, then."

"Yeah? You're not just humoring me or something?"

"Nah, it'll be good to have someone to pace me. I'll give you a head start on the intervals so we can end at the same time."

Peter's lips crack into the widest smile I've seen on him yet.

Twenty minutes later, we cruise out from the docks and, from the moment I dip my oars into the water, I feel good. Strong. My muscles respond to my intentions with an unexpected energy. My lungs feel clear and weightless, and my shell slices toward our line of buoys as effortlessly as a butcher's knife running through paper.

Peter starts our first interval fifteen seconds before me and I push hard to catch him, each stroke prying through the water in rhythmic progression until I overtake his bow just at the end of our row of buoys.

"Next one," I tell him as I let my blades skim across the surface in a bumpy swish.

Peter pushes up his glasses with a shoulder and grins back. "Give me twelve seconds next time."

"I gave you fifteen on this one."

He pulls on one oar to start turning his bow back around. "Sometimes I do my best work when things feel impossible."

I nod my approval. "Twelve it is."

My watch screams twelve seconds after Peter starts his interval. I hit my first stroke hard and fast. Although Peter will have a good view of me as I race toward him, I decide to avoid looking for his stern when I check my line. Still, I hear the splash and groan of his strokes as I gain on him. An image of my bow ball coursing up the side of his hull flits through my mind and I drive my legs harder, pushing past the initial flood of acid that already has my blood feeling like it's on fire. My shoulders burn. Peter's stroke rate picks up as we near the finish. With a few meters to go, I pour on the gas, pumping my legs and core as hard as they'll take me.

We hit the end buoys. I glance to my side. My oarlocks are nearly even with his, but not quite. Peter won that one.

"Very nice," I say.

He can barely contain his smile through heaving breaths. "Again?"

The sun is high in the sky by the time we coast back toward the docks. The inlet radiates harsh light, and a mix of sweat and briny water has darkened my shirt. It's rarely warmer than temperate in Berkeley, even in the summertime, but today is unusually hot.

"Best practice I've had in a while," Peter says as he braces an oar against his knee and lets his boat drift to the dock.

"Me too." I heave off my seat and dip both legs into the water by my hull, letting the cool liquid soothe my heated skin. He's right—this practice was great. Maybe it went so well because I was setting pace for Peter. Maybe it's my new commitment to Adrian's coaching cues. Maybe it was corn dogs and mini golf and everything that happened after. "I can tell why Adrian keeps raving about you and your quad. You're going to kill it at Nationals."

I think I must have said the wrong thing, though, because Peter's smile falters.

"What?" I ask.

He still hasn't gotten out of his boat, and he runs a hand through the water without looking up. An eddy ripples behind his fingers. "What do you do when you think you might fail?"

"I'm not sure I . . . Sorry, what do you mean?"

Peter frowns at his eddy as the current swallows it. "I'm just—how do you get yourself to keep going when the pressure gets big?"

I swallow because I can't help but think about the way this conversation echoes the one I had with Adrian last night. "Is someone putting pressure on you?"

"No. No. It's just like . . . my dads keep getting calls from coaches at all these big schools, big names, and they're saying they'll be there at Youth Nationals, watching. And Coach Adrian and my parents are great—just happy for me and everything. But I feel like . . . what if I'm not as good as everyone thinks? Does that make sense?"

The high-pitched screech of a seagull rings through the still morning air.

"Yes," I say. "That makes sense."

"What do you do?" he presses. "When it feels that way."

Peter looks up at me full of hope and crushing expectation and, god, how do I live up to what he needs? Talking to Adrian about this stuff is one thing, but a seventeen-year-old kid is something else entirely. I don't know the right thing to say. That everything will be okay, win or lose? That he should be proud of second place even if he expects to get first? Those would be lies and we'd both know it.

The truth is that the pressure only increases. Winning only makes losing that much harder. Striving for excellence means never being satisfied. Sometimes, the price we pay for success is giving up our contentment.

"Rowing is rough," I say, trying to find a way to tell the truth without being disheartening. Besides, a variation of this line seemed to help Adrian yesterday, so why not Peter? "Sometimes that's just how it's going to feel."

Instantly, I know I've said the wrong thing because Peter's eyes slip from mine. The sheen of expectation in his face dulls.

"Yeah," he says. "It is. I still love it, though."

"Of course," I say, floundering to find better words. "I'm sorry. I'm sure your coach has better advice on this stuff."

He nods. "He tells me he believes in me all the time. That helps."

"Good," I say. At least someone knows what they are doing with this kid because it definitely isn't me. "That's good."

Peter lifts himself from his boat and hoists it out of the water. "Thanks for practicing with me," he says, before stepping over his oars and striding up to the boathouse.

. . .

I'm still haunted by that conversation when I scale Mom's porch steps. The warm chorus of my childhood awaits me on the other side of the door: a whistling tea kettle, Mom's feet dancing across the hardwood floors, and a symphony of chimes piped from her ancient stereo.

A peal of Mom's laughter rises from the kitchen, tinkling in near harmony with the music.

"Don't be ridiculous," she says as I close the front door. She has her phone cradled on her shoulder so she can pour a cup of tea. "I'm not flexible enough for that pose."

I toe off my sneakers and move past the kitchen, aiming for the stairs. Adrian will be back from his recruiting event in a couple of hours and, since I didn't have much time to think on the water, I still haven't decided what to say to him. Plus, I didn't see Mom when I came home to change before practice and she's sure to have noticed I didn't spend the night in my bed. I might be an adult, but it's the first time in my life I've ever done something like that.

Despite my best efforts, though, the creaky floorboard by the couch announces my presence.

Mom spins, facing me with lavender-colored eye masks. Abruptly, she tells the person on the line that she needs to go.

"Kath." She lets her phone drop to the counter. "Good morning."

There's an edge to her voice. Is she going to admonish me or something? I'm old enough to stay out all night if I want. Besides, it would be unlike her to lecture me. Usually it's the other way around.

Then I catch her fingers twining through the belt of her robe. Wait a second. She's not angry. She's anxious.

"What's going on?" I ask.

Her fingers still. She drops the tie.

"What do you mean?" Mom dabs a ring finger against one of her eye masks, feigning nonchalance.

"Who was that on the phone?"

"No one." She drops her finger. A pink hue slides into her cheeks.

My brain flits to a memory that's half-hazy with the smell of corn dogs and pavement warming in the sun. *She might be abstaining from love, but she's certainly giving it some glances, if you know what I mean.*

"Hang on," I say. "Was that Rob?"

"No. No. It wasn't."

Her cheeks have deepened to the same shade of red as the array of chili peppers in the basket above the countertop. This is strange, though. I've never known her to be secretive about her love life.

She crosses her arms, pulling her robe tighter. "Where were you last night?" she asks over my silence, like she's challenging me in return.

"With Adrian," I say because *I'm* enough of an adult to be transparent.

Mom's defensiveness dissolves. She claps her hands together in something that can only be described as delight. "Oh? How wonderful."

"I suppose."

"What's the matter?"

I let out a long exhale. I usually try to avoid Mom's relationship advice. When I was in college, she always seemed disappointed to hear I wasn't dating anyone. When I told her about Maxwell, I expected her to be overjoyed. But then she started asking irrelevant questions about how my stomach felt when I was around him. Somehow, I think she might be the only person who could understand my stance on relationships and—possibly—the only one who never will.

"I'm just—" I start. "I'm not sure where this could go."

Mom lifts an eyebrow. "But you're open to it? To him? To the possibility?"

"I don't know," I say. "I'm only here for the summer, hopefully anyway. And I'm worried about Pan Ams. So, I don't know how open I am."

I leave the rest unsaid. That it is a bad idea to get involved with someone whose presence feels like standing next to a damn bonfire.

Mom studies me for another moment, then smiles softly and pats one of the place mats at the table. "Sit."

I hesitate, but only for a moment. I'm going to see Adrian later today. I don't want to head back to the boathouse without a plan. Besides, it won't hurt to hear her out.

So, I let my bag descend to the floor, cross into the kitchen, and sink to a creaky seat in one of Mom's antique chairs. She hunts around her cabinets before setting two vintage teacups on the place mat in front of me—they're white china circled with pink and blue flowers. She pours hot water into both and then adds her Irish breakfast tea bags. Serious tea for a serious conversation. The last time she got out this setup, I'd just told her I'd decided to make the incredibly unorthodox choice to give up my scholarship, drop out of college, and move to the training center.

I wasn't as anxious for that conversation, though. I already knew Mom wouldn't have a strong opinion either way—she just wanted to hear me out and give the conversation the weight it deserved. Unlike with relationships, Mom has never tried to give me much advice about rowing. I think she mostly trusted me to find my own way. I've always appreciated that and, after my recent conversation with Adrian, I appreciate it even more now.

Mom takes a seat across from me and spoons sugar into her cup. "I know my yoga wasn't exactly for you, but there is some wisdom from my classes that I'd like to share."

I take a sip from my steaming mug and try to keep an open mind. Yesterday, I hurled a ball at some milk bottles on the optimistic hope that it might make me row faster. I have no high ground to judge relationship advice dispatched from her yoga classes.

"There's so much about the yoga practice that appeals to me," she begins. "But the theme that resonates with me most—the one that I try to infuse into every class I teach—is about *presence*. Finding our centers on the mat. Grounding ourselves in the here and now. Focusing on our breath—constant and also always changing."

She sips thoughtfully. "I'm sure you, of all people, would understand why."

I tilt my head. "Why?"

"You've been with me through my big changes, Kath. My ups and downs. Triumphs and defeats. I suppose for some you were too young to truly understand what was happening, but you seemed to see so much, even when you were tiny. It hasn't always been easy to have you witness all that. But I hope what you might take from it is a lesson about change. Life. It's fleeting. All we have is this moment, right now. I'm fortunate enough to be in a happy one. But I can't know how long that will last. So, I will enjoy every moment I have."

A couple of weeks ago, this speech would have sounded a bit ridiculous to me. Not because it isn't true that the present is important, but also because life is nothing without goals. But maybe the mini golf and corn dogs have addled my brain, though, because there is something in there that resonates.

"So," I say cautiously, "you're saying—to stay focused on the present with Adrian?"

She nods. "Maybe this summer is all you have. But that doesn't mean you can't enjoy it."

There's something both comforting and oddly rational about this idea. Maybe there *is* a solution here. Something that will prevent me from getting consumed by Adrian. A way to be with him without losing control of myself in the process.

Adrian and I shouldn't have a future. Hopefully, I'll move back to the training center after Pan Ams. He will either stay here or move to Florida for the junior development job. We're only together for the summer. Maybe that fact—that we *can't* have a future—makes it easier. We can enjoy each other's company and then go our separate ways. Knowing that this will end will make that inevitable end easier. Knowing this will keep me from losing control.

"Mom," I say, "I think you've just given me some very good advice."

She leans across the table to pat my arm and press a kiss to my temple. "I'm glad."

Twenty-Two

Adrian texts me when he gets back to his office in the boathouse a couple of hours later. I find him hunched at his desk wearing his recruiting uniform: a crisp button-down with sleeves rolled up to the elbows. Through his half-open door, my eyes snag on the muscles descending his forearms. My fingers curl around the doorknob as I remember the way those muscles flexed under my fingertips.

I take a steadying inhale, trying to get a grip.

Adrian glances up. A cautious smile unfurls.

"Hey," he says.

"Hey yourself." I bump the door open wider with a shoulder.

"I'm glad you came by." His face is unreadable as he watches me press my back against the door to click it shut. "Your note . . . It was very you."

"What does that mean?"

"I have no idea whether to be nervous or excited about this conversation."

I lower myself into the guest chair and Adrian shoves aside a stack of books so our line of sight isn't obstructed. As he waits, I press my palms into my thighs, trying to hide the fact that I'm wiping away a sheen of sweat.

"I don't want to be cryptic," I tell him, "but I think that depends."

"On what?"

"Whether you're up for . . ." I gesture a finger between us. "A next time."

Adrian's laugh unfurls with the ease of a ringing bell. "You had me worried there."

"Is that yes?"

"Yes, it's a yes. I would repeat last night"—he mimics my gesture—"as many times as you asked."

My mouth erupts in an uninvited grin. I shove it back, though. We're far from done with this conversation. "Right. Well, I have forty-six days until I leave for Pan Ams." I keep my tone light even as I continue to choose my words carefully. "So, if we see each other every other—"

"We're making another program here?" he teases.

"No. I'm just clarifying my intentions."

"Your intentions?"

"About us."

A line creases between Adrian's eyebrows. "Go on."

My fingertips start shaking slightly and I squeeze them against the armrests. I'm not sure why I'm nervous. If he says no, then I'm free to move on with my summer, unencumbered by this thing that's grown between us.

"I would like this to be casual," I say. "It can only last for the next month and a half—until I leave for Pan Ams. After that, I'll hopefully get my spot back in Southern California and you'll either stay here or take the junior development job in Florida—"

"I'm not getting that job," Adrian says.

I have no idea why he believes that, nor why he seems to equate *not getting the job* with *not wanting the job,* but I guess this isn't the time for a debate.

"Right," I say. "Well, either way, we'll be far apart. I can't do long-distance."

Adrian has his arms crossed against his body and his face frozen somewhere between a smile and a frown.

"That's a lot to take in," he says.

"I know," I say. It's a lot for *me* to take in, even though I'm the one saying it. "Look, I want you to know that this would be new for me, too. For me it's always been . . . a serious relationship or nothing. And for a long time, it was nothing. I never wanted to take a chance with dating because I knew it would just distract me from training. And then I tried something serious, but look how well that turned out. With you and me, I'm wondering if an in-between could work. Casual."

Adrian's eyes are dark and expressionless as his finger taps against his elbow. My chair creaks under my shifting weight. The wall clock ticks, counting down the seconds until his verdict. He considers for so long that I convince myself he's going to say no. He's going to turn me down and I'm going to deserve it. I have no right to ask this of him and it's unfair to both of—

Adrian's expression shifts. He pushes out of his chair, rounding the desk until he's standing in front of me. I have to crane my head back to look him in the eye.

He leans one hand against the armrest of my chair. "Tell me. What exactly do you mean by *casual*?"

My brain momentarily freezes before I can make out some words. "I just think that since there can't be anything long term between us, we should be up front about it." I try to remember what my mom said about being centered, finding focus. Something about a yoga mat? It's hard to remember with him this close. "I want to be present for this—this summer. The now."

Adrian lowers his other hand to the other armrest, cocooning me in citrus. His pupils are so big they've nearly swallowed his irises, and he holds my gaze for long enough that I feel a flush rising across my cheeks. He lowers his face until it's nearly level with mine, burning through the space left between us. That familiar desire for him edges back into my body like a ship gliding into its home port.

"I can agree to the terms of your contract," he says.

Anticipation flutters through me, like a little breathless bird.

"But before you start outlining a calendar," he adds, voice low, "I have one amendment."

"An amendment?"

"Mm-hmm." His breath traces a warm path down my neck. My eyes close. "There will be no schedule."

And then his mouth is taking mine and my hands are pressing into his pecs and he's lifting me out of the chair and my legs are wrapped around his torso. Heat vacuums through my body as I grab hold of his neck, push my fingers into his hair. Adrian spins us until my butt lands on his desk, sending a scatter of papers and books off the edge.

I try to drag him closer, to pull his weight on top of me as I lie back, but he pushes a hand to my collarbone and holds himself upright.

"I have something for you," he says.

Despite the fluttering in my chest, I raise an eyebrow.

He laughs in a low rumble. "No, not that. Well, yes, that. But also this."

He reaches into a drawer by my hip and hands me a folded paper. Propped on one elbow and still lying almost prone on his desk—which is not the least awkward position I've ever been in—I unfold it.

It's Adrian's recent health records.

Above me, his green eyes catch mine. That familiar electric crackle erupts through my middle, shuddering down my spine in rippling waves.

"I thought you'd want it in black and white," he says. "In case you decided there would be a next time."

Something unlocks deep inside my chest. I'm not sure I've ever felt this accepted, this well understood. I don't think I've ever felt this *safe*.

I want to say thank you. Or to pull up my last tests on my phone. Or to tell him I'm as religious about my birth control as I am about my sleep logs. Or to find some other—better—way to express my gratitude, but there are too many thoughts jostling through my mind.

What falls out of my mouth is "How do you know me so well?"

Adrian smooths a thumb across my forehead, down my cheek, until he's cupping my face in his fingers. "You're easy to know."

"That's not how people usually feel about me," I say.

"And yet it is how I feel about you," he tells me.

It hits me deep—a stab of pleasure straight to my chest. My head goes light and I flutter my eyes closed, overwhelmed with the paradox of him, of us. This simultaneous feeling of being completely unsteady even as I feel so safe, like I'm sheltered in the warm cabin of a sailboat tossed at sea. I arch myself into him, and Adrian meets my lips with his. His fingers find the back of my head and my mouth falls open.

This kiss is new. There's a depth to it, an openness from both of us that I don't think we've ever given each other before. It feels like I'm unlocking a part of myself and he, in return, is opening a new part of himself to me.

Tongues entwining, our lips move in a harmony. My knees fall open wider and I lock myself into him, bringing our chests together until there's no space left between us. So close I can feel that he's hard. Heat gathers between my legs. I'm almost breathless and probably wet.

I'm buzzing with impatience. We have only a handful of weeks left. How can I wait even a minute longer?

"Adrian," I say against his mouth. "This is a next time."

"It is," he agrees.

"No," I say, pushing a hand to his solid chest, forcing him to look into my eyes. "This is a *next time*."

His pupils dilate. He swallows. Hard. "Is my desk on the pre-approved list?"

I drag my teeth across my lower lip and Adrian's eyes follow the movement.

"I think," I say softly, "that we should throw that list in the trash."

He inhales. "Damn."

I try to press back up into him, to draw him down on me with my knees, still hooked around his torso. But he closes my wrists in one hand and holds them tight above my head, pinning me down on the smooth desk.

"Are you sure?" he asks.

Am I? On the one hand, it's terrifyingly new. But on the other, all we have is the rest of this summer. And if this is what being present means, then I'm all for it.

"All I want is to take every moment with you that I have," I say.

Adrian closes his eyes and I wonder if what has crossed his

face is physical pain. But then his mouth is on mine again and there's urgency and desire so deep and furious that every swipe of his tongue against mine feels harder and more desperate than the last.

He pushes at my shirt and I tear away his. Our bodies run against each other, skin brushing like silk on silk. One hand on the back of my neck, Adrian gathers one of my nipples in his mouth and runs his tongue over the surface. I gasp as tingles race through me.

He smiles against my skin, and uses his free hand to pry my pants loose, pushing them into a heap at the base of his desk. Even though he's still clothed from the waist down, the heat gathering between my thighs is throbbing so intensely it's almost painful.

I tug at his belt and struggle with it for a moment before Adrian clicks open the buckle and sweeps down his zipper. He releases himself and my breath stills.

Well, fuck.

My eyes lift to his face and he's gazing down at me, pupils blown out, breath hard. I reach for him and he grabs me, hitching my hips up, dragging me forward. He holds himself against me so that all I can do is arch into him, claw at his back.

"Still okay?" he asks as he settles between my thighs, holding back from the place that I want him.

With him this close to me—hovering, stalling—I can barely form thoughts, let alone words. But my mouth manages to verbalize my enthusiastic consent.

"Yes," I say. "*Please.*"

Adrian cradles me from behind, guides up my hips to angle them higher. Then he sinks inside me. Pleasure flashes through me so intensely I nearly cry out. Instead, I rise up and sink my teeth into his shoulder, channeling every urge to scream into the press of my lips against his smooth skin. My vision blurs around the edges as he moves deeper, and I nearly gasp from the friction.

Adrian's hand finds the nape of my neck, long fingers digging into my hair. He tips my head higher and kisses me deeply, tongue sliding over mine. Our chests press together, heartbeats throbbing, and I relax, until it's no longer too much.

I move once, twice. Sliding experimentally until we're moving together, finding rhythmic waves. Like somehow, even though this is our first time, we both know just how good it can feel and we're racing each other toward the top of that mountain. Maybe we also both know that—even without a schedule—there are only so many times we're going to do this, only so many times in a summer that we'll touch each other, taste each other, move together.

His movements pick up and this time I can't help it—I cry out from the pleasure that's coursing through my body. If I'd known it was going to feel this fucking good I never would have had the willpower to resist him. I would have peeled off that unisuit and taken him on one of the ergs. Maybe I should regret all the days I spent not doing this. But I'm too full of incandescent pleasure for regrets.

My legs coil tighter around his torso, like I can physically hold him so close that I'll never have to let him go.

"Adrian," I say.

He traps my wrist with a hand and catches my eye. His eyes are as bright and beautiful as the day I met him. But this time every part of him is mine—open and strong and so fucking good—and maybe I've known I wanted him like this every moment since then.

"More?" he asks, breath hard around the word.

"There's more than this?"

He laughs as he presses kisses up my neck. “A bit, yeah.”

“Yes,” I say. When I’m with Adrian it feels like the answer is always the same. “Please. More.”

Impossibly, he sinks deeper. A gasp falls out of my lips. He’s been holding back. I have to force out a breath to relax again.

“Okay?” he asks, smoothing his thumb against my forehead, slightly sticky with my sweat.

“Not regular good,” I pant. “So good I could scream.”

He laughs again and then he’s gliding slow and purposeful. I shiver in the wake of each movement, loosing little breathless gasps. My fingernails dig into the expanse of muscle across his back. He pushes and pulls, punctuating each movement with his lips against my throat. My chest rises to meet his, spasms of ecstasy vibrating through us both.

“Adrian,” I say again, and this time I’m not asking for what I want right now—I’m pleading to drain every drop from him, to wring ourselves dry with every kiss, every breath.

He picks up the pace, and all I can do is hang on to him, lock my hands into the muscles at the back of his arms, hug myself tight to his shoulders.

I’m coming undone, unwinding, thread by aching thread. I want this. Not just now, not just today. I want this feeling again and again and again. Like I could never have enough of it. Like I could never have enough of him.

He lets his forehead fall against mine. I can feel tremors racing across his arms as I squeeze myself closer to him. He moans, low, and with such intense pleasure and desire that my body seizes. I’m unraveling, uncoupling, snapping loose from every one of my threads. I feel myself contract around him, arch my back, and it’s enough to loosen him, too. He pulses into me as we both ride the wave, cresting and breaking apart.

Tremors descend over my spine, my limbs, as the feeling

ebbs and recedes. Adrian breaks away from me slowly, warms my neck with another kiss. His lips come away moist with my sweat.

"Holy shit," I whisper.

It's the only thing I can say. But what my brain—still in a liquid haze of confusion—really means is: *I want to do this forever.*

Twenty-Three

38 DAYS UNTIL PAN AMS

I'm not ready to say whether or not Adrian's method works, but I've found it surprisingly easy to shift to an entirely new gear.

Last Thursday, I left his office with a lingering kiss and a promise to see him after I finished my solo cross-training session. And then, I did. We spent that evening cross-legged in front of a giant set of Connect Four before tucking into meatballs that Adrian simmered in red sauce for a solid hour. Afterward, I stretched and foam rolled while he attacked his training programs, notes and books strewn across his coffee table in a manic pile. Then he ripped off my pants with the same fervor.

On Saturday, after morning practice, we rented matching green cruiser bikes and rode over the Golden Gate Bridge, whips of hair assaulting our foreheads. That afternoon, when I pushed my fingertips off the dock, I realized my cheeks were still sore from smiling.

Instead of going straight back to the bays after practice the other day, Adrian and I spent an hour sitting on the dock, watching Rohan's TikTok videos as we kicked our feet through the water, stirring up eddies behind our knees. Some—like the ones where the kids keep shouting the same few lines (song lyrics?) before pushing one another off the dock—felt like inside jokes I didn't understand. But others, like the ones where the kids answer "common questions about rowing," were hilarious. My favorites, though, were of Rohan talking directly to the camera with surprisingly personal reflections on our sport. Like when he describes the agony of erg tests and early-morning practices. Or complains about the banal torture of unloading a trailer. Or when he explains why, despite it all, rowing gives him life.

When I kicked off my shoes by the door a couple of hours later, Mom smiled knowingly and asked if I'd be "spending the night away" again.

"Does it bother you that I'm not around much?" I asked, pausing by the stairs as she chased a tea bag with a spoon. It'd been a week since I'd spent the night in my own bed, although my sleep tracker hadn't yet complained about my deep sleep ratios. "I could stay here tonight if you'd rather have me at home."

"Not at all." A faint smile tugged on her lips. "You seem happy. And that is nothing but a good thing."

Sofi certainly agrees.

"Getting laid is good for you," she declares during our next FaceTime chat. "Like hydrating and sleeping ten hours, but even better because you already do those things."

"Don't forget," I whisper, trying to scan her background for other people. They have a couple of hours until practice, but I can tell she's walking the trail near the boathouse. "Don't tell Carla."

As much as I might understand that I can keep "Adrian the

man" and "Adrian the coach" separate, I don't think my coach would.

Sofi frowns at me. "You've said. I don't get why this is a big deal."

The lighting on the screen changes and the telltale view of steel rafters and racks of shells come into view behind her curls.

"Why are you at the boathouse?" I ask, officially desperate to change the conversation.

"My grips were kind of slimy this morning even though I changed them a couple of months ago. I don't know if I just need to clean them again or if I should go ahead and replace them so soon."

"Oh. How have you been cleaning them?"

She tilts her head. "Soap and water. Why?"

I wince slightly, wishing I'd remembered to tell her about this before I left. "I usually give both of ours an extra scrub with a bleach-and-water solution on Saturdays when you're at PT. It helps disinfect them, especially in the on-season."

She stares at me for long enough that I wonder if I've overstepped, probably bowled over some boundary. It's her equipment, after all. I shouldn't be messing with it just because I'm overzealous about disinfecting my own.

"I'm sorry," I add quickly. "I haven't talked to you about this in years. Just assumed you still wanted me to do it."

She nods slowly and then swallows. "Now I know, I guess. But I should go, see if I can find the bleach." I'm about to tell her to use a ten-to-one ratio when she adds, "I'll talk to you later, okay? Keep me updated on everything."

Then before I can explain myself, she hangs up and I'm left staring at the blank screen. Sofi has always been one of the few people in my life who doesn't mind that I'm overbearing, even seems to appreciate it sometimes. But, with all this distance between us, I wonder if she still feels the same way.

I try to forget about the grips. Instead, I think about just how many days' worth of stuff I can fit in my overnight bag. Given how frequently I change my clothes, it's not many. Adrian keeps saying I should leave more stuff at his apartment, but doing that would definitely not be *casual,* so instead I'm vacuum-sealing socks as I catch up on Rohan's TikToks.

In the first from a couple of days ago, a coxswain jumps off the shoulders of two of the taller guys, like some kind of clumsy Cirque du Soleil situation. In the background, I'm talking to Adrian. Even though the conversation was mundane, I vividly remember it. We were going over session goals and, after he listed various technical cues, he reminded me, yet again, to get out of my head and into my body. As I watch myself now, I realize that, instead of pulling a face, I look contemplative. Like I'm actually trying to figure out what the hell he means.

I smile and flip to the next video. My phone speaker fills with the grind and thuds of a skateboard park where, apparently, the guys have gone live. A few of them clumsily attempt tricks on the ramps while others huddle around the edges, alternating cheers and high fives. In the corner, Peter stalls at the edge of a rail, determination etched across his face.

He nods to himself, then tips forward. The board flies toward the camera lens as he gains momentum down the ramp, then rises, turns, and flips. He's careening back down. The camera zooms in on his speeding body. Cheers ring out from the crowd. Peter chances an enthusiastic grin. But as he turns, his wheel trembles. Then loses contact. Throws him off-balance.

His arms windmill, but he's moving too fast. He stumbles, falling forward so fast that I barely catch a view of his straight arm shooting out toward the ground.

There's an audible crack.

The kids swarm toward him. The screen goes blank. My sock bag hits the ground.

I'm already calling Adrian.

. . .

The hospital room would be blindingly white were it not packed with people. When Adrian pushes open the door, it nearly checks someone in the back. Kids shuffle around, allowing us to forge a path through their anxious faces. From his position near the head of the bed, Rohan blinks despondently, no phone in sight.

Adrian lands by Peter's side, wearing calm and confidence like a shield big enough to cover the whole room.

"Skateboarding?" Adrian asks. All traces of worry that haunted his expression when I first met him at the automatic doors have been replaced by sure movements and a steady voice.

"I blame peer pressure, Coach," Peter says. He's trying to keep his voice light, but he can't hide the strain. He strikes me as even smaller, even younger.

Rohan scoffs and reaches out a fist, as though to punch Peter's shoulder, but then thinks better of it and drops his hand.

"Where are your dads?" Adrian asks, glancing around the faces in the room.

"Talking to the doctor some more." Peter swallows, eyes locked on his splinted arm. "She said they can put the cast on in a few days and I'll need to wear it for at least six weeks."

My heart sinks on his behalf, even though I couldn't have expected much better. If he's lucky, he'll be getting out of his cast around the time Youth Nationals ends.

Adrian *must* be thinking the same. If I were in his place—if I'd just found out that the stroke seat of my fastest boat, and best bet for a medal, was injured—I'd be fighting against the chokehold of frustration. He has to be running through contingencies, wondering how he'll fill Peter's spot, and contemplating worst-case scenarios. Yet, if he is, he betrays none of it.

"No surgery, though?" he asks.

Peter shakes his head.

"That's good," Adrian says. "It could have been worse."

Peter squeezes his eyes shut and pinches the bridge of his nose with his still-healthy hand, like he's forcibly trying to tamp down his tears.

"Hey, guys," Adrian says lightly. "Can you give us some space for a minute?"

The kids—who apparently didn't get the memo about keeping their expressions neutral—seem to be made of frowns and angst. One by one, they shuffle out of the room, sneakers squealing into the silence. I step away, intending to follow the others, but Adrian's hand shoots to my forearm, stilling me.

"Stay?" he mouths.

For the first time since we entered this hospital room, I find actual emotion in his face.

My heart dissolves. He's showing up for Peter—being strong and steady for Peter—and asking me to show up for him, too. I want to do that. I want to stay for him.

So, I nod and retake my position by his side. Although we try to avoid physical affection around the kids, his hand remains clamped to my arm. As discreetly as I can, I brush his fingers with my own.

The door clicks closed as the last boy leaves. Adrian squeezes my arm gratefully and then releases me so he can drag a chair to Peter's bedside. He sinks down, elbows resting on knees. Peter's eyes are still squeezed shut, like he's trying to close out the suddenly too-big world.

"Let's talk about it," Adrian says.

Peter tries to take a deep breath, but he chokes on it instead. A tear seeps through his tightly closed eyelids.

Adrian sets a hand on his athlete's clenched fist. "Rowing will still be here when you're healed."

The tear slips to Peter's chin. "I won't be able to race again this year."

"You have another year as a junior," Adrian says. "I know it doesn't feel like it right now, but I promise you can come back next year, better and stronger and more resilient."

Peter blinks open his eyes. His blue irises are rimmed in scarlet. I hate watching him break, watching him accept defeat.

"I'll lose *at least* three months of training. That's what the doctor said—I might only be in a cast for six weeks, but I won't be able to row again for at least three months. Maybe a lot more." He inhales shakily. "I'm going to fall behind and I'm never going to catch back up."

To say I sympathize with this would be an understatement. I can't stomach losing a single week. A single session, even. Three months is an eternity.

"God, I'm so sorry," I blurt.

They both turn toward me and my throat seizes. I shouldn't have said anything, particularly not in that tone that suggests Peter is right to be devastated.

"I mean." I try to clear the thickness in my throat, but it's hard with both of them watching me. Peter guarded and Adrian with esteem that I'll never live up to. "I mean, I know injuries are rough. I know how it feels."

Peter's expression shutters.

I wince and mouth "I'm sorry" to Adrian.

I'm about to try to beeline for the exit again, but he squeezes my fingers. "What do you mean, you know?"

My mouth helplessly works. "I probably shouldn't say any more," I tell him. "I'm not great at this stuff."

But Adrian shakes his head, gaze locked on mine. "Tell us your story, Kath."

"My what?"

"Whatever happened to you. The reason you said you know how an injury feels."

He gives me another encouraging smile, like I have something worthy to say. And, god, even though I'm positive I'll never live up to this man's esteem, he makes me want to try. So, I nod and steel myself.

"I made the Junior Worlds team," I say softly, "but I never went."

Peter blinks open his eyes and watches me with a daunting mix of solemnity and respect that would level me with uncertainty if Adrian weren't still holding my hand. He runs a finger across my knuckles and I keep talking.

"I broke my ankle," I explain. "We were doing a trail run a few weeks before we were scheduled to leave. I slipped on a wet rock and twisted my ankle. It was such a simple thing. It should have been a mild sprain. Freakishly, it wasn't."

I smooth a hand over my braid, remembering that soul-crushing day. A thick coach with an even thicker mustache crossed his arms and, voice heavy with disappointment and frustration, told me I needn't bother getting on the plane with the team. That I might as well go home instead.

"I never went to Junior Worlds," I say, "because the next year, I turned nineteen, and I was no longer eligible."

Peter winces, perhaps contemplating the reality of an even worse situation than his own.

"It sucked," I say honestly. "It was the first—and last—time

I've seriously considered quitting. I lost a huge amount of fitness in those months. And I felt so alone with it."

I hadn't met Sofi yet and my mom tried to help, but she didn't really appreciate just how monumentally devastating it all was. She kept insisting everything would be fine and would get better with time, but for months, it only felt like the world was ending.

And then, almost suddenly, it didn't.

I started walking and then cycling and then I got back on the water and, yes, it was slow and frustrating, but I just kept going because life was better with rowing in it. The early mornings. The discipline. The routines.

In my darkest moments, I was never able to internalize what my mom was saying, about how things would change, about how this too would pass. But maybe, at some level, those words did penetrate the recesses of my mind, because eventually it was okay. Mom was right. It did pass.

I continue: "Ultimately, I didn't quit because I couldn't. I'm bound to this sport." I've thought of a way of saying it, in the days since Adrian and I talked about this. An eloquent way to put my feelings into a single sentence. "In my life, a rowing shell has been a lifeboat."

Another tear has tripped down Peter's cheek, but his mouth has turned up, and his eyes are fixed on mine.

"I don't know," I continue, "whether you feel that way or not. If you decide to quit after this, you can. That wouldn't be a bad choice or the wrong choice. But if you decide you want to keep going—well, just know that this injury doesn't erase your future. It wasn't the end for me. It doesn't have to be the end for you, either. Not if you don't want it to be."

Peter swallows and nods ever so slightly.

"Thank you," he whispers.

And, oh, he's looking at me like I finally did something right. Maybe I haven't erased all the fear, but I've managed to plant a small seed of hope.

I glance down, ready for Adrian to fill in the rest. But he's not looking at Peter. He's still twisted in his seat, staring up at me.

The intensity of his gaze—the mix of adoration and maybe even reverence—might crack me in two. A splintering, shearing sensation grinds through my chest. Adrian's fingers inch up my hand, circle my wrist.

"Can you call in the others?" Peter asks.

"Okay," Adrian says, but his voice is thick.

"And tell Rohan he can get out his phone again," Peter adds. "I didn't want him to, before. But I can take it. Besides, our TikToks aren't just about happy stuff. We want to be real, too."

Adrian smiles, like this is all the confirmation he needs that Peter will be just fine.

We swing open the door to find the kids piled outside in a mob of anxiety. An adult—one of Peter's dads, probably—nods at us from across the hall. Adrian exchanges a few sympathetic words with him before we duck out the way we came, back down the halogen halls and into a lamplit courtyard.

My watch buzzes even as I register the deep darkness outside. I'm supposed to get into bed in the next fifteen minutes so I can get at least two hours of REM sleep before midnight. Yet I'm also wondering if Adrian needs a sounding board to work through the big questions presented by Peter's injury.

I tap his elbow, drawing him to a stop. "Do you want to talk about the quad?"

He turns, pushes his hand through his hair, and I finally see the mess of anxiety and indecision that I'd expected in the hospital room. Still, his eyes cut to my watch. "Don't you need to go?"

I drop onto a stone bench in the courtyard and pat the empty seat next to me. "This seems more important."

Adrian sinks down. "Thank you. And for the story. That was extraordinary."

"You weren't so bad yourself," I say. His kind of unconditional support is rare, especially among coaches. I know Carla wouldn't have found a way to be that kind and level.

"We're a good team."

"Yeah," I say, and my heart surges with affection. "So, the quad."

Adrian lets out a shaky sigh. "The quad."

"Do you have any thoughts for a good replacement?"

"A few ideas, yeah," he says. So, he did think about this in the hospital room. I never would have been able to tell. "Matt is the obvious choice. He does well in the stroke seat of his eight."

Adrian says this with less conviction than I'd have expected considering Matt is absolutely the right choice on paper with his experience sculling, consistent rhythm, and clean technique. Then Adrian frowns—the same expression he gets when I quote textbook advice that he has a gut reaction against.

"What are you thinking?" I ask.

He swallows and his eyes skate away from me. "Matt is the obvious choice. But I don't know if he's the *right* choice."

I consider this for a long moment. Matt is one of the strongest rowers on the team, and in many ways, he reminds me of a younger Maxwell: strong, exacting, and demanding. Then I think about the angry meltdowns Maxwell had when their coach announced his retirement, and how much his sour mood affected the rest of the team. Or the way a single one of his disappointed headshakes could turn my entire day upside down.

"I think I see what you're saying," I tell him. "The other three guys have spent months learning to swing with Peter, and work as a cohesive team. It's going to be a huge deal to change all that with just over a month to go. This late in the game, technique isn't as important as personality. You need someone willing and able to adapt to the others rather than insisting they all change to fit him."

Adrian nods, and the gesture simmers with relief. "Exactly, Kath. That's exactly it."

"You need someone with heart," I say. "Someone with empathy and charisma."

He needs someone like Sofi. He needs someone like *himself*.

"How about Rohan?" I ask.

"Rohan?"

I sit up a little straighter. "He's not quite like Matt, but he's still got a strong technical base. His stroke is a bit different than Peter's, but he's got the skills and personality to meet the other guys in the middle. And he's *definitely* got the heart."

Adrian pauses, expression going faraway for a moment. "It's a lot to ask. It would be a big step for him."

"I bet he can take it." When Adrian still doesn't answer, I add: "Is something else wrong?"

He shakes his head like he's clearing it. "No. No. It's a really good idea." He smiles at me, approving, and my heart melts just a little more. "It's just an unconventional choice, but I think you're right—it's the best choice we have. I'll talk to him."

I watch Adrian's face, torn between lightness at the way he's trusting me and wariness at the uncertain look in his eyes. "All you can do is ask."

"Yeah. And the worst that can happen is he'll say no."

Twenty-Four

35 DAYS UNTIL PAN AMS

For reasons I don't fully understand, Adrian waits three days to talk to Rohan. When he finally does, it's well past our last practice of the day, when—after the usual informal social hour—all the other kids have finally headed home. I've just finished wiping down my shell and giving my boat shoes an extra clean. I'm feeling happy with my performance today—or at least content. I've finally been progressing nicely. Nothing revelatory, but it's progress. Whether it will be enough to beat either the Brazilian or the Canadian, I don't know.

With my newly freshened shell back in its berth, I forge back toward the bay doors of the dusty boathouse. As I approach the exit, though, I find Adrian and Rohan, rimmed in the low light of sunset. The conversation doesn't look like it's going well. Rohan has his arms folded tightly around his torso and Adrian's mouth is etched with a frown.

I take another step, aiming to bolt past them, but Adrian catches me mid-stride with his eyes. He shakes his head minutely, as if to warn me away. So, instead, I tuck myself into the shadows between the rafters and wait.

"I just—" Rohan's voice is strained, higher pitched than I've heard before. It's certainly not filled with the easy charisma that he exudes in most of his videos, even the ones where he's *being real*, as he says, "I just don't think I'd be good at it."

"You don't have to do anything you don't want to do," Adrian replies. "But I want to make sure you know that you're just as capable as the others in the boat. I wouldn't be asking you if I didn't believe in you."

He's using that steady, confident voice again. It's as smooth as sun butter.

Rohan, however, does not seem to be swayed. "I don't know, Coach," he says.

"Look," Adrian says. "Do you trust me?"

There's silence, but I imagine Rohan nodding. How could he not?

"Good," Adrian says. "Sometimes it's hard for us to believe in ourselves. I understand that better than you might think. But, here's the thing, *I* believe in you. Anytime you're doubting yourself or feeling unsure, you can think about that."

He's not even giving me this speech, and it *still* sprays my skull with riffles of pleasure. There have been dozens of times in my life that I've needed to hear words like those. After any number of tough training sessions, after I broke my ankle. In Italy. Especially in Italy.

After an agonizing silence, Rohan says, "You might believe in me, but you don't know for sure that I can do this. You can't."

My stomach twists on Adrian's behalf.

"You're right," Adrian says. "It's a risk. There's always a risk in trying something new or pushing yourself to the next level. Why don't you take some time to think it over?"

I hear the telltale squeak of a shoe.

"Coach." Rohan's voice sounds strained and breathy. "Maybe—maybe this isn't the right time, but I . . ."

His voice rises with the vowel and he clears his throat.

After another moment passes, Adrian gently prods, "Go ahead. Whatever it is. You can say it."

"I've been thinking I should quit."

What?

"What?" Adrian asks.

"I don't think I want to keep rowing."

My brain stutters on this pronouncement. I admit that I haven't always appreciated Rohan or that camera on his phone, but I have started to feel like I understand him. And his passion for this team. He's often the first person to arrive at practice and nearly always the last to leave. On more than one occasion, I've seen his mom get out of her car to tear him away from the docks. And the way he talks about our sport in his videos—well, if it's an act, then Rohan is one of the most talented actors of his generation.

Now he wants to quit?

"I—I've been thinking about it for a while," Rohan continues, although if this is true, there hasn't been a hint of it in his reflections on TikTok. If anything, it seems like he's been happier than usual—more excited, more energetic, particularly since his follower count started ticking up. "My parents think that practices are taking too much time away from family stuff."

"And that's how you feel, too?" Adrian asks. "Not just what your parents want?"

"Maybe it's for the best."

It's not an answer, and I'm sure Adrian knows that, but he also stays quiet, perhaps unwilling to challenge Rohan's parents, even implicitly. I drum my fingers against my thigh, concern building at the idea that I am at least partially responsible for this turn of events. There aren't any footsteps to suggest they've left, but the silence has stretched for far too long. A beat later, I lean forward to chance a glance at the pair. Rohan is looking down at his shoes. Adrian has his face tilted toward the boathouse, expression flat.

I've been around coaches for my entire adult life, but I think I'm just beginning to appreciate how difficult this job really is. Not just the technical aspects or even the soft skills, like communication and empathy, but the weight of it. The balance between uplifting your athletes and doing what's best for them, even if they might not always appreciate the bigger picture. And then the incredible responsibility of shaping that bigger picture in the first place.

Adrian closes his eyes slowly and rubs at the back of his neck. I have exactly two choices.

I could stay away. Maybe I should. I don't want to be an interloper between coach and athlete. I don't want to insert myself where I don't belong.

Or I could try to help.

Then he opens his eyes and looks directly at my place in the shadows. I catch his gaze and tilt my head in question. He nods, so slightly that Rohan might not have caught the gesture. For me, it's enough.

"Hey," I say, stepping out from my hiding place.

Rohan spins.

"How long have you been lurking back there?" he asks with more suspicion than I'd like.

Instantly, I'm second-guessing this decision. "Sorry. I overheard your conversation and I thought . . . Well, I wondered if you would be up to talk to me about it?"

Rohan doesn't answer. Shit, maybe this was a mistake. The

stakes of this conversation are too big for me. Telling Peter about one of my own experiences is one thing. Navigating a path here that both respects Rohan's autonomy, but also helps penetrate the root of his decision . . . I don't know if I'm equipped to do that.

"It's your choice," Adrian says to his athlete. "But I do think you should hear Kath out. She's been in your shoes before—leveled up more times than I can count. She knows what it feels like to be kicked down and get back up. She's someone worth listening to."

Rohan frowns, then folds his arms and lifts a shoulder. "Fine."

With that, Adrian gives me an encouraging smile. I'm still terrified, but I already know what I should do. I made the decision to step out of those shadows. Looking at his face—his green eyes fixated on mine, full of confidence, never once wavering—I know I have to at least try.

"Did Adrian tell you I was the one who recommended you for Peter's spot?"

Rohan's eyes ping between us without dropping an ounce of skepticism. "Why?" When I don't immediately answer he adds, "Because I *know* it isn't my rhythm. And there are at least three other guys who would beat me in a seat race, so definitely it isn't my speed."

He's still staring daggers at me, but something about this response crystallizes my understanding of the conversation. At the end of the day, this is about rowing. Maybe I don't know how to navigate the emotions of a seventeen-year-old boy, but I sure as shit know how to talk about crew.

"Why do you row?" I ask.

Rohan frowns, clearly caught off guard by the question.

"I can go first," I say. "I row because it gives my life stillness and order. My friend Sofi—she's the Olympian I've told you about—she loves to be part of a team. Your coach . . . he doesn't race anymore, but he likes helping other people achieve their full potential. He likes to figure out what makes his athletes tick and use that to help them succeed."

Adrian raises a single, surprised eyebrow in my direction. It's enough to tell me I nailed it, even though I'm making some inferences. But I was pretty sure I'd be right about this. It's one of the many things I like about him.

Rohan is now staring at his hands.

His coach nudges him softly with an elbow. "How about you?"

"It's fun," he says in a voice that's almost comically glum.

"Really?" I ask. "Why?"

He shrugs, almost like he isn't going to answer. "My friends all do it."

"And?"

"And it's fun to goof around with them and stuff, especially early in the morning. My jokes are funnier when people are tired." An involuntary smile tugs at the corner of his lips. "And I like making TikToks. I never really—I never actually meant to be any *good*."

"So, what's changed? It doesn't sound like you stopped finding it fun."

Rohan frowns. "It would be different."

"You mean . . . it would be different if you move up boats?"

He freezes, shoulders rising like he's just realized he's trapped and is calculating escape routes. Slowly, he lifts his eyes to Adrian, searching his coach for a reaction. Yet the only betrayal of his feelings is one of his fingers, which taps gently behind his back.

"Is that what it is?" he asks gently.

Rohan, appeased by this, nods, sinking into the motion with the relief of truth. "If I move to the faster boat, I'll have to take it more seriously. The jokes, the videos. I'll end up distracting the team. Or letting them down. My parents have been asking lately whether I'm sure I want to keep going with all this, especially with senior year and everything. I keep telling them yes, but . . . I don't know. Maybe it's better to quit than face all that."

"But you don't have to move up," Adrian says, and though his voice is even, I can nearly hear the anxiety in its depths. "You can stay in your boat and keep making the videos."

"If I did I—" Rohan pauses, and Adrian encourages him onward with a gentle nod. "I would feel like I'm letting you down."

"Saying no wouldn't let me down," Adrian says. "It's your choice."

"Plus," I add, "I don't think you should give up TikTok."

Rohan squints at me.

"I'm serious. Remember how I said I suggested you take the spot? Well, it was because of TikTok. Your energy, your enthusiasm, your *jokes*. I mean, I don't find them all funny, but the other guys laugh a lot."

Rohan's lips twitch. "They aren't all funny. Sometimes they don't land."

I return his smile. "Yeah. Well, I think that's exactly what the quad needs. Fun. It's like my friend Sofi. She doesn't sit stoke seat, she's in two. But she's the glue that holds the rest of her crew together. She's always cheering, even when everyone else is in despair. She knows that sometimes the best way to get through something tough is to make her friends laugh." I should know. She does it with me all the time. "I think that's what the quad needs right now, too."

Rohan rubs at his thumb, looks at Adrian. "You agree with this?"

"Absolutely," Adrian says. "Kath is right. What the boat needs is fun. And that's exactly what your videos can do."

Rohan wavers for another moment, looking between us, searching for the catch. Reorienting himself, perhaps, to this new reality. I wait, holding my breath.

Then his face breaks into a grin. He tugs his phone from his back pocket. "Can I tell the other guys? I have an idea for how."

My breath releases in a whoosh. Adrian nearly laughs.

"Yes," he says. "Tell them we can circle tomorrow on some game plans."

Rohan flies toward the stairs, phone already aloft. This situation had nothing to do with me—it was Adrian's weight to bear—but my muscles are still weak with relief. It's like this small corner of the world had tilted for a moment, temporarily thrown off course, and now, with Rohan's phone squarely back in his hand, everything is upright once more.

I turn to find the full force of Adrian's approving smile zeroed in on my face. It feels like I'm standing on top of a fucking mountain—air thin and body exuberant with my accomplishment. I'm a junkie for this feeling. It's a million times better than apple pancakes.

He tugs at my elbow. "Very nice."

I release myself into the curve of his chest and we twine our fingers together, holding hands as we gaze at the spot Rohan just vacated. "You set up the shot. I just took it."

"You still found exactly the right thing to say," Adrian says.

"I only told him the truth."

"Yeah? You were *entirely* truthful?"

I swivel to look up at him. "Of course. That's why it worked."

Adrian's lips are pinched like he's withholding a victorious smile. "So, you're ready to admit that having fun is good for training?"

"Maybe. Why?"

"Because I think it means you're ready for something else."

"What? Even more fun?"

"No," Adrian says. "I think you're ready for a challenge."

Twenty-Five

34 DAYS UNTIL PAN AMS

Halfway into an eight-kilometer trip, I'm tossing in a wave, desperately reciting a new mantra about *nuts and cheese*. For Adrian's challenge, we're using one of my endurance sessions to head out into open water. Our destination is Angel Island, which sits nearly halfway into the massive and wave-tossed San Francisco Bay. Adrian has promised snacks when we arrive. That's just about all that's keeping me going.

It all started out well enough. We left the peaceful calm of the inlet with sun already warming our shoulders and glimmering off the water in rippling jewels. I soon hit the swinging strokes I usually find in my endurance sessions and was able to lose myself in rhythm, arms and legs moving together in unconscious harmony.

The problems started when we passed our first shipping container. I dutifully angled my bow perpendicular to the boat's wake so it would roll along my hull instead of ramming into it, tossing me side to side. Unfortunately, just as I crested the second wave, a motorboat zipped past, throwing off more wake at a completely different angle. I was caught in the crosshairs, waves slamming into me from both directions so that there was nowhere to turn.

I eventually got a grip without further incident, but ever since, I've been on edge, paddling with more anxiety than ease.

Nuts and cheese, I repeat to myself. Just four more kilometers until nuts and cheese.

"Parker?" Adrian asks. He's a dozen or so feet from me, bobbing atop the waves with the ease of a surfer waiting behind the breaks. "How're you doing?"

Before I can answer, another unexpected wave rams my hull. My boat jerks and my breath catches. My next stroke is awkward, plunging into the surface at an odd angle. I quickly feather it to keep from catching a crab.

"Kath," Adrian says. "You're okay."

Clearly, my nerves are visible. I scan the horizon, searching for a bit of calm water, an escape from this situation. My stomach plummets as I register more ships and a towering sailboat streaming toward us, more wake flowing off its back end.

"This isn't going well." I try to take another stroke forward, but my knees are quaking so hard that the hull seesaws. "I'm getting nervous and—"

"You need to stop fighting the conditions and trying to solve the problems with your brain," Adrian says. "Out of your head. Into your body."

Another motorboat thunders toward me.

"I don't know what that means," I say desperately.

My hands are vises on the grips, my knuckles ashen. My abs are clenching so hard it's like I'm trying to blow out a thousand birthday candles.

Trying to reassure myself, I mentally retread our safety precautions. I'm a strong swimmer. We both have our phones, radios, and life jackets stashed behind our seats. I'm practiced at getting into my boat from open water. And if all else fails, Adrian has a volunteer at the boathouse ready to hop in a launch and drive out to rescue us.

Yet none of this logic dispels the quaking of my knees or the fluttering of my heart.

"Katherine Parker." Adrian's voice bites over my vibrating mind. "You've got this. You get to *choose* to be okay."

He's wrong. Everything is spiraling out of control. Getting worse by the moment. My hands are so sweaty I'm losing my grip, not just on my oars, but on my mind. Reality disintegrates around me, colors and shapes pulling at odd angles. I'm so lightheaded that it feels like I'm disconnecting from my body. What happens if I pass out? I could tip and hit my head. I could drown. I could—

"Take a deep breath," Adrian commands.

I can't. "What?"

"You need to suck in a big gulp of air. Don't worry about anything else. Take a breath. Do it now."

As I keep moving my blade in panicked, feathery strokes, my lungs drag in air, a choking, spluttering feeling that rattles through my torso.

"Good. Inhale again."

I take another stroke and suck in more air. It snags in my tight throat.

"Again."

I breathe again. It's deeper this time, nearly filling my lungs, instead of the half inhales I've been taking for the last few minutes.

"Breathe in again, but now focus on what you smell."

My lungs expand as I suck in air through my nostrils.

Salt water.

Motor oil.

"Again," Adrian says. "But this time what you feel."

Cool grip pads under my palms. The soles of my feet against the footplate. Wind on my face. The smooth motion of my legs as I take another stroke, gliding up and down the rails.

"Sounds."

The call of a seagull. A revving roar spilling from a motorboat engine. The blast from a far-off barge.

"Breathe again, Kath. One more deep inhale."

I suck in another breath. It shoots a ripple of calm across my mind.

"And what do you see?"

My eyes find Adrian over the rocking waves. He's paddling steadily in front of me, keeping himself close enough that he doesn't need to shout for me to hear him. The sun glints off his sunglasses. His hair moves with the flutter of a breeze. His forearms flex, strong and solid, as he rolls through his next stroke.

You. I see you.

Adrian nods. "There you go."

I flex my fingers against the grips, feel the weight of my seat, let my back and legs move with the rhythm of a pendulum. Waves toss me underneath, but bit by bit, I'm gliding, slicing instead of tossing. I'm finding the calm rhythm of progress.

"Yes!" I hear Adrian yell over the wind.

I pick up the pace, and the bow drives forward. Sunlight glitters in the footprints of my oars as we approach the next set of waves. But this time, as I crest the first one, I focus on my breath. I take a deep inhale. And my boat rises.

"That's it, Kath!" Adrian yells beside me. "Out of your head! Into your body!"

I pull. And we fly.

. . .

Warm sand pricks the backs of my legs. I'm spread out like a starfish, chest heaving and heart full. Our shells and oars are sprawled near the waterline and we're surrounded by craggy rocks that slice out from the hillside, carving out our own private beach.

Triumph courses through my humming veins as I, yet again, replay the image of myself sailing over the rise of waves and crashing through the breaks. For the first time in the longest time, the glide of my legs and the rhythm of my oars were unstoppable. Inevitable.

I've experienced this magical feeling many times since I started rowing. The one where everything aligns and the boat and I start flying—like we're working together instead of at odds. Since I can remember, though, I've always believed it was something that happened to me. Something that either clicked or didn't. That it was out of my control.

But Adrian taught me an important lesson today. That feeling is a choice. Not something I arrive at through a checklist or a rubric or a training program. It's not a place I get to by eating lemon bars or touching my oarlocks.

I get there by getting out of my head and choosing to connect with my body instead.

Those words would have made no sense to me a few months ago, but now they are obvious. Life-changing.

"Kath."

To my side, Adrian's watching me, sitting with the crook of his elbows hooked around his knees. His Lycra is damp, clinging to the long lines of his rigid torso. His biceps and quads are still swollen from our exertion. He tilts his head and lifts his chin, eyes lingering on mine.

A tingle traces from my spine to my hairline.

Sometimes, I'm shocked by how easily I react to this man. All it takes is a glance or a tip of his chin and my skin is already buzzing. Maybe that should scare me. But, sitting on this private beach with a pair of skylines over our shoulders, I feel too safe to be afraid.

"I've never been more impressed by you," he says.

My next breath sharpens in my lungs. "Even though I panicked?"

"*Especially* because you panicked." I tilt my head in question and he slides toward me until his knee grazes my thigh. "The accomplishment isn't that you did it. It's that you did it even though you were afraid."

"I couldn't have without you," I say truthfully.

Adrian touches the inside of my elbow and drags his fingers along the veins of my forearm, like he's tracing a stencil. I've always been self-conscious of how prominent those veins are, but his touch is so soothing that I can't help but melt into him.

"I can only encourage," he says softly. "I can't paddle for you. I can't change your mind for you. You did that."

When his eyes raise to mine again, his pupils are heavy. One of his hands is braced next to me, close enough that I can feel the heat of his body rolling off him. I inch my fingers into the spaces between his, drawing up tiny piles of sand underneath.

He swallows. I watch it descend the long line of his throat.

"So, do you admit it?" he asks.

"Admit what?"

"That you're extraordinary."

My heart thumps, misses a beat, then resumes its steady pattern.

Extraordinary.

It's not a word I've ever used for myself.

Hardworking, yes. Strong, sure. Obsessive, definitely.

I am all these things and more to make up for everything I'm not. I don't have an aptitude for my sport like so many elite athletes do, either in some perfect combination of genetics or effortlessly flawless technique. It's taken me a decade of hard work to overcome that fact.

And yet. Sometimes when I see myself reflected in Adrian's eyes, I feel this prick of awareness. It's like I'm expanding, escaping the boundaries of what usually makes me myself. Today, still sprawled out in the sand, muscles softening, the coarse edge of triumph humming along my skin . . .

Today, just maybe.

Even though it's not something I can put into words, maybe I can still feel it to be true.

"Kath," Adrian says, eyes glued to my lips. "Tell me you know how strong you are. Tell me you know how *special* you are."

Wind shivers across my face. Adrian's hair caresses his forehead, and all I can think about is him. How strong and extraordinary he is. The warm press of his fingers to my chin and the way he tips my face toward his. The heat that's spinning out from my chest. The coarse sand that's clinging to our muscles.

When I drop my eyes, all I can see is that Adrian is hard.

Slowly, almost experimentally, I slide my fingers up the hem of his Lycra. He releases himself toward me, and our mouths fuse together. Adrian's tongue moves against mine and his hands slide against my damp unisuit. I can feel every one of his movements through the glossy material: across my back, along my hips. And I can feel him, too, the cords of his biceps, the ridges of his abs, only partially covered. But I know too well what's under that thin material—and even still it's too much.

I yank at his shoulder straps and he shrugs out of his kit, peeling it off the length of his torso. He kisses my neck as his hand curves around my spine and his fingers pull down each of the straps on my shoulders in two smooth motions. My skin shivers as it's exposed to cool air.

I'm not someone who usually engages in public displays of affection, let alone whatever this is about to become. I probably should care that we're on a beach, but given the rocks, we're not visible except from the water, and I don't see any other boats nearby. Besides, I'm too feverish, too drunk on my own strength and the intoxicating power of Adrian's touch. Too safe in the warmth of his arms to feel anything but comfort.

So, when Adrian works the fabric off my chest, I reach into the spandex still covering his thighs, and pull him free of the fabric. He groans out my name as I pump my hand. His breaths are sharp by my throat and I'm heady with this feeling, too—the electrifying power of making him unravel. Adrian's hands climb into my hair as his forehead drops to my collarbone. His lips tremble, and, god, he's even more beautiful like this. Like seeing him this vulnerable and malleable just reminds me how fucking strong he is.

"You're brilliant," I say as his head tilts back.

He murmurs my name as I move my hand faster, overcome by the ways this man has showed me how to trust my own power. On an erg, when he gently touches my shoulder to correct my catch. On a dock, when he squats next to my boat and tips my chin toward his. On the water, when he screams out my name.

And right now, his breath coming in groans as his legs twitch. His tight fist pressing to his forehead when he tells me he's close. I move faster still, and Adrian bucks into my hand as he mumbles some swear words intermixed with my name.

And he comes undone.

After, Adrian lies back in the sand, bringing me with him. With one hand, he cups his head and with the other, he traces the calluses along my palm.

"You still haven't said it," he reminds me.

I tip my chin toward his face. "And I don't think I'm going to."

Adrian's fingers, which are still working circles over my palm, inch up my forearm to the crook of my elbow. He tugs gently and I tip until we're facing each other. His hand coaxes lower to the dip and rise of my waist, made more prominent by this angle.

"There's a chance," he says as his fingers move along the bunched material of my half-removed unisuit, "that it makes you even more attractive."

"What does?"

He tugs me closer and I follow the glide path easily, zippering into the pocket of his chest. His breath is warm and sweet on my cheek and his scent is so intoxicatingly familiar that I ache with it.

"That you don't know how special you are."

I tip my head so I can look at him from slightly hooded eyes. "Because of some cliché about womanhood and innocence?"

A laugh snaps out of him. "No. Because it means I get to be the one to convince you."

My next breath hitches as Adrian flips me onto my back. For a long moment, he hovers above me: eyes boring twin holes into mine, one hand pressed to the sand by my braid, the other cupping my cheek. His thumb traces across the hard plane of my cheekbone and I can feel the fluttering in my chest as my heart takes off with breathless anticipation.

"You do like a challenge," I say.

Adrian laughs again and then he's kissing me and I'm all out of quips because he's already hard again. Two weeks ago, this would have taken me by surprise. Now? I know better.

I tug at Adrian's shoulders as he traces my jawline with his tongue. His hands work down the rest of the smooth material of my unisuit. For some reason, it reminds me of the way my shirt hitched in the wake of his exploring touch when we danced—the first time our bodies pressed together.

"You know what else I like?" he asks into my hair.

Before I can make a joke about a well-organized weight room, Adrian eases his hand into my spandex, and because I never wear underwear on the water, his fingers are already on me. My next breath comes out in a low gasp, unbidden. Making noises like this was never something I used to do, at least not unintentionally. But now, under Adrian's light touches and soft circling fingers, it feels like I'm sighing and gasping on a daily basis.

He runs his teeth over his lower lip, watching my face as I flutter my eyes closed again. "I like the way your cheeks go pink when you're doing squats. Or when I'm doing this."

His fingers circle again and my hips buck into his hand. Warmth courses down my skin as my thoughts turn feverish and fierce.

"Adrian," I say, and the word is almost as inadvertent as a groan. Like he's drawing it out of me and I don't even know what it is.

Somehow, Adrian does, though, because his fingers release me for just long enough that he can push my unisuit down my thighs until it catches on my knees. When I try to kick the material loose, Adrian stills me, leaving my legs pressed nearly closed together.

He takes me in. His eyes trace a long, slow line from my face down my chest to the place where he's positioned just above my thighs. I can feel my heart thrumming with anticipation, and there's heat radiating over every part of my skin. I shift, bound legs fighting to close the distance between us, but Adrian holds himself above me without ceding any more inches.

"I like you like this, too," he says. "You're most beautiful when you want something."

"Adrian," I protest.

If he weren't so maddening I'd be able to appreciate how beautiful he is right now—lips full, cheekbones shadowed, eyes flaring bright in the sun. Instead, though, all I can think about is how good it feels to have him inside me. And the fact that he's currently not.

Adrian lowers his mouth to mine and draws a kiss across my lips. It's wonderful and pleasurable and also pure torture because it's not nearly satisfying enough. I arch into him, begging without words. Perhaps he listens to my silent pleas or maybe he just wants this as much as I do because, with one hand pressed to the ground, he repositions himself. Then, slowly, he pushes inside me.

My hips arch into him as my fingernails find his shoulder blades. He lowers himself to his elbows, and with the motion, he draws himself the rest of the way. And, oh god, everything feels so full and tight it's like I'm the personification of a twanging string. He moves up and down, dragging through me in slow, agonizing strokes.

I strain upward toward him. His mouth drops to mine, then travels to my jaw, my throat. He kisses the mounds of my shoulders, runs his nose down the crest of one of my biceps, traces his fingers over the ridges of my ribs.

"So fucking beautiful," he whispers into my neck as he pushes into me again.

When he slides back, eyes locked on mine, I think maybe I can see it, too. Or at the very least, I can see the yearning in his expression, because I know it's exactly how I look at him. He runs his hand down my thigh muscle and pushes the unisuit the rest of the way off my legs, freeing them. I lift up a knee, curling around his back and Adrian thrusts into me again, deeper this time. I let out an unrestrained moan.

He groans in answer.

"And so strong," he says. "You . . ."

He trails off, barely finishing the word because our breaths are coming in heavier now, like we're both sprinting to an unseen finish line. I kiss him back, fiercely, and our tongues move together as he glides in and out of me. Unrestrained, I move with him, letting the rhythm of our strokes sail through our bodies like we're back in that bar in Italy dancing to the deep thrum of bass. Like we're on twin ergs racing each other to a sweat-soaked finish. It's all blurring together—the heat and sweat and flecks of sand and Adrian's hands on me, Adrian's hands everywhere as he sinks deeper, moving like a rolling wave.

It's the same breathless, paradoxical moment of disassociation and focus I just had rolling across the waves in the bay. This time, though, there's nothing but Adrian's tongue tracing across my neck, the drip of sweat that's descending his collarbone and tucking between his pecs, and, most of all, the fullness of the pleasure coursing through me.

I'm lost in this moment and I think Adrian is lost with me, because he keeps opening his eyes, finding mine, before closing them again. His mouth strains against words he can't form, either because his tongue won't move the way he wants it to or because his brain has stopped working, also.

"You," he manages finally as he gathers one of my hands into his and presses it to his chest, his strokes deepening until I'm pulling taut and there are unrestrained words bubbling out of me now, too. They're rising up alongside the friction of pleasure rising up against my skin.

It's another thought—this one carrying the heavy fullness of truth. Something I know not just with logic, but intuition. Not just with words, but feeling. Something that maybe I can answer aloud, because right now, safe in Adrian's arms, I feel emboldened enough to admit it. To him. To myself. His hips stutter.

The change in tempo is just jarring enough to rip me apart, rip the word out of me that's been pressed against my lips and hovering on my tongue.

"Extraordinary."

Twenty-Six

"I meant what I said, you know." I have the back of my head pressed against Adrian's thigh, and when I swivel to look up at him, the San Francisco skyline fills the space beyond his shoulders. "You're a brilliant coach."

Adrian laughs and elbows me. "Thanks, Kath. You're a fantastic athlete."

"No, I mean it." I grab his hand, forcing him to make eye contact. I should have told him this a while ago and I don't want what I'm saying to be lost in jokes or passion. "I've never had meaningful progress this quickly before. You're probably one of the best coaches I've ever worked with. Certainly, the best possible person for the junior national team."

Something unreadable passes over his face. "There's no way that's true."

"That you're not the best person for the job?"

"That—" he begins, but cuts himself off. "That I'm one of the best coaches you've ever had."

He's staring at the horizon now.

"You don't believe me?" I know we had a rocky start. I ignored his advice and, possibly worse, actively questioned his knowledge and abilities. "I'm sorry that I haven't said this before. I've known it for a while. Sometimes it takes me some time to admit when I'm wrong."

Adrian shakes his head, eyebrows pulling together as he finally looks at me again. "I appreciate you saying that, but no, that's not it. It's okay that you took some time to warm up to me. Besides, I made some mistakes early on, too. It was trial and error and some of that didn't land exactly as I'd hoped."

"What is it, then?" I ask.

Adrian goes back to trailing his fingers across my skin, working a thumb into the muscles at the front of my shoulder—the ones that are always tender to the touch.

"Nothing," he says. "Everything is fine."

But it's not. I can tell by the flex of his jaw and the way he's been avoiding my eye contact. I look up at his chin, mentally rehashing our conversation and trying to remember the moment where he tensed.

"You don't believe you're a great coach?" I ask. It seems impossible that he wouldn't see this for himself. He's always treated me with so much confidence—too much sometimes. Even when I questioned everything about him and his strategies, he looked me dead in the eyes and told me to trust him. Surely, he knows that he's good. Great, even. He wouldn't have applied for the junior national team otherwise.

"I do well for myself," he says. "Certainly, with my team. With you, too, apparently."

"And you'll do remarkable things with the juniors. We've got some serious contenders to medal at Junior Worlds next year. I know you'll be the right person to help them get there. They'll be lucky to have you—if you decide you want it."

Adrian's expression flickers again. He pats my shoulder. "We should head back before your muscles get too cold."

Then, without waiting for me to move, he slides my head off his lap and stands, brushing sand off his legs as he forges toward the waterline.

"What is happening?" I ask as Adrian pushes his scull into the water, waves gently lapping against his shins. "Are you mad?"

"No. I can't get mad about a job I'm not going to get."

Before I can respond, he's squatting into his seat and paddling away. I hurry after him, wet-launching my own boat and trailing after his strokes. I'm not letting this go. Not only because of my own curiosity, but more importantly because I need an answer to the evaluation question about Adrian's interest in the job. Shouting at him about this across the water is probably not my best move, though. So, I wait until we've traversed back across the bay and our oars are resting on the docks.

Then I say, "I'm sure you're going to get the job, Adrian. I mean, I probably shouldn't tell you what I've written in your evaluation so far, but it's very positive. One could say it's glowing."

"Thank you." He yanks his boat out of the water and hoists it onto a shoulder, effortlessly carrying it uphill toward the boathouse.

I can't carry my boat quite as fast, so I have to wait until we've both released our sculls into their berths before I can add, "I think you'd enjoy it, too. You'd love the challenge. You'd get to work with athletes who are more serious and committed. Best of all, you'd be working alongside a team. You'd have people to bounce ideas off of, people to make decisions with you."

It's something I've been thinking about for a while. Adrian could have handled Peter's injury and Rohan nearly quitting without me. Still, I could tell he enjoyed having someone on his team. I'd like him to have support like that permanently. Even after we part ways.

He frowns down at the hull of his boat, then smooths a thumb across the surface. "I must have dinged this on the beach," he says.

It's the tiniest scratch—one that would sit above the waterline. Still, Adrian doesn't say anything else, just trudges off toward the locker where he keeps the boat repair materials and returns with a tub of epoxy, sandpaper, and patches.

He's avoiding me. Obviously. Maybe I should stop pushing because it's not my place. We're not really together. We don't have a future. It's not like him taking the job would give us one, either. My training center is about two thousand miles away from the junior development center. If anything, Adrian taking this job would solidify what I already know—we have no real future.

Rather, I want to push because I think this job would make him happy. And because I believe in him.

"What do you think, though?" I ask. "About having a team?"

Tongue clenched between his teeth, Adrian finishes using his sandpaper to buff out a small area around the scratch. "I don't see the point in thinking about it if I'm not going to get it."

"Why are you so convinced of that?"

He doesn't answer, just tucks his sandpaper away and pulls out a popsicle stick, which he uses to brush on a thin coat of epoxy.

I let out an impatient sigh. This might be the most infuriating conversation I've ever had with the man, and I have no idea why. "If you're so set against it, why not withdraw?"

"I'm not set against it," Adrian protests. "I just—I don't want to withdraw. It would crush my mom. Staying in the running is my way of doing this one thing for my dad."

I tilt my head, still not understanding.

"For the last few years before he died," he explains quietly, "I stopped trying to make him proud. I shut down the conversation every time he brought up anything to do with rowing or my career. I *disappointed* him. And now he's gone and I need to at least put in the effort to do things that would have made him proud. Even if I ultimately fail, I'll have done what I should have been doing all along."

"I see," I say.

"Do you?" he asks, sounding genuinely curious. "You seem so . . . blissfully unconcerned by your dad's feelings. I mean that in a good way."

"Yeah," I say. "But it wasn't always like that."

It took me years to get over the crush of disappointment every time I was supposed to see my dad, but something came up and he said he couldn't. Eventually, I started fighting back against the idea of visiting with him at all, but only because I wanted to stop feeling that way, not because I didn't care. As a junior, every time I finished a race or stood on a podium, for just a moment, I'd wonder what he'd say if he were there. Even after all the times he wasn't. I've had about two decades to learn to separate my emotions from my dad's choices. Adrian has had only a couple of years.

Adrian nods, but he's still frowning. Maybe I've taken all of this too far. The whole reason he never dated a rower before was because he didn't want to be pressured by someone he cared about.

"I'm sorry," I say. "I know you don't want me to push you. I'll drop it."

Adrian stares at the popsicle stick clenched in his fist. "But you wish—You would rather that I had a better job."

"*No*," I say, angry with myself for eliciting this reaction. I grab Adrian's hand, popsicle stick and all, pinning it in mine so he can't escape the sincerity of what I have to say. "Absolutely not. I don't care about your job description or your team's medal count or whatever the hell else. I like you because you are an enthusiastic, caring, and supportive man and that will be true no matter what title you have."

He smiles and looks up at me and my heart flutters with it. "Thank you."

"You're welcome." I let go. "Sorry I took your high-tech tool hostage there."

"I kind of liked it," he says with a wink, before hunching back over.

Even though he's focusing on his patch and this conversation absolutely could have gone better than it did, my chest feels reassuringly light. Not only because of the way Adrian looked at me, but also because we had a disagreement that didn't leave me feeling like I want to flop on a couch and sob into a balled-up napkin.

Behind me, I hear a shuffle of footsteps. I glance around to find Rohan peeking at us from behind an open bay, concern apparent in his brown eyes.

My eyes cut to Adrian's hunched shoulders, but thankfully he's still absorbed in his task. Trying to keep it that way, I murmur something about needing a calorie deficit and forge toward Rohan's concerned face. When I reach him, I tap his elbow and angle him wordlessly toward the stairs at the side of the boathouse, out of sight and earshot from his coach.

"How much did you hear?" I ask when I've planted myself in a seat a few steps above his eyeline.

Rohan remains standing, arms crossed, head tilted. Unnecessarily defiant. "He's leaving?"

Well, I guess that answers that. "Probably not. But if he were, would it be so bad?"

"I *just* moved up boats." Rohan's voice is barely more substantial than a whine. "It's hard enough with him around. I can't do it without him."

"I realize this isn't ideal but—"

My words snag as Rohan's eyes stab me accusingly.

"I wouldn't have even agreed to move up if I'd known I had to do it without my coach," he says.

My jaw clenches as I appraise him, realization setting in. If there's something holding Adrian back, maybe it's this. Maybe he knows how his kids would react and, even if it's completely unfair, he's willing to sacrifice his own future to avoid temporary pain for them.

"What grade are you in?" I ask.

Rohan's forehead crinkles. When I don't elaborate, he says, almost hesitantly, "I'll be a senior in the fall."

"A senior. So, you graduate next summer. And then what'll happen in September?"

"I'm hoping to get into UC San Diego with early admissions, but I'll have to see."

"And are you trying to make the varsity team at UCSD?"

Rohan lifts a shoulder. "I haven't decided yet."

I let out a long breath. "Right. So, let's say Adrian doesn't take this job. And, for a while, everyone is happy and together. Then, in less than a year from now, you'll leave for college, right? But Adrian will stay."

Rohan's eyes slip to his shoes.

"Yeah," I say. "I'm sure you already know this, but your coach cares about your feelings a lot. Maybe even more than he cares about his own."

"I didn't think of it that way."

"That's okay," I say, tamping down my frustration until it dissolves. "You get to feel your feelings, too. They are just as important as anyone else's. But I also hope you'll think about his. Because there might come a day that Adrian needs *your* support. When that day comes, I hope you and the other guys will rise to the occasion."

Rohan swallows, scuffs a toe against the ground. "I'll think about it."

My phone vibrates in my fanny pack. I stand and fish it out. "That's all I can ask."

We head back toward the bays and I click open the screen. Then nearly plow face-first into the bow of a boat.

Maxwell.

I press hard on the message, and hit the delete button. But not before I see the first few words.

Can we talk?

The words set off a montage in my mind with scenes from that day in Varese. Sitting on the dock and blinking at my freshly minted ex-boyfriend. The race. The finish—a tornado of despair and pain and ache.

"Kath?" Adrian, outside the bays, holds his hand like a visor and squints against the sun.

I shove the phone away. "Hey."

He smiles as I reconnect with him, our eyes snapping together in easy contact. "Your hull has a scratch, too. Want me to start on it while I wait for my epoxy to dry?"

"That would be really nice," I say, following him back into the quiet darkness of the boathouse, trying to ignore the tendril of anxiety that's coiling around my stomach.

Twenty-Seven

20 DAYS UNTIL PAN AMS

Over the next couple of weeks, my progress becomes undeniable.

My erg tests get faster. My splits improve. I finally *feel* good. My boat slices instead of dragging. My oars are light in my hands. Even my mind feels unburdened. Like when I start an interval, I'm able to focus on the swing of my strokes instead of getting lost in a quagmire of thoughts.

Through it all, Adrian has been there to scream encouragements on the water and whisper affirmations off it.

Last Thursday in the erg room, after the kids went home, I was midway through an interval, quads pumping, breaths coming in hard and fast, and I panted out: "It feels so good I could scream."

Adrian bent low and said, barely above a whisper, "Excellent. Because you look so good *I* could scream."

I nearly abandoned the erg right then and there. I only kept tethered to the machine because I was on fucking *fire*.

After I set down the handle, I swiveled toward Adrian's shining eyes and beaming smile and all I could think was: *You are brilliant.*

I nearly asked him, yet again, about the job. But I stopped myself. I've resolved not to push about it anymore. Just like he's my temporary coach, I'm his temporary girlfriend—it's none of my business what he decides to do with his life after we go our separate ways. Besides, these kinds of mental boundaries are the reason I'm able to keep my role as his evaluator separate from our romantic relationship.

After practice, Mom announces that I have a visitor.

It's been three workouts since I last showered and my arms are streaked with white—dried rivulets of salt from sweat and brackish water. I kick off my shoes and pad toward her voice, half expecting to find Adrian sitting at her kitchen table. Instead, it's only Mom in here, sipping on some kind of herbal concoction out of a mug the size of a cereal bowl.

"Upstairs," she supplies as I grab a handful of cheese sticks and a hard-boiled egg from the fridge. Somehow a pair of eyelash curlers have migrated into my pile of mozzarella. I can't imagine why she needs those cooled, but I guess they aren't hurting anyone there.

"In your room," she adds.

I bite off half the egg and say, "Are you being weird and cagey on purpose?"

She mocks innocence, eyebrows high, as she blows a riot of waves across the surface of her tea-bowl. "No idea what you mean."

"You're not using complete sentences. You never miss an opportunity for an adjective, let alone a noun or a verb."

Her mouth quirks. "Perhaps you should head upstairs and see."

"Okay," I say suspiciously as I pinch a cheese stick between my teeth and shove the rest into my back pocket.

When I swing open my bedroom door, I'm rammed by a head full of curls with an accompanying set of muscular arms.

"Sofi!" I scream, nearly choking on my cheese.

Despite our differences in height, Sofi's hugs are vise grips of affection, like she's trying to make me pop or squeal. I don't care if it's slightly painful, though. I've missed this woman way too much to do either.

When we spring apart, she catches my hands in hers and squeezes my fingers.

"Fuck your grip is strong," I say as my hands collapse under hers. "What are you doing here?"

"Don't get too excited. I'm only staying until tomorrow morning. I had a meeting with one of my sponsors in San Francisco, kind of a last-minute thing."

"You didn't say anything," I say. "Why didn't you say anything? I could have had everything ready for you."

"I like to catch you off guard."

"To keep me guessing?"

She lets go of my hands so she can flip her curls off her shoulder. "To support Adrian's campaign to loosen your pathological need for order and control."

I give her a look before collapsing to a seat on my twin bed. "You two haven't even met and you're already conspiring against me. I'll have you know that I went for a run today instead of getting on the erg just because Adrian said so. And I didn't even think twice about it."

Sofi lowers her chin and gives me one of her devious smiles. Then she dances to my closet and tugs open the door, motioning like she's revealing a vowel.

"You still color-coordinate your spandex," she says, waving up and down at the hangers. Before I can protest, she skips toward me, slaps away my legs from the edge of the bed, and lifts the edge of the comforter, revealing the crisply folded sheet. "Your bed has hospital corners."

"I like how it feels on my feet!" I protest.

Sofi smiles and drops to a seat next to me. "I know. And I'm kidding, mostly. I know how well you're doing. I've seen an unusual number of TikTok videos with you dancing."

"Wait what?" I grope for my phone, and fire up the app in question. "What kind of dancing?"

"Relax. It was practically a shoulder shimmy and you were in the background—those kids are definitely the main event."

"Why did you say unusual number, then?" I ask, still thumbing through Rohan's feed.

"One is an unusual number. I've never seen you so much as snap your fingers to music when you're sober. You are looking great in those videos, though, and I don't just mean the dance moves."

I relax minutely and let the phone fall back to the comforter. Ever since the open water paddle, Rohan has caught a number of my successes on camera: The day I crushed my last pull-up record. The day I raced one of the kids' quads—and nearly beat them from a half boat length behind. The day I tried again to stand up in my boat and managed to stay aloft, eyes fully closed, for nearly half a minute before falling back into the water with a laugh. Adrian is in the background of nearly every one, alternating between screaming and beaming in some kind of stunned, doting silence.

"Thanks," I say. "Apparently, and I'm quoting here, I make 'great content,' not only when I'm falling. Rohan says his page views have skyrocketed."

Sofi lies back on the bed, facing my Olympic flag on the ceiling. "Nice spot for those rings. I believe it. Your videos have become a thing back at the training center. Mostly among the rowers, although the other day a volleyball player came up to me in the dining hall and asked if I knew you."

"Wait." I grab her knee as uneasiness slides through me. "Is *everyone* watching them?"

"You worried about Maxwell?"

"No," I say, although possibly this explains the three missed calls I've deleted from him over the last few weeks. I wish I could remember everything Adrian and I have done on camera. It's not like there have been any overt public displays of affection—we're careful not to do any of that in front of the kids—but I don't know what Rohan has caught when we thought no one was looking. "Does Carla watch?"

Sofi scoffs. "Carla doesn't need TikTok to know what you've been up to. I keep her in the loop. Why does it matter?"

My chest relaxes slightly as I push myself up from my seat. "No reason. I mean, it doesn't. I need to take a shower and tell Adrian I won't be coming over tonight, but then we can go to dinner?"

"Sure," she says, but she's still eyeing me as I close the door.

I take Sofi to an Indian restaurant downtown that spices its chicken within an inch of its life. She insists we sit on the same side of the booth so we can really "soak up each other's company," which doesn't bother me at all because I didn't even know how much my heart ached for her until just now. So, we sit crammed together, elbows jostling as we dunk hunks of meat and puffy bread into green sauces and lick dribbles off our fingertips between bouts of laughter. Around the time that I'm digging into my third portion of chicken and Sofi has lifted her plate to lick sauce off the edge, my phone pings.

It's Adrian. He's sent a picture of an azure sky with a dozen technicolored kites flying above a marina. Underneath he's typed a couple of sentences.

> Don't want to interrupt your dinner too
> much, but saw this and thought of you.
> What do you think?

We've been looking for something new to do for my next day off. Since I'm getting close to competition, it has to be low key enough that I avoid injury, even a minor one, but also unique enough that it'll feel like a real break. I can already imagine sitting in a folding chair and using a hand to shield my eyes against the sun as Adrian runs a kite across an expanse of grass.

I bite back a smile as I write, *It's perfect.*

Sofi nudges me with an elbow. "I see that look."

She's smiling at me, but it's not her sideways teasing smirk or her wide laughing grin. It's an expression filled with contentment and tenderness.

"He's really good for you," she says, and her eyes haven't left mine. "I know I said it before, but it's deeper than I realized."

I drop the phone face down on the table. "Sure. For now."

"I don't think that'll stop any time soon."

I drain the rest of my water without looking at her. "I just mean soon I'll be back in the training center where I belong."

"Right, of course." She shifts. "Where you can row on our perfectly flat lake with Carla shouting at you from her launch."

"Yep. And where I can remind you to hydrate, in person."

Her smile fades, but she tries to hide it by taking an aggressive sip of her soda water. It's exactly the same look she gave me when she realized I'd been messing with her grips.

"I'm sorry," I say quickly. "I'll back off. I'm not trying to be annoying."

"Why would you be annoying?"

"Or overbearing or whatever it is I'm being."

Sofi squeezes her eyebrows together for a moment before releasing a small sigh. "It's not you that's annoying. I'm annoyed with myself for being so dependent on you."

"What are you talking about?"

She picks up her paper napkin and starts tearing at the edge, watching her hands as she works. "You know, a few weeks ago, I realized my boat shoes didn't smell right and I couldn't figure out why. I wondered if maybe I've been sweating in practice more than usual or if something weird is going on with my feet. And then one day I saw one of the guys spraying down his shell and I realized something." She looks up from her torn napkin. "But you already know, don't you?"

"I always deodorize your shoes when I do mine."

"Yes. Exactly. And sure, it's not like I don't clean my shoes *ever*. The rest of the girls and I have all that stuff on rotation. But still. You've been doing this extra thing for me for years and, as it turns out, the natural scent of my shoes isn't lilacs."

"Jasmine, actually. Sorry, why is this bad?"

"Because I can't be useless without you."

I set my hand atop hers, stilling her fingers from fiddling with that napkin. "Sofi. You are *not* useless."

She huffs a sigh. "Fine. Not useless. But I can't depend on you like this. I can't need you. You might . . . you . . ."

She slams her mouth shut and instead squeezes my fingers, gripping my hand through the papery fabric clenched in her palm.

I swallow. "And I might not even come back."

She nods, eyes shut and lips drawn. "I'm sorry. I don't want you to put even more pressure on yourself because of me. I know how you are and—" She presses fingers to her closed eyes. "Damn it. I didn't mean to spill all this out to you. Please forget I said anything."

"I will not forget you said anything." I wrap an arm around her shoulders and hold her close. Sofi is the strongest person I know, not only on the water or in a weight room, and not only when she's screaming encouragement in the boat or literally holding up my broken spirit when I'm falling to pieces. But she shoulders so much alone, and I hate that she thinks she doesn't deserve the same devotion in return. "You can't always be the one to support other people. You have to let us help you, too."

She nods and lets me hold her, but when the waiter comes by to give us the bill, she pulls away to wipe her eyes and yanks out her credit card and won't even have a pretend fight with me about the bill. I don't know what more I can say, but I'm also not sure I got through to her.

After dinner, we walk arm in arm down Shattuck Avenue and Sofi tries to distract us both with half-hearted jokes. I take deep inhales of fresh air and Sofi's lavender shampoo as I try desperately not to think about the fact that, in about three weeks, I'll line up next to the Canadian and the Brazilian.

And beating one of them isn't just about me.

. . .

"Did you book a hotel room for Toronto yet?" Sofi asks the next morning. The air mattress is folded and back in its faded gray bag. She's got her duffel by the door and she's helping me move my desk back to its place by the closet. We lift in unison and, despite our remarkable muscular control, it tips slightly, sending notebooks and highlighters scattering across the floor.

"Yeah," I say, stooping to clean up the mess. "Although I paid for it with credit and I'm not entirely sure how I'll afford the bill next month."

She crouches next to me. "Can't you cancel? I got a double, so you can—What's this?"

She's holding up Carla's rubric. My draft notes hang from a constellation of Post-its littered across the page.

"Oh, um . . ." My brain hunts for a compelling, alternative explanation for a cover sheet labeled "Job Evaluation for Adrian Crawford." Coming up short, I flail out a hand, attempting to wrest the papers from her. But Sofi's brow furrows and she bolts upright, eyes scanning.

"You're evaluating Adrian for a job?" She steps farther out of my reach. "When did this happen?"

"A while ago." I yank the papers out of her hands and smooth out the one about *character* that was bent on its descent to the floor. "Please don't share that. Carla asked me not to tell anyone."

Sofi still hasn't blinked. "But you're *sleeping* with him."

I set the rubric on the desk and shut the roll top like this motion will let me close this conversation, too. "It's not a problem, Sof. I can keep it separate."

"Keep what separate?"

I face her, arms crossed. "Adrian the coach and Adrian the man."

"And . . . how exactly do you do that?"

"When I work on his evaluation, I just think about his coaching. And when we're together outside of practice, I don't think about the evaluation."

Sofi has her face screwed up so tightly it's like she's readying to use her eyeballs as a can opener. "That is not how it works."

I drum my fingers against my elbow. "You won't tell Carla, right?"

"Of course not. You're going to tell her."

"I—what?"

She stares back flatly at me. "You're going to tell her. At this point, you can't unfuck Adrian. So, that's the way you can make things right."

I step back, nearly ramming the desk with a hamstring. What the hell is she saying to me? After weeks of agonizing over this, I made a choice to be with him—one that I made with much prodding from Sofi herself. And now she's going to question my decision? Make it seem like it was the wrong thing to do? I don't want to rehash this.

"This really isn't any of your business."

Sofi's eyes flash dangerously, and she holds my eye contact, idly picking at her calluses without looking down. We've rarely gotten into fights, but when we have, they've been epic. I'll be the first to admit I'm a fairly stubborn person, but Sofi gives *strong-willed* a whole new meaning. She can hold a grudge for years. This, coupled with her often very strong opinions about right and wrong, could mean we're on the precipice of a fight that's so massive, it will last for months. I can't lose her for months. Right now, I can't lose her for minutes.

"Look," I say, "I'm sorry that—"

"Here's the deal," Sofi interrupts. "I haven't seen you in six weeks and I'm not going to again for another three. I've missed you so desperately that you could probably tell me you've committed murder and I still wouldn't walk out that door without a hug and a tear and a slap on the ass for good measure. So, do I think this is super shitty and pretty unethical? Yeah. Do I love you anyway? Also, yes. But I trust you to do the right thing eventually. So, I'll leave it at that and I'll see you in Toronto, yeah?"

There's pressure behind my eyeballs as I pull Sofi in for another crushing hug. This time, impossibly, she grips me even more tightly.

"You're the best," I say.

Her fingers cling to my shoulders like she's a bird and I'm her branch. "I know."

"And I love you so much," I whisper.

"I love you, too." She buries her nose into my shoulder. "Also, you forgot to put on deodorant."

Twenty-Eight

7 DAYS UNTIL PAN AMS

I decide to do one last erg test. As always, Rohan catches it all on video: The intensity and triumph on my face as my legs pump out the final meters. The display screen moving slowly into view. Kids cheering in the background. Adrian yanking me into a tight hug.

It's a personal best. The first one I've gotten in nearly a year.

I'm still watching the video on repeat—I bet I'm personally responsible for a third of the twenty thousand views it's gotten so far—when I click my bike lock closed outside my mom's house. Usually on Mondays I go to the weight room right after practice, but today I'm going to do a long stretching routine first. It's what my body needs.

As I reach the door, salsa music blasts so loudly that it's competing with the kids screaming encouragement in my earbuds.

I'm still grinning when I pull open the door.

Then freeze.

Inside, Mom is sashaying back and forth, hips moving to the music. But she isn't alone. There's a man towering above her, and she has a palm pressed to his sternum. Somewhere in the back of my mind, I realize the video is still playing because I can hear myself let out a scream as I cross the finish.

The man twirls Mom in a cyclone of scarves. She's so lost in the moment that she doesn't even see me standing with the door half open, mouth gaping.

He whispers something into her ear. She laughs, then tips her chin toward him.

They kiss.

I lose my grip on the knob. The screen door slams shut.

Mom whips around. The man's eyes snap to my face and I register the familiar salt-and-pepper hair.

This isn't just any man. This is Rob. Her *business partner.*

Mom's hand remains on Rob's chest, but pink sweeps up her cheeks.

I remove my earbuds and swivel my shoulder bag so I can bury my phone inside it.

"Katherine, darling." Mom is clearly trying to sound casual. "You remember Rob?"

I nod and try to muster a smile. "Yes, hi. How are you doing?"

He stuffs his hands in his pockets. "Fine, yeah." He glances at my mom. "Would you like me to get out of your hair?"

She squeezes his forearm. "I think that might be best."

Rob stoops, just slightly, like he's aiming a kiss toward my mom's cheek. But then his eyes ping toward my face and he straightens.

"I'll see you tomorrow," he says. "We'll go over the month-end accounting."

Mom nods tightly. "Of course. Tomorrow. Accounting."

"Good to see you again, Kath," he says, as he passes me on his way to the door.

I force another smile. "You too, Rob."

When his footsteps fade down the porch, I spin. Mom has her hands up, bangles and shawls cascading from her arms like a hippy surrendering to a SWAT team. She murmurs my name, perhaps bracing for a speech. I'm not angry, though. I'm just disappointed.

I heave a sigh. "Your *business partner.*"

"It's not what you are thinking."

I eye her as she sinks onto the couch. The same one that she'll lay on for days the next time her heart gets broken. This trip has been so different from all the others. Mom has been level and stable—not flying high on some new romance, but also not crashing after an old one, either. And the studio, too. Every morning, I've watched her cruise out the front door with a smile, and every evening she kicks her feet onto the ottoman with that exhausted, but full, feeling of a day well spent. After years of flitting from job to job and man to man, she's finally found purpose.

"Mom, you're doing well. You're doing so well. Are you sure you want to throw that away?"

Her lips flatten. "How am I 'throwing it away'?"

"Because if you get involved with this guy, you'll eventually break up. And if you break up with your business partner, you'll either have to buy him out or dissolve the business or, at the very least, find someone to take his place, which will put that business under threat."

"What do you mean 'you'll eventually break up'?"

I frown. "Mom. Come on. Your track record is clear on this."

"No, it isn't. I haven't dated Rob before. So, we have no track record at all."

"You know what I mean."

"And you know what I do. Rob is nothing like anyone else

I've been with before. He is caring and kind and supportive. He lifts me up, he doesn't push me down."

I can see she really believes that. But I've heard it all before. Or, maybe not that list of traits exactly, but all of the guys have had good qualities. Most of them have been handsome, several exciting and adventurous, some passionate, others generous. "Sure, but . . . Rob isn't the first guy in the world who is *nice*."

She throws her hands up and then lets them drop as she stands. "Kath, this is the reason I didn't tell you about him. *Exactly* this."

"Wait," I say. "How long has this been going on?"

She blinks and I can practically see the recalculation happening behind her eyelids. "Some time."

"Was he the one on the phone a while ago?"

Her mouth purses. "I wasn't ready to tell you then. I'm not even ready to tell you now."

My throat lets out a strangled sigh. "Because you already knew you were doing something wrong."

"No," she says. "Because I knew how you would react."

I shake my head. Maybe there's no point in pushing back on this. If she's been seeing Rob for over a month, then she's already too deep in it. I'm about to give up when Mom says, "There's nothing wrong with falling in love, you know."

"There is if you keep getting hurt," I say. "Have you forgotten how many breakups you've gone through? Because I haven't. I haven't forgotten a single one."

Especially not the first one.

I've lost them both. I hear the words as if she's speaking them aloud. I feel her arms circle me as the slamming door is still echoing and I'm trying to hold my slight shoulders steady enough to support her. I still feel myself fighting back tears, bit-ing at the inside of my cheek so hard I draw blood, because I know I'll only make it worse for her if I show just how much Dad leaving is hurting me, too. I can feel her coarse hair in my fingers as I whisper that everything will be okay, even though I know it won't because she lost almost everything she has ever loved. Because now I'm all she has and I'm too small and too young to take care of her.

"Just because I've failed in the past doesn't mean I should give up on it for the rest of my life. You of all people should understand that. And, with the last few weeks, I thought maybe you were finally getting there. I suppose not, though."

"What does *that* mean?"

"You and Adrian," she says. "You're finally *with* someone. Falling in love. Experiencing the highs and lows that come from real, genuine affection and not that box-checking nonsense you did with the last guy. I was hoping that falling in love with Adrian would have changed your perspective a bit."

My next breath stalls. "What? That's not what's happening."

"No?"

"No. Nobody is 'falling in love.' We have an expiration date. Like you said, I'm being present."

She blinks at me like there's something caught in her mascara. "Being present doesn't mean that you don't have feelings for him."

"Right, sure, but it does mean that I won't end up heartbroken. I won't be hurting while I'm racing at Pan Ams because I knew from the beginning that it would end. I've protected myself."

Mom looks back at me with an expression that can only be described as pity. "You are such an intelligent person, Kath, but the world—life—they are not black and white. Not everything fits in a box with a neat label. It's messy. It's grayscale. It's *emotion*. That's true whether you want to see it or not."

In the last few months I've gotten pretty good at understanding Adrian when he talks to me in cryptic code, but apparently these translation skills don't extend to my mom. "Sorry, what?"

"It doesn't matter what label you put on it or what you decided in advance," she says quietly. "It will still hurt when it ends."

A thick feeling rises up my throat. The world suddenly seems like it's moving too fast, and Pan Ams is streaming toward me like a launch with a broken motor. I swallow again, trying to push that feeling back down. We've gotten derailed here. This conversation wasn't supposed to be about me and it certainly wasn't supposed to be about *Adrian*.

I cross my arms, square my shoulders, quell the tremble in my fingers.

"Does this mean you're going to keep seeing Rob?" I ask.

She watches me for a long moment, lips pressed into a thin line. "Yes, I'm going to keep seeing Rob."

"Fine," I say, scooping up my bag. "But I don't want to pick up the pieces when it all falls apart."

Before she can respond, I fly upstairs to my room.

. . .

Mom's words are still haunting me the next time I see Adrian.

The truth is I *did* think that the expiration date would make leaving him easier. As much as I hate it, I realize now that leaving Adrian is going to hurt. I'm going to miss the way he smiles encouragingly when I'm afraid to try something new, and the tingle of his high fives after I do it anyway. I'm going to miss the way he touches me, like he's full of reverence, and the way my chin fits into the divot in his sternum. I'm going to miss the way he tastes like citrus and how he always presses a kiss to my forehead when he thinks I'm already asleep.

"You okay, Parker?" Adrian asks.

I blink up at him from the squat rack. Apparently, I've spent the last two minutes of rest staring at the middle distance between the barbell and the rubber flooring.

I swallow, but it's like I'm trying to push down a mouthful of agave syrup.

"Uh, yeah," I say, ducking under the bar and letting the cool metal settle across my shoulders. Thankfully we're alone in here—the kids aren't strength training today because they leave for Youth Nationals a few days after I land in Toronto. Rohan absolutely would have caught that awkward moment on camera. "I'm fine."

He snorts. "Extremely convincing."

"Just worrying about Pan Ams," I say as I rise onto my tiptoes to lift the bar off the rack. It's not that I don't want to tell him how I'm feeling. But talking this through with him would be confusing and possibly hurtful. It also might give him the wrong idea and I don't want to mislead him.

I drop into my first squat, trying to focus on my sets. The weight room has always been my sanctuary—a silent corner where the world makes sense. A place where every day, every moment, is organized methodically. Reps organized in sets. Sets organized in circuits. Predictable. Orderly.

Under Adrian's careful watch, this weight room now smells of Lysol and rubber instead of sweat and rust. Rather than towers of mismatched bar plates shoved into corners, dumbbells and plates are organized by size in neat rows. I still love this place. But the best part of being here is Adrian, his presence, his enthusiastic confidence when I'm repping pull-ups, the way he yells in triumph when I let the barbell crash to the floor after a clean-jerk, the fire in his eyes when he urges me to finish just one more rep on the bench row and how my chest immediately clenches in response.

The weight room back in the training center is objectively better—cleaner, higher tech, more orderly. I need that place. I love that place. But it won't have *him*.

My glutes burn lightly as I finish the set. I rack the weight, trying to avoid Adrian's eye contact in the mirrors.

He slides to a seat on the bench across from me. "You want to talk about it?"

I duck to pick up my water bottle, take a swig, and lean against the rack. "You were right before, you know. About my mom and Rob."

"Oh, yeah?"

"I refused to let myself see it because she was finally, *finally* happy with her life and career. As well as I know her and as many times as I've seen her make the same mistakes over and over, I didn't think she would be careless enough to risk that for, what, a few months of happiness with a guy, only to have it all come crashing down when they break up."

Adrian tilts his head. "Are they having problems?"

I swat at the air. "Not that I know of. But they will. Inevitably."

"Well," he says, "you don't know that until you know that."

"No. With her, I know. She's been in about a dozen serious relationships since my dad. And those are only the ones I know about. This thing is doomed from the start."

Adrian rises slowly from his seat and moves toward the rack of dumbbells so that his face is angled away from me. "Rob is a new person, though. Why can't this time be different?"

"Probably not, though."

"But it could be," he presses.

"I mean, sure, in theory it could be. But I don't see the point of taking the risk."

"I think that if you've taught me one thing this summer, it's that there is a point in taking risks," Adrian says quietly. "In taking chances. In not quitting before it's over."

He traces a finger across one of the plates and a creeping, tingling sensation runs up my neck, a heightened awareness that something has shifted. "We're not talking about my mom anymore, are we?"

Adrian turns to me, smooths a hand across his hairline. "Kath."

My heart rate accelerates. "First name? Must be serious."

His fingers curl around a dumbbell like he's holding on. "I want to say something and I don't want you to say anything back, okay? Just hear me out and, maybe, take some time to think."

"Okay?"

"I know we said—you said and I agreed—that you want us to have a clear end date. And I know you have goals, really important goals. I don't want to get in the way of those. But I also want to say that . . . I think we could make this work. Berkeley isn't that far from the training center. I can fly down to you once a month and I'll see you when you're here after races. We can video call and text. It's not ideal, I know, but . . . but I think it's worth *trying*. I think we shouldn't quit before it's actually over."

There's a low ringing in my ears. "You . . ."

"Please don't react right away, okay? Take a few days."

I nod, stomach twisting. A handful of days is all we have.

"You'll think about it?" he asks.

"Yes," I say slowly. "I'll think about it."

Twenty-Nine

2 DAYS UNTIL PAN AMS

I'm boarding a plane for Toronto the day after tomorrow, but I still haven't responded to Adrian's proposition. He hasn't pushed me for an answer, but I can feel the expectation, the hope, every time we broach the subject of our individual futures. Meanwhile, every day, I weigh pros and cons. I make list after list. I've tried to imagine my life in vivid detail both ways: saying goodbye to him permanently or saying yes and attempting long-distance for who knows how long. Either one sounds untenable.

At this point, all that's keeping me from a complete meltdown is the promise of spending my second-to-last dinner with Adrian. He offered to take charge, but I thought it would give me some calm to plan things instead.

I'll head to his apartment to make dinner: salmon with steamed greens and rice. Then, just for fun, I'm going to crush him at a game of Twister. A couple of weeks ago, I found an antique-looking copy while helping Mom organize her hall closet and I've been saving it as a surprise.

Getting dressed was a good distraction, too. Over FaceTime, Sofi coaxed me into a pair of jeans, a colorful top that's fitted around my middle and flowy around my wide shoulders, and some heeled boots.

Now, I'm sitting on my bed, putting finishing touches on my final draft of the evaluation for Carla, which includes a cover letter that I'm editing on my phone.

Downstairs, the doorbell rings in a muffled sonata of chimes.

Rob, maybe? But, no, Mom already left for the evening. She didn't say where she was going, but an hour ago, she flounced out of the front door with a jingle of bracelets and about three accompanying words.

The doorbell rings again, this time with the demanding urgency of someone who has held the button for longer than socially acceptable.

I guess it could be Adrian? I was supposed to meet him at his apartment, though. He wouldn't ring like that—or get the time and place wrong—unless something has *gone* wrong. I cast aside my notes and jog down the stairs, taking them in twos.

When I pull open the door, my body goes cold.

Maxwell.

He's wearing a polo shirt that makes him look like he belongs in a country club, not standing on a faded welcome mat surrounded by antique wind chimes and overgrown succulents. For a reason I can't possibly fathom, he's holding a bouquet of red roses.

His eyes are obscured by reflective sunglasses, but he flashes a set of impossibly white teeth. "Hey there. You look fit."

I cross my arms, a half-protective measure to shield my lacy top from his eyes. "What are you doing here?"

Maxwell moves forward expectantly, like he's stepping in for a hug. Reflexively, I step back. He ends up just far enough into the threshold that he's both crowding me and still blocking the door from closing.

"I brought these for you." He tugs off his sunglasses and presses his bouquet of roses into my hands.

My fingers awkwardly close around the still-damp stems. I'm too stunned to do anything else with them.

"Can we sit?" he asks.

Cool evening air from the open door raises the hairs on my forearms. "Just tell me why you're here."

His eyebrows tighten. I have no idea why I once found those eyes attractive. Or really, any of him. His hair is too coiffed. His facial hair is too clean. He even has his collar upturned slightly, like it's been accidentally ruffled. I've seen him spend a half hour pressing that shape into place.

"You wouldn't answer my calls or texts," he says, as though that explains why he flew five hundred miles to stand at the threshold of this living room.

"Because we broke up."

"Right. That's what I want to talk to you about."

I don't say anything.

A flicker of doubt creases Maxwell's expression. He forces a smile and rubs at the back of his neck. "Okay. I guess I deserve some of that reaction."

He folds his arms, collects himself. Maxwell, if nothing else, has an excellent game face. He can get himself psyched up for basically any challenge—it's one of the many things that makes him such an accomplished athlete. He's gearing up like that now, with the quiet intensity of a champion golfer approaching their last hole.

"Katherine," he says, back straighter so he's nearly two

inches taller. "I won't sugarcoat it. I'm man enough to admit when I've made a mistake. And, with you, I did. You and I—we're right for each other. We make sense. I shouldn't have denied it."

I think my mouth might be slightly agape, but I'm not sure I have the wherewithal to snap it back into place. "You . . . I'm sorry, what are you saying?"

"I'm here to pick up where we left off." He turns up the corners of his mouth in the self-assured smile of a man who doesn't feel any remorse. "I rented a car and I have my bags. We can fly to Pan Ams together."

He rented a car? He's going over *logistics*?

"You said—" I start. Shake my head. "I'm sorry, just so we're clear. You want to get back together? With me?"

Maxwell takes another step toward me, like he's misreading my confusion for excitement. "I was wrong about you. About us, too. I've seen you in the videos. It's really impressive stuff." He yanks a small notebook from his back pocket and riffles through the pages. "And, I made some notes for you. Your times are great, but that chin tilt is still holding you back. I wrote down a bunch of new drill ideas to fix it. If you get them in daily before you race next week, I think it could make a big difference."

He holds out the notebook and touches my upper arm, like he's angling me toward it. "I'm willing to bet you can do this, Kath. You can win this thing next week. And I can help."

As his words permeate the thin membrane of my mind created by sheer shock and disbelief, I'm struck with a sudden clarity about just how ridiculous this is. No, not just ridiculous. Sad. Sad because, two months ago, this stunt probably would have worked. I was so caught up in predictability and familiarity that

I might have taken him back just to avoid the terrifying vastness of change.

That fact, more than anything else, throttles my disbelief into anger.

I twist to extricate my arm from his grasp.

"Maxwell," I say, my voice cold as I squeeze the damp stems. "You broke up with me on the docks at my last World Cup final. Maybe that wasn't the only reason I bombed that day, but it doesn't matter. You *hurt* me."

He frowns, thick eyebrows knitting together. "I know, but I was going through a tough time, Katherine. That week was especially hard. My coach had just announced he was retiring. Losing him was a huge deal."

"I'm well aware of how difficult it is to lose your coach," I snap.

He folds his arms. "It doesn't sound like you are."

"Let me assure you, *Maxwell.*" I spit out the word with enough venom that Sofi would be proud. "I absolutely am. Or maybe you forgot that I, too, lost my coach this summer."

"Right, then you should also understand what a difficult situation I was in and why I might have made a mistake. I already told you I was wrong. I don't know what more you want from me."

"Let me be clear," I counter. "I want *nothing* from you."

And then, just because I can, I drop the bouquet and stamp my foot on the shower of petals. I am so fucking glad Sofi insisted I wear boots tonight because this would be far less gratifying in sneakers.

Maxwell's placid expression morphs into incredulity. He takes in the detritus of petals littered at his feet. That, more than anything else, gives me a purr of satisfaction.

His eyes go dull and hard. Slowly, he flips his notebook closed and sheaths it back into his pocket. "Is this because of that guy?"

"The . . . What guy?"

He huffs. "The guy from TikTok. The high school coach."

Involuntarily, I step back. Even though I've spent the last two months trying to convince Adrian he can do more, my stomach hardens at the casual way Maxwell just wielded his title like an insult.

"I have no idea what you're talking about," I say.

"Don't pretend. I've seen the way you two look at each other."

My heart is a painful drumbeat hammering against my rib cage. Maybe I should be worried about who else figured out the true nature of our relationship, but I can't think beyond the sneering asshole who just insulted the best man I've ever known.

My hands close into fists, like I'm ready to throw a punch on Adrian's behalf. "I'm not pretending anything. Yes, the high school coach, Adrian is his name, and I have been—" I don't know how to put this, so I settle on the easiest, vaguest, explanation that will still put Maxwell in his place. "We're together."

"Are you in love with him?"

I feel a telltale churn of my stomach. "What?"

Maxwell sneers. "And how is that going to work, exactly? You're going to date across the state? Fly up here on the weekends? Lose hours of sleep and training time so you can travel back and forth? Or"—he lowers his chin and aims for the kill—"are you planning to stay in Berkeley and give up rowing to be with him?"

It's like I have rocks in my lungs and I'm having trouble getting a full inhale around them. I suck in a breath as hard as I can, willing my body to calm, refusing to give Maxwell an inch in this conversation. He can't have the upper hand. He can't know how precisely his missiles are landing.

"That's really none of your business," I manage.

He shakes his head. "I thought I was wrong about you. I thought you were serious about training and racing. I thought you had what it takes to go all the way. I guess not."

"It's time for you to leave," I say, my voice quivering. "Now."

Maxwell's eyes snap from the strewn petals to my face. "I'm already gone."

The front door slams behind him.

I throw the lock closed and spin, landing with my back against the wood. A sob struggles against my throat. I slip down to a seat. Knees hugged into my chest, I squeeze my eyelids shut, trying to close out his words.

He isn't worth a single more tear. Mom is right and Sofi is right and I am right—he's a jerk and a conceited asshole. He also . . .

He also isn't wrong.

Adrian and I *can't* have a future. At least not one that doesn't put my Olympic hopes in jeopardy. Maybe it's been okay while we're both living in Berkeley. But trying to be in a relationship across hundreds or thousands of miles is impossible. It would mean putting dozens of cracks in my schedule. Nights of missed sleep spent on the phone or on an airplane. Missed calls. Missed practices.

There's an even darker possibility, too. I could arrive in Toronto with hope for our relationship. But that would be a disaster because there is a version of my future where Adrian and I don't end up far away from each other. That's what will happen if I don't perform my best in Canada. I'll lose my spot for good. I'll be back in Berkeley forever.

I can't race with that possibility in my mind. I can't afford to preserve a shred of hope for that outcome and end up subconsciously sabotaging myself.

Mom was right when she said I was lying. Here I am, doing the same thing that she is doing with Rob. I've been committing the exact same crime that I lectured her about.

But I'm not her. I won't choose a man over my dreams.

Thirty

With my stomach climbing into my throat, I knock on the door to Adrian's apartment.

"One second!" he calls.

When I glance at my watch, I realize I'm on time for our date. He's expecting me. That, somehow, makes all of this even harder. Like giving someone bad news on their birthday.

The door flies open like Adrian couldn't get to it fast enough. His hair is still slightly damp and curly from the shower. He's wearing my favorite button-down, soft baby blue, and he has the top two buttons undone and the sleeves rolled up. Did I tell him I like it when he wears his shirt that way? I don't remember.

I don't remember anything, actually. Because Adrian has pinned me with his green eyes and the flecks of gold deep in their surface are nearly glowing. Because Adrian is looking at me like he's thirsty and I'm made of nothing but water.

He reaches out and twines his long fingers through mine.

"You look beautiful," he says softly.

A sharp ache lodges into my chest. I should have changed

before I came over. I should have wiped off this stupid makeup and gotten back into my spandex. I was in too much of a rush to get this over with.

"Thank you," I manage.

Adrian's fingers tighten. "What's wrong?"

"I—I need to talk to you about something."

He tugs at my hand, like he's trying to pull me inside. I stay rooted to the spot, keeping to the safety of the doorway. If I go into that apartment, there is a good chance I won't be able to do what I came here to do.

"What's going on?" he asks. "Is someone hurt?"

I shake my head. That sudden, traitorous tickle settles behind my nose, but I force the tears away.

"I need to—" I have no idea how to say this. How to say anything.

"Whatever it is, we can figure it out."

"I can't do it," I blurt out.

Adrian blinks. "Can't do what?"

"I've thought about what you said, about us making it work long-distance. And it won't. It can't. I'm sorry."

He releases my fingers and my hand goes unnaturally cold in the place he was just touching. He's still staring at me, expression frozen somewhere between confusion and hurt. "Why?"

I clear my throat. "Because I need to train and travel and race. Berkeley might be my hometown, but I'm hardly ever here. Between coaching and recruiting, you take a day off every two weeks. We can't build a relationship on twenty-four-hour visits twice a month."

He opens his mouth to protest, but I put up a hand.

"But also, I'm worried that if we try, I'll only end up undermining myself. Long distance is stressful, it's hard. The emotional toll will be bad enough, let alone the physical one when I come to visit you. I'll lose recovery time. I'll miss practices. It will put everything back in jeopardy."

"I can come to you," Adrian says. He's trying to hide it, but I can hear the emotion in his voice. It nearly breaks me in half. "You don't have to fly up here."

I close my eyes, shake my head. "It wouldn't be fair to put all of it on you. And that's not even to mention the expense—how can you afford to buy a plane ticket every month?"

"So, you just want to *quit*? You don't even want to try?"

"In this case, trying could mean failing, not just with you, but also in the rest of my life. I could lose everything I've wanted. Everything I've worked for."

"Kath." His eyes search mine with a desperation that nearly pushes me off-balance. "Don't do this, please. You *never* quit. Never. You soldier on, despite the hurdles. When you get knocked down, you always pick yourself back up. It's one of the reasons I love you."

I swallow a gasp.

The lights of the hall brighten, the world coming in and out of focus.

"You . . . love me?"

Adrian runs his hand through his mop of brown hair. "Damn. This wasn't what I had in mind for saying that to you, but fuck it." He steps forward, coming so close I'm wrapped in his familiar smell.

"*Of course* I love you." His voice is low and insistent. "I love your passion for rowing, for life. I love how you lift other people up, encourage them to be the best versions of themselves. I love your quiet confidence, your focused inspiration, your honesty. I love how you've made me feel, even for a short time, like I'm not alone anymore. Like we're a team. Like we can take on anything. Together. We can take this on, too."

Everything is splitting, splintering. My body is a rock that's shearing off, piece by piece, and exploding into an abyss below. I'm breaking apart and all I can think—all I can do—is flatten my arms against my body and try to hold myself together.

Adrian *can't* love me. Because I can't love him back. I can't afford to. I can't race with a broken heart.

"It wouldn't work," I insist.

Adrian slowly closes his eyes.

"I'm not saying that because I don't care about you," I say, desperate to make him understand. "But the logistics are insurmountable. And that's not even to mention if you move to Florida. Instead of two hours, you'll be a six-hour flight away."

Adrian blinks open his eyes, and there's a hardness in them that wasn't there a moment ago. "I'm not moving to Florida."

"You keep saying that. I don't understand why. Is it because of the kids?"

"The kids?"

I had been hoping I got through to Rohan, that maybe he would talk to Adrian, too. So far though I'm not seeing any evidence of that. "Because you don't want to leave the kids?"

"No," he says quietly.

It's so direct I know it's the truth. This is about much more than the kids.

"Is it because you're afraid?" I whisper.

He jerks back. "Why would you say that?"

His expression is twisted like I've rammed him in the chest with an oar and it's all the confirmation I need. I understand now.

It took me two months to see because he hides it so well. In some ways, Adrian is an extremely confident man. With his team. With me. But when it comes to taking a new step, moving forward in life and pushing beyond the bounds where he is comfortable and confident? That's where Adrian shuts down.

Instead, he approaches his life with the same strategy he uses in a game of Skee-Ball. He shoots right down the middle, always aiming for the hole that he feels most comfortable sinking. He's scared to want the job because he's scared of aiming for the fifty and hitting the ten instead.

It's no way to win at Skee-Ball. More important, it's no way to live a life.

"Why did you want the lemon bar in Italy?" I ask gently.

"I don't—Why is that relevant?"

"When we met. You said you didn't want to just give it to me because you needed it, too. To cheer yourself up."

"I don't know what you're driving at."

"It was for the interview, wasn't it? The interview with Carla and the rest of the board. Tell me, when was it?"

He pauses, jaw working. "The day you raced in the final."

"Yeah," I say softly. "So, you bought the lemon bar to cheer yourself up because of an interview that hadn't happened yet. You weren't just expecting to fail. You were *planning* on it."

Adrian swallows so hard his throat dips with the motion. The rest of his body language hasn't changed—his arms are still crossed, creasing his forearm muscles, and his jaw is so tight I can see the muscle working by his ear. I'm probably overstepping a boundary here because this isn't my place to push, but I don't think I can stop.

"Remember when I told you that you're one of the best coaches I've ever worked with?" I say. "It's true, but it seems like you don't see it, too. Even though you're also a person who does nothing but believe in the people around you. So, why can't you turn that around? Why can't you believe in yourself?"

"That's not true," he says quickly.

"That you can't believe in yourself?"

"That I'm better than most of the coaches you've worked with."

"Right." I lift my shoulders. "You're right. Because you're better than *all* of them."

He swallows, shaking his head like my compliment was some kind of insult.

"Look at how much progress I've made this summer," I argue. "Look at all the ways you've helped me improve. The open water challenge. All the changes in my routine. You even convinced me to let my chin tilt."

It happened a few weeks ago—one day after our trip to Angel Island when we were messing around in the erg room after practice.

"Stop fighting your instincts," Adrian said.

Just like that first day on the ergs, he pressed my chin higher with his index finger, pinned me in place with his eyes, and raised my face to his. My heart practically erupted under his touch, his confident gaze. And finally I tried. I let go of the steady stream of textbook advice and coaching cues, and I let my chin lift the way my body has always wanted. And it felt amazing. Like letting go. Like being set free.

Right now, though, my words do nothing to dissipate his tension. In fact, he clenches and unclenches his jaw, fixing me with a leaden stare. "You said you wouldn't push, Kath. You said you didn't care about how successful I am or what job title I have."

"And I still don't. I'm not pushing you because I care about you achieving some status. If you want to coach high school for the rest of your life that is absolutely valid and worthy. And you know what? I'm not even pushing because I want you to be happy, although I do want that with every fiber of my being.

"I'm pushing because you won't even let yourself consider it. I'm not telling you what choice to make—I'm telling you that you *have* a choice. That if you want this junior national team job, you should go for it. Instead of shutting down the idea, you should consider how excellent you already are.

"And why can't you see that about yourself?" I ask, feeling frustrated for the first time since we started talking. He's so brilliant it's almost offensive that he can't see it. "Why can't you admit that, if you wanted it, you could skip over juniors entirely and be the damn *national* team coach? That, here in Berkeley, you've barely scraped the surface of your potential? That you're capable of so much more?"

"Because I will never be more!" He slams a fist against the doorjamb. "This is all I'll ever be."

Adrian lowers his shaking fist and raises his eyes to mine. "I *quit* in high school. I've never even sat in a team boat since that day. I've never gotten back on a starting line. So, what right do I have to coach the athletes who have dared to push themselves so much further than I have? The ones who *aren't* quitters. I don't. I can't. This is who I am. High school. This is the top for me."

My stomach lurches, heart skipping like a record scratch. I want to yank him into a hug, to scream out that he's wrong. I'm itching to smooth his hair and insist with my touch that he *is* more. But I can't do that, not when none of this conversation changes our future. Not when it's already going to be nearly impossible to walk away.

So, instead, I ask, "Did someone say all that to you?"

"What?"

"Did someone tell you that you're a quitter? That 'high school' is as good as you'll ever be?"

He pulls in a deep breath through his nose and his eyes track lower. "He said it would define me. That it would hang around my neck for the rest of my life. He was right."

I have an irrational urge to shove Adrian's father off a bridge. "Only because he made you believe it," I say desperately. "Not because there's any real truth to it."

Adrian's eyes are distant again, but I can't walk away from him like this. I won't leave him with nothing but hurt and regret. I want his life to be better because I was in it, however fleeting our time together might have been.

"I want to read you something," I say.

Before I can lose my nerve, I fish out my phone from my back pocket. I click open the Notes app with the draft of my cover letter for the recommendation to Carla and USRowing. It's not polished yet, but this has to be enough.

"To the Board of USRowing," I read. "My name is Katherine Parker. I'm a five-time junior national and national team member and NCAA Champion. Two months ago, I was given the honor to evaluate Adrian Crawford for the junior development lead coaching position.

"Coach Crawford's technical skills are as strong—in many cases stronger—than every other national team coach I've ever known. He's up-to-date on the literature, not just in rowing and sports science, but in related fields. He applies the research to his programming with energy, enthusiasm, and excellent attention to detail."

The phone starts shaking so hard that the words are blurring. But that was the easy part. The objective part. I take a breath and push forward, trying to keep my voice level.

"But it isn't Coach Crawford's hard skills that make him exceptional. It's the soft skills where he truly shines. He's passionate. He treats his athletes with kindness and respect. He understands individual needs intuitively and deeply. Then, instead of asking his athletes to change for him, he adapts *himself* to them. He knows when to push, when to ask, and when to cajole. He puts his athletes first, no matter how he's feeling. Possibly to his own detriment."

I hear Adrian take a shaky inhale, but I plow forward.

"I am undoubtedly a better athlete for having trained with him. He has made me a stronger and faster rower. He has made me a better *person*.

"I can only begin to imagine what he could accomplish at the service of USRowing. And so, it is in the strongest possible terms that I recommend him for this position."

I stare at those final words for another long moment, afraid to raise my gaze. I can hear Adrian breathing, though. Deep, even breaths.

When I finally find the courage to look up, his eyes are still fixed on my screen, his thumb running laps over the calluses across his fingers. His expression, however, is unreadable. Lost in thoughts that I can't see.

"I appreciate the recommendation," he says with a voice that is carefully neutral.

My heart sinks.

"I didn't—" My throat closes over the next words and I try again, unsteady. "Adrian, you are more capable than you think you are. You once told me I was extraordinary, that you wanted me to see myself like you see me. Well, I *know* you're extraordinary, and I just wish you could see that, too. I wish you could see yourself like I see you."

He inhales slowly, holds it. "I don't think there's anything left to say."

He's shutting down again, and I need to accept it. His future isn't my concern, anyway. It never was.

I step back beyond the edge of the threshold, everything melting at the edges like it's been doused in acid.

"Okay. Yeah. I guess not." I try to find his eyes, but he's staring resolutely at the door handle. "I'm sorry. I'm sorry this couldn't be more. I'm sorry I don't have more to give."

Before Adrian can answer—before I start to regret this enough that I change my mind—I turn. And I walk away.

Thirty-One

5 DAYS UNTIL PAN AMS FINAL

Away from Adrian, time and space warp like I'm watching the world through a fun house mirror. My chest aches as I do squats in the airplane's cramped bathroom. Tears well in my eyes as I get back on the water in Toronto and start my first of three days of acclimatization. Eggs turn to ash on my tongue in the morning before my heat.

Every moment that passes, I tell myself I'm forgetting his face a little more. The ripple of heat from his touch. The way electricity charged through my bones when he looked at me.

It's just that every night, when I'm lying in bed willing myself to sleep, I can feel the flutter of his breath against my shoulder and the pressure of his arm against my chest.

Then the tears come storming back.

· · ·

"You haven't sent me that recommendation yet," Carla says.

I'm midway out of her tent when her words bring my dragging feet to a stop.

We've just finished going over my race plan for the final. When the week began, I was petrified that the heartache would kill my performance. I was convinced the relationship—and the end of it—would make me lose. Yet, evidence is mounting to the contrary. On Thursday, I placed second in my heat, but only because the Canadian was racing in the lane next to me. Today, I won my repechage by more than a boat length, placing me squarely in final territory.

On Saturday, I'll race in the final and, today, Carla and I talked strategy. Throughout our conversation, I went through the motions. Stroke rates, race plans, analyzing the tape from the Brazilian's heat. It matters to me because I still desperately, unequivocally, want to go home. Yet in the wake of my loss, everything else has lost its sheen—the buzz of nerves and anticipation that normally fills my mind in the days leading up to a big race isn't there.

Instead, I'm empty and aching.

I spin and face Carla full on. "I know. There's a question I'm not sure how to answer."

It's the truth, but it's also a lie. It's true I don't know how to describe Adrian's interest in the job, now more than ever. But that's not the reason the recommendation is still sitting in my email drafts. Every time I think about sending it, I hear Sofi's voice in my mind.

How could you possibly be unbiased, Kath?

And yet. I *can't* come clean. If I tell Carla about my relationship with Adrian, I'm almost certain I'll lose her deal. That would mean I'd need to race tomorrow on my own merit. I'd have to beat *both* the Canadian and the Brazilian. I'd have to win.

"Which question?" Carla asks.

She's staring at me intently, more intrigue in her expression than I'd have expected. Does that mean she already knows?

I wipe my sweaty palms against my spandex shorts, hoping she doesn't see the truth in my eyes. I can barely say Adrian's name without getting pummeled by sadness. "The one about his interest in the job."

"And what's the issue?"

I pause, heart thudding, considering how much to say. I don't want to undermine Adrian's chances, but I don't think he'd want me to lie, either. I also don't know how much he shared with me as his evaluator versus his confidant. I don't know where the line is anymore.

"I'm not sure how much he wants it," I say, trying to keep my explanation simple. "I asked and—his answer was complicated. I never got a straight response."

Head tilted, Carla crosses her arms and taps an index finger against her elbow. "I think you should leave it blank, then."

"Oh," I say, stunned by the simplicity of that solution.

"You've filled out the rest?"

"Yes. It's unequivocally positive. On every metric, Adrian is the most impressive coach I've ever worked with."

It hurts to say. That doesn't make it untrue.

"Present company excluded?" Carla asks.

Even as my mouth goes dry, I lift my chin, thrust my chest forward. Carla never shies away from telling us the truth and I know she'd expect no less from me. "Coach, I think he's even better than you."

She stares at me as my heart thuds against my rib cage so hard it's almost painful. For a long moment we're accompanied only by far-off sounds of the finish line announcer and the occasional roar of the crowd.

Then Carla's lips crack in the slightest smile. "That's just what I hoped you'd say."

. . .

The final is tomorrow.

I still have an hour until my bedtime routine, which means I'm in the hotel's restaurant, trying to shovel down a salad with chicken breast and sweet potatoes. Sofi is having her tried-and-true pre-race dinner of steak and potatoes. My lemon bar sits between our plates.

Since I arrived in Toronto, Sofi has been my only constant. When I got off the plane, she let me dissolve into tears in the crowded terminal, rubbing circles on my back as I sobbed. Despite our disagreement back in Berkeley, she steadfastly refused to let me spend the last dregs of my savings on my own hotel room and made me share her double. When I won my repechage with my cheeks streaked in tears, she pretended it was a perfectly valid emotional response to a victory.

She also, blessedly, hasn't questioned me further on that recommendation. Despite my conversation with Carla, I still haven't sent it. There's only one reason for that now.

"How are you feeling?" I ask Sofi.

Like me, her final is tomorrow. Her eight is the three-time defending Pan American champion, which puts a whole different kind of pressure on her crew. Victory is expected. Anything less will be falling short.

She swallows a bite of potatoes, and sets down her fork, expression carefully neutral. "Good."

"Sofi," I say firmly. She's been avoiding talking about herself all week, and I haven't pushed her on it because I know she doesn't like that. But at the same time, I don't want her to hold back if she's worried about affecting me. "You can lean on me, too. I can take it."

Sofi turns her water glass in its ring and then takes a drink without looking at me. "Not now. Not when your problems are bigger than mine."

"Yes, even now." I reach across the table and grab hold of her forearm. "Maybe there will come a day that I will be so broken I can't find a way to lift you up, but that's not today. I'm here for you. And that's my decision. Not yours."

"Even if what I have to say could make everything even harder?"

"Even then."

Sofi's gaze traces a long arc across the table between us before she raises her eyes to mine. "Okay, here's the deal. I've been thinking about this ever since I left Berkeley. And I decided it's true that I'm capable of living without you. If I needed to, I could figure it out on my own. The boat is stressful as hell right now, and Missy keeps falling apart, and I seem to be the only one who can talk her down, and, yes, I could handle it all without you.

"But, you know what, I don't want to. I want you back in the training center. I want you to hand me prefilled water bottles and spray my stinky shoes so they smell like fresh linen. I want to lean on you and let you lean on me right back. Not figuratively or over FaceTime. In real life. But I also didn't want to admit any of that to you because I don't think you need any more reasons to be nervous on that line tomorrow."

"That doesn't make it harder," I say softly.

"It just makes the pressure even bigger."

I shake my head, and look at my friend—my powerful, nearly indestructible best friend. "All you've done is tell me I'm not alone."

Sofi's smile stutters and she squeezes my hands together so tightly, I lose sensation in my fingertips. "I love you."

I use a shoulder to wipe my eye. "I love you, too."

My phone pings. I release Sofi so I can fish it out of my pocket, assuming it'll be Mom. Our conversations were still strained when I left, but I know she's been watching my races on YouTube because she's been texting me encouragements all week. It's felt a little performative—tinged by our fight—but I appreciate that she's still trying to be supportive.

But the message isn't from her.

I drop the phone.

Sofi glances up, fork paused. "What? What's happening?"

"Adrian." My voice sounds distant in my own ears. "I don't think I can look."

"You want me to read it to you?"

Nauseous pain rises up in my gut, spinning and whirling like I'm on one of those horrible carnival rides. "I don't think I want to know."

"It might help."

I bury my face in my palms, digging my fingertips against my hairline. So far this week, my heartbreak hasn't derailed my performance. Somehow, I've been racing well, despite all the pain. Whatever is on that phone could change that, though. Because no matter what this message says, it will reopen the painful wound that hasn't begun to heal.

The chair next to me scrapes back. Sofi's arm curls around my waist.

"Maybe it will hurt," she whispers. "But that doesn't mean you shouldn't see what he has to say. He's earned that much."

Another ping.

My gaze travels from the lines of her muscled forearms to my black phone case. Then I take a breath, unlock the screen, and nudge it toward my friend. "Read it for me?"

Her lips remain pursed as her eyes scan the message. She sets the illuminated device face up in front of me. "You should read it for yourself."

With shaking fingers, I pick it up.

> Good luck tomorrow, Parker. You'll be extraordinary. But just in case you don't believe it right now, you should know that I believe it enough for the both of us.
> Just remember: Out of your head. Into your body. You've got this.

The words slice through me from scalp to toes. My skin starts buzzing all over, and the sensation is so intense I can barely feel Sofi's fingers as she squeezes my shoulder. I can barely feel the tears that track down my cheeks and drip off the end of my chin.

The world is folding in on itself. I'm upside down and all my blood is rushing to my head. Like I'm underwater, fighting to find the surface.

"I'm in love with him," I whisper.

"I know," Sofi tells me.

"I love rowing, too."

"I'm sorry, Kath," Sofi says, squeezing me still closer. "I'm so sorry."

"There's no keeping it separate."

"What?"

I'm still staring at that screen as the dull blade of realization slowly sinks in. Adrian the person and Adrian the coach are irrecoverably tangled in my heart. Some of his best qualities as a coach—loyalty, passion, dedication—are also his best qualities as a man. At least some of the reason I fell for him was that I was impressed with his coaching.

Writing about any of that inevitably involves my heart.

"He's a great coach," I say. "And he's a good person. I don't know where the line between these things is anymore. Maybe I never did."

"Yeah. I know all that, too," Sofi says gently.

Somehow, it doesn't sound like *I told you so.* It sounds like *I love you.*

My fingers shake as I scrub my tearstained cheek. "Will you hate me if I make tomorrow even harder on myself? On both of us?"

She leans her temple against mine. "It's barely possible, but it will only make me prouder."

My chin quivers with a nod and I pull my phone toward me, clicking open the draft email to Carla. I type more at the end, words flowing easily, not like the painful starting and restarting that overcame me as I tried to draft the rest of it over the last few weeks. The message whooshes away.

Even though she didn't ask, I set the phone in front of Sofi.

The email is as I read it to Adrian, except that I added a new ending:

> While I stand by this recommendation, the problem is that this assessment is biased. I am in love with Adrian Crawford. I realize coming clean about this means I'll need to win tomorrow to regain my spot outright. Still, I owe everyone the truth.

Then I get up from the table, lemon bar discarded, ready to face my race.

Thirty-Two

DAY OF PAN AMS FINAL

On the starting line, I take a small stroke to touch up my bow, ensuring it's aligned with the line of buoys dotting the water behind me. My heart hammers at my throat. I want nothing more than for the buzzer to release me from this breathless purgatory.

"Rowers ready?" The starter's voice crackles through the air as he calls through each of the athletes on the line. "Canada."

The Canadian's eyes remain fixed, a silent assent for the race to start. Her gaze is glued on her feet like she's made of focus. Like she already knows she's unbeatable.

I close my eyes and flutter an oar, trying to stave off thoughts of Adrian. I should be focused on this moment. This race. Not the man I love.

His voice—soft as velvet—invades my mind anyway. *Out of your head. Into your body.*

Fighting thoughts of him is as fruitless as paddling to the edge of a waterfall and trying not to get sucked over. So, instead, I let myself think of him. The way his eyes shine when he smiles. The way he bellows out my name when I'm picking up speed. The text I sent him last night—the one that he still hasn't answered.

Thank you, I said, but if I do this tomorrow, it will be because of you.

It's true whether he wants to admit it or not. Somehow, this is reassuring to me, too. Maybe because it makes me feel like I'm not alone on this starting line. It's not just me and the boat and the pain. Somehow, Adrian is here with me, even if it's just an echo of his voice.

Out of your head.

My lungs expand. My heart slows from an erratic gallop to a cool canter.

"Brazil."

Camila takes deep breaths, so loud I can hear them over the rustle of wind.

Phantom fingers graze my chin.

I let my chin lift—the way it wants, whether or not I can change it. Like I'm looking to the sky for my power.

"United States of America."

I open my eyes. Bring my knees up, seat forward. Poise my oars above the waterline.

"Attention."

Wind whispers across my damp skin.

The starter buzzes.

I move.

My shell slices forward. Stroke after stroke, I launch off the balls of my feet and we pick up speed. My back muscles heave. Water rushes by my hull in jeweled ripples. My legs jam against the footplate, my body pushing and pulling. I'm lost in the symphony—the prayer—of this moment.

The boat has a life of its own. Together, we kick into a higher gear, speed climbing so effortlessly it's like we're weightless. A memory flashes through my mind: Adrian asking if I had a secret motor attached to the rudder. Even though I'm already breathing hard, my mouth twinges in a half laugh.

The crowd roars. Cowbells clang.

A thousand meters to go and I'm flying. I'm already in pain, I have been for some time, but I'm also tied for first place—cruising even with the Canadian. I can hear her breathing, the skim of her oars across the waterline, the determination in each of her strokes. She glances at me. I think I see her smile. Then she picks up the pace.

Her boat drives forward, suddenly leaping ahead by half a length. Her stroke rate is higher than mine now, a drumbeat of determination and strength.

And my pain starts transitioning to agony.

It began, as it always does, in my legs. A flood of lactic acid descending both quads, setting them aflame. Then it spread to my arms. At first it was as harmless as a heating pad, but it's quickly growing to an inferno. It's like I've plunged my limbs in boiling water and I'm just trying to hold them under the surface as long as I can.

The Brazilian gains on me. She's pulling like I saw in the video—like her stern is on fire. She's picking up at the very moment that I'm falling. That I'm breaking.

Seven-fifty to go and the fire has breached my lungs. Every choking inhale only deepens it, like oxygen stoking the flames.

I risk glances to my sides. It's not just Brazil and Canada. I've dropped into fourth, just behind the Chilean.

Hopeless. This is hopeless.

Adrian's face surges into my mind. *You don't quit, Parker. You never quit.*

All I want is to quit now. All I want is for it to stop. Nothing is worth this agony.

But Adrian screams at me to pick it up. He tells me that I only need to go a little farther, only need to push a little more. *I believe in you enough for the both of us.*

I keep pushing.

Take a breath.

I force in breath after breath. I make myself lean into the fire instead of shrinking from it.

Five hundred to go. I'm floating above my body now, pain so intense I've disconnected from it. My nerves unshackle from my muscles.

The Canadian is half a boat in front. The Brazilian is just behind her. My bow is nearly even with the Chilean's oars. This is it. This is happening no matter what I do. In fewer than five hundred meters, this is going to end one way or another.

I have a choice. I can keep fighting, keep trying to muscle out each stroke, each breath. Or I can listen to him. I can let it go. I can find my flow.

And, the most revelatory thought of all: It's my choice. It's in my control.

Into your body.

The world goes quiet.

It's like someone turned down the volume. The cheering crowd fades. Cowbells clang at the end of a long tunnel. Instead, the sounds I hear are my own. My labored breath. The slide of my seat. The rhythmic beats of my oars slicing water.

I pick up speed. Water runs faster past my hull. I drive my legs harder, accelerate my strokes. Wind rips over my face, throwing hair across my forehead. The boat jumps forward, stern bouncing slightly against the subtle waves rocking the surface of the water. We move together, in tandem, in symphony, in poem.

It hurts. Nothing could be more painful than this. But I'm not leaning into the flames anymore. I've become the fire.

My bow passes the Chilean.

A hundred meters to go. Maybe ten more strokes.

I start emptying the tank. I'm going to give this everything my body has left and so much more. I pour my entire being into this race, every fiber of my soul. It's my determination, my lists. It's calm in the chaos. Every ounce of passion and heart I have to give.

My lungs sear against my ribs. My triceps are mutilated agony. Every inch of my lower body burns, from my spent quads to the arches of my feet. But still I pull.

If this isn't passion, then I don't know what is.

Five more strokes.

I pass the Brazilian.

I pull because I believe in myself. I pull for my best friend. I pull because I love rowing. I pull for the man I love.

Three more crushing strokes. I'm nearly even with the Canadian.

My back muscles heave with every inch of strength that's left.

Two more. This race is ending. This race will never end.

One. I wrench out the final stroke.

And let out a feral scream.

Horns blast in rapid succession as our bows cross the finish.

My forehead falls to my knees. I suck in air, gag on the vomit rising in my throat.

It's the best race I've ever had. It's the best time I've ever gotten. It's better than I could have ever imagined two months ago.

It's second place.

I still lost my spot.

. . .

Even after my cooldown, acid lingers in my veins. When I crossed the finish, I was in too much pain to wrap my head around what just happened. In the minutes since, the pain has ebbed and a tangle of emotions has taken its place.

I don't want to process it all alone.

Sofi won't be on the dock—she's already starting her warm-up ahead of her own final. Anyway, as much as I'd like her support, there's someone else I want more right now.

When I raced, Adrian's voice was so vivid in my mind it was like he was sitting in the boat with me. Like every moment we spent together this summer was just as bright and focused and light today as it was before our painful separation. I want nothing more than to talk to *him*. To share my joy over my success and to commiserate about the impending implosion of my entire life. To tell him the truth of what I feel for him.

Before my boat has even touched the dock, while my arms and legs are still heavy with acid, I brace my oars so I can flip through the messages on my water-dappled phone, searching for our most recent exchange. He never responded to my last message, but there's so much more I want to say anyway. I want to tell him what he means to me. I want to tell him how he's changed me.

I click off Do Not Disturb. Before I can get to the exchange with Adrian, though, my phone pings with an unread email. Carla has responded to my recommendation.

When I click it open, I find only four sentences:

> I appreciate the honesty, but the board decided to offer Adrian a job, anyway. He accepted.

What?

My ears start ringing with the whine of my mom's antique tea kettle. In my haze, the side of my boat lunges toward the dock. I barely pull up my oar before I land against the wood.

He took the job?

Even as people flow around me, competitors shouting, coaches enveloping athletes in hugs, I sit, stunned, staring at the words still on my screen. How is this even possible? Less than a week ago, he was adamantly against it.

I force my eyes back down and read the rest.

> You're right about the deal, though. Come to my tent so we can talk after your race.

Adrian is moving to Florida.

I'm going back to Berkeley.

I pull up his contact page and consider calling him. But then I stop myself. There's a reason he didn't tell me himself and a reason he didn't respond to my last text. He might have initiated contact, but that doesn't mean everything is okay between us.

I still need an explanation. I have to understand what the hell just happened.

If Adrian took the job, he would have told his kids about it first, right? I haven't seen them since that last practice in Berkeley—when Rohan gifted me a video montage of my top ten moments from the summer, and Peter surprised me by showing up at the dock and diving in for a one-armed hug. I haven't seen any of their videos since, haven't been able to bring myself to watch, but I'm sure Rohan would have an opinion about all this, one he'd be willing to share with the entire world.

I flip to TikTok.

The first few videos from the last week or so are normal—practices, songs, dances. Then I get to one filled with Rohan's face. He's walking up the stairs at the boathouse, forehead still dotted with sweat from practice. He announces that their coach has called an emergency team meeting.

This is it.

The next video centers on Adrian, standing in the middle of the erg room. The camera pans and I can see guys sprawled across the floor, rolling back and forth on seats. Peter is there, too, cross-legged with one arm in a cast. Even on the tiny sliver of screen, Adrian's smile is like a steel rod through my sternum.

He tells the kids that he was offered an opportunity to coach elite athletes. It's far away so taking it means he wouldn't see them much anymore. He wants to know what they think before he accepts.

Kids eye each other uncertainly, as if looking for clues to their own feelings in their peers' faces.

"What would we do without you?" someone asks. I recognize him as a shy redhead that sits in the bow seat of Adrian's fastest quad.

"East Bay Rowing would hire someone new," Adrian replies. "But you might be without a coach while they look for a replacement."

A muffled harmony of grumbles rises up through the room.

"No one could ever take your place!" someone out of view shouts.

A chorus of agreement meets this declaration.

Adrian winces.

"How soon?" another asks.

"Unfortunately, I'd need to start immediately," Adrian admits. "I negotiated with USRowing to let me fly to Nationals so I can be there for everyone racing, but you'll be on your own right after."

A chorus of grumbles and thumbs-down follow. I hate what I see in Adrian's expression—the pain their disappointment is causing.

"I'm sorry, guys," Adrian says. "I know it's not ideal. I've got some thoughts on contingency plans, like about how you can support one another until the club gets a new coach in here."

This is met with only another harmony of consternation.

"We need you."

"No one else would be as good as you."

"What about next year?"

The camera jostles as Rohan stands. His voice bites out through the clamoring crowd. "Do you want the job, Coach?"

Adrian looks at him. Right at the camera. Right at me.

"I would be lying," Adrian says, "if I said the answer was entirely yes. It's a really big promotion. It's an almost overwhelming challenge, so I'm not positive that I'll succeed. But—" He takes a breath and rolls his thumb over his palm. "I want to give it a try. Someone I trust told me that I'm selling myself short. That I'm better than I think I am. I'd like to see if that's true."

My heart lurches with love and pride.

The angle changes as Rohan plants his phone in someone else's hands. The video catches his face. He crosses his arms and the frowning teens filling the room turn. Even though this happened more than a day ago now, my lungs still as I await his verdict.

Rohan looks around the room, administering his attention to each person's face. Then he says, "If he wants it, then I think Coach Crawford should take this job."

My breath releases in a rush. On the video, faces uncertainly swivel toward one another. This, apparently, is not what the other kids expected. Still, Rohan tips his chin defiantly, waiting for someone to challenge his verdict.

One of them rises to it—Matt, a petty kid with a mop of curly hair and a splash of acne. "And just leave us? He'd let us taper alone and only show up for the medal ceremony? What kind of coach would do that?"

Rohan wheels on him. "He's the only reason any of us qualified for Nationals in the first place and the only reason any of us has a shot at medaling. He got us this far. We can go the rest of the way ourselves—supporting one another. Figuring it out. It's what he would do for us if the tables were turned. It's what he's always done for us."

"Yeah," Matt spits back. "Except now. When we need him most."

"Actually," Peter says, low enough that if the room weren't already quiet, he might not have been heard, "when *he* needs *us* most, we'll be there for him."

My heart stutters as silence descends once again, even thicker this time.

Rohan nods, pleased, then turns to Adrian. "I think you should take that job, Coach. We'll be fine. We want you to be happy."

Adrian looks around the room. The stunned silence has shifted—an occasional nod. A half smile.

Another guy jumps to his feet. "I agree with Rohan and Peter. You should go for it, Coach."

"Yeah, we think you should do it!" another yells.

"We support you."

The kids break out into applause. Adrian blinks and raises a knuckle to his eye.

The video ends.

I'm so happy for him. I'm so *proud* of him.

But I'm so devastated for myself. It's all turned out even worse than I thought it could.

I love Adrian. I love rowing.

I've just lost both.

Thirty-Three

Choking back tears, I stagger uphill, dump my shell into some slings, and pull out my phone. There's really only one person who I can turn to at this moment. Still, my thumb hovers over the name, indecision stalling me.

Mom and I have only talked superficially since our fight about Rob. I don't know how she'll react to me calling her now, unburdening on her about heartbreak—the very thing that has driven us apart.

Yet I have no one else to help me process the deluge of emotions that are threatening to break my carefully constructed dam.

The phone rings as I wedge myself into a sliver of space between a couple of tents. Back here, I'm somewhat protected from the crackle of the loudspeaker and the wind that's snapping flags like whips.

"Kath, hello."

Grass stabs the backs of my bare legs as I sink to a seat. "Mom. Can we talk?"

She's silent for a long moment and I find myself holding my breath, waiting for her verdict. I hear her take a few steps across a hard floor. A door closes. A chair creaks.

"Tell me what happened," she says, voice soft.

I sob. A heart-wrenching, obliterating sob. Phone still pressed to my ear, I pull my knees into my chest and brace my forehead against them, cocooning myself in a tight ball.

How can I explain what just happened? What I've lost. What I'll never have. Where I went wrong. Where did I go wrong?

"Kath? Are you hurt?"

I shake my head on my knees, rubbing my forehead against my still-damp skin. "No. Not—not physically."

A sigh rushes out of her—both relieved and even more concerned. "Tell me."

With heaving breaths, choking sobs, and more tears, I get out the words. I tell her about the breakup, Adrian's text, and coming clean to Carla. I tell her about the race: the beautiful, majestic, best-of-my-life race. How it still wasn't good enough. I've lost my spot for good—no way back now.

And then I tell her that Adrian took the job in Florida. I tell her, truthfully, that I want him to be happy and I want him to succeed. But . . . it makes things even more impossible between us.

Altogether, it's almost certainly the end of my rowing career. It's definitely the end of us.

"Are we just doomed to repeat the same mistakes endlessly?" I ask aloud when I've finished.

So far Mom has remained silent, offering only small sounds of understanding. When she answers, however, her voice is sympathetic but skeptical. "What do you mean?"

"You and Dad. Me and Adrian."

"I don't see the similarities."

A vinyl tent flutters in the wind, punctuating each of my shaky inhales. "This is what happened to your dancing career. You fell in love with Dad and gave up dancing for him. Then he left, anyway."

"Your dad left," she says, gently but firmly. "He left because our relationship didn't work for him. That's not what happened with you and Adrian."

"It's the same ending place, though. It's always a choice between *what* you love and *who* you love. And even then, there's a good chance you'll lose both."

"Kath . . ." I don't hear doubt in the word. Just caution. "That's not true."

"Yeah it is, Mom." I know we aren't talking about me and Adrian anymore. Not only. "Look at your life. You spent years dating men who weren't right for you. And you never had time or bandwidth to devote to anything else. But then, being single simplified everything for you. It made it possible for you to start the yoga studio. To be successful and happy."

Mom sighs. In the distance, I hear the crackle of the speakers as the announcer rolls through finishes.

"Sweetheart," she says. "I wasn't single when I started the yoga studio."

"I . . . what?"

"Rob and I have been together for almost a year."

The world tilts. I hold the phone pressed to my ear, fingers chilled in the wind that's gusting through the tents and sending the damp hairs on my legs into prickling goose bumps.

"Rob and I met and hit it off," she continues. "We spent those first few weeks talking constantly and, eventually, talking about almost nothing but our biggest, most terrifying dreams.

Two months after our first date, we started the business. Was that too fast? I'm sure some would say it was. But you know me, always full steam ahead."

"Why didn't you tell me?"

"At first it was because, well, because you never like the men I date. I told myself I'd wait until it got serious. Once it did . . . then I had a thousand new excuses. You were busy with qualifiers, then World Cups. You had too much on your mind to be open to him.

"Then when you came home for the summer, I told myself you just needed to meet him first. I'd tell you after you could see for yourself how different he is. Then I saw you with Adrian, and I thought maybe, if you were finally happy in your own relationship, you'd see that I could be, too. The truth is"—she expels a breath—"I delayed and delayed because I was afraid you would judge me. Or reject him."

My throat tightens. "And then I did both."

"Yes. You did."

Cold rushes through me as I remember my reaction when I found them together. I acted like her relationship was shameful. Like she had to answer to me for it.

"I'm sorry," I whisper.

"I'm not telling you that because I want an apology—at least not right now. I'm telling you because there's something I want you to understand."

"Okay?"

A long pause stretches between us. It reminds me of her last dance performance. I was so young when she retired, but I distinctly remember this complicated solo. The curtain went up, the room hushed, the music started. There was this pause—this infinitesimal beat where Mom remained perfectly still, but somehow, I knew she was collecting herself. Taking a single breath before plunging in.

That pause is laden with possibility. Like the top of a stroke. Like the last deep breath before a starting buzzer.

"Rob supports me," Mom says. "He challenges me. He fills in my gaps—takes things on that feel overwhelming to me—and I do the same for him. He's good with spreadsheets; I'm good with people. He gave me the confidence to open the studio in the first place."

"You're saying . . . ?"

"I'm saying Rob is *the reason* that business exists at all."

A prickle scales my arms as my mind zips over memories from this summer, categorizing and re-cataloging. Some things make more sense now. Like the confidence that she's had in starting a business—a terrifying new endeavor that has to have involved all kinds of skills she doesn't possess. How successful and well organized the yoga studio seemed when I visited. She did that—but it makes more sense to know that she didn't do it all alone.

"I want you to see that's how love—healthy love—is," Mom continues. "It makes you better, stronger, in the other parts of your life, too. Yes, love can tear you down. It can hurt, it can make your life worse. But if you find someone who lifts you up instead, it makes the other parts of your life better. Even if it ends."

Clearly, we're not talking about Rob anymore. "You think that's how it is with me and Adrian?"

"I know it is," she says. "I watched your race. I saw your training over the last two months. You went from dragging yourself out of the house in the morning, and going through the motions because you thought you had nothing else, to practically skipping out the front door. You fell back in love with rowing because you fell in love with Adrian. You've always known how strong you are, but you lost faith in yourself. You found that again, too. That's exactly what I'm talking about. That's the kind of love that lifts—the kind that adds instead of subtracting.

"When you find the right person," she says emphatically, "it's not a choice at all. When you find them, *who* you love will make you better at *what* you love."

My throat has gone dry. The tears on my cheeks have evaporated. A sinking certainty creeps up around me, like I've been standing in a field and the grass has grown around my feet, but I didn't notice until it was brushing my fingertips.

She's right—it's exactly the way the last two months have felt. This building sensation that everything has become fuller with Adrian in my life. She's describing today, too. The race. The way I pulled harder, went faster than I'd ever done before.

Just yesterday, I told Adrian that my success today would be his, too. I was talking about his coaching: his technical advice, his passion, the way he's helped me get out of my head. But the truth is so much deeper than I even realized. My life—my rowing—is stronger *because of* him.

"I need to—" I clear my throat.

I don't know what, exactly. All I know is that I have to find a way to make it work, no matter how many thousands of miles stand between us. Surely, having him in my life, even infrequently, is better than not at all. Surely, it's all worth the risk.

"I need to go," I say.

"We'll talk more soon," Mom says. "I love you."

"I love you, too," I say. "And thank you."

With shaking fingers, I hang up. Turn toward the edge of tents. This isn't a conversation I want to have over the phone. I could get on a flight to Berkeley today. But what if Adrian has already left for Florida? He said he was starting the new job immediately.

I frown at my phone's screen, then pull up a message to Rohan.

Do you know where Adrian will be tomorrow? I need to talk to him as soon as possible.

My phone pings with a response almost immediately.

Isn't he with you?

I stare at the words, uncomprehending. Before I have a chance to respond, I hear my name. I spin in slow motion toward the shaft of blue sky between the tents. The world is tilting again, but this time with a kaleidoscope around me falling, dropping, descending. Clicking into place. Landing on one still image—a face amid streaking primary colors.

Thirty-Four

I sprint toward Adrian, arms pumping, legs windmilling. A dozen feet separate us, but I can't possibly get to him fast enough. I land against his chest in the breath of a heart-beat, my body colliding like a compass finding her true north.

"Kath," he says, laughing into my damp braid.

His hands wrap around my shoulders, dragging me toward him. I cinch myself into the pocket of his arms, letting our bodies fit together like puzzle pieces. Inhaling his citrus smell. Feeling our hearts beat together.

"How are you here?" I whisper into his chest. "*Why* are you here?"

Adrian pulls away so he can grab my hand. Our fingers braid together, tethering me in place. The world might be crumbling, but Adrian is here. Adrian is real.

"I wasn't expecting you to be this happy to see me," he says breathlessly. "I have a whole speech ready. I was hoping for happy *after* the speech."

I squeeze his hand. "I want that. I want to hear it all. But I have a speech for you, too."

"Should we arm wrestle to decide who goes first?"

I grin. "We already know I'll win."

He laughs. "Okay. Go ahead."

Thoughts are tumbling through my mind like an avalanche gaining steam. I could have used a few hours to try to put everything into a semblance of order. I don't have that, though, so I'll just have to speak from the heart.

I take a step back, still gripping his hand, but far enough that I can look into his jade eyes. They hold me steady, fixing me to the ground with enough certainty that I know I can speak.

"You once told me," I say, "you admired the fact that I have never quit rowing, even when it's gotten tough, even when it's felt impossible. For a long time, I thought that was because I had no other choice but to row, that I am no one without this sport. But, recently, I've realized that's wrong. I row because I love it, because it makes my life better. I love the kind of life I get to live with rowing in it, despite the hardship and the pain."

I can feel the emotion rising in my throat, and my eyes are already wet, but I don't care. I don't bother to collect myself. I just need to get these words out, no matter how they sound.

"That's how I feel about you, too," I say between gulps of air. "My life is better with you in it. Loving you has made me a better rower and a better person. I know you're going to be in Florida and I'm going to be in California. And I know that won't always be easy. But I still want to be with you, regardless of the distance, or the stress. I'm sorry I quit on us. I shouldn't have done that. But, if you'll forgive me, if you'll have me, I want to take it back."

Adrian's mouth parts slightly, his warm fingers coiling ever tighter around mine. "Sorry, did you just say that you love me?"

My mouth explodes with an unbidden smile. "Yes. Yes, I love you. I'm sorry I didn't say it before. I love how strong and steady you are. I love your enthusiasm and support. I love the way you've pushed me to be better, reminded me of how strong I really am. You're the best coach I've ever worked with. You're the best man I've ever met."

Adrian reaches out to touch my face, thumb catching one of my tears. My cheek sinks into his palm.

"Too much?" I ask.

"Never. As usual, you are nothing but extraordinary." He holds his hand on my cheek for another long moment. "But we need to sort out some logistics. We seem to have different impressions of just how much distance is going to be between us."

"What do you mean?"

A smile lifts the edge of his mouth. "I didn't take a job in Florida, Kath. I took a job at your training center in California."

"What job?" I ask.

"The men's national team coach retired earlier this summer. USRowing has asked me to replace him."

"The . . . men's *national* team," I say, still in disbelief.

"There's only the one," he says with a laugh.

My mind works over snapshots of memories: Maxwell freaking out about his coach. Carla's insistence that I keep my evaluation secret and her caginess about why. Her email, Rohan's TikTok. They weren't specific about what job he'd been offered.

Adrian. He's not just taking on a challenge. He's taking on *the* challenge.

"Wait, and you're okay with that?" I ask.

Adrian's eyes gleam with a smile that is both timid and heartbreakingly self-assured. "I wouldn't have been two months ago. Maybe even two weeks ago. I didn't admit this to myself until recently, but I've been—I've been comfortable with where I am.

I have a life that I love, but also a life that I can *handle*. But that's a double-edged sword, isn't it? Because I've also been afraid. You were right about that. I was afraid because I was so sure I was going to fail. Again."

"What changed?" I ask, barely daring to breathe over his next words.

"You," he says with enough conviction that I pulse with joy. "I was making you take all these risks, forcing you out of your comfort zone, but I wasn't doing the same for myself. Then I watched your races here and I was so impressed and so *proud* and—I guess that's how I finally saw it. What you said sank in. Maybe I can coach national team athletes because I've already done it. This summer. I coached the strongest, fiercest, most obstinate national team athlete I've ever met. I helped make her better. And if I can do that, I can do just about anything."

Tears leap to my eyes. I'm so desperately, viciously proud of him. At the same time, I'm lost in a haze of recalibration. Berkeley might be only five hundred miles away from the training center, but it's still five hundred miles. Adrian is smiling like the distance is inconsequential. Of course, it's worth it. He's worth it. It is easier this way. But it still won't be *easy*.

"But, Adrian," I say, "you need to know I lost my deal with Carla and USRowing. And then I got second in the final—it's not enough to get reinstated outright. I needed to win."

Adrian shakes his head. "That's not what Carla told me when she offered me the job."

"She didn't?"

"No, she specifically mentioned that you'd be in the training center, too."

I'm so confused. My mind is racing for a contingency or an explanation. Clearly, I'm missing something. "I don't understand. How could I possibly have my spot back?"

The sharp falsetto of Carla's voice stabs at us from around the corner of the tent. "You would understand if you had come to talk to me when you got off the water like I asked."

She rounds the corner, eyes flaming, hair sprawling wild in the wind. She's at least a few inches shorter than Adrian, but she still seems to take up as much space as he does.

Her eyes pin me like a nail to a board. "Katherine Parker, I've been looking all over tarnation for you."

"I'm sorry?"

She folds her arms, but even so, her eyes skate over my fingers, still twined with Adrian's, and a smile tweaks her lips. "We need to discuss your residency."

"Okay?"

"I submitted my recommendation to the board this morning. I said they should reinstate your residency at the Olympic Training Center effective immediately. They voted to confirm you an hour ago."

Am I hallucinating?

I'm certainly not attached to the ground anymore. I'm rocketing upward, above the tents, into the sky, into the stratosphere.

Desperately, I look to Adrian. He's smiling at me, broad and expectant. I'm still floating, my heart is still rattling around in my chest, hammering in my ears over the buzzing, over the wind, over the shouts of spectators as the next race descends the course. But Adrian's smile is a single star in a moonless sky.

"You . . ." I swallow. "You asked them to overrule before you even saw me race?"

"Yes," Carla says. "Before your race."

"Why would you do that?"

"Don't you remember what I told you," she asks, "when we discussed this in Italy?"

My mind leaps back, pulling me into the sinking moment in

her tent when she broke the bad news. The memory has been reduced to no more than a blur at this point.

So, it takes me more than a moment to say, "You said the board was concerned about my lack of flexibility."

"Right," Carla says. "And we have it on good authority that's changed."

I look to Adrian, but he shakes his head. "Not me," he says.

"Sofi has been giving me regular updates," Carla tells us. "She brags about you so much it's frankly gotten irritating. That said, I can always trust her to tell me the truth. Plus, there's everything I've seen directly, too—your willingness to work with Adrian, the way your views changed in that recommendation, the flexibility you've demonstrated this week."

My chest is expanding under the pressure, a balloon of hope and happiness. Even still, I'm worried that Carla will take this too far. Even though I've changed some, I'm still *me*.

"I still like routines, though," I say. "I like making plans and sticking to them. I still do a long stretching session every night and eat the same stuff for breakfast every day before an endurance session. And I have specific supplements I like to take and—"

Carla taps a finger against her windbreaker. "I saw an uneaten lemon bar at the hotel last night. That was yours?"

I nod sheepishly. "Yes."

"And you didn't need it?"

"Not anymore."

She smiles and nods. "Like I told you. Routines are good. Being so inflexible that you can't live without them—that's the problem."

My chest lifts, spinning outward like I'm in orbit. I look at Adrian, daring, finally, to believe this is real. That this is happening. The sight of him pulls me in like gravity.

"We're both going to live at the training center," I whisper.

He bites back a smile. "Well, I get to live in a coach's residence and you will be in the dorms, but otherwise, yes."

"And you are only coaching men so this is"—I look to Carla—"fine with USRowing? No problem with an athlete dating a coach?"

She nods. "Adrian could never switch to coaching women. But otherwise, yes. USRowing is aware of the situation and has deemed it acceptable."

I grope for Adrian's hand and thread our fingers together. "This is really happening."

"It really is," Adrian says, his eyes on mine. I feel like I swallowed a sparkler and the lightning streaks are glittering through my insides. "And I would like to kiss you."

I shove myself into his arms.

Epilogue

8 MONTHS LATER
(4 MONTHS UNTIL OLYMPIC TRIALS)

On Tuesdays, Sofi and I get off the water before the men's team. We walk, arm in arm, up the long hill that slopes from the docks to the complex, air filled with the smell of sagebrush and the bursts of our laughter. Unisuits still damp, we push our trays through the gleaming metal of the dining hall.

With full plates, we usually snag two seats by the massive bay windows that overlook the water shimmering in early afternoon light. Sometimes, I prop up my phone against my water cup and we catch up on Rohan's videos. Peter got back on the water a few months ago and he's been making tremendous gains already—his splits are nearly as good as they were before he broke his arm—and their new coach keeps making oblique comments about Junior Worlds.

But instead, today, Sofi and I talk as we sneak glances out of the windows. If we sit right in the corner of the room, I can usually catch a glimpse of Adrian's launch streaming after the men's shells.

I'd be lying if I said this new job has been all sunshine and rainbows. It was a huge promotion, after all. One that was met with a fair amount of skepticism by the men's team, most notably from the guy in stroke seat of the eight. In the first weeks after we moved here—in the dark of Adrian's living room, both of us huddled under a throw on the deep couch—he second-guessed nearly every one of his decisions on and off the water. I reassured him as best I could. With time, I knew he'd overcome the challenges.

And he did. In the months since, Adrian has won nearly all of his athletes over with easy charm, obscene attention to detail, and a refusal to back down from even the most demanding rowers. Now I can hear nothing but confidence in the thrust of his voice as it carries across the water or while he confers with his assistant coaches after practice.

When Sofi and I finish eating, we linger at the table, sipping on hot tea with lemon, letting it warm our limbs as the rising sun heats the bay windows. Sofi's phone buzzes a few times, and she glances at it before setting it upside down.

"Everything okay?" I ask.

She inhales, then lets it go. "Missy had another difficult practice, and it sounds like she's still having a rough time of it. But I think I'll let Carla handle this one."

I watch her as she takes another sip of tea.

"You don't want to rush over there and single-handedly talk her down?" I ask.

"Nah, I have a PT appointment that I'd rather not cancel. I'll get the next one."

I'm still smiling at her when Adrian strides into the dining hall, lanyard swinging from his neck and a plate balanced on his clipboard. He leans over to press a kiss to my temple before taking a chair across from Sofi. There's a rightness to this moment, a feeling of peace so deep and absolute it almost steals the next breath from my lungs.

"I'm due at the med center in ten minutes," she announces and swivels toward Adrian. "But I wanted to stick around long enough to say that Kath killed it in practice today. If you wait for her to tell you about it, she'll hem and haw for an hour first."

Adrian grins. "Killed it?"

"Yeah," Sofi says. "Like, she didn't just beat it up a little. Practice is lying face down in the lake with no pulse."

"Vivid, Sof," I say, as Adrian laughs.

We did an important one today—three by three thousand. The same benchmark workout I did the first day I ever practiced with Adrian. The one where he insisted I get on the water without my usual tech and then read out my times with that wide, infectious grin.

"How were the splits?" he asks.

I push up the sleeve of my sweatshirt. Back at the boathouse, as Carla read them out, I wrote my times on my forearm in blue ink pen. Not because I was going to forget them or because I didn't believe they were real, but so that I could spend the next twelve hours looking down at my arm and smiling.

"Holy shit, Parker," Adrian says as he curls his long fingers around my wrist. He blinks up at me. "You're extraordinary."

Pleasure unfurls inside my chest like a flower opening for the sun.

"Yeah," I breathe.

Sofi hides a smile. "I figured you'd want to swoon." She stands and hoists her tray off the table. "Which means my work here is done."

As she marches off toward the med center, Adrian's eyes linger on mine.

"Seriously, Kath," he breathes. His hand is still closed around my wrist, my forearm facing up so that my messy handwriting is smiling at us from the table. "These aren't good times. These are *Olympic qualifying* times."

"I know," I whisper back.

For a moment, we sit like that, eyes locked. The force of Adrian's love and approval radiates off him in soft waves.

"I have something for you," he says and reaches under his plate for a white paper bag, which he sets on my tray.

I peek inside to find the yellow edges of a sugar-dusted pastry. "I didn't see lemon bars in the dessert case today."

"I got this in town."

"Are we celebrating anything in particular?"

"Other than the fact that I'm looking at a future Olympian?"

I elbow him. "Don't jinx it."

He raises an eyebrow. "Superstitious?"

"Always," I say. "At least a little."

Adrian nudges the bar toward me and I take a bite. It's flaky and lemony and it brushes the tip of my nose with a dusting of sugar.

"To answer your question, we're celebrating the fact that it's a Tuesday," Adrian says. "And I'm sitting at a table with the most powerful, inspiring woman I have ever met. And I love her, and through some miracle, she loves me back. And we're looking out over the water where I get paid to do a job that I never dreamed I could have. Is that enough of a reason?"

I smile back at him, just as broadly. "I think that's an extraordinary reason."

ACKNOWLEDGMENTS

Thank you to Lauren Spieller, my agent, who somehow is, all at once, fierce, dedicated, and kind. Thank you for believing in me and this book and steering us both to the best possible home. I remain convinced that you could walk on water if you decided to try. My deepest thanks also to Hannah Teachout, brilliant editorial assistant, whose insights make me sit back and whisper: "Yes, *that's* how it's supposed to be." I can't believe how lucky I am that you found me. Thank you for always being in my corner.

A huge debt of gratitude to Sydney Collins, my editor. At some point, Kath describes racing in single sculls as a lonely endeavor. "You have your coach and your training partners," she says, "but no one is *with* you." This, often, is how it feels to write a book. Or rather, that is how it used to feel, before I started working with you. Thank you for your brilliant edits, which uncovered layer after layer of depth in these characters. Thank you for your support and encouragement. Thank you for being *with* me.

Thanks so much to the team at Dell that shepherded this book into the world, including Annette Szlachta-McGinn, Saige Francis, and Meghan O'Leary. Thank you also to my copy editor, Whitney Bak, for the brilliant edits that drew out so much meaning and clarity from my words. (I didn't realize copy edits could be brilliant until you got your hands on this book!) Thanks also to my proofreaders, Allison Linden, Hope Clarke, and Vicki Fischer.

I'm also so grateful to be working with Emily Siegmund and Brianna Kusilek. Thank you for your enthusiasm for this story, and your patience in answering my many questions. I'm thrilled to have your brilliance behind this launch!

Many thanks to Michelle Weiner, my film agent, for championing this book and connecting it with the perfect creative team.

So much gratitude to the brilliant people who shaped this book into the stunning thing it is, inside and out: cover designer Carlos Beltran, illustrator Sarah Maxwell, and interior designer Betty Lew. This book is beautiful, and that's entirely thanks to your artistry and thoughtful choices.

Deep appreciation to my several subject matter experts, including Jo Palmer, for your helpful insights and incredible reservoir of knowledge. Special thanks to Stephanie Arpin for pointing out all of the ways that rowing is not like kayaking, for being patient with my absurdly specific questions, and for your enthusiasm for this story. Any remaining errors are most certainly my own.

Many thanks to all the early readers of this book. Natalie Moss, thank you for your generous feedback, sharp insights, and for pushing me to add, what turned out to be, the most important scenes in the book. Lauren, thank you for lengthy phone calls, endless support, and putting up with my regularly scheduled despair. You continue to believe in me enough for the both of us, and I'm beyond lucky to have you. Rebeca Civatti, thank you for lengthy critiques, even lengthier PenguinTalks™, and most of all, teaching me to be a better writer. It's humbling to think about where I'd be without you. (Probably still trying to write books without character arcs.) Fija Callaghan, thank you for your sharp and witty insights and being my first friend in this business.

And my family. Thank you to my mom—one of the most supportive, caring, and generous people I've ever known. You didn't just convince me my goals are achievable, you convinced me I'm worthy of reaching for them. To my sister, Lauren, who once replied, after I described the long odds of publishing: "If anyone can do it, my sister can do it." You're an extraordinary woman and I'm so viciously proud of you. If you happen to read this before the actual text, I apologize in advance that it doesn't include any dragons. And to Bobbie, who has joyfully and enthusiastically read every book I've ever written, even the ones that (let's be honest) weren't very good. I'm so grateful to have you on this journey, in books and life.

Most of all, to my husband, Cam. Thank you for living up to your middle name. Thank you for sharing in the joy of my milestones and calling them *ours.* Thank you for loving me, exactly as I am.

ABOUT THE AUTHOR

CAMERON STONE ADAMS

In a past life, Ann Adams was a junior national champion, national medalist, and resident of the U.S. Olympic Training Center in Lake Placid, New York. Today, she lives in Sacramento, California, where you can find her analyzing public policy and going for moderate hikes with her husband and overly enthusiastic cockapoo. Mostly, though, she's writing stories—especially those about women falling in love and finding their strength.

ABOUT THE TYPE

The text of this book was set in Electra, a typeface designed by W. A. Dwiggins (1880–1956). This face cannot be classified as either modern or old style. It is not based on any historical model, nor does it echo any particular period or style. It avoids the extreme contrasts between thick and thin elements that mark most modern faces, and it attempts to give a feeling of fluidity, power, and speed.